Keys of Candor

Sea of Souls

By Seth Ervin and Casey Eanes

Keys of Candor: Sea of Souls

Copyright © 2016 Seth Ervin and Casey Eanes

Editors: Laura Stallings and Susan McDonald

No part of this book may be reproduced or utilized in any form by any means, electronic or mechanical, including photocopying and recording, or by any information storage and retrieval system, without permission in writing from the authors.

ISBN-13: 978-1523889990 (paperback)

ISBN-10: 1523889993 (paperback)

Keys of Candor: Sea of Souls / by Seth Ervin and Casey Eanes

978-1523889990 (paperback)

1. Good and evil. 2. Adventure fiction. 3. Fantasy fiction.

For my beautiful wife and my <u>three</u> amazing kids. - CE

For Mom, my storyteller, and for Dad, my guide.   -SE

TABLE OF CONTENTS

CHAPTER ONE	1
CHAPTER TWO	15
CHAPTER THREE	34
CHAPTER FOUR	48
CHAPTER FIVE	64
CHAPTER SIX	76
CHAPTER SEVEN	88
CHAPTER EIGHT	102
CHAPTER NINE	117
CHAPTER TEN	132
CHAPTER ELEVEN	142
CHAPTER TWELVE	155
CHAPTER THIRTEEN	169
CHAPTER FOURTEEN	187
CHAPTER FIFTEEN	198
CHAPTER SIXTEEN	210
CHAPTER SEVENTEEN	226
CHAPTER EIGHTEEN	243
CHAPTER NINETEEN	260
CHAPTER TWENTY	272
CHAPTER TWENTY-ONE	289
CHAPTER TWENTY-TWO	302
CHAPTER TWENTY-THREE	312
CHAPTER TWENTY-FOUR	327
CHAPTER TWENTY-FIVE	343
CHAPTER TWENTY-SIX	362
CHAPTER TWENTY-SEVEN	393
CHAPTER TWENTY-EIGHT	414

MAP OF CANDOR

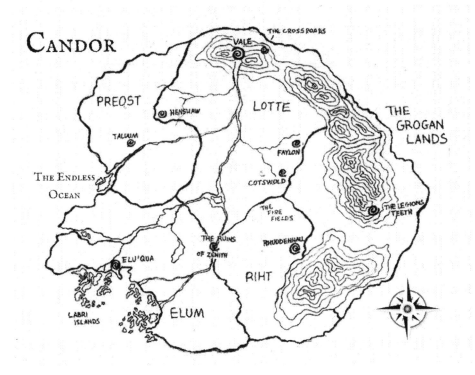

Artwork by: Calandra Usher

CHAPTER ONE

"Stop!"

Seam's voice cut through the chaos of the chamber as he stepped toward Kull's shattered body. The avalanche of blows cascading over Kull ceased and the mob of soldiers pulled back. Kull fell in a heap, the black stone floor shining red with his blood. He opened his eyes terrified that there was only a swirling darkness.

I'm going to die. The realization was not fear-filled, but welcome. Kull forced himself to breathe, his lungs slowly taking in ragged, thin breaths on the cold stone floor. His mind grasped in vain for clarity as he lifted his head off the floor to open his eyes, but they had long-since swollen shut.

"I said stop!" The king's command quieted the room. In an instant, Kull remembered. *Sacrifice.*

Seam locked his bloodshot eyes on his enemy and slowly staggered to his feet, lumbering toward Kull like a hunter surveying his snares. He wiped blood from his lip and spat against the ground. Dark thoughts of revenge swirled through the king's mind as he tallied up his injuries; the stabbing, the gunshot wound, and the humiliation of being held at ransom. Seam promised himself that everything he had endured would fall back on Shepherd's son, one-hundred fold.

Blood seeped from his wounds, but he would not relent. It was not enough to keep him down. Sheer power rushed from the iron bracer locked on his right wrist bearing the Keys of Candor. He strode toward Kull, filled with the ancient, forbidden strength radiating from the relics he wore on his arm.

"Step back and let me look at him." The king's smile went crooked. Seam's bruised face looked little better than Kull's. The whites of his eyes were badly damaged, a streak of demonic crimson orbited around his brown irises. His long brown hair was tousled and caked with drying blood. Newfound mania swept over Seam as his boots slowly thumped across the floor toward his prize. *His sacrifice.* He paused, towering over Kull before leaning down next to his face.

"Look at me," he whispered, almost tenderly. Kull refused, turning his head away. Seam growled, wringing his hand through the Kull's hair. "Look at me!" he screamed, pulling Kull's face forward.

Kull fought to open his eyes, but even that was impossible. Seam slammed Kull's face back down on the ground, the cracking sound unleashing a torrent of pain. He could feel Seam's black boot hovering directly over his face. Kull pushed a trembling hand to Seam's foot, and he grasped at his ankle with what little strength he had left. *So this is how I die.*

Seam's heavy boot slammed down on Kull's hand. Kull's mouth opened in a silent scream, his vision evaporating in an instant.

Seam ground his boot down without mercy as the bones in Kull's hand began to pop.

"You have been very brave today, Shepherd. Very brave, indeed. You will soon learn the price for such defiance!"

Seam relented, lifting his foot and turning his gaze to the guards surrounding them.

"Pick him up and bind him. I don't want him making another move without me ordering it."

The soldiers obeyed, scraping Kull from the ground and dragging his limp frame back to the room's central pedestal where only moments before his father had been chained. As they locked him into place, Kull's mind raced to think of some way to escape, that there might be some hope, but his body was an unwilling partner. Seam's men had rendered his body useless, and every movement brought a deep, paralyzing anguish.

Seam stood up and gazed into the vacant mirrors. "Leave us." The command was quick, and instantly the host of soldiers vanished. Kull swallowed hard as he accepted the fact that he could not escape. No one was coming to rescue him. Wael, his father, and the girl with crimson hair had long since left the Spire, their escape bartered with his own life. Dark thoughts stormed in his mind.

He thought of his mother, his father, Ewing, and Adley. He hung there bound, his mind gazing deeply into the abyss of all he would soon lose. It would soon be over. There would be no more fighting. Kull struggled to take a calming breath and felt the cold metal amulet still hanging from his neck brush against his bloody chest, his mother's last gift to him. *You kept your promise. You fulfilled your oath. So be it.*

Seam limped to the console, and Kull heard the large datalink display hum again with life. Hosp's voice slithered through the cold room.

"What happened, Seam? Where are all the prisoners?" Hosp's voice was direct and irritated. "*Where are the keys?*"

Seam huffed at the inquiry and pointed to Kull. "*The keys are mine.* We have all we need for now, Hosp. The others are of no consequence." The High King held the bracer aloft, his face alight in the cold green hue of the screen.

Hosp's eyes narrowed and his face fell into a scowl, "How can you brush off losing these terrorists? This is no simple matter, Seam!"

"Oh, but it is." Seam slammed a button on his datalink. "Let me show you how simple all of it is, dear Hosp." Seam leaned his head down to the device bound on his left arm. "Bronson, send in the guards assigned to guarding the mirror chamber."

A small electronic question cracked back, echoing through the room. "Sir?"

Seam roared into the device like a madman. "You heard me! Do it now!"

"Yes, sir." Seam's servant stammered under his master's rage. The electronic voice shot back to the High King, "Beor and Kalam of the Groganlands were assigned. I'll radio them both to report back to you immediately." Seam nodded and closed his eyes, his bruised and broken face reflecting back from the two panes of glass that stood like monoliths in the pinnacle chamber.

Kull grew restless, unable to stomach the stagecraft of the tyrant. He willed his body to stand and push through his pain. He threw himself weakly against his chains, crashing again to the floor.

He coughed violently, his lungs screaming with protest, but he forced himself to speak. His voice trembled, but it grew with each word. "If you're going to kill me, Seam, just go ahead and do it." He threw his arms out against his bindings a second time. His voice grew like oncoming thunder. "You need guards to kill me?" He glanced at the face of the Surrogator. "You think you need *him*? Kill me yourself you COWARD; sacrifice me to your monsters in the mirrors! Do it yourself if you can." Rage shook through him as he spoke, and the urge to fight again swelled within him.

Seam kept his back to Kull, but raised his head and laughed. Hosp's face was painted with confusion as he peered through the datalink connection.

Hosp's words whisked through the room, "What exactly *are you doing*, Seam?"

Seam stared back at the huge face of the Grogan Surrogator on the screen and sneered. "I'm issuing a new age for Candor, Hosp." Seam turned, pinning his blood-red eyes on Kull who stood trembling, filled with rage and fear on the metal platform in the center of the room.

"You think I want to kill you, Kull Shepherd? Oh, you are sadly mistaken. You might wish I had killed you before the end, but now I have much more *useful* plans for you. *Useful and extensive plans.*"

The chamber door opened and two guards stumbled in, their faces like ghosts. The men loafed toward Seam and offered a trembling salute. The taller one, the one who had been so coarse with Adley, spoke first.

"Officer Beorn, reporting for duty."

The shorter stout soldier saluted the king a second time, his voice barely above a whisper. "Officer Kalam."

Beorn continued, "Your command, sir?"

Seam smiled, his eyes flashing bright with sudden interest. "Yes, my friends, please come up to the platform. I need to ask you a few questions."

Kull could not look away as the two men dutifully followed orders. He knew what was coming.

Seam smiled widely, his face like a crocodile's. "You both were assigned to keep watch over the prisoners." The two nodded in silent agreement as the signs of fear flared on their faces. "Then answer me this," his finger shot out toward Kull, "how did *he* get out of his bindings?"

The taller guard nodded. "Yes, sir. He was secure, sir, I assure you. We checked his bindings twice." He glanced over at his fellow soldier who nodded, his face full of panic.

Seam shook his head, his eyes like daggers. "How did he use this under your watch?" Seam tilted his head, motioning for an answer as he held up the lock pick Adley had slipped to Kull.

Beorn stammered, searching for an answer, some explanation that would work, but he came up short. "I'm sorry sir, but... I... I don't know." Beorn glanced at Kalam, whose face remained stoic and disinterested.

Seam spoke, shaking his head. *"That's a pity."* Seam's black blade sliced through the air and severed Beorn's head in one swift motion. An explosion of blood poured out of his lifeless body as it fell to the ground. His body's red reservoir rushed out with each fading heartbeat to fill the troughs hewn in the metal floor.

Seam stared at the remaining officer as he wiped his blade clean. *"Now. Officer...what was your name again?"*

Shock kept the soldier's feet nailed to the ground.

"Kalam...sir."

"Yes. *Officer Kalam.* I want you to think very hard. It is of critical importance that I learn how Kull Shepherd received this lock pick."

Kalam's wild eyes stared at the blade in Seam's grasp. His life depended on his statement, and his mind exploded with dread. Out of the chaos, the answer revealed itself. *The nurse.*

"The nurse, sir. The nurse you ordered for the prisoners must have slipped it to him."

Seam threw the pick across the room, balled his fists and screamed, "I...ordered...no nurse! What was her name? I want it now!"

Kalam stuttered as he labored to remember the girl's name, her clearance code, anything that would help him.

He spoke, his words fumbling with cowardice, "I...I don't know, sir, but she was young. She had brown hair."

Seam's brow creased in fury as he grasped Kalam's shoulder. He lifted the blade to Kalam's throat as he spoke through clenched teeth.

"That is of no use to me, Kalam. Do you know how many young brunettes are running around Candor?" His blood red eyes broke from the soldier's. "I have no time for this. You have failed me." He looked into Kalam's face and his face softened. Pity replaced the look of rage. "You'll have only one more chance to serve me well."

Relief washed over Kalam for a moment. He exhaled with joy, but as he lifted his eyes, Seam drove the ebony sword through his chest. Kalam wheezed for breath and grasped at the blade's hilt before falling to the floor, joining his comrade at the king's feet.

Seam wrenched the sword from Kalam's chest, wiped the blade clean and returned it to his side. He was careful not to sully his boots as he stepped over the bodies beneath him and made his way back to the datalink screen. Hosp's voice droned through the speakers.

"This is what you wanted to show me, Seam? That you can slaughter my soldiers at your whim?"

Seam shook his head. "Failure will no longer be accepted under our rule, Hosp. These two paid for their errors. So will all who choose to idly serve us."

Hosp sneered, "Killing them does not bring us any closer to capturing those who have escaped!"

Seam chuckled, "The terrorists who escaped are of no consequence. *We are in possession of the keys.* All the keys! And we have *two of the five celestials.* Those fools are powerless. Let them run and hide." Seam glanced at the river of red flowing into the etched troughs. "Killing your soldiers has other uses though."

Hosp shifted forward in his seat and gazed past Seam. Kull followed the Surrogator's eyes toward Arakiel's mirror. The blood of the two soldiers had begun to pool at the feet of both the mirrors. They sizzled with an inferno of white fire as the sacrifices were absorbed into the nightmarish glass. Kull pried his swollen eyes open wider, forcing himself to look.

A frail figure of a stooped old man appeared within the second mirror. As the portal took in more and more blood, the man's tangled and matted white hair became as black as night. Thin arms grew and swelled with strength, and the man's frame magnified. Soon his figure filled the entire pane of glass. He sighed, stretching and flexing his arms as he leveled his red eyes with Seam. His voice exploded through the room like a thunderclap, making Kull's mouth go dry with fear.

"Who has awoken me?"

Aleph above. Kull's mind raced with the image of the skeletal serpent in the desert pit. *That voice.* The voice of the beast and the man standing in the mirror were the same. *That was him.* The realization brought a new onset of agonizing fear.

Seam smiled and stepped forward, bowing his head before speaking.

"Arakiel, first of the Dominion. I, High King Seam Panderean, have woken you, and I welcome you to join me."

The giant behind the glass sneered, pointed at Seam and balked. The whole room rumbled, and Seam felt the pinnacle beneath him sway from its height.

Seam fell to his knees as Arakiel's voice exploded with absolute authority, each utterance from the deity ripping through the entire room like a bomb. It forced Seam to cover his ears and grit his teeth in pain. "**You *welcome me*? Then you are clearly a fool. King or not, I join no one.** *No mortal dare commands me.*"

Seam flicked back the robe hanging over the bracer on his arm and held it toward the mirror as he growled, "That changes today, Serub. I am the Keeper of the Keys, and you and all your kin are now under my authority. *You are bound to me.*" Seam's face twisted in ecstasy at his own display of power as he continued, "Now, you are welcome to *join me,* Arakiel. Will you leave your mirror, or will I leave you to rot?"

Arakiel's chiseled face remained stoic. "Rot? You use strange words when speaking to a god." The warrior's face filled the mirror, morphing its countenance to that of a hideous boar. When the beast spoke, it felt to Kull that the entire Spire would collapse beneath them. "**I WILL NEVER ROT, FOOLISH KING. A THOUSAND YEARS ARE NOTHING TO ME. I WILL NOT SERVE YOU, EVEN IF I STAY LOCKED IN HERE FOR MILLENIA.**"

Kull glanced at Seam, who continued facing the beast in the glass, unfazed. He stood proud like a pillar, and for a moment Kull found himself amazed at Seam's prowess.

Seam narrowed his eyes and pursed his lips tightly. "Oh, *you will serve, Serub*. I will see to that."

Seam bolted for the mirror and thrust his right hand, gilded with the keys, into the glass. The glass gave way, rippling like water, and Seam made contact on the other side. Seam's eyes widened as his fingers quickly wrapped and locked down onto Arakiel's throat. The glass portal shimmered as the king tightened his grasp on the god that dared to oppose him. Arakiel bellowed in agony as Seam growled through gritted teeth.

"*You will serve.* Either we can work together or you will force me to display the power that has been destined to me. The choice is yours, *Serub.*"

Kull could not turn back his gaze as the once massive man began to shrivel beneath Seam's grasp. As Arakiel's strength waned under Seam's grip, the king's countenance began to change. He was flushed with new strength. His visible cuts and bruises from Kull's previous attack healed in an instant, and his skin became fresh and radiant with an unnatural light. Seam hurled the spirit to the floor behind the glass portal and pulled his arm back from the mirror, staring down at the bracer, shocked in the realization of its newfound potential. Seam stood in silence, captivated by his glorious keys. Hosp's face froze with a dumbfounded look of confusion as he muttered to himself, observing Seam's meteoric rise.

Abtren's beautiful form filled the vacant mirror next to Arakiel's and her voice cut into the room, "*High King*. My brother and I understand your power. We have long awaited our awakening, but we thirst for freedom, and we know that you are the only one who can grant it. Please forgive my brother's boldness and allow us to work together."

Seam sneered and kept his back to Abtren as he gloated over Arakiel's thin and wilted frame.

"Diplomatic words, Abtren, but I want to hear a promise of allegiance from Arakiel's own lips."

The ragged and ruined body of Arakiel glanced up, his lips quivering as he strained to speak, his once triumphant voice whittled down to a whisper, "*Let it be*."

Seam clasped his hands and smiled. He turned to face Kull and glory in the fear that grew on his face. Seam basked in it as if Kull's anxiety were the shining sun, allowing his steps to linger. Kull fought the chains binding him, desperate for escape, but there was nowhere to run.

Kull spoke, his voice defiant despite the fear that locked around his heart, "I should have cut you down when I had the chance. You are insane."

Seam shook his head and clicked his tongue, "Tsk, tsk, tsk. Call me insane if you wish. You will barely matter after I'm done with you. You too will serve me, despite your rebellion." He glanced back at the dead soldiers' bodies. *"All will serve me, in the end."*

His fist smashed against Kull's face. The blow sent Kull to his knees. He fought to regain his footing and set his eyes level with Seam again.

Seam snatched Kull's chains and unlocked him from the floor. He jerked the chain hanging from Kull's neck and forced him to the ground as if he were a dog. Kull wheezed and gasped in desperation as Seam kicked him in the gut. Blood poured from Kull's face, blurring his vision as he fought his way back to his feet but his damaged body refused to obey.

The king dragged Kull across the blood-soaked floor by the chain shackled to his throat. Kull scratched at the chain, and his feet flailed as Seam hurled him to the foot of Arakiel's mirror. He pressed Kull's cheek to the cold glass and leaned in next to his ear. Kull's heart threatened to hammer through his chest. He could feel a dark, famished energy seeping from the Serub's portal.

Seam whispered in Kull's ear, "Believe me. I would enjoy letting every last drop of your precious blood feed the beast inside, but I have decided to make you far more useful."

A fire sprung from Kull's shoulder as Seam dipped his blade into Kull's flesh. The piercing pain silenced the aches that had paralyzed Kull's body before. Black shadows squeezed into his vision and white-hot stars shot across his mind. In one swift motion, Seam lifted Kull to his feet and slammed his face back into the mirror.

"Watch what your blood has awoken."

The intense heat of the mirror burned and Kull could feel what little strength he had being siphoned away as the withered form of Arakiel blossomed again to full strength within the glass prison. Ice shot through Kull's veins as the Serub's horrible eyes met his own. The being rushed the mirror's edge like a rabid boar.

Seam jerked Kull from the mirror and threw him into the floor in a heap. There was no more fight left in Kull, no strength or energy remaining. He helplessly lay there, waiting to see what would unfold.

Seam growled with vile ambition, "Now. It is time to claim my destiny. *Candor is mine.* Come first, Arakiel, Lord of the Five! Come first and usher in the New Dominion of the Keeper of the Keys!"

Kull watched as Seam slammed his bracer through the mirror, which gave way like water. The keys bound on his wrist lit with unnatural colors, shades and pigments that Kull had never seen before. Kull opened his mouth to scream, but no sound dared retreat from his lips. As the Serub stepped out of the mirror and onto Candor's soil, Seam could feel the heavy hand of destiny upon him. The king held his arm between the two realities waiting to withdraw it until the red-eyed terror emerged on the other side. When he did, the mirror once again became solid, reflecting the room like any ordinary looking glass. Kull's mouth went dry with fear as the two leveled their eyes toward him and Seam spoke again, his voice laced with despotic rage.

Seam extended his index finger toward Kull like a weapon and glared upon him with a sick, twisted glee. "I command you, Arakiel, as your Keeper to *expel him."*

Arakiel, who stood two heads above the High King, glared down at Seam with consternation chiseled on his face. A long black snake of a tongue licked his lips as he spoke, his voice echoing through the chamber, "**No mortal has dared asked for this upon another, on this world or any other. This is a judgment reserved for the enemies of my kin.**"

Arakiel glanced at the second mirror where Abtren was standing. Her ivory skin gleamed like the sun and her eyes filled with a blossoming of kaleidoscopic colors. "**Does this one,**" Arakiel glanced to Kull, "**deserve this fate, sister?**"

Abtren nodded and paced the mirror's edges like a ravenous wolf. "If the High King wills it, it must be so, Arakiel. He is the Keeper! Do not tarry any longer! *I wish to be free.*"

Seam spat his words at the Serub, "Listen to your dear sister, Serub, if you wish your stay on Candor to be a pleasant one! Expel him, or you will go back into your mirror."

Arakiel gritted his teeth, his eyes burning like embers toward his new master. He growled and stepped forward to Kull. Kull's soul quaked within. *What is he going to do with me?*

"Know this, Seam Panderean of Lotte. Once this punishment is finished, it cannot be undone."

Seam laughed, "I would not want it any other way, Arakiel. *Now do it.*"

The Serub stretched out his hand, and Kull felt an invisible turbulence shake through his body. It was as if an earthquake channeled through Arakiel's hand, its full force directed at Kull. Like a ship caught in a hurricane, Kull felt something within him collapse under the weight of the storm. He felt himself being blown far away and he gasped at what he saw through the chaos. He could still see the Serub standing over him, as his broken body lay on the ground. Kull realized he was seeing *himself* lying on the floor, along with Seam who stood gloating over him. He saw his body whisked away, and Kull's perception soared up and away from that place and time.

What is happening to me? Kull felt like he was falling, but instead of going down, he was falling up and out. His perception left his body, the Serubs, and Seam in the Spire. He felt a flurry of substances and places move past him, but he could only absorb brief glimpses of what was happening. He saw a bird's-eye view of Zenith, alight in the desert night. He saw the Continent, all of Candor lying before him; a broken landscape shattered across an orb, floating in the darkness of space. Then there was only darkness. The darkness filled with screams, crying out for justice and restoration.

The screams echoed through the void until everything went completely black and collapsed into nothingness. A final jolt seared through Kull's consciousness until everything stopped.

"Stop!" Hosp screamed through the datalink. The cold, calculating voice that Seam had conspired with for so long evaporated and gave over to hot rage. "What are you doing? HOW DARE YOU COMMAND LORD ARAKIEL TO DO THIS?" He slammed his fist down on the console and stared down on the High King. "Do not forget all that I have provided you, Seam. You may hold the keys to control the Serubs, but you cannot control the populace of this world. You need me; do not forget our allegiance and our plans."

Seam shook his head and turned to the Surrogator's screen. "Plans must change, Hosp. It is time for you to decide who you will serve, for soon *all will fall under my bidding.* Order will return to this continent, even if I have to build up an army to do my bidding. *You know that my potential knows no bounds.*"

Hosp's eyes narrowed as Seam spoke. The snake like man leaned into the datalink screen before speaking, his words short. "Do not free Abtren until I am present. You owe that to me. I will be there soon."

Seam nodded with smiling defiance. "Fine, as you wish." The datalink screen went black and Seam stood next to Arakiel whose hulking figure seemed to fill the entire chamber. The king questioned the god like a child. "Did you do it, Serub?"

"**It is done.**" Arakiel's face showed no pleasure and no allegiance to his new master. He simply stood like a hulking golem, awaiting another task from the magician who controlled him.

"Good, let me see the quality of your work." Seam's eyes fell on Kull's body. He held up the bracer of the keys and spoke out his command. "Kull Shepherd of Cotswold. Arise."

Kull's broken body shook, seized with some dark power. The empty husk inhaled a ragged, choking breath and raised its head. It stood up like a fumbling marionette and turned to face the High King. Eyes vacant and dormant, Seam stood before this new creation and smiled, inspecting it as if it were a gift given on his birthday.

"*Very good*, Arakiel. Kull will prove to be an excellent servant for me now." Seam walked away from Kull's hollow body and stared out into the night horizon that lay before his perch on the Spire. "*All will serve.*"

CHAPTER TWO

The fortress monastery of Taluum lay hidden deep within the thick pine forests of Preost. Though it was filled with thousands of people, the nexus of the Alephian order had no major inroads. The city, carved and hollowed out of a natural outcropping of stone, was so well hidden within the dark green conifers surrounding it that it was invisible until one was standing at its gates. Willyn paced the rough-hewn floors of her room and peered out a window overlooking the pine trees gently rustling in the wind. The sweet smell of pinesap drifted in through her open window and filled the small room with its crisp aroma.

A solitary cardinal flitted its wings on a branch outside her window. Willyn stared at the small flame of a bird as it bobbed along the branch, unaware of its curious observer. After a few moments, the bird flapped its wings and disappeared through the thick canopy enveloping Taluum.

"Fly away, little red. I am not far behind you."

Willyn sighed and sat down at the small wooden desk in her room. She glanced around. It was a beautiful room with gorgeous wood plank floors, stone walls, and handcrafted furniture. Most would consider it a quaint paradise, but it felt like a prison cell to Willyn. She flipped open her datalink and scoured the live feeds. Her eyes stopped on a channel dedicated to the Red rebellion within the Groganlands. The channel was a difficult one to follow, surfacing sporadically only to disappear and then reappear again under a new handle. The current feed had a video of executions taking place within Rhuddenhall.

Rhuddenhall. So much had happened since Willyn had left the Rhuddenhall, chasing Grift Shepherd into Elum. She had been wrong about so many things, and the grief of all she had lost seized her chest with pain. *Hagan.*

Willyn drew in a deep breath and extinguished her emotions. As her nerves settled, she aimlessly scrolled the feeds. The executions in the Red City were troubling, but there was something more sinister in the images. Willyn looked past the executioners and into the on looking crowd. They were not protesting. They were celebrating. The resistance to Hosp and his regime was fading. She could read it on faces in the crowd. The tides were turning. She slammed her fist down on the small desk. "Two months! It has only been two months! How can they forget so quickly?"

How can they forget my family? How can they forget what we've done for them? What Hagan did for them? Willyn's heart felt like it was wrenched out of her chest, and she shook her head in disbelief. *It took so little time.* Only a couple of months had passed and people were cheering the execution of the Reds, calling them terrorists for defending their proud heritage.

She stood, turned off the datalink in disgust and stared out over the dancing pines. Her mind flitted back to the cardinal who flew free. *It's time for me to leave. To restore the Sars. To save the Groganlands.*

A gentle knock on her chamber door interrupted her thoughts.

"Come in," Willyn whispered.

A young girl stepped into the chamber and bowed her head, her hair held back tightly in a bun. "My apologies, Madam Kara, but the Mastermonk has requested your presence." Even through the monk attire and her ash covered face, the girls' beauty and grace was striking.

Willyn shut her eyes and sighed. "Did he give a reason? I haven't heard from anyone in days."

The young girl shuffled her feet and briefly closed her eyes. "No ma'am. If it would please you I could ask. Should I send a query?"

Willyn waved off the request. "No. None of that is necessary. When and where does he want to meet?"

The girl straightened her back and answered, her voice delicate but firm, "Now, ma'am. In the sanctuary."

Willyn scoffed, "Now hardly seems like the time to try and hold a prayer meeting."

The youth surprised her with his quick, stern response. "I don't mean to speak out of turn, my lady, but he does not seem prepared to pray."

Willyn's eyes narrowed and she nodded, dismissing the girl's overly polite attempt at bluntness. "Fine. I will be there."

The young monk bowed and whisked herself away behind Willyn's door. She was once again left alone in her beautiful coffin of a room. Her mind flickered back to the memory of being bound in Seam's control, awaiting an unjust fate in the Spire. Her memories were chaotic. So much had happened so quickly, and if it hadn't been for Shepherd's son, they all would have died that day to serve as chum for the sharks in the mirrors. Death had felt as inevitable as an avalanche threatening to fall. Taluum had offered her safety and rest for months, but she couldn't shake the feeling that the avalanche was still coming, threatening to consume them all. She wasn't used to hiding in wait.

I have to fight.

Willyn stepped through the massive wooden doors of Taluum's sanctuary and walked up the aisle cobbled with river rocks. The organic trail led to an altar composed of massive hewn tree trunks. The structure was unlike any Willyn had ever seen, and its composure made her heart dance in her chest. The buttresses that flew overhead were not made of stone, but of the trunks of ancient oaks, bent and bowed to form the rafters hanging dozens of feet overhead. Strung within the living sanctuary were seven white chandeliers lit with beeswax candles. No temple in Candor could match the simple elegance and awe of Taluum's sanctuary. As Willyn walked up to the altar, her face fell on Grift and Wael standing together in the bright candlelight. It had been weeks since they had formally gathered, but now after what felt like years both men's faces were painted with purpose.

She did not waste time with pleasantries as she gruffly addressed the monk as one would a servant, "You summoned, Mastermonk?"

Grift's eyes flared with contempt, but Wael's eyes smiled at Willyn with no reservation. "You are quite right, Madam Kara. Thank you for joining us at such short notice. We have much to discuss. I trust that your accommodations here in Taluum have been satisfactory?"

Willyn nodded curtly but said nothing. She glanced at Grift whose eyes seemed distant. The Spire had changed him.

Wael continued, "Good. Follow me." He beckoned his friends as he stepped up onto the altar's floor, decorated with a beautiful mosaic of river stone, each rock painstakingly etched with ancient runes. Willyn was shocked to see Wael slowly lumber up to the altar. The Mastermonk carried a noticeable limp, and leaned heavily on his ironwood staff, and though his face was strong, his body still carried the toll of Seam's torture.

He stopped at a tapestry hanging on the far wall. The daylight from the sanctuary's distant windows cascaded down on the fabric wall, and Willyn was struck by its shocking beauty. The fibers stitched within the rug seemed to vibrate with light, as if woven with gold. Willyn's eyes danced on the image of white ephemeral beings twisted together. Their forms were like that of a burning cloud. Their faces were painted in serenity, full with peace and filled with secret knowledge.

However, Willyn could not look away from the beast beneath the creatures' feet. The monster's face twisted with rage. Its eyes were filled with fiery hatred, and it wore a crown made of horns. It crouched over a pile of bones, the remnant of its victims. The beast's power burned through the woven fiber, but its gruesome display of might did not seem to affect the beings standing over it. Willyn's heart quickened, but she did not understand. Wael slipped beside Willyn and peered up at the tapestry, nodding as he spoke in a hushed reverence.

"This work is older than our Order. It was made by the last of the faithful Predecessors. It showcases the guardians that live in this place, even now."

Wael carefully rolled the tapestry away to reveal a locked iron door. Willyn's mind was awash with questions, but she still couldn't shake off the eyes of the burning beings that danced upon their foe. *What does it mean?*

Wael slid a key into the iron door and twisted the lock to life. Wael stepped through the portal and lit a small torch, ushering Willyn and Grift through the passageway.

"We must not tarry here. There are very few who are aware of this passageway, and we must not risk being seen."

Wael locked the door behind them and plunged them into the dark hallway. The walls were timber, the sides of a living giant tree trunk that grew perfectly into this secret chamber. The floor held a steady downward slope and the party descended, following the Mastermonk into a passage draped in silent shadows. The trail soon began to twist and branch off into a confusing maze of organic tributaries. At each intersection Wael would stop and examine the wooden walls before continuing.

Willyn quickly surrendered to the thought that she was lost beneath the castle city. Her navigation skills were worthless in the labyrinth beneath the sanctuary. As they continued to descend, there were no discernible features that could serve to orient her. Whatever Wael was examining was not evident, and from the look on Grift's face, it was not obvious to him either. With one quick turn, Wael led them out of the hallway made of living wood and into an earthen grotto. The walls opened slightly, and they were surrounded by a hollow chamber of rock and earth. The light of Wael's torch flickered, revealing a wooden trap door hidden in the river rock floor.

Wael spoke and pointed at a trap door. "We are nearly there. Stay close."

"Where are you taking us, Wael?" Grift's voice sounded haggard and worn. Willyn examined him in the dim light, shocked at how he sounded. For the first time she noticed how poor the warrior from Lotte looked. Thin, disheveled. His eyes seemed to be sunken back from his frame, and Willyn marked the weathered look of grief that clouded his face.

"Soon, Grift. I promise to discuss this matter with you both soon, but we must be silent here."

The trapdoor led to a steep ladder carved into the stone that emptied into a small, dark chamber. The thought of being at least fifty feet underground with a maze between her and the open air caused a claustrophobic tightness to twist in Willyn's throat. The chamber was a dead end with no exit other than the stone ladder rising behind her.

Grift's face filled with frustration. "Wrong turn, Wael? Why have you taken us here? What is so important that we have to crawl around underground to discuss?"

Wael did not respond but instead felt with his fingers around the carved out stone and knelt to the ground. He spread his hands across the walls before settling on his unseen mark. His hands pushed into the wall and, remarkably, the stone gave way. Wael pushed the hidden barrier, causing a rush of stale air to wash over the party. He turned and stiffened his back as he locked eyes with Willyn and Grift.

"*Do not speak.* Only listen to what I say." The monk's wide, white eyes stared through the dark, demanding their allegiance. "Do you understand?"

You must be kidding me, thought Willyn. *This is getting stranger by the second.*

Both Willyn and Grift nodded, and the three entered the hidden cavern. It too was carved out, and in the center of it was one solitary pane of glass mounted in the floor. A portal.

Aleph above. Willyn's mind exploded with fear, and her heart hammered in her chest. The monks had been hiding one of the monsters Seam was searching for underneath their own sanctuary.

Wael placed himself between Willyn and Grift and the mirror. He turned and lifted his gaze to his two allies. Grift bristled at the sight of the mirror and stepped forward, pointing a defiant finger past Wael as he spat with a fit of rage.

"How long did you intend to wait before telling us you had this thing? It has been two months, Wael! Two months! My son died and we have been sitting around in Preost for two months! We could have destroyed this mirror weeks ago! But we've been sitting here at your instruction, all while my son rots in the grave and my wife lays dying in Lotte!"

Wael's stoic face shattered and his body stiffened against Grift's words. The monk's voice swelled and consumed the entire room. "You think I don't understand your pain?"

The monk's eyes welled with tears as he spoke, "Be glad, Grift Shepherd. Your son spent his last hours saving your life and fighting for you! My daughter spent her last hours betraying me." He pointed his long finger at the mirror standing behind him. *"Trying to free these demons!"* He paused and finally whispered. "Do not speak of loss. Grift. Not to me."

The words sent Grift reeling. He turned away, his voice muted. When he did speak, his tone was meek. "Wael. My friend. How can you really be sure about Vashti?"

Wael sighed and wiped his eyes, the tight knot in his throat relaxing. "There is much I have not told you," the monk glanced between them both, "because I could not rest until I knew the truth. During these past two months you know scouts have been trying to discover safe passage out of Preost, but they have been doing more than just that." The monk's eyes were grave. "The borders...the borders are tight with Seam's men. Only two of my scouts found safe passage."

"What else have they been up to Wael? What are you hiding?" Grift stepped closer to Wael and peered into the monk's eyes.

"I told them to journey into Lotte to the place where the mirror of Abtren was hidden. *They found her there, Grift.* Her body. She was where I feared she would be. *Seam sacrificed Vashti to Abtren.*"

"So she was murdered, just like Kull?"

Wael shook his head and lowered his face, "No, Grift. She knew what she was doing. She had stolen several of our protected manuscripts from our scriptorium. She led Seam to Abtren. She was working as his ally to unlock the Serubs from their prisons, until..." he paused and swallowed, "she was no longer useful to him."

A chilling silence fell over the three as they all absorbed the truth of Vashti's betrayal. Behind them, a slow, menacing chuckle crawled through the room.

Willyn's eyes shot to the glass pane, only to see the image of a feeble old man, hunched over with a twisted spine that matched the smile etched across his smirking face. The old man's red eyes dripped with malice as he glanced from Grift to Willyn only to settle on Wael. His brow twitched as his chuckle grew to a raspy laugh that echoed through the entire chamber.

"So glad to hear your daughter's life was not wasted, monk. It won't be long until your blood feeds me."

Wael slammed his ironwood staff to the ground before shouting back at the apparition.

"In the name of Aleph, be silent! We did not request your party."

The man in the glass rushed to the mirror's edge and slammed his palm on the portal. He breathed in short gasps. A long black tongue flickered out beneath his teeth. Red fire burned within his eyes. He spoke, his voice like a thousand growling beasts speaking in unison, his face twisted with wicked rebellion.

*"THEN WHY ARE YOU HERE? You hold no power over me, and **that name** certainly has no control over me. Try again, monk."*

The old man sank back away from the glass, ran his long black tongue over his lips and chuckled. The wrinkles in his face began to tighten and fade as if he were being restored. Willyn stared at Grift and then Wael as fear fell over her. *How was this happening?* Without blood the beast in the mirror was strengthening. She stared at Wael and Grift in hopes to find an answer.

The being in the pane laughed as he examined the three. "I see that I have nothing to fear. Candor is full of ripe fruit, ready to pick." He stared at them with his eyes alight with power. "I long for the harvest, and it is fitting that *you would come to beg at the master's feet.*"

Wael stepped forward and bellowed back into the glass, "THERE IS BUT ONE MASTER! HIS NAME IS ALEPH!"

The man's eyes sunk from red to pools of black as he stared at Wael, his frame growing within the mirror, becoming more and more agitated with each mention of Aleph's name.

"That insect is already dead, Wael, Mastermonk of Preost." The being's voice filled with the sound of a rushing river. "I HAVE CRUSHED HIM BENEATH MY MIGHT. Nothing in the entire universe will ever compare with the feeling of destroying *that failure.*"

Grift stepped forward and stood beside Wael, placing a hand on his friend's shoulder.

"Save your lies, Serub! Aleph is not the one trapped behind a pane of glass. If you are so mighty then step out and face us now. Aleph bound you to your prison, and we will die before you step back out again."

The Serub's eyes widened with ecstasy at Grift's challenge. His smile grew to reveal a clean row of white daggers hidden within. He spoke, "If you wish to die, Grift Shepherd of Lotte, that can be arranged."

The walls of the room exploded into a hot inferno of red flames. Tendrils of heat wrapped around the three where they stood, and the mirror went black as midnight. The heat came in an instant, excruciating and inexplicable. The room's walls of solid stone began to melt around them in a bright orange glow.

Willyn managed to pull Grift through the fiery wall and back into the empty grotto. She turned, ready to plunge herself back in to get Wael, but she stopped as the Monk screamed at the Fallen in the mirror.

"Save your lies and illusions Serub! This ends now!"

Wael was standing in the furnace, unchecked by the flames. He lifted his ironwood staff and smashed it through the mirror. The glass exploded in a shower of crystal, and the flames immediately extinguished. The room returned to normal, dark and cool. Grift and Willyn stood blinking in disbelief outside the room, staring at the sea of glass scattered on the floor. Wael was hunched over his staff, weary but elated, with long white tendrils of smoke still flowing off him.

Grift stepped back into the room and let out a laugh, "We should have done that sooner, Wael." Wael nodded but there was no smile on his face. Willyn stood, her face hesitant, gazing at the shattered glass scattered on the floor. *So that is how we defeat them. Break their mirrors.* The thought fell hollow in her mind. *How could the Serubs be so fragile? Why keep the mirrors, if they could be so easily destroyed?*

Willyn's mind found the dreadful answers to her questions as the ground beneath her began to pulse with energy. The shards of glass vibrated with an electric intensity, and they hovered in the air, carefully joining together piece by piece. Large sections of the mirror floated above the ground and slid back into place at the center of the room. As the final pieces of the portal joined, the maniacal face of the Serub was waiting for them on the other side.

The Serub's eyes set onto Willyn and he smiled, "I can feel your fear, and it is quite…intoxicating." He rubbed his hands across his chest, and a voice clattered in the recesses of her mind. *Willyn Kara, the true Sar of the Groganlands. Oh, how beautiful and mighty you are.* The Serub's form continued to change, and his worn, decrepit features fell away, leaving only a striking and handsome young man. She was bewitched by his beauty, and Willyn felt the odd foreign sensation of her heart pounding with desire.

Willyn looked for Wael and Grift, but they were gone. She was alone with the handsome man in the mirror. He spoke, his voice no longer cruel, but sounding like a thousand bells chiming on a wedding day. "I could feast on your fears," he said with a calm smile, "or on your rage for an eternity." All of this inexplicably sounded wonderful to Willyn, and in that moment she wanted nothing more than for that to be true.

The Serub smiled, his eyes greeting hers, consuming her mind. "Yet we could do much more, Willyn Kara of the Groganlands." She could hear his voice, but his lips did not move. *"I know who you are. I know what you want. You, you want to free your people? I can make that happen...and so much more."*

Willyn's mind filled with rapture, and she saw herself donning the Helm of Rodnim the First. She was the Sar, and all of Rhuddenhall praised her as she sat on the Sar's throne. *You could have your revenge.*

Willyn found herself standing in a high place. She knew it instantly, the large crop of reaching red rock. Hangman's Pass. The wind blew through her shimmering red hair, and she looked down. Below, Hosp's lifeless body swung from a chain. She cranked her head and laughed, every care on Candor diminishing before her might.

Willyn found herself again facing the beautiful eyes of the young man, and his lips moved. "I can give you everything your heart desires, Willyn, if only you free me from this prison."

Willyn spoke, her mind petrified by the starlight in his eyes. "What of Seam? What of the others?"

The Serub laughed, and Willyn stared longingly at the mouth that once bore the razor sharp fangs of a monster. *That was a bad dream. That was not real.* She felt herself longing to feel those lips against her face as he crooned in her ears. *"Seam Panderean is a worm, and my kin...they hold no sway over me. I am their true master, and they fear me. Arakiel would wish me to be imprisoned forever because he knows what I can do. I am ISPHET, the Lord of Chaos."*

Willyn's whole body shook under the power of the Serub's name. *"What would you have me do, Isphet?"*

Behind her, Willyn could hear whispers that felt familiar. She turned, only to see an empty room.

"Pay no attention to them, Willyn. Find Seam Panderean, and cut him down. You can be the Keeper and the Sar of all Candor!"

The whispers behind her grew. She distinctly heard Wael's voice, but it was almost impossible to distinguish his words.

"Ha...Hag..."

Hagan.

Willyn's mind spun and she stared at the beautiful man in front of her. "What of Hagan? Can you bring him back?"

Isphet said nothing and looked away from her.

"Well, can you?" Willyn's mind snapped back into a cold, dispassionate reality. "You can't, can you?" She screamed at the apparition. "YOU CAN'T, CAN YOU?"

"LIAR!"

Grift and Wael stood over Willyn as she thrashed violently, slamming her head against the stone floor. Grift looked back in the mirror. The Serub had disappeared.

"What's happening, Wael?" The monk's face was frozen with fear as he stammered out a whisper.

"I should have never brought us down here." Wael lay on the floor next to Willyn and put his hand on her forehead.

"Release her, Isphet, Fallen of Aether! By the name of Aleph, Lord of your kin, release her!"

Grift jumped back as Willyn's eyes rolled open to reveal the red eyes of the beast within the mirror. Willyn opened her mouth, and the monster spoke through her, laughing maniacally, "SHE IS MINE, MONK!"

Grift's mouth went dry with fear, and he stared at Wael who began reciting the prayers of Aleph in the old tongue. The monk worked with a panicked fury. Grift rushed to help him hold her down on the ground, but he did not know what to do. Like a spark on a fuse, the answer came burning within his mind.

"Hagan, Wael! Remind her of Hagan!" Grift did not know if it would work, but everything in his bones told him that it was the only answer that made sense.

Wael nodded and screamed into Willyn's ear as she thrashed on the floor.

Wael sat up, his forehead covered in a cold sweat. "In the name of Aleph, release her! Willyn think of Hagan! Do not believe whatever lies he is telling you."

Willyn's eyes rolled open, and the beast growled, "SHUT UP, MONK. SHE IS MINE."

Without thinking, Grift slammed his fist into Willyn's face and screamed the name of his fallen friend.

"Hagan, Willyn! Come on! Fight for Hagan!"

An eternity seemed to pass, but suddenly the thrashing stopped. Wael glanced back to see the apparition reappear in the mirror. He grabbed Grift's arm.

"Get her up! We have to get out of here."

Willyn woke in her lush, clean bed, her head throbbing with untold pain. The light streaming outside the window was enough to make her scream, and she groaned aloud as she rolled over in clean white linens.

She felt hands fall on her, and she began to throw her fists. "GET OFF OF ME! GET OFF OF ME!"

A familiar voice called out to her. "Willyn! It's me!"

Willyn forced her eyes to open and tried to focus on the two blurred figures standing before her.

Grift spoke, "Are you okay, Willyn?"

Willyn was not okay. Her head felt like it had been run over by a truck. Nausea washed over her as she spoke. "Ughh...my head." It felt like everything behind her eyes was on fire.

A deeper voice spoke. "Willyn, what did he say to you?" Willyn's mind heard the words, but she could not understand them. *Who was 'he?'*

The question came again, the deep voice penetrating her mind with terrible clarity. "What did he say to you, Willyn?"

The recollection came quicker than lightning. *The Serub. The beautiful, terrible Serub.*

Willyn shuttered as she spoke, "He offered me everything I ever wanted. If only I would release him."

She looked back at the sound of Wael's voice, her eyes focusing on both he and Grift. "Am I going to be okay? What happened to me?"

Wael glanced at Grift and spoke, "I believe you will be fine. I should have never taken the two of you down there. In all the times I have visited the chamber, and they have been few, the Serub has never displayed himself, but it is obvious that Isphet is...less predictable than I supposed."

Grift shuddered, "Aleph above, how could Seam align himself with those things? What in all of Candor would make him want to do this?"

Wael's firm hand fell on Grift's shoulder. "The Serubs are very powerful, even in their captivity. Seam Panderean, no matter his motives, is completely under their sway, believing he can control them."

Willyn looked at Wael and spoke, her mind rushing with the sight of the man she saw in the mirror. "Does Seam control them?

Grift looked at Wael gravely. "The Order always taught that he who holds the keys controls the Serubs."

Wael nodded but measured his words. "The Keeper of the Keys, according to the prophecies and scriptures, can control the Fallen, but as we've seen today, that does not mean that we have a full understanding of these subjects. Take our encounter with

Isphet. He has restorative powers that I did not realize, powers that are never mentioned in our sacred texts."

"What do you mean?" Willyn asked.

Wael's eyes were grave. "We have known that the Serubs gain strength through blood, but Isphet's power surged without a single drop of blood coming near his mirror. Isn't that interesting?" Wael furrowed his brow as he pondered the encounter. He blinked, "I am sorry to you both. It was foolish to have taken you below, but you needed to know the truth of what we hide here in Preost."

Grift shook his head, dismissing the apology. "What exactly is our plan now? It's obvious that the Serubs are stronger than we thought. We can't even destroy the mirrors. And Seam's filling the datalines with propaganda about his alliance between Lotte and the Groganlands."

"What is he calling it?" Willyn knew there was some name for this alliance, but she could not place it with her foggy mind.

Grift turned and spoke. "His New Dominion. Men and women across Candor are lining up to support him and his cursed regime. We know he is seeking the remaining mirrors. What do we do? We have already wasted almost two months hiding trying to figure out how to even get back out of Preost, much less take down Seam's new kingdom."

Wael paced the floor, his face ignoring Grift's critique. "This time has not been as wasteful as you think, Grift. Since our escape from the Spire, I have been very busy, searching for answers." Wael's hands trembled by his side as he leaned on his staff. "The portals cannot be destroyed. They never could be."

Willyn chirped, "Then why did you break the mirror, Wael?"

Wael smiled, his face knowing, "For confirmation, dear Willyn. I trust the records of the previous Mastermonks up to a point, but I needed confirmation." The Monk's face turned grave as he looked at her, "I just wish they had told me about Isphet's strengths as well."

Willyn's face flushed at the sound of Isphet's name. "So what now? How are we going to fight something we can't destroy?"

Wael stood and silently stared at the two.

Grift broke the silence. "Wael, there has to be something else! Something hidden in your scriptures on what we must do!"

Willyn slammed her fists down on her bed and forced her aching body to stand. "We don't have time to read more old manuscripts! Sure, *we* might be safe here, but I am watching my people get slaughtered every day at the hands of the men trying to free those things." She steadied herself by the window, allowing her eyes to focus in the dimming daylight.

Willyn came to her answer. "*I have to leave.* You said the scouts finally found a couple ways out. I have to defend my people. My place is with them, not hiding here in Taluum searching for answers. I have to get back what is mine."

The ghostly whisper of the Serub flickered in her mind. *I can make that happen.* Her face went pale, and she shook the voice away.

Grift stepped next to Willyn and put his hand on her shoulder. "I agree." He stared at Wael. "We have to take action now, Wael. We might be weak and outnumbered, but hiding here won't do us any good. The Realms are already backing Seam and his New Dominion. Soon his influence will control the entire continent. You've seen the same datalink feeds."

Wael nodded. "I have seen the same reports. Candor is being swayed. I agree with you both. It is time to take action." On his face a secret answer burned within and a wide smile grew. "I believe I know how to strike."

Willyn leaned forward excited "What's your idea? How do we fight back?"

A look of determination swept over Wael's face. "We cannot destroy the portals, but there is nothing preventing us from taking them and hiding them again. We can accomplish that. Even if we die, their hiding places will die with us."

Willyn shook her head. "I don't know, Wael. The Serubs are not defenseless, even in their mirrors. We've seen that today."

"What choice do we have, Willyn?" said Grift.

Willyn snapped, "We make the only logical choice we have. We make for the Groganlands. I will rally the Reds to take back my Realm. We need an army to fight Seam's Dominion." She stared at their stoic faces. She continued, her voice passionate, "Seam only has two of the five mirrors. How quickly can he find the rest?"

Wael shook his head. "With Arakiel in his possession and control Seam will soon have the knowledge of all of the other Serubs' locations. Arakiel was the last to be hidden away by the Sixth."

Grift's mouth fell open. "Whoa. Wait a minute, Wael. The Order has always held that the Keeper imprisoned the Serubs in the mirrors. What is this talk about a sixth?"

Willyn rolled her eyes. "What are you two talking about?"

Wael stared at Grift, his face tense and his brow creased with worry. The monk shook his head. "The time has come to share a truth known only by the Mastermonks. The Sixth, the Exile, was indeed the first Keeper of the Keys. The Sixth was the only one of the Celestials to regret his decision to abandon Aleph. As penance to Aleph, the Sixth locked his kin away, deceiving them with illusions that they could control and destroy Aleph himself. That was all a lie. So with a lie he locked them away in the mirrors of his own making and hid the keys with the Order of Keepers so they could never be unlocked again."

Grift stood silent, his eyes wide.

"So there is a Sixth Serub? Is it locked in a mirror, too?"

"No, and he is not what you should call a Serub. He is the Exile. The Sixth, completely unlike his kin. Due to his work, Candor remained safe for hundreds of years as he lived in hiding."

Willyn asked the obvious, "Well, where is he?"

Wael nodded. "He still walks the continent disguised as a man. He has gone under many names, but has always secretly aided our Order and Aleph's work on Candor."

"How does that help us now, Wael?" Grift said. "It doesn't change the fact that we need to do *something* now. Whoever the Exile is, he isn't here, and we don't have the luxury to wait on him."

Wael weighed the words and finally nodded his head. "You are correct; we cannot sit and wait any longer." The monk turned first to Willyn. He wrote on a small scroll of paper and handed it to her. "These are the coordinates to an encrypted datalink channel. I'll be running coms to you as you approach the Groganlands." Wael stared at her, his penetrating eyes making her nervous. "Head for Legion's Teeth. There have been rumors of another mirror held there for many years, rumors that must be investigated. Go and see what you can find."

"You are sending me to the Teeth? What good is it for me to go to the mountains? What about the Reds? I have to seek them out and rally what forces are left!"

Wael nodded. "I will search the archives to validate the exact location, but you must go to Legion's Teeth first. Find the mirror, then rally the Reds. The Reds are no good if the Serubs are unlocked. I will arrange that you are escorted in secret to the city."

"Escorted?" Willyn scoffed at the idea. "That's ridiculous. Who are you going to get to escort me, monk?"

"Someone I would trust with my own life. Make for the railcar to the Teeth. He will be waiting for you. Contact me as soon as you get to the Groganlands."

Willyn's face scowled at the monk's command, but she nodded and tucked the coordinates in her pocket. "What about Grift?"

Grift coughed and spoke up. "I need to get back to Lotte and bring back Rose. She's not well, and I need to be with her now. She doesn't even know about..." his sentence trailed off. Grift rallied and continued, "While I'm there I'll touch base with Ewing. He's been working on an underground trade network of resistance.

He'll have contacts we can leverage, so we can expand our reach into Lotte and Elum." Grift swallowed hard and glanced at them both. "I won't be long, but I have to go. Once I get Rose safely into Preost, I'll make for Elum. If there's a mirror there, I'll find it. I'll move as fast I can."

Wael nodded and sighed, handing a small chip for his datalink. Take this. This should show you the fastest and safest route my scouts found into Lotte. Be cautious, Grift. Get to Rose and find Ewing. We will need his assistance." Wael paused and looked at them both. "It's not ideal, but it is time for us to separate. Go now with Aleph's blessing. I'll be in touch with you both via datalink."

Willyn turned for the door but paused and called back to Wael. "What are you doing? Are you going to move our friend downstairs?"

Wael's face locked with purpose as he shook his head. "No. This location is guarded by more than stone walls. I will seek the Exile."

CHAPTER THREE

Gulls cackled overhead as the Elumite frigate carrying Seam and his detail pushed further out into the Endless Ocean. The green, foaming waves slapping against the hull gave way to bottomless, blue churning water. The shore dipped beneath the horizon, and Seam closed his eyes. He breathed in the salty air as he paced the ship's deck. Bronson stood silently by his side.

Seam spoke, his eyes dancing across the magnificent view of the ocean. "You are awfully quiet today, Bronson."

Bronson shifted and stood straight as if being called to attention. "My apologies, sire. I...I am only homesick."

Seam gave his Captain of the Guard a sideways glance. "Why did you not bring your family down to Zenith? I would have seen that your expenses were paid. You would have had every opportunity to be with them there."

Bronson nodded and gave a humble smile. "Your generosity knows no bounds, sire. It was my desire that they stay in Lotte, my lord."

Seam turned to face him. "And why is that, Bronson?"

Bronson felt his heart slam against his chest, but he forced himself to remain composed. His mind flickered with the images of the gorgeous woman in the glass. The woman who he now knew was free and walked again among mankind. The woman whose mouth held a valley of bleeding daggers that made him want to kill himself. Cold beads of sweat formed on his brow as his king questioned him. Everything within him wanted to scream out the true answer for his decision. *I would rather die than to have my children near the nightmares you are unleashing.*

"I'm afraid that my wife and children are very content in Lotte. It is all they have ever known." Bronson feigned a smile, praying to Aleph that Seam would accept the answer.

Seam nodded. "I understand. Mother will not come to Zenith either. She would change her mind if she could see what we were building."

I very much doubt that, thought Bronson.

Seam continued to stare out over the horizon. "I'm going to the bridge. We can't be far now."

Bronson nodded. "Very good, my lord."

Seam patted Bronson's shoulder and climbed the metallic stairs, making his way to the ship's control room.

The High King entered the bridge with few pleasantries. "Captain, how far are we from the coordinates I provided?"

The burly captain slid his chair to a nearby panel and blankly stared at the screen for a few moments before turning back around. He ran his hands through his long, greasy beard, calculating nervously.

"We appear on course, sir. We should arrive within the hour."

Seam glanced down at the coordinates on the screen before peering back out over the empty horizon. "Very good. Make sure your divers are prepared as soon as we arrive. I don't want to waste any time."

The captain grunted as he shifted in his seat and tipped his head. "They will be ready. Any details on this mission, sir? I'd like to prepare them for what might be ahead."

Seam turned for the door before replying over his shoulder, "I will inform them once we arrive."

Seam's datalink buzzed to life as Hosp's face appeared across its screen. His cold gray eyes shifted from side to side and his nostrils flared as he spoke. "Seam, what is the status of the third mirror? Arakiel and Abtren are *growing restless*."

Seam did not bother to make eye contact with Hosp. Instead, he peered out over the bobbing waves. "Where is your patience, Hosp? Do you still doubt my abilities after all we have accomplished? We are within minutes of the coordinates Arakiel provided."

As he was speaking the frigate slipped into a halo of perfectly calm water. The waves came to an immediate halt, forming a perfect ring of water stretching nearly five hundred feet in diameter. Seam leaned over the ship's railing and peered into the calm waters as they rippled away from the intruding vessel. As he focused on the center of the circle he could feel an electric charge inch up his arm, resonating from the bracer and its keys. He lifted his sleeve and smiled as he flexed his fist and felt his skin absorb the energy radiating from his wrist. The keys were calling out to the mirror resting in the waters below. Seam called through his datalink to the bridge.

"We are here! Shut down the engines and deploy the divers."

Seam stood beside Bronson as four divers clad in black wetsuits emerged from below deck. The captain of the ship cut the engines as commanded and fumbled down the stairs to join the men at the frigate's edge.

Seam stepped to the railing and peered over, allowing his eyes to focus into the deep abyss. He had not noticed it before, but the water's color had shifted. What was once clear blue now looked dark as midnight. He turned and pointed into the water as he addressed the divers.

"Gentlemen. Below us rests an object of extreme importance for our alliance. A very important artifact that must be treated with the utmost care. Resting somewhere within these waters is a mirror."

One of the divers shifted and smirked. Another shot a glance at the other crewmembers and spoke.

"A mirror, sir? Does it bear any special markings? Any other furniture that we need to pull out?" The diver's remark sent a low chuckle through the troop.

Seam shook his head. He constrained his frustration to a whisper as he stepped close to the inquisitive man.

"This is no piece of *furniture,* you fool. This mirror is a lost piece of our continent's history and it is extremely valuable. Now you will do your job and get in the water or you will not make it home." The divers' chuckles evaporated in an instant.

Seam stared at the men and then turned to look at Bronson. "Just so there won't be any mistakes, I am sending my own Captain of the Guard down with you."

Bronson's face went white.

"He knows exactly what we are looking for."

The divers nodded as Bronson fought the urge to faint. He approached the king and whispered. "Sire? Me in the water?"

"You heard me, Bronson. Now go suit up." Bronson bowed his head and nodded.

Bronson joined the dive team in an ill-fitting rubber suit and fidgeted with his oxygen tank lines as he addressed Seam. "Sir, if I may beg for relief once more. I am not properly trained."

Seam leaned in close to Bronson's ear and whispered. "I trust you will not fail me, Bronson. Failure is *not* an option. Do this *for your family's sake.*"

Bronson swallowed hard and suppressed the urge to throw Seam and his insanity into the midnight waters below. "Yes, sir. Understood."

The ship's captain dropped a gate in the railing and kicked a ladder over the ship's edge before walking back to the diving crew.

"Well, you heard the king. Hit the water, men. Careful to keep the thing in one piece." He turned to Seam and offered a smile before spitting a wad of dark tobacco overboard and hiking his sagging trousers. "Don't worry, sir. These men are the best divers in all of Elum. We will have your mirror up in no time."

Seam squeezed the frigate's railing and offered a thin smile. "Thank you, captain. I trust we won't have any issues."

Bronson's eyes strained to focus through his goggles. The cold, murky waters clouded his vision. It was like swimming in an ink well. He fired up his dive light and tossed the beam from side to side beneath the water's surface as he tried to gain a sense of direction. The other divers circled around him and fanned out as they pushed into the deep waters. Two of the men had towlines attached to their belts. Bronson kicked his flippers and pushed himself further into the depths following the lead of the others. He swam away from his king and closer to another monster buried in the depths of the sea.

You can stop this all now. The thought pervaded Bronson's thoughts. *This is your chance.* As Bronson and the divers plunged further into the deep, the reality of the situation lay on him like a lead weight. There were three possible outcomes. He could somehow stop this mirror from ever making its way to the surface or he could die trying and sink into the Endless Ocean. The last and worst scenario is that he could fail and live to face the consequences. The thought of Abtren alone was enough to come to a decision. *I will not willfully allow another one of these abominations on Candor.*

Resolve quickened in Bronson's spirit and propelled him to find the mirror before any of the other divers. He observed the other divers were swimming in a large circle, slowly covering an organized perimeter. With each pass they drew closer, tightening their search. *The center.* There was no need to search the perimeters of these calmer waters. The mirror would only be in one place: the center of the search area.

Bronson did his best to guess where the center would be. Breaking formation, he pushed downward, leaving the other divers behind. The depths swallowed him, and he could feel the pressure of the Endless Ocean surround him. He swam for what seemed like a long time until he was finally at the sea's floor. He looked around, swirling in the depths for the mirror, but there was nothing there except dull gray sand. He scanned the gloom, desperate to find the cursed object. *This isn't right. I know it is here.* Bronson shot his light from side to side, its beam barely penetrating the thick black water. He looked back up toward the surface, trying to orient himself using the other divers. Their searchlights looked like nothing more than fireflies blinking in the midnight sky. He outpaced them by a good distance but he realized he had drifted too far to the edge of the search zone. To be so deep was disorienting, so he turned toward what felt like the center and swam hard, hovering over the sea floor. A strange realization came over him. *There is nothing alive in this water.* No fish, no seaweed, not even shells littered the sand. As he pushed toward the center of the search zone his datalink lit up and Seam's voice roared over his headset.

"Bronson, how is the search progressing?"

"Still searching, sir." Bronson mumbled through his mouthpiece. "I think..."

Bronson stopped mid-sentence as he nearly swam into his own reflection. The shimmering plane of glass stood proudly, lodged into the sandy floor.

"You think what?" said Seam.

"Apologies, hard to speak in this thing. Think it may be hard to find." Bronson shined his light on the surface, doing his best not to stare too deeply into the mirror. "I will let you know once I find it."

"Very good," Seam answered. Bronson sighed as the datalink went dead and he was left alone with his one opportunity to stop Seam's insanity. Bronson shot a glance overhead and lowered the intensity of his searchlight, hoping to prevent the other divers from realizing his discovery.

Bronson's eyes darted across the ocean floor as he tried to think of what exactly to do. He grasped at the knife on his belt. *I can kill the divers. No. It won't work. Seam will get more.* As Bronson fought for answers, his eyes found what he needed. A large stone was lodged in the ocean floor not far from the mirror.

A broken mirror is no good to the King. Bronson's heart raced as he swam to the rock and loosened it from its resting place. Bronson strained and finally lifted the rock off the ocean floor. As he moved for the shimmering glass, he glanced up, ensuring the other divers would not see his treachery. They were still far enough out; they had not tightened their perimeter enough. This was his chance.

Bronson tightened his grip on the rock and whispered a prayer to Aleph. "Let my death be quick for I know my king will blame this failure on me. End my life quickly, Aleph, so I may rest in Aether." He held the rock and tightened his grip. "Remember and bless my children." Bronson grabbed the mirror's edge and cut off his light. Using feel to guide him he slammed the rock into the pane of glass like a hammer. The first hit thudded against the glass with little effect. The deep waters made it difficult to gain momentum but Bronson continued to fight, smashing the rock against the mirror.

Bronson furiously attacked the mirror until he felt the portal give way beneath the hand he used to anchor himself. As the glass snapped within Bronson's grasp, a jagged edge of the broken mirror sliced into Bronson's leg. Bronson let out a muffled scream and cut his search light back on. *Aleph, no.* His light revealed a cloud of crimson rising from his leg, but he could see that his work had been successful. The mirror had shattered with a large section broken away from the base.

As Bronson dropped the piece of mirror from his hand, it passed through the blood pouring from his wounded leg. The shattered pieces of glass ignited with an uncanny glow and shot through the water, rejoining with what had just been hewn away. *The mirror was healing itself*. The water around him began to bubble and Bronson felt a searing heat. *The water is boiling.* Bronson desperately kicked himself clear from the water that raged with life, his eyes locking onto the mirror that was once again pristine.

The water roared, stirring the sand and silt on the ocean floor into a tempest.

Through the sand, blood, and rushing water Bronson's headlamp shone on the face of a beautiful young woman trapped within the glass. She stood tall with a waterfall of black hair and piercing blue eyes. Bronson pushed away from the penetrating gaze as fast as he could manage, turning his face away from the monster that he knew was waiting inside. He would not dare to look at the face of another Serub as long as he could will it. As he pushed himself backwards, he slammed into something. He turned, his heart in his chest, only to see the dark mask of one of the other divers.

The diver carried the towline. Bronson's eyes locked on the line and quickly weighed his options. *She can't go up. She can't be freed.* The fellow diver tried to plunge into the vortex past Bronson, but was whipped back from the violent current. It swept him end over end through the water. As the diver tumbled by, Bronson reached out to cut the line to his oxygen tank and push him back toward the surface, a pillar of bubbles erupting in the depths.

He watched as the diver steadied himself only to realize his line was compromised. He swam rapidly for the surface. *One down*, Bronson thought. The other three divers descended and closed in on the scene, pushing for the mirror. Two of the men planted anchors in the ocean floor and reached out to attach their lines to the third diver, the one who carried down the last towline. The two then hooked their lines to their own belts and used themselves as counterweights as they moved with skillful precision to pull the third diver toward the mirror.

The middle diver thrashed between the rushing waters but successfully grabbed hold of the mirror's edge. Bronson swam to one of the anchors in the sea's floor and slashed it with his knife. The line snapped with a resounding POP, whipping into one of the divers, sending him careening through the darkness.

The towline diver motioned for Bronson to come over and help him secure the mirror, but as Bronson made his way toward him he felt a massive blow connect with the back of his head. The anchor line had whipped across his skull, and the darkness of the water overtook Bronson as he lost consciousness.

Seam stood proudly as the shimmering mirror was lifted out of the dark waters. He could not hide his delight. He scanned the water and counted the four divers joining the crew. *Only four.* Bronson was missing.

The diver responsible for hooking the mirror ripped his mask away and looked to the others. "What is this thing? What was that all about?"

The oldest of the men pulled back his mask and chuckled nervously. "I've never seen anything like that. Nothing causes that kind of a stir. It was like a tornado down there."

The diver that hooked the mirror looked to Seam, searching for answers. His eyes were wide and he gasped for breath. "But did you see her? I swear there was a woman in that mirror! This thing ain't right."

The other diver gave a mocking laugh. "What? A woman? The pressure got to you, Murdock. Those rapids knocked you silly."

The diver slapped at the water. "I swear, man! Some woman was in that mirror. Her eyes. They were crazy blue." His comrades went silent, and Seam's lips pursed in anticipation. "Look, I know what I saw. Look at it!" The diver pointed to the mirror that was hanging overhead, but it simply reflected the evening sun. Murdock stared at his companions. "Come on, guys, you know I don't play around. I swear I saw something."

Seam clenched his fist and paced to the edge of the ship. He stared at the four divers as they chattered over the mirror's retrieval. "Where is Bronson?" The men looked at each other and returned vacant stares.

One of them dared to speak, "He hasn't resurfaced?"

Seam shook his head and pointed to the water splashing around the divers. "Get back down there and find him! Do not come back to this ship unless you have him with you. We will not leave without him."

As if on cue, a figure resurfaced from the water behind the other divers. Bronson swam slowly over to the ship, and the divers helped heave him up to the deck. Red-hot blood painted the ship's deck, pooling from beneath his body.

Seam screamed, his eyes flaring at the ship's captain. "Medic! Get a medic over here immediately!"

An alarm sounded as two medics rushed to Bronson's side. In the commotion no one noticed the river of blood running toward the freshly discovered mirror. Seam looked from the mirror to the blood making its way across the deck. He rushed to put his foot down against the stream. As Bronson's blood pooled around Seam's foot the High King called for the crane operator. "Hoist the mirror! Get it off the deck!"

"What, sir?" The man at the crane's controls called back, eyes wide from his cockpit.

"I said lift the mirror! Now!" Seam yelled.

"But, sir, you just had me drop it."

"I said lift it now!" Seam's voice ripped from his throat, and his eyes locked on the blood continuing to inch toward the mirror's edge.

The crane operator gunned the engine, which roared with an explosion of black smoke, ratcheting the mirror off the deck just as Bronson's blood slipped below the pane of glass. The ship's captain bumbled over, his face alight with questions. He glimpsed at the mirror. "What seems to be the problem, sir? Did you not want the mirror on deck?"

Seam composed himself and took a deep breath before answering. "Captain, this mirror is of extreme importance, and my Bronson's blood was about to soil and tarnish it. I need you to have your men cover it and store it away below deck. I will inspect it shortly."

"Fair enough," answered the ship's captain. "As you wish. Come on, men! Drape it and then lower it into the holds."

Seam stood staring at Bronson as the medic poured over his injury. *That was close, Seam,* he thought to himself. *Too close.*

Bronson hovered over a steaming cup of tea with a wool blanket draped over his shoulders. He tilted his head back against the wall and closed his eyes. The fluorescent lights within the boat made him feel nauseous, and his ears would not stop ringing. He rubbed at the thick bandages wrapped around his thigh.

The door to Bronson's cabin slid open, and Seam stepped into the room. Bronson's heart pounded, and he tried to swallow the knot forming in his throat. He wanted to sip at his tea and pretend nothing was out of place, but he could not swallow. He could barely breathe.

"Bronson." Seam's voice was quiet, and it made Bronson's skin crawl. "What *exactly* happened?"

"Um. Sir. I don't know." Bronson refused to lift his eyes to Seam. He knew his treachery was about to be punished. "I'm drawing a blank."

"I need you to think very hard. What did you see down there? How were you injured?" Seam's brown eyes pinned Bronson to the floor. "The other divers were fine. They said you were the first one down." Seam's voice crawled like a predator ready to pounce.

Bronson fumbled for answers as he stared down into the brown tea sloshing in his cup. *What do I say?*

"Something did happen down there, sir. "

Seam's eyes squinted. "What happened, Bronson? What did you see? Was it, perhaps, a woman?"

The mention of the woman in the glass stopped Bronson's breathing as he choked back his emotions. The woman's pitch black hair and blue eyes were unforgettable, her face burned in his memory. Bronson knew exactly what he had seen, but he shook his head, lifting the brown tea to his lips and taking a heavy slurp. He would not even acknowledge the abomination that he knew was hiding on the other side of the mirror. "No woman, my lord, just a lot of violent waters. The mirror was surrounded by a wall of raging water that was boiling hot. Unlike anything I've ever seen. Once we got close to it, it went crazy. One of the towlines broke loose and must have caught my leg."

Seam nodded and sauntered closer to Bronson. He turned and looked to the cabin's door and then kneeled to meet his eyes.

Bronson spoke back up to try and combat the awkward stare. "I don't understand it, sir. How does an underwater vortex simply appear out of thin air?"

Seam chuckled and stiffened his back. "Don't you mean thin water, Bronson?" Seam smiled and laughed. "Witches, sorcerers, and other religious fanatics, Bronson. They must have cursed the area where they hid the mirror. But as you can see, with some ingenuity and teamwork it is now safe."

"If I might ask, my king," said Bronson. "Why the mirrors? Why curse them? Why hide them? What are they?"

Seam smiled as he stared back at Bronson. The smile made Bronson's skin grow cold.

"I think it is time I show you something, Captain Donahue."

Bronson's heart threatened to break free from his chest as he stood in the central cargo hold alone with Seam and the mirror pulled from the dark waters. Seam pulled back the fabric wrapped around the portal and sighed as he stepped back. He stood with his arms crossed and examined the glass's smooth reflection.

"They can't know that they were right, Bronson," said Seam.

"Uh, who, sir? Who can't know they were right?"

Seam turned and pointed overhead. "The divers. The divers claimed that they saw a woman."

Bronson tried to feign ignorance and shook his head. "What do you mean?"

A grin crept across Seam's face as he pulled back his glove. "Let me show you, Bronson. I would like you to meet her. *Nyx*. One of the five deities that will be assisting in reshaping the face of Candor."

Before a word could leave Bronson's lips, Seam cut his hand and pressed it against the mirror's edge. The dark hold illuminated with hot, blinding light, and Bronson cursed his life.

Nyx approached the mirror's edge and looked straight at the High King and then toward Bronson. Her eyes were a crisp, cold blue like the Endless Ocean. Bronson's whole body shook with uncontrollable fear, and he shielded his eyes.

"High King Seam." Nyx's voice sounded like the tides, rolling like thunder. "The Keeper of the Keys. I am glad you have finally come."

Seam's eyes dilated with the sound of the Serub addressing him with such respect. "So your kin have spoken to you about me?"

The Serub produced a meek grin and nodded, whispering, "Yes, my Keeper. My kin and I speak of many things, even behind our prison walls. You will encounter no resistance from me, as I know the merit of your cause. I would see Candor at peace. I will gladly aid you."

Seam smiled and nodded and glanced back at Bronson. "Now you see, dear Bronson, the scope of my plan. The divines will lead our world into a new age, and I alone will rally their power." He pulled up his sleeve to reveal the iron bracer where all of the Keys of Candor rested.

Bronson's eyes went wide, and he nodded, feeling as though he could die. There was no more guessing, there were no more secrets. Seam had revealed his intentions and he planned for Bronson to follow dutifully.

Aleph above. For weeks Bronson had only assumed that Seam had one or two of the keys, not all five. *I thought I had more time.* As his mind whirled through the implications of his new knowledge, the Serub's eyes locked on Bronson, pinning his heart to the wall.

She spoke, and Bronson knew that his plans were doomed. "You. You were the one who tried to destroy my mirror."

Bronson's mouth went dry, the fear of death wrapping around him like a straightjacket. He looked at the High King, but it was as if he had not heard a word the Serub said. In fact, it was as if the High King was frozen, unable to converse or hear anything that was transpiring.

He stared deeply into the ice caverns of the woman's eyes as time stood still. Nyx spoke, filling Bronson's mind with an ultimatum. *You think me a monster, Bronson Donahue, Captain of Lotte?* Bronson could not look away from her glacier colored eyes. They froze everything, even time itself in their tracks. He could not blink, react, or run. He could not move. All he could do was stare, falling deeper into their depths like someone slipping into an icy river. The color of her eyes flickered red for the briefest of seconds before pooling into a blackness that Bronson had never seen on Candor, a dark warning flare that sapped all of the light from the chamber.

Today, you must choose which monster you will serve, mortal. Will it be your precious king? If you remain loyal to him, I assure you he will kill you, himself. I need only mention what I saw in the depths of the Endless.

Bronson felt the pieces moving. He knew she had him in checkmate before he could say a word. He swallowed hard and hung his head. "You leave me with little choice."

CHAPTER FOUR

The bustling city of Vale gave little notice to the old man shuffling down its cobbled streets. The man avoided the open storefront windows and kept his head down, his hat pulled over his wrinkled brow to shield his eyes from the burning sun. The only feature about Arthur Ewing that stood out was his new chrome leg that shone like a mirror in the hot sunlight, as well as an annoying alarm that buzzed madly around him, hidden away in some unknown pocket of his thick coat. Ewing scrambled, his hands desperate to stop the contraption, cursing the datalink's shrill cries. A few Lottian strollers chuckled at him with mild amusement.

"Stupid contraption won't shut off," he grumbled as he ducked into an old bank building that had been vacated years earlier. The alarm's volume only increased when he ducked into the tower's entrance, its noise bouncing off the walls of a long, darkened hallway. Ewing's anger boiled under his breath as he fumbled for the screeching datalink in his pocket.

Arthur failed to spot Adley waiting at the end of the hall as he fought to find the mute switch. She rushed toward him with wide eyes and grabbed the device from his hands. In a fluid motion she silenced it, all while ushering Ewing into the quiet, nondescript room at the end of the hallway. Wood paneled walls were the only accent to an otherwise bland room that held a table and a few overstuffed office chairs. Ewing made his way to the nearest chair and wiped his feet on the shabby carpet while Adley cracked the door, examining the hallway before locking the two inside.

"Did anyone follow you?" she asked.

"No one. I'm alone," Ewing said.

Relief filled Adley's eyes. She examined the datalink in her hands. "So this is it?"

Ewing was already loading his pipe and grumbled, "Course that's it. Didn't you hear the cursed thing? Been trying to shut it up for three blocks now!"

Adley allowed Ewing to take a few good draws on his pipe before she bothered asking any more questions. She examined the small datalink and activated it. The screen blinked with life and indicated a transmission feed was active.

"You're absolutely sure this one is encrypted?"

Ewing blew smoke out of his nose and glared at her. "Aye, it's good. *Unregistered and encrypted.*"

Adley's eyes did not relent. Ewing threw up his hands in disbelief. "You need to trust me on this, Adley. I have a contact who handles these *things* for me. Do you honestly think this is the first time I've had to *be discrete?*"

Adley nodded as the last of her reluctance gave way. Ewing came behind her and motioned with his eyes for Adley to accept the incoming feed. With a flick of her finger the screen shifted and revealed Bronson Donahue's face on the other end.

Ewing spoke through his clenched pipe, a wide smile growing on his face. "I am glad we were finally able to get in contact. I trust since you are answering our call that my driver is safe?"

Bronson's voice chirped back, the speaker making him sound metallic and tinny. "Arik is fine. He should be back anytime now."

Ewing smiled. "Let's not say names on this call. I trust my contact, but it's best not to take any chances. Good news, we've progressed this far. Let's make this brief. What news do you have? How are things progressing?"

Bronson's eyes said enough. He whispered, "Things are not good. As you know *his* governmental power is increasing daily. There is no political infrastructure in place to curb his ambitions, and no will in Zenith will dare defy him. His word is law, and anyone who raises questions. They are...snuffed out."

Ewing coughed and his eyes narrowed. "What about *the glass*? What word on that?"

Adley's brow pinched with questions as Ewing continued.

Bronson shook his head. "He has a majority of them now. Three of the five."

Ewing sat back and rubbed at his aching leg just above his chrome prosthetic limb. Adley could read the worry on his face. He let out a quick, smoky breath and leaned back over the datalink screen.

"Okay. So there are two left. There is at least that. There is still some time. Where is *he*?"

Bronson glanced over his shoulder and lowered his voice. "He is here again in Zenith. We just arrived."

Adley hurried over to the datalink and blurted out the one question that had burned in her mind ever since she had escaped with the others from the Spire. "What about Kull? Did he survive?"

Ewing snapped and threw his arms in the air. "NAMES. No names!"

Bronson blinked his eyes and shook his head, ignoring Ewing's scolding. "I'm sorry. I have no knowledge of your friend. Any evidence of his whereabouts is gone. I haven't seen him since the episode in the Spire. I don't want to imagine what *he* did to him. I'm so sorry."

Adley nodded and turned away from Bronson's face. She handed the device back to Ewing.

Ewing sighed, ran his hands through his hair and rubbed at the wide bald spot at the crown of his skull. He dropped his head and took in another deep breath before responding to Bronson.

"You are doing so much for us. You have my thanks." Ewing glanced at Adley who was still standing away from the screen, her eyes vacant. "*Our* thanks. Is there anything we can do to support you?"

Bronson checked back over his shoulder and whispered, "Yes. I need you to hide my family. I need them moved." Bronson's voice began to tremble. "I don't think I have much longer here. Someone saw me do something. Just get my family to a safe place. Please!"

The plea floored Ewing. "What do you mean? I will certainly help, but what is going on?"

Bronson's face had lost its color and he began to whisper again. "I can't explain it all here, but one of *his* allies knows my intentions. One of *them* saw me try to break the *glass*."

Adley spun around and paced back to the datalink screen. "What do you mean? What in Aleph's name are you talking about?"

Bronson kept checking over his shoulder before giving a quick reply. "No time now. Get your datalink to Wael or Grift." Ewing winced at the sound of the names, but said nothing. Bronson continued, "We need them. Tell them what I said." Bronson looked back over his shoulder and the screen went dead.

Ewing and Adley stared at one another as Ewing closed the datalink. He furrowed his brow and pursed his lips as he rolled the last few sentences from Bronson in his mind.

"Adley. This is bad. *Very bad.* I have to get this datalink to Wael as fast as possible."

Adley snatched the device from Ewing's hands. She ran her thumb over its screen and flipped it open. She entered a few commands and the small machine beeped an error code. "It won't work, Adley. It's completely locked down. Designed to only operate on a linked channel. One line in; one line out."

Adley gripped her fists and paced the floor. "Well, how are we going to get this thing to Preost? They have border guards everywhere and they have started monitoring all datalink communications."

Arthur rocked on his prosthetic leg before taking a few clumsy steps toward the door. He propped himself against the doorframe and looked back at the girl who had been his sole companion for the better part of two months.

"They are going to have to come to us, Adley. I have a feeling they are already on their way, but I need you to trust me."

"But who is going to come, Ewing? What hope do we have? If they try to cross the border they will be shot on sight." Adley's eyes streamed with fresh tears, her mind full of grief.

Ewing dismissed the emotions and took another draw on his long stemmed pipe. "It's time that we get back to Cotswold, Adley. We need to check on Rose."

Grift sat alone with his hood pulled up around his face. He kept his distance from the others riding in the van. He was more than happy to let his credits buy him silence and a blind eye. After trekking through the dense forests of Preost, he was relieved to pay for a quiet ride with a traveling band of peddlers that happened to be making a rare pass through Preost. He slipped a small scrap of paper from his pocket and rubbed his thumb over the faint penciled sentence. "Return now. Be quick. -AE"

Ewing managed to get a driver into Preost and all the driver had was the note. The poor kid had no other details except that he was asked to deliver the piece of paper and make it look like he was coming to pick up some evergreen lumber. He did not know who Rose was or how she was doing. In fact, he hardly knew of Cotswold. The kid's ignorance had frustrated Grift, but he knew Ewing kept him in the dark for his own safety.

Grift tucked the paper away and glanced around the open hold of the caravan. He never allowed his eyes to settle or lock onto anyone, but he listened to their different chains of conversation hoping to pick up on the news of Candor. It did not take long before he overheard two men chatting about the rebuilding process in Riht.

"Place is crazy, I tell you. Looks like a brand new city."

"Don't care. Never stepping foot in the place. That whole Realm is cursed. Still on fire, ya know."

"Eh. I'll be stopping by quite regular. The new government forming there means lots of trade with plenty of rich 'uns."

The convoy rolled to a stop, and the driver hopped out and called to his occupants. "Sun 'bout to drop, men. We make camp for the night."

As the men and women pulled tents and blankets from the caravan, Grift slipped away, plunging deep within the forest. He figured they were about five miles out from the first established checkpoint. He had pored over Wael's files on the main thoroughfares in Candor. Wael's scouts had been meticulous, noting the number of troops and patterns of patrolling Dominion soldiers. Grift combined this new data with his own soldier's field map. Using both, he knew a checkpoint was right up the bend, and he needed to avoid it. He pressed through the dense canopy on foot, trusting his intuition and slipping away from the others with little notice. He traversed through the thick canopy in silence, his heart aching with the realization that he was getting closer to Lotte. The signs that surrounded him confirmed this. The thick pines were beginning to thin out, giving way to a growing number of oaks and maples. Soon, Grift knew that the forest would recede into patches of meadow and fields of tall, lush grass. He kept marching, stopping to check his worn soldier's map only once. Even in the darkness, Grift knew he was on the right path. The birds' songs changed from the joyful chattering of the forest to the lonesome calls of the plains; bobwhites, whippoorwills.

Grift's mind filled with hope at the lonely sounds. Lotte was not far. He was almost home. The sounds of the field birds brought tears to his eyes, making him ache for Cotswold. For Rose. *For Kull.* The pain of losing his son was more than Grift could process. It was enough to make him want to lie down and die, to give up, but he would not allow the tempest within him to gain any ground. He had to keep pressing on. He had to keep fighting, if only for Kull's sake and memory. *You can't go there now,* he repeated to himself. *You can't ever go there.*

After several long days and sleepless nights wandering through the wilderness, Grift finally made it to a large opening that spread before him like an ocean. The clearing came together over the bend, the patches of fields merging into a vast, open prairie that stretched as far as the horizon. Many miles away, Grift could see the outline of the Asban Mountains that stood over Vale. He had done it. After so many months, Grift Shepherd had once again stepped into Lotte. He drew in a deep breath and sighed.

I'm home. Despite the torture of the last few months, the sight of home gave him a glimmer of deep hope. He walked another mile or two, choosing to make camp by a small stream, taking in the gorgeous space that was his home. He laid his head back, his eyes squinting under the bright sun hanging above him. Whatever sleep he would get would be in the daylight. Moving at night would help to avoid the border patrols. As the sun ran its bright circuit, Grift gave in to the exhaustion that followed him like a ghost.

When Grift woke, he could barely see the markings of his field map in the fading twilight. He squinted, running a thin red line on the worn paper to a supply cache for the roaming Lottian guard details. He estimated the route from where he thought he was; ten miles. The town nearest to the cache was Tindler, a small manufacturing village that bought lumber from either Preost or the Asban regions to process. Tindler would give him a chance to resupply and find out more news before making his way to Cotswold.

The last contact Grift had with anyone in Cotswold was before Willyn kidnapped him. The months away felt like years. He rubbed his face in disbelief, trying to erase the pain and loss from his mind and focus on his destination, but the flames swallowing his hometown had never stopped burning in his mind. *Is anything left in Cotswold?* The thought made him shudder, and he buried it.

Grift forced himself to stop walking down the dark path in his mind and focus instead on the cache. Folding his map, he calculated the distance. *One full night and I will be there,* he thought.

He set out, heading southeast just as the stars began to fill the sky. Lotte had trained and developed a sophisticated system of border patrols to protect the Realm from outside threats. Patrols would leave their stations and circulate across the vast border of the Realm in a synchronized, yet unpredictable pattern. *Like a tree's lifeline.* That was the easiest explanation when training new recruits. If you were to look at the border patrol of Lotte, it looked like the inside of a felled tree, concentric lines of guards patrolling the Realm. The capital, Vale, was the most heavily guarded, protected by nearly a hundred different patrols that endlessly marched through the wilderness of the land, when not stationed at a town or city. Grift's military career began in the wilderness, walking midnight border patrols during the Rihtian and Grogan conflicts forty years prior.

He was thankful that he was only trying to get to Tindler, far outside the tightening circles of the patrols that orbited Vale. *You are still very close to the border,* he warned himself. He shoved the thought aside, trying to ignore the fact that the cache he sought brought with it a high likelihood of unwanted exposure. Determined, he kept marching through the darkness as his mind wrestled with things unseen.

"Thank Aleph." The small concrete bunker sat untouched and unspoiled by any recent patrol. It was loaded with rifles, ammunition, and canned food. Grift ripped open a can of peaches and threw back its contents. He swallowed the fruit whole, the sweet, sticky juice running down his face, covering his beard in a film of sugary syrup. He had gone for several days without any real food. He snapped up some readymade field rations and ate until his stomach groaned with displeasure.

After taking a few moments to digest, he examined the contents of the cache. In the back, beyond the food, weapons, and supplies was an object covered in a thick blue tarp. Grift made his way toward it, his heart hammering with unforeseen hope. *Please, just let it work.*

The contraption waiting under the tarp could hardly be called a rook in its current state, though Grift could clearly see that was what it once was. Recovered by the Lottians after some unknown battle with the Grogans, the machine had been crudely reassembled, making Grift wonder about its ability to run. There was not much to the thing—just an engine, a seat, and a thruster.

Grift got on the cobbled-together heap and kicked the throttle. The engine heaved, like a monster kicked awake from its slumber, but the engine turned over with a roar. The rook lifted off the ground, rumbling with life.

Not the quietest ride, but it will do.

Grift anchored the hovercraft, allowing the engine to run for a while. *Aleph knows it needs to run; the engine is knocking like crazy.* As the rook idled, Grift went about the cache and restocked his pack with more canned food, ammo, and water. Then he slung a rifle over his shoulder and holstered a pistol to his side. The welcome comfort of arming himself again was a bigger relief than Grift had expected. He trudged through the cache for some more weapons when the rook sputtered to a halt and crashed to the ground.

"Come on!" Grift ran to the rook and looked over its few dials and displays. "Ugh! No gas?" Grift could barely believe his own stupidity.

Grift ripped through several shelves before the blue gas canisters caught his eye in the rear corner of the hold. He ran to them, but his hopes were dashed when the first three were empty. He kicked them to the side just as his foot thudded against one container that was weighed down with fuel. Grift breathed a sigh of relief. He shouldered his pack and picked up the jug of fuel, not wasting time to refuel the machine. As he poured the fuel Grift's heart hammered up into this throat.

What was that?

In the distance, he heard the sound of voices. They were faint, but distinct.

"Did you open the cache?" a man said.

"Of course not. No one goes in those things," replied a younger sounding voice.

Grift threw the fuel to the side and hopped back on the rook. He kicked the starter, but the engine refused to budge. He pressed at the throttle several times to try and prime the engine, but still, nothing happened. He hopped off the rook and glanced around the door to the cache. Two flashlights bobbed across the field no more than one hundred feet away.

Grift mounted the rook again and pushed the starter over and over. "Come on! Work!" he shouted. "Work!"

As he pushed in the starter, the engine fumbled over itself and sputtered back to life. Grift slammed down the accelerator and the rook rocketed from the cache with a cloud of black smoke.

The two guardsmen dove out of the way as Grift flashed by. The rook was struggling to hit a good stride, but Grift laid in on the throttle. Shots rang out, but Grift was soon out of sight and reach. Grift slapped at the top of the rook, curses filling his mind. *They know someone is on a rook and I hardly have any gas. It will be a miracle to get to Tindler, much less Cotswold.*

With limited fuel, Grift threw out his plan to snake through the normal patrols. Instead, he decided he would dissect the routes and miss the soldiers he knew would be looking for him. He hammered the throttle and the crumbling rook roared through the night. Its speed would have to be enough. There was no other option.

Luck, it seemed, was on his side. Grift stopped on the ridge of a hill overlooking the outskirts of Tindler. He killed the engine, and the rook slammed to the ground in a dramatic chorus of spattering and wheezing. Grift shook his head and rolled his eyes. "They don't make 'em like they used to."

The moonlight provided just enough illumination to confirm his location, but little else. His mind ran through the scenarios. He needed gas, and quickly. It would be too dangerous to barter in the daylight. His face had been beamed on every datalink from here to Elum, and he wasn't about to risk having Seam on his trail. He squinted against the shadows, trying to discern if anyone was out on the street. Even in the moonlight the town seemed desolate and felt extremely dark. Grift started down the hill when he came to a sudden realization.

There are no lights on.

Grift blended in with the shadows, careful not to take any chances. He snuck toward the first building on the edge of town, hoping to find either fuel or someone with recent news. He found neither. Glancing into windows was like staring into an abyss. If someone was still living in Tindler, they did not want to be found. Grift could make out some evidence of earlier Grogan attacks, bullet holes and scorch marks, but it was superficial compared to the damage they did to Cotswold. There was no reason for the city to be abandoned. It was still very livable, yet there were no signs of life.

As he examined the buildings more closely, Grift noticed that many houses and buildings were left with doors still standing open despite the hour. The scene made no sense, but Grift forced himself to ignore the curiosity of the situation. *None of this matters. Find some fuel and make for Cotswold. Find Rose.*

Grift nodded, agreeing with himself. His footsteps were soft as he walked up the abandoned street. *A fueling station was here.* His mind was fuzzy on details of the town. It had been many years since his last patrol brought him to Tindler. In the dark streets,

Grift tried to navigate himself through a jumble of mixed up memories.

Getting close to the square now. Find some fuel and get out.

The small, open square expanded before Grift. He squatted, watching for any signs of movement, allowing his eyes to adjust to the darkness. Remnants of an Alephian monument sat crumpled in the square's center. The fountains that had surrounded it were also dormant, the smell of stale, stagnant water filling Grift's nose.

Grift scanned the square, and his eyes landed on what he had hoped to see. A single lamppost stood on the far southeast corner of the square. It wasn't lit, but Grift knew if he was going to find any fuel it would be at the filling station identified by the lamp.

No chance I am cutting across the square, he thought, his mind heightened with a sense of danger. *No cover. Western side of the square is too ruined. Too much rubble, approach would be too slow. Looks like the eastern side is it.*

Grift tightened his grip on his pistol and crept along the eastern border of the square. As he slid through the shadows, he kept checking his surroundings. Even with no lights burning in the town, the moonlight was enough to make Grift feel dangerously exposed. The small shop canopies offered some cover and when possible Grift cut down back alleys running parallel to the square.

After a few minutes, Grift was under the fueling station lamp. The old building's front door was hanging open, and the barrels out front were either overturned or busted open.

"Looks like someone beat me to it," grumbled Grift. He tapped on a few barrels but they all returned a hollow ring. He sighed and pulled out a small light as he approached the front door of the station. He stepped into the building and flicked the light on, sweeping it from corner to corner. The room was still and silent. The only sign of life were some cobwebs accumulating on the abandoned furniture. Grift slipped behind the counter and creaked open a door leading to the storage room.

"*Please, Aleph. Please.* I just want to get to Rose." Grift let his light wash over the storage room shelving. His heart peaked as he spied three unopened fuel canisters.

"Thank you!" Grift dashed for the shelf. He went to lift the first canister but it had no weight. *Empty!* The second canister calmed his nerves as it sloshed with valuable fuel. He holstered his pistol and lifted the last container, pleased to find that it was also full.

"Should be just enough as long as that piece of trash will start again."

Grift pushed out into the shadows and made his way back along the storefronts lining the square. As he was passing the halfway mark, a movement across the square caught his attention. Grift kneeled behind a small table and set the fuel down. He stared out over the small opening and waited.

Getting jumpy, old man. Seeing things out here in the dark. He shook his head and started to stand before glimpsing another movement, but this time it was distinct and obvious. Something was moving behind the rubble on the western border of the square. *Pale. Humanoid. Aleph.* Grift cursed beneath his breath and shrunk behind an overturned bistro table.

The shadows obscured the movement, and Grift could not tell if he had been detected. As badly as he wanted to rush and get to Rose he knew it would be better to wait. After several minutes, the activity subsided and the square was silent. Grift picked up his two jugs of fuel and slipped down an alley, adding distance between himself and the square. Within a few minutes, Grift was just a couple blocks from the town's edge.

As Grift neared the clearing, he lifted his arm to wipe sweat from his brow, but his hand slipped and one of the canisters fell, the metal jug clanking like a cymbal on the ground. Grift froze and pressed against the nearest wall, his heart hammering in his chest.

Nothing. There was no response to his clumsy mistake. Grift chuckled at his paranoia and lifted the fallen canister as he walked toward the clearing and his rook.

As Grift left the city streets and made his way into the hills, a thunderstorm of feet pounded against the ground behind him, echoing off the cobblestone streets. Grift sprinted, his mind pumping with adrenaline, but the fuel he carried was making running up the steep hill difficult. There were at least a dozen figures pouring out of Tindler, clamoring after him. They looked human enough, but Grift knew what they were. He cursed and churned his legs as hard as he could, but the morels kept gaining ground.

Desperate, Grift threw one of the canisters to the ground. He pushed on a little faster and spun on his heels, lowering his pistol on the abandoned tank. The morels pounced on the barrel, just in time for Grift to fire a shot. A violent fireball erupted, filling the darkness with an explosion of light. Most of the pack incinerated, their bodies thrown in pieces across the field. Grift kept scrambling for the rook, his lungs burning. He knew he had taken out most of the swarm, all while sacrificing miles of fuel, but the sound of shrieks and screams let Grift know this encounter was far from over.

He looked over his shoulder. Three morels were still pursuing him, roaring their way up the hill, their fangs barred. He ripped off five shots, sending one face first into the dirt. He turned to fire on another but he was too late. A morel that had once been a young girl made a titanic leap up the hillside and slammed into him, slashing at his hands. Grift swung all his weight into a spin as he smashed the remaining canister of fuel against the girl's face. The container let out a loud crack as it met its mark, crumbling the nightmare that was her face, before she stumbled to the ground, dead.

Grift eyed his pistol but knew he didn't have time to reach it. He kicked the downed morel in the jaw with a sickening crack for good measure and then turned to run for the rook. The last of the three pursuers was not moving as fast. From a quick glance, Grift could tell it had been injured by his firebomb. Ribbons of charred flesh hung from a mangled arm, and half of its hollow face looked as if it had been burnt away, but it was moving fast enough to keep him in a full sprint. It's half-ruined, singed body smoked in the night air, and one milky eye locked on Grift in pursuit. Its mouth opened and a dry horrible scream fell out, making Grift run in a panic for the rifle he had recovered from the cache. He grabbed it up and spun around unloading several rounds.

The monster's lifeless body quivered at his feet, and Grift let out a sigh of relief. His whole body was shaking, and he bent down to catch his breath. He steadied himself and picked up the dented fuel canister.

"You were worth it," he said to the container, his voice still wavering from the adrenaline soaring through him.

Grift turned and began pouring the fuel into the rook, doing his best to shake away the horror that still clung to him. As the last of the fuel dripped in, a searing pain exploded down Grift's arm, and he heard a ragged, moaning breath. He turned, and the bloodied, broken hollow that had been the face of the young girl was next to him, swiping her claws at him. He deflected one of the blows with the empty gas can only to receive another terrifying gash across his forearm. Grift screamed in pain and slammed the metal can across the girl's forearm, just as her claws ripped through the metal as if it were paper.

Grift hopped back several feet and slipped a knife from his belt. His eyes were wide with fear and he bobbed from side to side as the shambling girl stalked toward him, swiping her claws in the moonlight. The beast girl gurgled with heavy, drowning breaths as she approached, the one eye left in her skull never blinking.

She dove for Grift with outstretched arms, but he ducked to the side and stabbed his blade into the back of her thigh. The morel let out a shrieking howl and swiped again for Grift's arm but missed. Grift swung his knife into the creature's hand, but the girl did not relent. She pressed into him, pinning Grift against the rook, allowing the blade to slip deeper into her palm. She cooed at him, clicking her broken jaw and growling as she pressed her jagged, twisted teeth for his throat. Grift tightened his grip on his knife and pulled it out of her hand only to plunge it into the morel's neck. The morel ripped backwards in agony, but Grift grasped the back of her neck and slammed her face into the fuselage of the rook. He did not relent as he continued to hammer the morel's face against the metal casing time and time again.

Exhausted, Grift slung the limp body of his attacker to the ground. He rested his face on the rook and took in a deep breath, doing his best to remind himself that the creature he had to kill was not, in fact, a young girl. He opened a bottle of water and poured it over his hands and his face, trying to wash away the guilt he felt, only to finally vomit in the brush. He stayed there, heaving for a long time, until standing and wiping his mouth. *So much for this trip,* he thought. He turned and looked at the rook, whispering a simple prayer. "Please. No more stalling. Just. Work." He took one more breath and looked up to the starry night sky as he clicked in the starter.

The rook fired to life once more and lifted from the ground. Grift engaged the thrusters and rocketed away from Tindler as fast as the machine could carry him. He drove, the night streaming by his face like a blur, his mind haunted by the face of the young morel girl who stared at him with one mottled white eye. He shook his head, trying his best to let the tormented face go, but it held, burnt into his memory until the dawn came.

What is happening to Candor?

CHAPTER FIVE

The helm of Rodnim sat alone in a field of blood outside of Rhuddenhall. The ground was littered with the bodies of brothers and sisters that had slain one another just hours prior. The helmet's golden faceplate was spattered with the red drops of its Realm's citizens. The setting sun began to dip behind the horizon and cast its warm beams across the field of blood turning it into a burning, crimson ocean. The city was smoldering and the sounds of gunfire and screaming were still seeping from deep within its fortified walls. Willyn approached the lonely piece of armor and lifted it from the ground. She checked over her shoulder and began to clean the artifact. As she rubbed caked on dirt and blood away from the helmet, a voice startled her from behind.

"We can rule again, you know."

Hagan's voice was unmistakable. Willyn turned as quickly as she could and saw her brother standing behind her in his battle gear. He was full of life, and his stature exuded power. There was no sign of pain, no sign of death. Hagan was alive!

Willyn shook her head and blinked, but Hagan continued to stand before her. He stretched out his hand and took the helmet. He turned it over in his hands and studied its lines before gazing back to his sister. His eyes burnt hotter than the setting sun.

"Willyn. You know who caused this. We can fix this."

Willyn took a deep breath before stammering a response. "But Hagan. You died. This is not..."

"Lies, sister! Did you ever see my corpse? Hosp betrayed me. Betrayed our family! He betrayed our Realm! No. I never died. Now that he has turned his attention from me, I am stronger than ever. His poison would only last so long."

Willyn ran to hug her brother and wept into his shoulder. She did not want to let go of him for fear that he might be taken from her again.

"I should have never left your side. I was wrong. I thought Grift Shepherd had poisoned you. I was a fool."

Hagan held his sister's embrace and answered softly, "It is not your fault. This entire world was taken into the lie. But you have seen through it. It is time for you to join me and bring this Realm back into control; our control."

Willyn drew in another deep breath and stepped back, but when she opened her eyes she was not in Rhuddenhall. She was back in Taluum. The dream was gone, but she could still smell the bloody battlefield. As she glanced around the dark room and gathered her thoughts, Hagan's voice returned to her ears.

"We must fight. Find me."

Willyn did her best to keep from gagging. The quarters that the Baggers kept were unlike anything she had ever encountered. The railcar was stuffed to the gills with the migrants, all of them pouring in, invading her precious space. The air was soon a dense fog of sweat, smoke, and the indescribable patina of odors wafting from the busy and hardworking laborers. Willyn felt like she would either pass out or suffocate.

Willyn sneered as she twisted her charcoal hair between her thumb and forefinger, the black dye still smearing her fingers. It was not enough for her to have to ride with the Baggers; Wael and Grift both insisted she blend in as well, forced to conform and look like the very remnant of the people her Realm had proudly fought and nearly extinguished several generations ago. Willyn knew in her heart that nothing good could came from Riht, and the vagabond Baggers were no exception. Her hair color was not the least of her worries, however. Her armor, her weapons—all of it had been taken away. Except for the datalink she secretly carried with her, everything else had been left behind in Preost. The beige, course linen clothing she wore felt baggy and vulnerable. Without her armor she felt naked and exposed.

Willyn sat back and tried to wipe the black stains from her fingers. As much as she hated it, she knew there was no other choice. She was wanted for treason, and the Baggers were the only souls in all of Candor that no one would bother to ask for help locating a fugitive. Still, as new sets of eyes gazed over her, she couldn't help but feel that she needed to hide her face. She shifted and turned her back to the crowded rail car as she tried to focus on the mission: secure the mirror in Legion's Teeth and rally the Reds.

Willyn struggled to focus as she tried to run through her plan. A woman two seats down from her held a small, shrieking child. This was only a distraction compared to the man who sat beside her. Willyn glanced over to him, pursing her lips with disgust. The Bagger was a mountain of a man, whose face bore a long, intricately braided mustache. He sat next to her rumbling, his snores echoing over the clanging din of people who were talking, sneezing, singing, smoking, and chanting; all unaware that the rightful heir to the Groganlands sat in their midst. Despite her inability to focus on her mission to locate the mirror, there was one thought, one face, that refused to leave her mind.

Hagan. The vision earlier seemed all too real. She tried to convince herself that it was just a desperate dream, but the phantom thought would not stop haunting her, pushing her to dare consider that possibly he had survived. If it was true, then she would have no choice but to find him. The idea of reuniting with Hagan warmed her, but her mind was clouded with rage for the one person who was responsible for all her misery. *Hosp.*

What has Hosp done since I've been gone? Hate filled her mind like molten lead as she thought about all that worm of a man had put her through.

A loud chant rang out within the cabin of the rail car, disrupting her dark thoughts. The Bagger's language sounded like the twittering and tweets of the forest birds, sharp, but sweet.

"Ala, tro busim. Rey fell mey!" said a young Bagger as he made his way down the aisle of the cramped rail car. He held a large satchel of pinecones, each the size of grapefruit. He called out like a merchant at a festival, selling the strange product to his kinsfolk. He was tall, with a strong build, sharp eyes, and an unfortunate set of teeth. Willyn watched as the Baggers cornered him as he made his way through their car, inspecting his wares, shaking their head with a show of contempt, trying to haggle the price. The young man did not back down and was quick to point at them and argue loudly back at his customers. He was good at what he did, and soon many slipped him the credits in exchange for the pinecones. His customers slammed the cones on the ground, scrambling to feast on the roasted seeds within.

The young salesmen made his way to Willyn's side, and his eyes peered directly into hers.

"Ala, tro busim?" he stared at her, expecting a response.

Willyn's heartbeat ramped up with nervous energy. She did not know any of the Bagger language. She held up her hand and hid her eyes, hoping that the Bagger would leave her be. *Don't blow my cover. Don't blow my cover.*

"Eh treh fruh..." grumbled a deep voice next to her. The man next to her with the braided mustache had woken, and for the first time Willyn noticed the intricate tattoos he wore on his arms as he exchanged credits for the pinecone snack. *Black ink. Crows flying behind a cloud of shooting arrows.* The crows flew on the man's flesh, and arrows surrounded the swarm. Willyn had never seen anything that compared to the artistry on his skin. The young merchant stood over them for a second longer, his eyes scanning over her once more. Willyn closed her eyes, wishing that the train would start. It felt like they had been docked on the borders of Preost for a century.

"No snack for you, miss?" The common tongue made Willyn gasp as her mind filled with curses. She looked up at the young man and shook her head, her face blushing, painted with anger.

"No." It was short, quick, but Willyn could not risk any more exposure. It was obvious now that even with her disguise, she stuck out amidst the Baggers. Her skin was much too pale, and the contrast with her new, raven colored hair made her look like a phantom. Taking the hint, the young man left, but Willyn could still feel his eyes lingering behind her.

Beside her, the mustached strongman took the giant cone and crushed it between his fingers in an impressive feat of strength. Half of the rigid, spiky cone disintegrated in his palm, and his small black eyes looked to Willyn.

"Nut?"

Willyn shook her head as the giant man shrugged, picking out the nuts in his palm and crunching on them. "Name is Bri. Monk told me about you. Bri here to help."

Willyn's eyes went wide with anger, and she turned to look better at the once sleeping bear of a Bagger. *"What did you say?"*

The giant's face looked confused, and he spoke louder. "I am Bri. Monk sent me..."

Willyn reached out to him whispered, "I heard you fine. Did you say that Wael sent you?"

"Yah. 'Dat is truth. Monk sent me. I will help."

Willyn shook her head in disbelief. Fury and confusion washed over her as she scrambled for her datalink. Her fingers hammered over the keys.

```
:This? This is the escort you mentioned? A
Bagger? Anything else you want to tell me? Any
more surprises?
```

```
:So Bri has met you then? Good. He will
provide you with some additional protection. He
might seem simple to you, but I assure you, there
```

is more to him than you might suppose. He is a strong and loyal friend. He will serve you well.

Willyn's mind exploded with hot anger as she typed back on the encrypted line.

:I NEVER ASKED FOR PROTECTION. I DO NOT NEED IT.
:That remains to be seen. Bri is more than just muscle. He is a Bagger. He will help you navigate to Legion's Teeth undetected. There are many eyes searching for you. Follow his lead. We cannot risk your exposure. I will contact you soon, but we must cut this short. Do not waver in what you must do.

The screen went black. Wael had terminated the feed. Willyn quickly hid the datalink within her small bag as her mind fumed at the unexpected change in her plan.

Bri spoke as he continued crunching on the pine nuts. "What did monk say? Did he tell you that I am great warrior? This is true, you know." Exasperated, Willyn leaned her head back on the thin, uncomfortable seat.

This is going to be a long ride.

Squealing brakes jostled Willyn from a light sleep as the rail car rumbled toward the Zenith station. Willyn rubbed at her tired eyes and focused in on the growing landscape of the ancient city. Despite the panic surging through her, it was remarkable. The last time Willyn had passed by Zenith it was nothing more than deserted ruins. Steel skeletons of what had once been mighty towers and tumbled stone walls littered the lonely desert just months earlier. The corpse of a city had been resurrected and pumped full of life.

Tall skyscrapers covered in glass glistened in the desert sun like torches. They shimmered, giving the city the appearance of being made of light. Tents had sprung up on the dunes surrounding the larger buildings, and men and women were bustling about at a frantic pace. The most noticeable change was the Spire. The tall central tower was repaired, an ebony obelisk covered in black shining glass. It shot into the sky in stark contrast to the other buildings surrounding it, its prominent silhouette silently declaring dominance over the sky line.

Bri grumbled as he woke from a deep slumber and glanced over Willyn's shoulder.

"Different. Yes?" He sniffed and rubbed at his flowing mustache as he continued, "Stay very close, girl. Most danger here. People want you."

Willyn tore her eyes from the outline of Zenith and looked to Bri. "Stay close? You mean we are stopping here?"

Bri nodded. "Yes. Always stop here. Very busy place. Good work found here."

Willyn's heart raced and she reached for the spot where she normally holstered a pistol, but there was nothing there. She spat curses under her breath and looked back to Bri, eyeing his dull, dim-witted face.

"So you're really here to help?"

Bri smiled and bobbed his head. "Yes. Monk sent me to help. Stay with me and you are safe."

The mammoth of a man flexed his arms and stretched before standing and stepping toward the rail car door. The other Baggers scurried away and gave Bri plenty of space to move. He craned his neck and motioned for Willyn to fall in behind him. As she came close to him, a middle-aged Bagger woman reached out for her and tried to hand her a bead necklace.

"Ga la tay droman!" the women called out as she tried to force the necklace into Willyn's closed fists. "Tay droman," she shouted with a look of disappointment on her face. Willyn jerked back her hand and pushed in closer to Bri.

Bri leaned down and laughed as he answered the women. "Es la frehnan trume." The woman's look of insult faded, and she turned away to look for someone else to buy her beads.

"What was that all about?" whispered Willyn.

Bri chuckled, his voice booming. "She want to sell. You always *look yes*. Even if you don't buy." Bri leaned in and continued laughing. "No worries. I told her you can't speak. I told her you are quite dumb."

Willyn could not believe that a man who could hardly speak complete sentences in the common tongue was calling her dumb. The excuse for her awkward presence could be better, but if it kept people from asking questions she would go along with it.

The rail car swayed as it lumbered up to a new pristine platform and slid to a stop. The brakes hissed, and the doors slid open. Bri lumbered out the door into the swarm of bodies, and Willyn dutifully followed. The station's platform was buzzing with activity. Baggers were bartering with one another and yelling back and forth, laughing, singing and carrying on, creating another swell of noise. Foremen were positioned at the platform to recruit fresh arms and legs to assist with the continual rebuilding efforts for the city.

Guards clad in black and gold armor stood on the catwalks overhead. They paced, scanning the crowds with rifles in hand. The sight of their rifles made Willyn wish she had at least some weapon with her. She pushed in close to Bri and tried to use his massive frame to shield her face.

"Where are we going, Bri? Why are we here?"

Bri turned back and yelled over his shoulder, "Gonna get us some work in the Teeth." He leaned down and looked in her eyes. "Monk told me to get you to the Teeth, and you'd do the rest."

Willyn nodded, thankful that Wael had not revealed everything to Bri. She did not know how the giant would react to the knowledge of her searching for a Serub.

Bri continued, "I am good miner. Have to talk to a man over there." He pointed across the platform to another grouping of foremen that were distinctly Grogan.

As Willyn and Bri approached the Grogan work tables, a hand grasped Willyn's arm. She spun around to see a young Grogan man holding a finger to his lips. She did not recognize him, but the look in his eyes let her know that he knew exactly who she was. A knot rose in her throat as she waited on him to alert one of the nearby guards. Instead, he pulled close to her ear and whispered.

His voice was hard to hear over the din of noise surrounding them, but once the words registered they cut through the noise like a knife. "Come with me. Hagan sent me."

The mention of Hagan made Willyn go numb. *This is impossible.*

In a flash the man took off, threading himself through jumbles of laborers. Willyn rushed forward, pushing through the crowds, leaving Bri behind. She threw herself into a full sprint after the young Grogan. Every few feet the man would turn and motion for her to keep up.

The crowds thinned out, and Willyn finally approached the stranger on a desolate alleyway.

"What did you say to me?" Willyn said, staring down the Grogan. "What did you say?!" Her eyes tightened, scanning the man. He was Grogan. He wore the black body armor of her people, and his stature and dialect were enough to confirm his origin.

"I think you heard me quite well, Willyn Kara. Your brother, the Sar, sends his regards."

Pain seared through her, but Willyn's face remained as cold as stone. *Could this be true? How could this be true?* Willyn's mind strained to put it all together. The dream, the helm of her forefathers, all of it poured over her, but she held her composure, unwilling to flinch.

"Prove it." Willyn sneered, her face flaring with rage and revulsion. All of this charade had the scent of Seam. Nothing would please that roach of a king more than to see her lured into a trap of lies. She scanned the alley, preparing herself for an ambush.

The man threw a sheathed blade her way. It landed in the dry dust that caked the dirt road. Her eyes fell on it, and her mouth fell open. The foot-long dagger was none other than her brother's, bearing the mark of the Sar. *The lion wrestling the wolf. Aleph above.*

"Consider this your proof." The man's eyes gleamed in the desert light. "Your brother lives, Willyn. He is in hiding deep within the Groganlands. Deep within Legion's Teeth. He and his followers have made camp in the Eastern Caverns of the mines."

"Legion's Teeth?" Willyn stooped and picked up the blade. She yanked the knife from its red scabbard, her eyes flickering over the desert light that danced on the edge. She held it in her hand, allowing her mind to test the blade's weight. The inscriptions were unmistakable, the hilt crafted into an exquisite form by the painstaking polishing of a razorback's tusk. She leaned in, her heart hammering. There, burnt into the bone handle was the mark of her father, *their father*, Wodyn the Great.

The blackened, burnt image of the boar brought tears to her eyes, but Willyn did not weep. She threw the dagger onto the sandy alley and roared, "This heirloom proves nothing!" Painful memories washed over her. Of long days spent in a dank, dark Elumite prison. Of searching endlessly for Grift Shepherd. Of Luken rescuing her and delivering the worst news possible.

Luken. Willyn closed her eyes and forced herself to focus. *Luken...he had told her. He had told her that Hagan had died.* A thought crystallized in her mind. *Luken would not have lied to me.* She opened her eyes, leveling her gaze on the stranger.

The Grogan picked up the discarded blade, his jaw locked in anger. He shook his head and held the dagger. "How could you? I have traveled hundreds of miles to find you and deliver Hagan's message, only to have you disown your own brother, the Sar!" The Grogan spat at her feet. "You are not worthy to serve him." He took a step closer and sized her up. "You are not worthy of any of us."

Willyn had read his eyes. She dodged the blade's path not a moment too soon, the dagger's tip a mere inch from her face. The man screamed at her, cursing, "You are a traitor! TRAITOR!"

Willyn dodged several incoming jabs of the dagger, batting the man's arm and pushing away. Instead of running away she dashed straight toward her attacker. She slid underneath his legs as he screamed, swinging the blade in front of him like a madman. He was too late. In a flash she had slid underneath him and leapt up on his back, rocketing her boot across his groin. The man yelped, crumbling in a heap, groaning. Willyn rode him to the dirt, slamming her elbow into the back of his neck. He fell limp beneath her, and the dagger fell from his hand.

She thought it was over until she found herself flying through the air as her assailant pushed himself up, throwing her off with surprising force. She fell, face to the sky, just as the man turned, lifted his heavy boot, and stomped on her chest. Her lungs collapsed from the blow and she heaved for breath. Pain exploded within her as the man threw his fist at her, colliding with her jaw. She accepted the blow and countered with a sweep of the man's legs. He fell and Willyn pounced again, the rage within her boiling over.

She grabbed the man's throat and squeezed as hard as possible. The attacker looked at her with wild eyes and smiled like a madman. Willyn pushed every ounce of energy she had into her grip, and she saw the life of the man leave him, his corpse still bearing the insane smile. She held him there in the alleyway until she was sure it was over. The maniac was dead.

She shook her hands free, her whole body trembling. She rubbed her mouth, the pain of the punch still throbbing in her jaw, her eyes catching the blade he had presented. She stooped down and took the dagger, her mind still refusing to believe that it was real. She wrapped the weapon deep within her linen robes and left the alley without another glance at her conquered enemy. The hot desert air washed over her as she made her way back to the crowded station of Baggers lining up for work permits. Her hands shook with fury, but she allowed the shock of the encounter to wind its way through her. It would pass in time. As her survival instinct diminished, Willyn began to question what had just happened. *Could Hagan truly be alive? No. That could not be true... It was a trap. Either Seam or Hosp is trying to draw you out. To play you for a fool.* The answer was a sound one, but it did not satisfy the questions boiling in her mind. *Where did they find his dagger?*

Willyn turned the options in her mind: she could search for the mirror or break free and seek the truth about Hagan. She stood lost in her thoughts when a heavy hand landed on her shoulder. She turned, ready to fight, only to be startled by the booming laugh of the giant Bri.

"Why you play hide and seek here? Not very safe!" He slammed a friendly pat on her back that felt like a donkey's kick and leaned in to her ear to whisper. "You remember? Monk said you stay with me?" He stared deep into her eyes to confirm she understood. "Don't run off again."

Willyn nodded, but said nothing. Bri looked at her suspiciously. "You look like you roll around in desert sand. Why would you do this?"

Willyn shrugged her shoulders and opened her mouth just as the rail car whistle blew.

Bri's eyes pinched in the desert sun and dismissed the question. "No time. Doesn't matter. We must catch our car to the Teeth. We have only a three-day journey!"

Willyn cringed as she fell in line with the other crowds of swarming Baggers funneling into the tight quarters of the railcar.

CHAPTER SIX

The sound of pickaxes echoed through a dark, lonely mineshaft. Silhouettes moved through the shadows, no words passing between them. The miners at the end of the shaft were covered in dark soot from head to toe and heaved deep breaths through their thick masks, drawing in pure oxygen. The six men had no fanfare or ornate titles, but they were thrilled to be hand-picked to quarry into the lost pits of Legion's Teeth.

The six had been digging for months, clearing collapsed tunnels and snaking deeper within forgotten veins that had long been drained of their valuable ore. The never-ending tunnels of bedrock had been a monotonous blend of black and brown, but one man's pick broke away a large boulder and revealed a new color: gray. The men nodded at one another and focused in on the cement below. Within a few hours, they had chipped away at the barricade and a blast of stale air pushed past them, escaping from its sealed chamber.

"Light it up, boys," said the foreman as he motioned for two of the miners. "Drop in the light rods and back away."

The two men lowered in small light rods and flicked them to life. A serpentine crack of light shone up below the men.

"Back up!" The foreman's voice was stern. "I will inspect."

One of the two miners squinted his eyes and glared down at the light.

"I said back away, son!" The foreman pushed forward as the young miner glared into the crevice.

The subordinate looked up and glanced at the other men before speaking. "There is nothing down there but some old mirror."

A loud CRACK rang out and the mineshaft exploded with a violent light as a bullet crashed into the curious miner's skull. The foreman lifted his pistol and continued to fire on the other men until five bodies lay at the feet of their superior. He cursed and hurled the pistol to the floor as he kicked the corpse of his first victim.

"*I said to back away!*" He screamed. He glanced at the carnage and pointed to the other four men strewn out across the rocky floor. "Their blood is on *your hands*! I said to back away."

The foreman took a deep breath and looked overhead, examining the shaft above. He shook his head and screamed one last time as he wiped the blood that had spattered on the visor of his mask. He knelt and looked down through the opened crevice.

The miner flicked open the datalink on his wrist and dialed out. Gray eyes and a pale face met him on the other side of the screen.

Hosp's voice was filled with anticipation. "Any news?" he hissed.

The miner stumbled over his words. "Surrogator. Target has been located." The man looked over his shoulder as he swallowed and continued. "Cleanup is needed."

Hosp leaned forward in his chair. "Cleanup? What happened?"

"I did as I was instructed. The target was compromised so I eliminated the breach of intel." The miner answered flatly, his face white as a ghost.

Hosp's lips curled as he nodded. "Very good. Your next crew will help lift the target out." His grin inched wider as he squinted. "And don't worry. They will be disposable as well."

Seam rested his head against the massive mahogany throne towering behind him as he stared over the expanse of Candor. He smiled, knowing that his view was unlike any other on the Continent. His rubbed at his wrist where the six keys were locked tightly to his arm. It comforted him to feel them there; he could feel the power they were driving through his veins. He sat quietly and observed the world laid out below him. There was nothing beyond his view or grasp.

He turned and addressed the shadow lurking in the corner of the room. "Bronson tells me you are quite skilled at tracking and hunting. You are Cyric, correct?"

The man nodded, only his steel blue eyes peering out from behind the scarf pulled around his neck and face. "I am."

"Yet you have cancelled your contract?"

"I have my limits, and I never cancelled anything. Your helper and his requests breached my contract." The stranger peered out over the landscape. "But I know we aren't here to speak about that. You need something new."

Seam chuckled and sat forward in his chair. "You would be correct. I have a new proposition for you and it will pay far more than any of your former projects combined."

The man stepped forward. "I listen when credits are involved. Name your price and your target."

"One million credits," Seam deadpanned. "Bring me the Mastermonk, and you will have one million credits."

Cyric tilted his head and paused at the mention of the Mastermonk. "Wael?"

The name made Seam shiver, his memories snapping back to the questioning he endured next to his father's casket. *What is your duty to Aleph?* He shoved the memory away and spoke, "Yes, Wael of Preost. I need him brought to me...alive. I am far too pressed with other matters to bother chasing him down, but I want him contained."

Cyric shook his head, weighing the job. "I was raised up to believe it was not wise to interfere with the affairs of monks." He pulled down the scarf covering his face, revealing a grin. "But for a million credits I can bend."

"Very good," Seam answered. "Now, we are done here. You are dismissed. I don't want to see you again until you have the Mastermonk."

"One question, sir. Is this the only mark? It's well known there are other profitable bounties out for Willyn Kara and Grift Shepherd." The High King's face grimaced at the sound of their names.

"I have others in my employ. Focus on the monk."

"Very well," whistled Cyric as he turned to make his exit, quiet as a shadow.

A chime rang through the vast throne room. Seam lowered himself into the plush throne and shifted in his chair as he whispered, "Enter."

The large door swung open and Bronson stepped into the throne room. His face was thin and pale. The dark circles under his eyes were proof enough that he had not slept for days.

"What is it, Bronson?"

Cyric offered Bronson a nod as he slipped through the open door. Bronson sneered as the bounty hunter brushed by him and disappeared down the hallway.

"Sire, the..." he stammered, his mind in gridlock. "The...Synod. They seek an audience with you."

Seam glared at Bronson as he stepped down from the elevated podium holding his throne. "Send them in."

Seam turned his gaze toward the three as they walked through into the immense hall. Arakiel stood a foot taller than any man in Zenith, his face like a chiseled mountain. Huge muscles moved underneath the simple robe he wore, and in his hand he bore a gigantic iron spear. His sisters followed him, flanking his sides, moving in one accord.

Abtren radiated with such authority and grace that her presence still made Seam's heart pound in his chest. Her countenance was that of starlight on a clear night; magnificent, deep, and incalculable. She wore a white gown that glistened with gold thread, reflecting the rising sun just over the horizon. Her eyes were like hot embers, burning with a wild power. Seam did his best not to linger over her countenance.

Nyx, newly released from her glass prison, wore a dark gown of flowing purple. Long ringlets of black hair fell from her head, flowing over her shoulders like a waterfall of midnight. She was striking, resembling her sister in all manner of movement and composure. All, that is, except for her eyes. When Seam stared into them it felt as though he might turn to stone. She had no irises. Her cool, glacier eyes had long since transformed since her release. What was once the color of ice had given way to dark deep pits of sable, the colors of an impenetrable abyss.

Arakiel glared at Seam and slammed his knee to the ground. His voice was gruff and with no adoration. "Keeper. We have much to discuss."

Seam smirked at the sight of the hulking warrior-god on his knees. "Lord Arakiel, speak freely in my hall. Your counsel is most welcome here."

Arakiel stood and his voice boomed through the hall as he barged through any formalities. "It concerns our brother, Keeper. My sisters and I, we are...concerned."

Seam laughed and replied, "Bastion is..."

Abtren cut him off. "This does not concern Bastion, my lord." Abtren glanced at Seam, her kaleidoscopic eyes filled with trepidation. Seam glanced at Nyx. Her face was somber, matching Arakiel's concern.

Seam's mind clouded with questions. "Then what, exactly, does this concern?"

Arakiel looked at his sisters and leveled his gaze back on Seam, his thunderous voice full of malice. "It is a matter of one person. *Isphet*."

"Isphet?" Seam let the name roll in his mouth. He knew the name. The last Serub to be released. He marveled at the fear painted on the three Serubs' faces as they spoke of their kin.

Nyx took a step toward Seam and spoke. "Isphet is gathering strength, High King, and we don't know how. We have felt his presence *magnify*, and we feel him stirring with a new vigor.

Arakiel says that he was imprisoned in the forests of the land you call Preost. His power is—"

"You speak out of turn, sister," Arakiel growled. He stood over her, his fist tightening around his spear.

Nyx cut him with her cavernous eyes and said, "I will not hide the truth from the Keeper, Arakiel." She glanced at Seam. "I welcome my freedom from my glass prison. The truth is that Isphet is a threat to us all. His powers, left unchecked, could bring about our ruin. All of us." She stared at Seam, and his heart filled with revulsion. "Someone is working with him, High King, without your *guidance*. We must hurry, Left unchecked he could—"

Seam held up his hand to wave off Nyx's warnings and clicked his tongue. "Let him gain strength. If need be, I will drain all of his power from him once I am ready for him to be released. Let us not forget the power bestowed upon me." He held up his wrist that bore the precious Keys of Candor. "None shall oppose my will."

Arakiel stepped forward and proceeded with his case. "You are a *fool* to think you can understand our power, whether you bear the Keys or not. You did not shape this world with your own hands. You did not—"

Seam stepped up to the hulking brute. His hand burst forward and grasped Arakiel's throat. The chiseled form of Arakiel began to wither beneath Seam's grasp as the fury in Seam's eyes raged.

"You are right, mighty Arakiel. I *did not* shape this world in the beginning."

Arakiel's tight olive skin faded and slacked from his frame as he pawed at Seam's arm. The god's red eyes were like a raging fire plunged beneath a torrent of water. Seam held tight as his nostrils flared.

Abtren stepped forward. "Stop! High King, you must release him. He is not your enemy!"

Seam cut his eyes at Abtren, his hand still clamped around Arakiel's throat. *"Is he not? Anyone who opposes me is my enemy."* Seam glanced down at the husk of a warrior in his hands and sneered. He shoved the withered god to the black marble floor. He stood over him and wiped his hands.

"The world and all within it is under my grip now, Arakiel. I shape it and mold it as I please. Mind your tongue, mighty warrior, if you value your freedom here."

Seam clasped his hands together and leaned forward as he sat on his throne. "I may not know the entire history of this world, but I *do know* my destiny and my power. I do not fear Isphet. He will fall in line. *Just like his siblings.*"

Arakiel lay on the floor, gasping for breath like a fish out of water as Abtren stooped down to pull him to his feet. Nyx simply stared at Seam, her face a mix of adoration and worry.

A warm sensation ran through Seam as he sat on the throne. It was hard to describe, an electric current of power that riveted through him after he absorbed Arakiel's strength. He drew in a deep breath.

"What we must focus on now is your other brother, Bastion." Seam pointed toward the eastern horizon. "Arakiel has told me he is locked away within the stretch of mountains known as Legion's Teeth. I am ready to bring him home."

Seam stared out toward the horizon and tried to make out the silhouette of the distant mountain range. The arid deserts of Riht stretched over the eastern horizon and obscured even the massive grandeur of the Groganlands' red, steep mountains.

Seam turned back to Arakiel, Nyx, and Abtren and smiled. "We will leave Isphet for last. I have *special* plans for his recovery."

Abtren leaned her head to the side and cut her eyes to the window before replying. "If I may ask, High King. What exactly are your plans?" Her voice wavered with an intoxicating cadence, rattling through Seam's mind like a siren's song.

Stay strong, Seam thought to himself. Despite the keys, interacting with the Serubs was like swimming with sharks. It wasn't wise to linger in their presence any longer than necessary.

"You will know soon enough, Abtren. Our time is done here. You are all dismissed." Abtren nodded and stooped down with Nyx to lead her brother out of the throne room.

As they made their way out, Seam's voice echoed through the chamber. "There is one more thing. I need to speak with Nyx. Alone."

A puzzled look crossed Abtren's face as she glanced at her sister. Nyx shook her head and then looked back to Seam as he paced the floor toward a small door in the floor of the room.

Seam growled as Abtren lingered. "I said *alone*." Seam knelt and unlocked the trap door.

"Very well, *High King*," spat Abtren as she helped Arakiel to the door. She exchanged a quick glare at Nyx before exiting.

Nyx sauntered toward Seam. "Is there something *special* you need, my king?" She fell to her knees, her midnight eyes staring up into his, causing his insides to coil up with disgust. Seam faked a smile at her playfulness and held out his hand for her to rise. "The last beautiful woman that tried to seduce me died to feed your sister." He allowed his eyes to linger on her, ignoring the eyes that looked like the grave. "You are quite beautiful, but I require something very specific from you, mighty Nyx. That is, if you are who I believe you are."

Nyx slowed her approach and a look of confusion blanketed her face. "What do you mean?"

Seam cracked the trap door beneath him and stood to his feet. "You once were the *conduit*, were you not?"

A bright white smile broke on Nyx's face. "I am much more than a conduit, my king. I am the architect and handler."

"Perfect." Seam's eyes dropped into the small hold below him. "Then show me."

Nyx strolled to the edge of the opening etched in the floor and looked down. There, frozen in place, was the body of Kull Shepherd. His body lay in the dark chamber, crumbled on the floor. Yet, even to Seam's own surprise, the body still lived. Small, shallow breaths were the only sound that echoed from the empty husk hidden below.

Nyx stooped down and gazed at Kull. She turned back, her face turning toward the king. "Arakiel always did such a good job of cleansing them for me. You must realize how powerful our brother is."

A faint smile appeared on Nyx's lips as her eyes began to twitch and roll in their sockets. The pools of black gave way to an earthen brown iris, and for an instant, she assumed a more normal, human-like appearance. The simple change was enough to completely alter her beauty, and Seam felt his heart hammer within him. Nyx was just as mesmerizing as Abtren without her horrific midnight eyes.

Nyx stooped down as her eyes flickered between the light brown and abysmal black. Seam felt something shift beneath him and gasped. The body of his fallen enemy stood and gazed up at him.

Nyx's mouth muttered something unintelligible, and just as Seam was about to question what was happening, Kull climbed up and out of his holding chamber. Seam jumped back, staring at his foe and unable to speak. Kull took quick, shallow breaths and opened his mouth. A low, guttural moan fell out of his open mouth. For an instant Seam's mind clouded with fear and he took another step back as Kull approached him. Kull's body was once again full of life but his eyes were dull, hollow, and distant like that of someone gazing off into space without focus.

Kull continued pressing toward Seam and stopped just a foot from his face. A chill ran down Seam's spine as he examined the shambling specter of Grift Shepherd's son. He placed his hand on Kull's shoulder and looked back to Nyx.

"Are you providing him with any additional strength? Better vision? Enhanced senses?"

The thin smile that had sneaked onto Nyx's countenance faded as she answered. "No. His shell is limited to its own ability at first." She stepped closer to Kull and ran her hand down his arm.

"However, my king. As I told you, I am not only the handler. I am also an architect."

Seam allowed Nyx to read the confusion on his face as he stepped away from them. The Spire's wall-sized window showcased the shimmering, glass-covered city below him. "Speak clearly. What does being an architect entail, Nyx?"

Nyx ran her hand over the short brown stubble of hair on top of Kull's head. She opened her mouth and Kull's mouth opened in tandem. The two spoke in sequence, Kull's distorted and broken voice merged with hers.

"**I modify**," they both said as a grin stretched across Nyx's face. "**And improve.**"

Seam stood, his face knotted with both fear and revulsion. He shook his head. "Not *that one*. He remains as he is. There will be many more that you can tinker with, Nyx, but I have plans for him. He may be dead, but his body will continue to pay for what he did to me."

Nyx shrugged. "As you wish, High King." She paused, her face growing distant. "There are many still left here. What do the people of Candor call them?"

"*Morels*."

Nyx laughed like a child. "Ah yes, such a strange term for my abandoned children. They have been without their mother for so long, Keeper. Wandering with no purpose other than to survive." Her black eyes connected with Seam's. "They could still prove useful for you High King, yet...I recommend gathering a *fresh supply*."

Seam's eyes tightened. "In time, when it is necessary, Nyx."

Nyx nodded, another cold smile filling her face. She stepped toward the large metal doors leading to the hallway. "Are you sure you did not *need* anything else?"

Seam continued to peer from his perch, avoiding Nyx's horrible gaze. "No. That is all." He pointed to Kull. "But release him before you go. Your demonstration is finished."

"Very good," said Nyx just as the doors burst open behind her.

Bronson stumbled into the room, a cold sweat pouring from his brow. He panted for breath, but it was stolen away as his eyes fell on Kull Shepherd.

Aleph above.

He stammered and attempted to collect himself.

"Um, uh, my Lord."

Seam shot a glance at Nyx who slipped from the room. He placed himself between Kull and Bronson. "What is it, Bronson? What is so urgent that you dare burst into my chambers unannounced?"

Bronson could not tear his eyes away from Kull. *What had he said? Just days before? The boy is dead. Yes, that was it.* He had told Adley and Ewing the boy was dead, but now he was standing right in front of him. Seam grasped Bronson's face, breaking him out of his trance.

"What is it, Bronson?!" he screamed.

Bronson blinked, his body shaking. His lips somehow found the words. "The mirror. *Hosp*, sir."

Seam tightened his grip on Bronson's jaw. "What of Hosp and the mirror?"

Bronson tried to quit darting glances at Kull and finally focused in on Seam's wild brown eyes. "My intel has told me that he has unearthed the next mirror without your knowledge, sir."

Seam screamed. "What?!"

Bronson swallowed. "My sources say that he is planning to transport it to Rhuddenhall. For weeks, my spies have told me that the Grogans have been fortifying the city, but if this is true…"

Seam interrupted, "Then it appears like Hosp is trying to make a stand against me."

Seam closed his eyes, his face riddled with frustration. Bronson backed away from him and Kull, his mind still unable to process that Kull was alive. He tried to lock eyes with him, but the young man would not acknowledge his gaze.

Seam shook his head. "Very well, Hosp. At the end of the game the king and the pawn all go into the same box." He cut his eyes toward Bronson. "The game has just ended for the pawn."

CHAPTER SEVEN

Grift's rook burned out five miles from Cotswold just as the sun began to rise over the dark, cold horizon. As the machine sputtered, Grift hammered down the thruster, trying to steal the last of its energy. The engine finally gave up one last gasp before falling to the earth, careening onto the hard clay surrounding a dry streambed. The cold morning air enveloped the weary soldier as he abandoned the rook and sprinted over the foothills of the region he had known for so long. He cleared a familiar ridge and glanced down into the valley, his breath forming a pillar of cloud in the cold mountain air.

Grift stood, the cold morning breeze blowing through his hair, his heart hammering within his chest as he observed the ruins of his home. It had been nearly six months since Willyn tore him out of Cotswold. The battle had been terrible, but the shock of seeing the destruction that was left behind stole his breath away. Half of the town was nothing more than the charred skeletons of former shops and homes. Grift traced the remnants of the cobbled streets to the spot where his home once stood. The building that held so many memories with Rose and Kull had toppled over, falling in on itself. There were no signs of life in the town. Grift's heart sank as he ran his hand through his hair and shook his head. *They've pulled out. Just like Tindler.*

He sprinted for the town's remains, determined to find some clue to lead him to Rose. He was exhausted, but he would not will his body to stop. *You don't have much time,* he reminded himself. Thoughts of Rose's health goaded him to press on. He needed to get to her.

As he entered the valley, he bent down and looked at the ground. Large, iron tent spikes riddled the plain outside of Cotswold's retaining wall, but the accompanying tents were long gone. Truck tires had cut deep trenches in the fields, evidence that an exodus had taken place shortly after the attack.

Grift scanned the tire tracks and bit his lip. *Aleph. Help me.* The tracks were no help, weaving through the fields in no particular direction. They split up. His mind ran through the possibilities, but he did not like the conclusion. *Vale. They've gone to Vale for protection.*

A voice cried out over the empty plain. "Hey!"

Grift turned, his hand reaching for his pistol. He stared at the figure walking toward him. Grift read the figure in an instant and cocked the hammer back on his pistol. *Black and gold uniform. Dominion.*

He held up the pistol toward the figure as he slowly backpedaled. "Don't take another step!"

"Easy, easy!" the voice called back. The man held up his hands and continued walking.

"Did you not hear me, Guardsman?" Grift held the pistol right on the man's head and locked his jaw. "Stop!"

The figure stopped and called out, "Grift Shepherd, don't shoot!" The Dominion soldier lay down his rifle and laughed. "It's me! Ewing sent me here on patrol. I've been waiting for weeks for you to come." Grift's eyebrows arched with surprise, but his resolve did not sway.

"Who are you?"

"Rend." The man cocked his head, waiting on a response. "Rend Brinkley." Grift lowered his pistol, his mind remembering a name from what seemed an entire lifetime ago. He ran toward the Guardsman and wrapped his arms around the younger brother of his beloved friend, Tash. Tash had died defending Cotswold during Willyn's invasion. A smile erupted on his face.

"Rend! *Aleph above.* What are you doing out here?"

Rend's youthful face shined with surprise. "I told you, Commander Shepherd." Rend blinked and quickly threw up a salute. "Ewing sent me to wait on you. Once the refugees pulled out, he sent word for me, instructing me to wait in these ruins for you."

"*By yourself?*" Grift shook his head, the memories of morels in Tindler swarming through his mind.

"Yes, Commander. Though, as I'm sure you've seen... Lotte has changed."

Grift scanned the uniform hanging on Rend's shoulders, examining the golden insignia on his chest. He smeared a dirty finger over the golden emblem and smirked.

"So I see. Seam wasted little time creating this new world—a world in which I am a highly desired target. A terrorist of his mighty Dominion."

Rend's face clouded over with rage, and he spat on the ground. "Lies. Don't eat the lies of that jackal, Grift." Rend put a hand on his shoulder. "I never believed what he spoke about you or about the Mastermonk."

"Jackal?"

"*Seam.* What else would you call that murderer? Don't let my clothes fool you. I owe no allegiance to the King of Zenith. Just doing what I can to blend in, buy some time. And there are more than just me."

Grift nodded, his lips pursed. "So there is a resistance to the Dominion here?"

Rend laughed. "More than that, Grift, but I don't have much time to explain. I have to get you to the safe house." He pointed back toward the ruins. "I've got a fueled transport ready for us, but we need to move."

Grift nodded. He stared out over the field where he last saw Kull; where he lost his friend, Tash. He spoke, shaking the memories from his brain, his eyes wetting from the thought. "Rend. I am sorry for your brother."

Rend turned and nodded, his lips drawn.

Grift continued, "He was a good man, and my best soldier. I don't know how much you know, but the Grogans were deceived. The chaos they caused was just another one of Seam's schemes."

Rend shook his head. "I figure you speak the truth, Commander Shepherd, but my heart holds no love for the

Grogans, nor for General Kara. Deceived or not, my brother's blood is on their hands."

Rend looked away from Grift and took a deep breath before motioning for him to follow. "Come on. Let's get out of here."

Grift held his wife's brittle body in his arms. The skin of her face was nearly translucent and festered with red, irritated patches. Her chest rattled with each short breath. Her thin frame was tortured by muscles that would spasm and twitch as she lay her in cot. Wael's massive beast, Rot, guarded her bed, lying by her feet. Rot had been in the care of Arthur Ewing ever since Arik, Ewing's driver, had escaped the Groganlands. The massive dog was sprawled across the floor, but would sit to attention whenever anyone entered the room, ever watchful of Rose. The beast had even flashed fangs at Grift before realizing who it was as he approached his ailing wife.

Grift's tears dripped and ran down his bride's cheek. He leaned and kissed her forehead as she stared past him, lost in a stupor.

"Rose, I am here. I should have never left you." Grift's voice could barely escape his lips as he languished for long, calming breaths. "I am here," he whispered as he gently pressed his lips against his wife's chapped and cracking mouth.

A gentle hand pressed on Grift's shoulder. Eva Dellinger's tender voice followed. "*Grift*. Thank Aleph you are here. I have been fighting to keep her comfortable the best I can with what I have here."

Grift wiped the tears swelling in his eyes and turned to Eva and Ewing as they entered the room. Eva's long gray hair was pulled back into a frizzy ponytail, and her wrinkled face gave her a tired yet reassuring appearance. "Thank you, Eva. When was the last time..." Grift's question broke before he took in a deep breath and gathered himself. "When was the last time she spoke?"

Eva brought a damp cloth and wiped Rose's forehead and cheeks. She rubbed a creamy balm on her lips. "The last I heard her speak was before Kull left us. She was speaking to him. She has been in this state ever since."

Grift stood to his feet and slammed his fist against the wall. The brittle wood planks buckled beneath his fist. Rot shot to his feet and let out a rolling growl. Grift leaned his head against the wall and whispered to himself, "It is my fault. Her last words were used to beg Kull to find me. She needed me."

Grift turned and shook his head. "Thank you, Eva, and my apologies." He glanced at the wall. "I didn't mean–"

"No worries, dear," said Eva as she continued to care for Rose. "I have hit that old wall many times myself." Her eyes cut into him with a mischievous grin. "I'm just not quite strong enough to leave a mark." She squeezed the warrior's wrist. "She's not gone yet, Grift. She's still here. Her eyes still have strength."

Grift's throat choked as he fought back an avalanche of grief. "Thank you, Eva." Grift walked back to Rose's side, his mind scrambled with emotion.

"You're welcome. I am here to help, just call whenever you need me."

Rot lowered his hackles and laid back down at the foot of the bed. Eva slipped from the door and left Ewing and Grift standing over Rose. Ewing laid a heavy hand on Grift's shoulder and nodded his head.

"Eva's right, Grift. Rose hasn't given up yet." He pulled his friend close. "You shouldn't either."

Grift leaned back over Rose and looked into her eyes, but the blue eyes looking back were distant. His wife's eyes were staring through him, vacant and hollow.

He stood back to his feet and stepped close to Ewing, leaning next to his ear. "She has fought this thing a long time, Ewing. There was only one thing that ever helped."

Ewing's face bore a small frown. "What's that, son?"

"The Hand of Aleph. Wael blessed her and gave her his rune. Many years ago."

Ewing nodded and cleared his throat before answering. "Why is it not working now?"

Grift pushed back the thin blonde hair lying around Rose's neck. "Because she gave it to Kull. I saw him wearing it when he...saved me." Grift paused, purging those awful final moments from his mind. "She sacrificed herself to bless Kull while he was looking for me, Ewing."

Grift stepped to the lone window cut into the wall. "We'll need to be leaving soon."

"Who's leaving?" grunted Ewing. "There is much you don't know, Grift Shepherd. There is a growing resistance here in Lotte. I've seen to that, but I need you to help me rally it." Ewing grabbed his friend's arm and stared into his eyes. "We need you here. This resistance needs tending, and I can't do it alone."

"No." The answer was firm as Grift looked back at his friend with bloodshot eyes. "I am getting Rose out of here. I fought for Candor long enough. Now I'm fighting for her. We have to get her back to Preost."

Ewing straightened his back and hobbled forward on his mechanical leg as he raised his tenor. "Son. I know you want to get Rose back to Wael for a blessing, but have you not looked outside? Do you not remember the patrols? The cut and monitored datalinks?"

"I know!" snapped Grift. "This is not just about Rose, Arthur! This whole continent is in the hands of a madman! Do you really think Lotte of all places is safe for any of us? If it was, we wouldn't be holed up in a drafty shack in the industrial district, would we?"

Ewing shook his head. "I know it's not safe, Grift. I'm no fool. We have to do whatever we can." Ewing slammed his hand down on a table by Rose's bedside. "Running away and hiding won't accomplish anything. You'll rob this resistance of your leadership, Shepherd. Leadership that is sorely needed!"

"Last time I checked, I didn't volunteer for any position in your resistance, Arthur." Grift's voice was cold.

Ewing roared, his face flushed. "For Aleph's sake, Shepherd, do you think I've been sitting here smoking my pipe, waiting while you ran around this continent? I have spent these months gathering people against this madness. *This cursed Dominion.* If any resistance is going to survive it has to spread beyond this containment, and *I need your help.*"

Grift relented and sat on a small wooden chair propped against the wall. "Arthur. You've not seen what I have. Seam's plans go beyond mere political machinations."

Ewing's voice grew cold. "What do you mean, boy? Speak plainly."

Grift leaned in to reveal the awful truth. "Seam has all of the Keys, Arthur. He is unlocking *them* from the mirrors. From our count, we know he has at least two...if not three." Fear chocked Grift to whisper, his eyes locking onto his friend. "The last mirror is in Preost. I saw it and *I saw what was in it.*"

Ewing's mouth dropped open. "Aleph above." He paced the floor. "Why would he do that?" His eyes locked onto his friend's. "What did you see, Grift? What did you see in that mirror?"

"Ewing. The legends the Order had given us are true. The Serubs, the Keys. *All of it.* Seam is rallying his forces—not to unite Candor, but to gather the cursed mirrors of the Fallen. The last one he will need is underneath the very Sanctuary of Preost." Grift stared at his friend. "It's the only one in our possession right now. Willyn Kara is off to the Groganlands to try to secure one hidden in Legion's Teeth. At this point, it would be safe to assume that the High King has three of the Five at his beck and call."

Ewing's hands shook. He nodded his hands, his tongue licking his dry lips. "I understand."

"We can't let him get to the mirrors, Ewing. We have to protect them, but I am not leaving Rose. *Not again.* I don't mean to discredit your works in stoking a rebellion, but what good is a rebellion against the fallen gods?"

Ewing's face refused to soften. "I am not a devout man, Grift, but I fear only one god, and he does not walk on Candor." Ewing's mind swirled with thoughts, and he paced in silence. After what seemed a long moment, Ewing spoke, bringing an answer back to his beloved protégé. "*What good is a rebellion?* It's a spark. Our ancestors somehow overthrew these monsters in the past. *We can do it again.* We must. We have a spark, and I will not lose hope."

Grift shook his head. Ewing's face was stern as he pointed at Grift. "Get up. It's time to go. We need to meet with someone. This information has changed our plans significantly."

Grift slowly stood, his face drawn with exhaustion. He looked at his wife, hope far from his face. "It can't take long, Ewing. I am leaving within twenty-four hours. Who do we need to see?"

A mischievous grin stretched across Ewing's face. "The queen."

Grift watched the hovel that was hiding his wife slowly fade into the distance. The old mill house was one of the few still standing outside of Lotte's largest sawmill in an abandoned western industrial district outside of Vale. The setting sun cast a red hue over the industrial complex and draped tall shadows over the small houses. Sawdust and soot covered everything in sight. Three tall smokestacks reached up into the sky like rusted fingers stretching out from the metallic building, but no smoke lifted into the sky. Grift breathed a sigh of relief, knowing that the mill had not been open for operation at least since the Grogan attacks. Power had long been cut by the Grogan raids, and the roads surrounding them had been blasted out by mortar fire. It would be near impossible to drive lumber into the mill now. Rose and Eva would be safe here for the time being.

As Grift stepped out into the muddy alleyway, his comfort faded. His mind went dark with the thought of Dominion troops marching on the mill. He glanced at the Asban mountains. A wall of thick fog covered the spot where he knew Vale stood. *No one up there will protect this place.* Grift knew enough about the relative opulence of Vale to know that the rest of Lotte was on its own. With the exception of a few good barons within the aristocracy, as long as Vale was secure, there would be little help or concern for the regular people suffering within the Realm. He spat at the ground, his eyes still scanning the mountain covered with fog, and the thought of leaving Rose again made his heart ache.

Ewing snapped at him. "Hey! Are you coming?"

Grift turned, shaking his head. "Yes."

Grift slipped away and followed his friend to the outskirts of the mill. They were off to the tent city.

Grift spoke within his mind to Rose. *I will be back. I promise. Aleph...please.*

Ewing lit his pipe and puffed a blue ringlet of smoke in Grift's direction as they bounced in the back of a covered timber truck. "Don't worry, Grift. A soul hasn't come anywhere near the old mill since the attacks, plus they have Rot with 'em. That nasty old beast is scarier than any gun toting thug I've ever seen."

Grift shook his head, his eyes distant and heavy. "I'm leaving her again, Ewing. I finally have my wife in my arms and I leave her again."

Ewing patted his friend's arm. "This won't take long. You have my word. We will slide in under the cover of night, have our meeting, and work our way out. The queen can probably help make sure you find your way back to Preost... with Rose."

A smile forced its way onto Grift's tired face. "Thank you. I hadn't thought of that. I haven't thought clearly since...you have always been a good friend, Arthur."

Ewing puffed at his pipe and waved the smoke from his face. "Bah. Don't go blubbering about how wonderful I am." He leaned forward and flashed his yellowed teeth. "*I already know.*" Ewing sat back and chuckled to himself as the truck continued to push through the growing darkness.

The sun dipped behind the horizon, leaving the rolling hills dark and void. The logging truck carrying Ewing and Grift carefully lumbered toward a valley filled with small pinpricks of light. The hillsides sloped down to the tent city, and the fires burning below looked like tiny stars held in a large earthen bowl. The tents all rustled in the wind that was sweeping in from the west.

The truck pulled up next to the first row of tents and Ewing stumbled from the truck bed. He wobbled to the driver's door and leaned in to speak with the driver. "Keep the engines running. We won't be long."

Grift hopped out and pulled his hood over his head. *Too many people know my face.* Grift cut his eyes across the rows of green emergency tents and the people strolling between them. None of the faces caught his attention, but he still pulled the hood further over his brow and followed behind Ewing who happily sauntered through the rows of tents whistling at a few friends as if it was just a casual stroll through town. As Ewing continued to bark out greetings to the refugees, Grift cursed and drifted back. *Some cover you give, Arthur.* As Ewing drifted further away, Grift pushed through the crowded alleyway marked with deep, muddy footprints. The mob he pushed through held desperation in their eyes, but Grift did his best not to linger on their faces. He was able to scan them, and relief washed over him. It was not obvious that he and Ewing were together. He slipped down a row and kept parallel to Ewing's slow, relaxed gait until, at last, the two slipped into a small medical tent.

Adley was sitting alone on a cot with a small wood stove burning in the middle of the dirt floor. She looked up and smiled at Ewing. "Cold night, huh? Trying to get it warmed up a bit in here." Her eyes flashed as a hooded stranger entered the tent, and her eyes lit up with recognition. "Oh. Aleph, am I glad to see you!" She ran to Grift and embraced him, her eyes brimming with tears and a genuine smile on her face. "How are you?"

Grift forced a smile and nodded. "I've been better, dear. But we will get through all this." The words came quickly and sounded hollow in Grift's mouth. His eyes scanned the room. "Where is our guest?"

Ewing lifted the tent's cloth door and glanced outside. "Don't worry. She will come, but we won't have long."

Grift bit at his lip. "Security will have a short leash, Arthur." Ewing nodded as he relit his pipe and sat on a medical cot.

After a few minutes, the tent door rustled and a teenage boy slipped in. He flipped his hood back and glanced around the room. His young face was littered with sparse stubble and his shaggy blonde hair hung loosely around his pale face. His eyes paused on Grift sitting in the corner before scanning over Adley and Ewing. Grift reached for the pistol at his side, but the boy flashed back out the door as quickly as he had entered.

Ewing's hand pounced on Grift's arm and he flashed a smile to Adley. "*Easy friend*. That is Reuben, our queen's scout. Nice kid. Put your weapon away."

Grift's hands shook. *Gods*. He was more upset than he even realized. Coming back to Lotte, to Rose. All of it had been unsettling. The new reality had come with no warning. While he was fighting for his life, Seam's machinations had taken nearly everything he had. *Everything except for Rose*. He swallowed, composed himself, and slid his pistol back into his holster as he grunted, "Could've let me know before he burst in here unexpected."

As Ewing hobbled next to the fire the tent door pushed open again, but instead of a young boy, it was none other than Queen Aleigha. A long black gown washed over her thin frame, and her face looked as hard as the Asban mountain. She removed her hood, and on top of her head was a silver circlet that caught the light of the fire. Grift's heart panged in his chest. He dropped to a knee and lowered his head. She was all that was left of his fallen lord, Camden. The world had changed so quickly, and somehow his heart softened in her presence.

She stooped down and picked him up. "No pleasantries needed, Grift Shepherd. Not here. Not now." The queen's voice was tired as she addressed him. "Please stand, we don't have long."

Ewing snuffed the pipe he had been puffing and tipped his head to Aleigha. "My dear queen, I thank you for taking time to meet. I am afraid we have *unfortunate* news."

The queen's lips pursed. "Speak. What news do you bring me?"

Grift stood to his feet and stepped closer to the queen. "Your son. He is collecting the mirrors. Mirrors that have long held the Serub fallen. *The Five*. He is working to free them."

Aleigha's face went pale, and she stared into the flickering flames of the fire at her feet.

Grift continued, "He holds all of the Keys of Candor, my queen. The keys have the power to release them. Do you understand?"

The small fire reflected the ember of strength smoldering inside and shining within her eyes.

"I have feared this day." She looked back at Grift, to Ewing, and even to Adley who stood near the back of the tent. "This was his plan. I have had nightmares forewarning me of these events." She shook her head. "But I did not want to believe them...I even saw the first mirror." Anger flared on her face. "I should have had it destroyed that night!" Aleigha ground her teeth and stared into the fire, her rage electrifying the room.

Adley stepped forward and spoke. "There is still a chance, my queen. When I was in the tower, I saw that he had only two of the portals, though we have word he may have a third. With your help we can slow him down and destroy the mirrors that are left, before he can gather them all."

Ewing shot Grift a glance, his eyes wide open searching for confirmation.

Realization poured over Grift's tired mind. It flashed with memories of Isphet and the image of the demon's mirror healing before his very eyes. He remembered the intel gathered from Bronson Donahue, Seam's Captain of the Guard. He had three. *Aleph above, he has three of the five.* Rage threatened to overtake him, but Grift regained his composure and ran his hands through his hair. "No... it won't work."

Adley scrunched her face and shot a glance at Grift as he stared down into the fire. "What do you mean, no?"

Grift never broke his eyes from the flames. "I mean what I said. You can't destroy these things. The mirrors cannot be destroyed by anything we have on Candor. They have to be moved and hidden again. It is our only option."

Aleigha placed a soft hand on Grift's shoulder. Her eyes were gentle but resolute. "You saw one, didn't you? Where is it?"

After glancing back to the tent door, Grift whispered. "Locked under the protection of Preost. I have to get back to it. We have other allies at work, my queen. As we speak, Willyn Kara of the Groganlands is heading to secure another mirror, but we know your son has secured three of the five. We don't have time to waste."

The mention of Seam washed the life from Aleigha's face. She slumped her shoulders before shaking herself from her own personal terror.

"Don't..." Aleigha paused. "Don't call him that."

"Excuse me?" asked Grift.

"Don't call him my son." The room went silent, with only the sound of the crackling fire filling the void. "Now. What do you need? How can I help?"

Grift gave a stunned response, "We need safe passage to Preost, and if you have any datalinks that haven't been tampered with, that would be helpful."

Aleigha nodded, her mind awash with thought. She turned, glancing at the three of them.

"In three days I am sending a convoy of medical aid and healers to the border town of Henshaw. Preost lies just over the border. *Make sure you are on that convoy.* This is an aid mission, so you must be discrete. I can't say that I trust all of them. From there you will be on your own."

Adley exchanged glances with Grift and Ewing. "I will make sure the nurses have you ready for the trip." She bowed her head to the queen. "Thank you. We are indebted to you for your help."

Aleigha offered a faint smile and nodded. "May Aleph help us all." She lifted her hood back over her head and slipped back into the night.

Grift leveled his eyes with Ewing. "I'm going for her now. I will be back in the morning to prepare for the convoy."

Ewing lit his pipe again and took a draw before shaking his head. "I know. Be safe. And don't wreck my truck."

CHAPTER EIGHT

The ramshackle chorus of the railcar's metallic wheels clattered beneath Willyn as she sped away from the towering desert skyline of Zenith. Bri sat next to her, his eyes snapped shut. The quick swaying of the railcar had soothed the gentle giant to sleep so quickly that it startled Willyn as his titanic snores ripped through the cabin. She glanced around, doing her best to silence the peals of thunder coming from Bri's nostrils.

What was Wael thinking? Willyn could not believe Wael had not bothered to get her approval on the inclusion of Bri in her journey. He had insisted she have an escort; he could have at least let her have input in the matter.

She glanced around the cramped quarters she shared with the thirty other passengers, and her thoughts drifted. Disguised or not, she found it hard to relax in the presence of so many Baggers. Anxiety stemming from Seam's assassin in Zenith still made her heart twist in her chest.

Had it been Seam's assassin? Or could Hagan still be alive? She shook her head, clearing the doubt from her mind. It didn't matter. None of what the messenger said mattered. It had to be a trap; nothing else made sense. Hagan's supposed emissary was dead now. Dead and lying in an abandoned alley of Zenith, and she still had no one to trust. *No one.* If the mission to stop Seam was going to be successful, she knew she would have to be careful and make it happen on her own.

Focus. Her mind locked onto Legion's Teeth, onto the cursed mirror that she had to locate, and onto the Reds that she would rally.

Focus.

Willyn woke from a restless slumber just in time to see the pink hue of the easternmost point of Candor darken in the twilight. The jagged outcrops of rocky peaks shot up into the sky, their tops ripping through the clouds, standing crooked and perilous. Behind the Teeth lay only the other side of the Endless Ocean, as if the continent had sheared away from some cataclysm lost in time.

The railcar began to elevate in its grade, causing Willyn's ears to pop under the pressure. The ragged railway that weaved through the outcrops of the thin mountain pillars was the end of the line, and Willyn could feel it as the railcar struggled to navigate infrastructure that was long past due for maintenance.

Legion's Teeth was the original capital of the Groganland Realm, but had long since been abandoned for a more accessible and heavily fortified position against the Grogans' old enemy, the Rihtians. Rhuddenhall arose from the endless fortifications that were necessary to keep the Rihtians in check, leaving behind the ancient trappings of the warrior customs and architecture in Legion's Teeth.

The thin mountain pillars jutting into the sky still held cutout dwellings that housed a large number of Grogans. Willyn examined the outermost crop of pillars that the railcar passed. Up on the top of the cliffs she noted the bell keepers who looked down on the railcar like hawks. *They still keep the sentry.* The sentry keepers scanned any movement that dared to approach the Teeth, detecting allies and foes miles away from their vantage point. Her eyes scanned the rickety platforms that housed the faithful of her kinfolk, their rickety structures bolted to the tops of the world. Ancient bronze bells hung still in the cold mountain air. The last time she had traveled to the Teeth had been with Hagan and their father. She had been a little girl then.

The railcar reached the end of the railway, and Willyn observed the once proud colony that fought to cling to life. The wide rocky streets were filled with miners, laborers, and outcasts. Willyn watched the faces of the poor mining families flashed by as they peered out the fronts of their dugout, cave-like homes, watching the railcar pass by.

Willyn's mind filled with a mixture of both pity and disgust. *No wonder the Baggers fit in so well here. These Grogans have lost their hope. They have no pride.*

Willyn bit her lip and shook her head. *How do I rally a weak people with no hope? What do they have to fight for?* The reality of Willyn's mission pushed on her spirit like an anvil. A light mist fell on the mountain city, leaving the forlorn town even more gray and depressing.

As the old train screeched to a halt, Willyn wrapped a poncho around her shoulders and kicked at Bri's foot. Bri snorted and sucked in a large puff of air before stretching out his tattooed arms and yawning. He smiled at Willyn. "Ah. Thin mountain air. We're here. Good sleep."

Willyn followed Bri through the dirt streets of Legion's Teeth, trying not to trip over the broken bricks and stone jutting up from the roads. The train depot sat in a small dip in the rock, surrounded by roughhewn mountain homes and narrow, worn streets. The path carried them even higher into the mountain, to the heart of Legion's Teeth. As the two climbed the mountainside path, concrete structures protruded from the rocky cliffs. The tallest structure was no more than two stories tall, a massive bunker. A long artillery cannon jutted out from the thin slits at the bunker's roof line. Unlike Rhuddenhall and its towering gates, the strength of Legion's Teeth came from the walls Aleph provided, the mountains themselves. From this vantage point, no outside threat could penetrate the city of Legion's Teeth. The city was hidden deep underneath the craggy mountains.

The people inhabiting the mountain town outside the city were mostly downtrodden, dirty laborers. Despite this, just being back in the Groganlands bolstered Willyn's spirit. She regretted that her return must be in secret, as she hid from her own people.

Bri stopped in front of one of the larger concrete buildings that had a metal roof and large, sliding metal bay doors. "This it. This is mine hub. Ready to work?"

Willyn pushed past Bri. "More than I think you realize, Bri. Let's get inside."

The main hangar-like area inside the door was filled with a multitude of men and women. The scurrying feet kicked up a hue of red, dry dust that hung in the air like a fog. Most were dressed in black with red bandanas either on their head or wrapped around their upper arm. Their faces were covered with soot and mining dust, but few of them actually looked like miners. Instead of carrying picks or jackhammers, most of the inhabitants were shouldering rifles.

The Reds. These are my people. The thought quickened Willyn's heartbeat and brought a warmth that had been missing within her since she learned of Hagan's death. The internal question pricked her again, *"Is he really dead?"*

A whip crack echoed through the chamber, causing Willyn to snap with attention as the Reds turned in unison toward the newcomers.

A thunderous voice boomed in the chamber. "ALL RIGHT, YOU LOT!"

Willyn turned her eyes up to see a stout, barrel-chested man walking high on an iron catwalk above. A long, bushy black beard covered his face like a wilderness, and his eyes were wild, wide, and full of anger.

"I don't know what they told you down in Zenith," the man spat on the ground, "but you've been hired for something more than mining!"

Willyn glanced up to read Bri's face. He shook his head and leaned down to her whispering, "This...this is not the normal." Willyn stared at the foreman as he roared over them.

"In Legion's Teeth we do not serve the 'High King' of Candor who sits on his desert throne. Nor do we serve his Surrogator lapdog who whimpers in Rhuddenhall. We," he slammed his fist on his chest, "remain faithful to the old ways, the Grogan ways. We are the Reds, and we serve the rightful Sar, Willyn Kara!"

The Reds filling the room held up their fists and chanted, "Kara! Kara! Kara!"

Willyn's heart leapt in her chest, and everything within her wanted to announce her return. Bri's giant hand closed softly over hers. He looked at her and shook his head. His eyes said one thing: *Wait.*

Bri knows more than I thought. He knows who I am. The thought both comforted and disturbed her. What else did her companion know?

The foreman gave another crack of his whip, and the Reds ceased their chant.

"So, my dear Baggers, you have found yourself in a precarious situation."

Willyn held her breath. The faces of the Baggers were full of fear. The young mothers in the crowds gripped their children, their lips muttering silent prayers.

The foreman continued, "You are our ancient enemies, the displaced Rihtians who fought our countrymen for millennia. By all rights we should work you down into the depths of the mountains and leave you there to die..." The bear-like man paced around the rabble, his eyes soaking in the fear and trembling of the Baggers, enjoying his position as he strolled above them, safe on his catwalk. "But... now is not the time to open old wounds." His eyes scanned the crowd, his face as stern as the grave. "Let me be clear, we need you. The Reds need your help. On the authority of the Sar and her general here in Legion's Teeth, Rander, you will be given a choice."

Willyn's mind swelled with questions. *Rander?* The name was not familiar, but any person who would dare to play this game with her authority was either a fool or a madman. Neither option gave her any comfort.

"Swear your fealty to Willyn Kara, or leave. We only give this choice to you once. You and your family can leave, traveling down the mountain pass into the wilderness. Those who stay...if you betray us, you'll hang on the Pass. Do I make myself clear?"

The Baggers remained silent, shaking in the mining hub.

"Good. Those who will not serve the rightful Sar of the Groganlands, leave now."

No soul made for the door.

"On your knees, then. Repeat after me!"

All of the Baggers fell to their knees, the fear and adrenaline of the open threat slowly receding from their minds. The foreman continued and Willyn hid, kneeling amidst the mass.

"I swear my allegiance to the Reds, and their Lord and Master, Willyn Kara, the Sar of the Groganlands. By Aleph's name, I make this pledge. *Selah!*"

The Baggers repeated what they heard, for no more reason than to survive another day. Willyn did the same, her heart beating in her chest as her lips spoke her own name, and she wondered how many times her name had been invoked over the lives of innocent people just trying to survive. The thought of forcing her name on helpless Baggers twisted like a corkscrew deep in her gut.

"Stand up!" The foreman's foul face receded. "We know you have traveled very far. There is much work to do, but you must eat and rest. Tomorrow I will instruct you in your task. I am Viga and I welcome you. Follow your way through the hall to rest and eat now. Tomorrow we work!" With that, Viga left them and the Reds opened a large doorway that emptied out into a gallery of food vendors.

Bri chuckled and pointed down the large cement corridor. "Food that way. Don't get lost."

Willyn laughed at how quickly Bri adjusted to the circumstance. A realization shot through her mind. *They all are like this. The Baggers adjust as they have to so they can survive.* She thanked Bri and slipped down the long, wide corridor searching for a nook of privacy. A small hallway broke off from the main thoroughfare with markings for storage. Willyn snuck into the first unlocked door and dug her datalink from her pocket, quickly typing a message.

:Wael. I am here. The Reds have completely taken over the Teeth. They are swearing that they serve me. Rander, however, is the man in charge. Do you know anything about him?

A few seconds passed, and Wael's response flashed on the screen.

:No. We do not know that name. Proceed with caution. Learn what you can before you make your presence known. Your first task must be to find the mirror. Find it, then secure your place. I will be in touch.

Willyn typed her response in a flash.

:Understood.

Willyn snapped the datalink on her wrist shut. She stepped back down the narrow hallway and merged into the flow of migrant workers, following their noses to their next meal. As she followed the crowd, another large room opened around them. The cement floors gave way to red rock walls that jutted up hundreds of feet into the air, the ceiling held back by nothing more than steel beams shouldering the colossal weight of the mountain overhead. Tables lined the far wall of the marketplace, with smaller rooms cut out to house vendors offering an assortment of food, clothing, and wares.

The pleasant, smoky smell of Grogan cooking made her mouth water. The aroma of barbecued boar meat and stewed rabbit welcomed Willyn home. She fished in her pockets for a few credits and bought a roasted rabbit leg from one of the food stations. As she gnawed at the delicious, gamey meat, she sat at one of the vacant tables and positioned herself to examine the room.

After about five minutes, Willyn noticed a middle-aged man with jet-black hair and a long mustache stroll into the room flanked by six bodyguards. The man was no more than five and a half feet tall but looked as thick as he was long. The men around him were holding standard formation as he walked up to one of the vendors. He gazed at the food over his dark glasses before pointing at whatever it was he wanted to eat. Soon, Viga joined him and the formation and started shouting orders at the cook.

Rander. Willyn could read the formation in an instant. *Their formation is blatant.* Willyn knew that even if the mustached man was not Rander, it had to be someone important to the Reds, and he could lead her to him.

As Willyn started to rise from her seat, a rough hand caught her arm. "I see your eyes. Wouldn't trouble them. Not if you wanna live."

Willyn jerked her arm back and spun to face a young, portly Bagger. He flashed her a hollow-toothed grin before warning her again. "You best be careful. People been dying around here lately. Rander don't take much bothering to get in a fuss."

Willyn looked back over her shoulder as Rander and Viga slipped through the crowd.

"What do you mean?" She searched his expression for information. "Is he killing people? Is Rander murdering migrants?" Willyn cursed under her breath as Rander and his party turned the corner and disappeared.

The boy took a huge bite out of a roast pheasant, his jowls working furiously on the poor bird. He spoke between swallows. "No. He ain't killing. But someone is. Started with five bodies getting pulled outta hole deep in the eastern mines a couple days back. They was all shot in the head. Had gone missing a few days when a rescue dog found 'em. Barely got the dog out alive cause of the fumes. No one should be down in the eastern shafts." Willyn cocked her head, and the Bagger nodded. "Shafts there are full of poison. A few people went down to fetch the bodies, and they never came back."

Willyn raised her eyebrows, her mind whirring through the possibilities. "So someone is murdering the Baggers?"

"Baggers. Reds. It don't matter. People keep turning up dead down in the same spot. Don't know what's going on and it's got Rander wound tight." He leaned in, motioning for her to do the same. She did, meeting his solemn eyes. *I think the place is cursed. No one should be there no ways. It's been closed for years, ever since the accident."*

"Accident?"

"Yeah. Something about a ghost that walks the eastern shafts. Drinking the blood of miners, bunch of crazy stuff like that. The story has been passed around for years, and no one thought anything about it. It was all fine and good until a few of the kids decided to be brave and go exploring."

Willyn's heart throttled in her chest. "What happened?" she said, trying to sound disinterested.

The boy grabbed a cup of water and swallowed it in one gulp. He spoke matter-of-factly, "Five Bagger kids went in. None of them came back. They got trapped in the back of a shaft and couldn't find their way out. Strangest thing is the shaft was open. There wasn't a cave in or anything."

Willyn cocked her head. "So–"

The broad boy looked at her, his eyes distant, weighing the words. "The thing is they were all dead, but that wasn't the strange part."

Willyn leaned in, her ears peaked. "I heard that there wasn't a drop of blood in them. They were dried out like apples." He shook his head. "The doctors said it was because of the air, so they closed the shaft for workers ever since. Don't know if it is all true, but that's word round here 'bout it."

The mirror! The thought burst through Willyn's mind like a lightning bolt. *They've found it.*

Willyn's stomach turned. She was too late. The mission was a total failure and it had not yet begun. She ground her teeth before asking one more question. "Do you know if they pulled anything else out the eastern tunnels other than those five men?"

The Bagger scrunched up his face. "What you mean?"

Willyn looked around the room to make sure no one was listening in on the conversation and whispered, "Did they pull out anything of value? I mean, why were people going down there if they knew the danger? There has to be something down there that makes the risk worth it."

The Bagger shook his head. "Dunno. But word is people are still going down to dig even after all that happened. One of my friends said just yesterday some guy asked him to dig down there again tonight. Said they pay him fifty credits for one night's work. Good pay, but I ain't crazy. I wouldn't do it."

Willyn's heart raced. Her face flushed with warmth as she realized that she still had time. She controlled her excitement to a furious whisper. "Show me. I'll pay you a hundred credits. You just have to show me the way."

The Bagger's eyes flew wide open. "Are you crazy?"

Willyn grunted and pulled at his arm. "Just show me. Not all the way, just show me how to get to the eastern mine. I will handle the rest. And you tell no one about me going or you will be the next dead body down there. Got it?"

The Bagger chuckled and took another bite before wiping his cheeks and standing from the table. "Yep. All I heard was one hundred credits."

She led the husky Bagger out of the mess hall. Bri watched the whole conversation from a distance, reading their lips as he baptized his bushy mustache in thick beef stew. When Willyn left the room, Bri slurped down his last gulp and stood, trailing his ward in silence.

Willyn's face was covered with a large, awkward mask that hummed with mechanical life. She wore a heavy pack that supplied her with fresh air as she worked her way down the narrow path in the dark. Following the tracks in the forgotten mineshaft was easy enough. The dust and debris on the floor showcased the decisions that the now dead miners had made.

The shaft was a blanket of shadow that was near impossible to navigate, and Willyn was hardly prepared. After running off and leaving Bri and the rest of the Baggers behind, all she had for light was the screen of her datalink.

"No weapon. No map. Hardly any light. Not your best plan," Willyn whispered to herself as she pressed further into the mine. "Too far to turn back now. Should have taken something for protection."

Eventually the lonely cut of rock dropped into a steep slope. The slanting floor was coated with thick dust and debris. Willyn knew she was in the middle of the new dig site. The hair on Willyn's arms stood on end as she squeezed down the narrow walls in a steady decline.

The shaft soon ended and leveled. Willyn could see a large crevice running down the middle of the floor. She stooped down, examining it. The thin crack on the floor grew, appearing to open into a separate cavern below. The glow of her datalink did not provide enough light to examine the area below, but Willyn knew she was close. She could feel it.

She climbed back up the sloping floor and found a small perpendicular vein cut into the side of the mineshaft that she determined was deep enough to conceal herself. If what the Bagger said was true, there would soon be another set of miners walking into a trap.

The hours inched by as Willyn sat alone in the inky black depths of Legion's Teeth. She checked her oxygen tank and cursed as the gauge continued to drop. She dialed back the oxygen mix and slowed the airflow. Willyn fidgeted with the device as she prayed that the men would show soon, before she had to turn back to prevent choking out.

The time spent in silence offered the demons of her past a chance to torment her. The most common thought that continued to assault her was the face of Hagan. She kept thinking of his death and questioned what she could have done differently to save him. But Hagan was not alone in her nightmares. He was joined by Luken. Willyn kept replaying his death in her mind. The last she could remember of him was the explosion that sent him to the depths of the Endless Ocean. Two of the only people she had ever opened up to, been herself with, were gone. They were gone, but her nightmares remained. The two people that had once brought her comfort only tormented her quiet, lonely thoughts.

"Down here, you slugs." The gruff voice broke Willyn from her terrible daydreams. "One rule. No one drops in until I tell you to. Disobey and you will end up like the rest."

The voice was unmistakable. Viga was the one trying to dig out the mirror.

Willyn peaked around the corner of her hiding spot and watched the backs of four men bob up and down as they stepped down the decline leading to the shaft's dead end. Two of the men carried jackhammers, another was loaded with chains, and the fourth, Viga, carried nothing but a pistol.

The sound of jackhammers thundered up the mineshaft and vibrated the walls of Willyn's small hiding place. The thunderous din vibrated through the small shaft with growing intensity, scrambling Willyn's thoughts and plans. *Think, Willyn, think!*

The noise was terrible, making it almost impossible to cement a plan in her mind. There was no other opportunity to secure the mirror. Willyn slipped to the edge of the sloping floor and looked down into the shadows. The two men working the jackhammers were preoccupied, trying to open the vein in the floor wider, as Viga and the other worker stayed back. A cloud of dust enveloped the men as the rock floor was slowly eaten away.

Willyn slid down the descent, inching closer to the four silhouettes in the dust-filled dead end. Before the men became indistinguishable shapes in the cloud of debris, Willyn marked Viga and tracked his movements around the floor.

As she slid closer to her target, Willyn could not help but smile. The low light, the dust, and the rumbling of the tools provided the perfect cover. The jackhammers laid a blanket of noise that could disguise the sound of a stampede.

Viga still had his pistol drawn and his finger rested on the trigger. Willyn slipped in behind him and struck hard, grasping his wrist while kicking at his knee. Viga buckled to the ground, but his grip held tight. Willyn slammed her elbow into his mask, meeting the bridge of his nose twice, unleashing a torrent of blood from behind the plastic hood, before ramming her knee deep into his forearm. Despite the assault, he would not relent his grip on his weapon.

A shot rang out and illuminated the dusty corridor as the bullet ricocheted through the dark. The jackhammers stopped as the men ran from their posts. Through the cloud of dust, Willyn saw their faces behind the plastic masks: Baggers. They were probably fresh from Zenith. The other man followed suit, dropping the chains and retreating from the scene, leaving Willyn alone with her prey. Viga's strength and fortitude surprised her, and she cursed as he continued to try to wrench his pistol free. She refused to let go of his wrist, and she pummeled his face without mercy with her elbow.

"I order you to stand down, soldier. I am Willyn Kara!" Willyn screamed as she continued her attack.

Viga forced himself to his feet. He grasped Willyn by the throat and landed a head butt against her temple, avoiding any protection her mask could give her. An earthquake of pain shot through her skull. She had underestimated him; the man's strength was incredible. Willyn struggled to find a new angle of attack as Viga hurled her into the stone wall. The blows he landed on her stole the wind from her chest and sent her gasping for air.

She sucked in, trying to find a breath through her confining mask as she dove toward the middle of the room, her mind locked on the shot she knew was coming.

The shot rang out with an explosion of light and sound. The bullet careened across the room and left a white-hot trail in the dusty air. Viga turned to level his sights on Willyn again.

"I don't care who you are," he bellowed, his voice hollowed by the mask he wore.

Willyn's hand found a loose rock. She hurled the stone, and it connected with Viga's face, the shield of his mask cracking like spider webs right above his left eye. The blow stunned him long enough for Willyn to charge back in. She dove for the gun, using her knee as a battering ram. Viga actually let out a howl of pain but swung out, connecting a heavy fist against Willyn's face. Willyn stumbled back and felt her feet give way to the brittle floor. Fear flooded her mind as she felt her body lose control and freefall into a void. She swiped at the air before falling into the cavern, landing on her back. She braced herself for impact and heard her bones snap as she landed. Something had broken her fall in the darkness, but it felt like her leg had snapped in two. Her breathing mask broke away, and she lay in a crumpled heap, trying to orient herself in the darkness.

She tried to force herself to her feet, but every inch of her body screamed, recoiling from the trauma. She managed to roll to her back and looked up above. The opening she fell through was at least fifteen feet overhead. Through her blurred vision, she could see the silhouette of Viga trying to peer down and find her with his pistol.

The room was frigid and the air was motionless compared to the dust bowl that swirled above her. A chill ran through Willyn as she remembered exactly where she was, but the voice she heard stole her breath away.

"I've been waiting for you." A deep chuckle broke through the room. "You've been very, very busy."

Willyn rolled to her side and saw the outline of a mirror, its resemblance like those she had seen in the Spire and underneath the Taluum sanctuary. She cursed as large, green cat-like eyes glowed in the darkness locking on her. As she looked toward the glass, her heart hammered with panic.

A voice spoke to her, a whisper in her ear. "Do not fear him." Her eyes darted around the room, her mouth agape. The voice had been Hagan's, but as her eyes darted around the corridor, she knew she was alone.

The green eyes grew, shining an uncanny light in the darkness. **"You are here to release me. Surely you must be the Keeper of the Keys."**

Willyn froze, and her body shook with fear. She mumbled, trying to find the words, hoping and dreading that she was going insane and that the fall had rattled her brain. She blinked, trying to ensure the specter in the glass was really present.

Four shots rang out from above and Willyn tensed, waiting on the bullets to rip through her, but none hit their mark. *Surrounded. I'm surrounded.* After a few moments, a rope was lowered down into the room. Willyn swallowed as the wide green eyes from the mirror curved up into a wide, cruel smile.

The Serub in the glass spoke, his voice like the sound of the mountain. **"I can help you, if you will only release me."**

She turned her eyes upward, desperate to see who was coming into the chamber as her leg screamed with desperate pain. Willyn lay there trembling, joined only by her reflection in the Serub's mirror as a new enemy descended from above.

CHAPTER NINE

Seam stood alone, a pillar of black against the white horizon of the Rihtian desert. Gazing across the barren desert plain, his eyes lost focus, his mind deep in thought. The hot wind whipped through his long brown hair, and he breathed in deeply, savoring the heat of the desert air. He tallied all that he had accomplished in only a few short months.

Father could have never dreamt of it. He never saw the possibilities. He was blind to the potential.

A wicked web of past events and future realities jostled in Seam's mind. He had not slept for weeks, but he felt no weakness. The only price he paid from bearing the power of the Keys was that his mind *would not stop*. Every thought was crisp and clear like the dawn's morning rays, but they never ceased. Candor had been conquered, but Seam's mind knew no peace.

Peace. The word rolled around Seam's mind like a marble in a maze. *Hadn't that been the point of it all? Peace?* He looked down at the iron gauntlet he had stolen from the Mastermonk. Locked in place were the five Keys of Candor. *Peace comes at such a high price. It will continue to cost. It will always cost...*

In one swift motion, Seam opened his datalink, his fingers flying through memorized patterns.

"Bronson."

The tinny electronic assembling of Bronson's voice rang out. "My lord?"

"Bring me Nyx...no, no. Bring the entire Synod to my location. I want them to see this."

Seam looked back out over the desert sands as his mind wandered. *The path is set. My path is clear.*

Bronson spoke, a cloud of nervousness in his breath. "Yes, sir. I will see to their escort immediately."

"Very good," Seam said as he slammed the cover of his datalink closed and shook his head.

Bronson fears them...he has no idea. Seam beamed as he thought about the secret he had uncovered. The Serubs were no gods, despite their showcases of impressive power. How could they be? Weren't the gods supposed to be limitless?

He glanced down at his wrist, at the interlocked iron vines and sunlight that kept the Keys locked firmly in his possession. *They are chained. Held. Bound.*

Yes, Seam had realized the real truth since claiming his place as High King of all Candor, Ruler of the Dominion, and Keeper of the Keys. There was only one god on Candor. It was him.

Bronson closed his datalink, swallowing the knot in his throat. His position as Head of the Guardsmen was becoming harder and harder to manage, especially since the Serubs had been released from their mirrors.

The cost of keeping such creatures at the High King's beck and call was terrifying. Seam had long washed his hands of taking any responsibility for his newfound *allies,* choosing wisely instead to delegate the responsibilities of keeping the beasts *satisfied* to Bronson.

Bronson's frame had shrunk, and the uniform that was once snug began to swallow him. The things he had had to do to keep the Serubs appeased were things he could never forgive himself for. No matter how far he tried to distance himself from their evil, he knew he was no more innocent than the madman he served. Blood was on his hands and he knew it. In truth, he was worse than the king he so hated because of what he had to do.

Each of the Three were ruled by their hunger. Hunger that had to be managed and controlled per the High King's royal orders as he dangled Bronson's family by an invisible thread. Each Serub made their request known to Bronson and he was then chartered to procure the *resources* for each of the nightmares that dwelt within the shadows of the Spire.

Arakiel wanted warriors delivered to his chambers, ready to fight. Bronson found more than enough victims from the flocks of Grogans that poured into Zenith. Bronson did his best to avoid those who had fled for safety from the Surrogator's rule... those who secretly held Red sympathies. It was a losing battle. Arakiel was like all the other Serubs. As his powers grew, so did his hunger. What started as five warriors a week soon blossomed into ten, and then increased again to twenty.

What happened to them, Bronson could never confirm. All he knew was that he delivered them, always under the notion that they would be trained by an ancient teacher of the ways of war. They would enter Arakiel's chamber, the door would shut, and then the screams would begin. When summoned again into the Serub Lord's chamber there was no evidence of the murders and no bodies that required disposal. The routine of keeping Arakiel fed took on an uncanny normalcy, and Bronson reasoned away the crimes he committed with the knowledge that the warriors would *at least* die fighting.

Abtren's tastes were subtler. Seam had given her permission to seduce her prey within the denizens of the Spire. Thankfully, Bronson had little involvement with the deadly dance of cat and mouse. Abtren would move through the Spire, her kaleidoscopic eyes searching for her next victim, like a spider surveying its web. Sometimes she took one. Sometimes two. Sometimes more. Men. Women. It didn't matter. Few could, or would, resist Abtren's charms. Even to be in her presence for a few moments would cloud one's mind with potent desire. Her seductive voice caused an overflow of yearning to overtake whatever victim she had chosen, her lush lips dripping with a disastrous honey. Bronson thanked whatever grace was left for him that he did not have to contend with or manage Abtren's desires.

Of all the Serubs to serve, though, Nyx was the most wretched. She didn't *partake* as often as her siblings, but she would pull Bronson to the side and stare at him with her horrible eyes. Eyes like those of a wolf hiding in a sheep's skin.

"Bronson," she would call. *"I am getting quite bored. I think it is time that you find me a new playmate."*

Children. Children were the delicacy that Nyx wanted most. No matter how much he protested, Nyx would only need remind him of his debt to her, and he obeyed, praying that his compliance would prevent Abtren from revealing his attempted treachery to Seam. Bronson had a hand in children dying so his own could live. The double standard tortured his soul.

Bronson did not allow his mind to entertain the thoughts of what happened to them. He could not allow himself to go to that place. The only thing he did was give the credits to the mercenaries who handled the collection. He refused any further involvement.

Bronson cursed as he thought about his new position, his new duty. He had been trapped in an unimaginable hell all because the king's primary mercenary refused to deal in children, claiming that this violated his contract. The man had actually pulled out the digital contact on his datalink and cancelled it in front of his face. Cyric's refusal to feed Nyx infuriated Bronson because Seam had so quickly delegated the torture onto him instead. Bronson paid what it took to delegate the task to others, but the credits still came from his own hands.

The new responsibilities wore on his mind, fraying his consciousness unmercifully. His precautions to maintain some foothold to his sanity were not enough. Darkness began to break through the walls like a flood. If he saw a child in the city streets of Zenith, it sent his mind reeling with an explosion of grief and regret. He stopped venturing out much by day, and when he did, he made every attempt to stay away from populated areas. For days, he would feel his hand linger on his pistol. *Wouldn't it be easier if you just ended it all? Why damn yourself further?*

When the doubts and judgments arose in his mind, he turned to drink. One bottle. Three. Ten. It didn't matter. The alcohol never seemed quite stiff enough to chase away the faces of children that haunted his mind. Needle tracks on his arms were the evidence of the drugs that would help dull the agony. He would take anything as long as it kept the screaming orphans out of his mind.

Bronson had seen to his new responsibilities very efficiently. No matter how much he tried to fight through the reasons of why he kept up the charade of loyalty for Seam and his Synod, he knew the truth. He could feel hell tugging at his soul. Aleph's judgment would be swift and terrible for the zookeeper of nightmares. He was sure of his coming punishment. The beasts he kept were never satisfied. Their thirst for blood would never be quenched.

When he was alone he would practice a deadly ritual. He would hold his gun in one hand and bring the stiff cocktail of drugs and whiskey to his lips. He could not taste the explosive heat that he flushed down his throat, nor could he feel the numbness that he so wanted to experience. His mind was a dark, twisted alleyway of unending agony. He would hold the gun to his head, cock it, and take another swig of drink. There he would stay at the edge of blowing away his brains, weighing out his options as the hours passed by through the night. He thought of the resistance, of Seam, of how far he had fallen. He thought of his wife, of his children who felt like the embers of a dream life he had nearly forgotten. He had long abandoned drinking his whiskey from a glass and would bring the full bottle to his lips. In a few minutes, it would be like him; empty.

What are their names? What are the names of your children? His drugged frenzies made his family seem so distant, like a candle floating in the vastness of an ocean. *How long has it been since you last saw them? When did we last speak?*

He slammed the gun down on the table screaming, "WHY!? Why me?" The question ripped through room. He took another swig of whiskey before slamming his fists on the desk and screaming at the ceiling. "Answer me! Have I not served you? Have I not SERVED?" Bronson flipped the table and sent it hurdling across the floor. He stooped over the pistol and pushed it under his chin, tears flooding his face as he fell to his knees. "I can't. I can't. This is too much. *I am already damned, I can't.*"

His finger slowly pressed on the trigger, but the face of his children flashed in his mind, forcing him to pause. His hands trembled as his soul raged within, weighing his desperate option, but he could not pull the lever. Not without knowing that his family was safe. They were his only reason to live.

He owed it to them to stay alive, no matter how far he would have to plunge himself into the abyss. Even if he lost his soul through the process, he had to stay alive to see his family protected. Broken prayers would burst from his mind as he sobbed, gasping to come to grips with his reality.

Aleph, I understand the cost of my actions. I will not plead for mercy upon myself, because there is none left for you to give. I ask only for the sake of my family. Keep them from these nightmares. Protect them from the monster I have become. Have mercy on them, and if it pleases you, allow me to see them one last time before I die.

Seam strolled down the side of the dune he had been perched on to examine the desolate field below. The sand crumbled and slid beneath his footsteps into the windswept bowl below him. As he carefully stepped down the hillside, his datalink chirped. Hosp was waiting, fidgeting on the other end of the connection. Seam glared at the gray-eyed visage on the screen.

"Seam." Hosp's thin, whispering voice drifted in the desert heat. "I need to ask for your assistance. I fear that the Red resistance is growing too strong. It threatens our opportunity to procure the next mirror."

Seam looked back out over the field and sneered, refusing further eye contact with his sniveling ally.

"Hosp. How is it that in the months following our collection of the keys I have united all the Realms, rebuilt the city of Zenith, and kept three *gods* in check while you..." He stared into the screen, his eyes vicious. "...while you fail to unite the Groganlands?"

Seam stepped into the hot, deep sand and pushed further into the valley. The scalding sands were open, flat, and void. Seam's foot fell against something solid beneath the sandy debris. The feeling brought a smile to his lips, distracting him as Hosp responded over the datalink.

"Seam. With all due respect, you have never had to wrestle with the Grogan people. They are a stiff-necked people. Lotte was firmly in your grasp, and Elum has no qualms with your leadership as long as their trade is not regulated. I doubt the monks in Preost formally know how to respond to your rule. You have no idea how tense the situation is here. The Grogans are the hardest Realm to seize, *and you know this*. It is a task that I think you would rather avoid."

Seam stared deep into the screen, his face stern and eyes dripping hate. Hosp did not relent. "These people are deeply patriotic and loyal to the Sar. I will overthrow this resistance, but *I need your support. I need your resources*. With the proper *investment*, I can quell this rebellion within a week."

Seam leaned down to dig his fingers through the white sand and laughed.

"One week, Hosp? Is that all? Such big words for someone who has not dampened the Reds' fury in two months."

Hosp's eyes glared through the screen at the High King. "I know where they have headquartered, Seam. I know where the Reds have made their base."

Seam continued digging away at the sand. "And..."

"They are in Legion's Teeth, Seam."

Seam's hand grasped what he was searching for and in one swift motion he pulled it up from the desert floor. He stared into the hollow eyes of the bleached skull he unearthed, cocking his head at the skull's face as sand poured out from its open sockets.

"Well, at least you have them cornered. That should suit us well." Seam stopped, threw the skull down to the ground, and turned his full attention to Hosp. "Fine. I will help you if only to get the next mirror. I would recommend you make yourself useful and gather what forces you have. I will be bringing in an army to take Legion's Teeth."

Seam could tell that his words made Hosp wince. Seam continued, "Where will we make our rendezvous, *my friend?*"

Hosp's face strained as he tried to come up with solutions to a problem that would not be solved. "Meet me, High King, at the Hangman's Pass in three days. I will be looking forward to your arrival."

"*Be ready, Hosp.*" Unwilling to continue the conversation, Seam ended the transmission. His eyes turned, gazing toward the empty eyes of the skull he had discarded, his mind again lost in dark thoughts.

Where is Bronson?

Bronson crept up the spiraling staircase in the center of the Spire, climbing to the pinnacle where he knew he would find the Synod. The edge of his most recent drink was wearing off, and it had been nearly two days since he had any pills or injectables to help calm his anxiety. Each step on the metallic staircase brought a sharp pain between his eyes. He needed to find something to drink, but he knew Seam would not entertain any delays. The steel stairs clanked beneath his heavy boots and the sound pinged off the walls, building an incessant ringing within Bronson's ears.

As he shoved open the doorway into the pinnacle complex, Bronson stumbled into one of the mercenaries he had paid the day before for Nyx's *feeding*. The man's scarred face churned the acid in Bronson's stomach as a wave of nausea washed over him. He was able to compose himself until looking down at the small child chained to the thug's arm.

She was a young girl, no more than six or seven, with dirty matted brown hair and a face smudged with stains of poverty and destitution. The Bagger child stared up at Bronson, her eyes brimming with fear and questions. Bronson's soul was pierced with a pain that overwhelmed him, and he buckled over and vomited.

Her eyes. The thought forced Bronson to look away. They were the same eyes as his daughter's. Bagger or not, she shared his youngest daughter's eyes. The realization was too much, and Bronson fought just to stand and grab the man's arm as he was starting to drag the girl toward Nyx's chamber.

"Not this one," he growled. The mercenary paused and arched his eyebrows. Bronson did not relent, his eyes cutting a strong glare. "You heard me." He wiped the bile from his lips. "Not this one."

The man jerked his arm away and tugged at the girl. "Already paid me, Donahue. Said it didn't matter; boy or girl."

Bronson slammed his hand against the wall and forced himself up on limp legs. "*I said not this one, you cur.*" He glanced fearfully at the child who rendered him so helpless and back at the hired rogue. "She doesn't want *brown eyes*. Not this time. Go and find another."

The mercenary looked nervously over his shoulder to Nyx's room and sneered. "Should have said something earlier. Now I wasted all this time." He jerked the girl away from the Serub's door. "Come on, pretty. Time to put you back in the gutter I pulled you from."

Bronson said nothing as they left the chamber. He ran his hands over his face as he tried to catch his breath. As the two disappeared down the long hallway, Bronson fought the tears streaming in his eyes. *One life. At least I can save one.* The faces of the dozens of others broke through the wall of his mind, threatening to drown him. *Oh, but the others!* Bronson's stomach threatened to overflow with vomit that was no longer there. He dry-heaved in the hall with no control.

When the episode relented, his mind went back to his last real encounter with Seam. "Don't fail me, Bronson," Seam had said, "I want to make sure your family remains safe. But..."

But. That word had held him in his personal hell for months. The king was using the people that Bronson loved the most to motivate him to commit these horrors on others. Nyx, too, had trapped him, threatening at any moment to reveal his true intentions to the High King should he be bold enough to displease her. As he stepped down the hallway to gather the Synod, he thought through his options. It would be his death or the death of his family. Either way there was no victory. If he were to die, his family would have no one to protect them. An honest question met him in the hallway.

How much longer can you keep this up?

Unable to answer, Bronson swallowed deep and stepped into Nyx's room.

Seam leaned against the rook he had used to travel through the desert and stared out over the rolling dunes. The heat of the white sands rippled the view of the horizon with a scorching wall of heat, making it difficult to distinguish the details of the oncoming convoy. Soon, Seam was able to spy the river of black transports hovering over the sandy landscape, swimming through the desert like dark ships on a sea of sand. The transports were escorted by a platoon of rooks that flashed up and down the line, constantly monitoring the formation. Two Grogan titans lumbered in the front and back of the formation, the hulking war machines pushing up pillars of sand and dust.

The titan running point touched down a few yards from Seam, its base sending a shudder through the earth as it made contact with the ground. The act of landing sent out a blast of sand that surrounded Seam before drifting off into the dry valley below. The rear bay door lowered and Bronson exited, his eyes tightening in the intense light of the desert. The Synod followed closely behind. Abtren, Arakiel, and Nyx sauntered off the titan and took time to absorb the landscape. A dark smile was set on Arakiel's lips as he stooped to the ground and sifted some of the sand through his fingers.

"I take it you remember this place?" asked Seam.

Arakiel stepped past Seam, his height mountainous in comparison to the High King. He looked out over the valley with his blood red eyes and breathed in the hot air.

"Oh yes. I remember this place quite well."

Abtren and Nyx joined Arakiel at the edge of the dune. Abtren locked eyes with Nyx, who stole a quick glance at Seam. The two looked back out over the sunken field before Bronson broke the silence.

"Sir, I brought them as asked and I also gathered together every support vehicle possible per your orders." Bronson leaned in close to Seam's ear with his face full of concern. He whispered, "Do you think it is safe to have them outside the Spire, sir?"

"We are quite fine here, Bronson," answered Nyx as she drew her eyes shut. "We are not dogs on a leash. We understand Seam's powers. We will not try to defy him."

Arakiel shook his head and scowled, but said nothing. Abtren cut her eyes at her sister.

Seam read their faces but remained unperturbed. "You are right to speak in truth, Nyx, though I know your kin bristle under my leadership." He turned and walked down the steep dune, leaving the Synod and Bronson at the soft peak. "It doesn't matter. I am more capable than any Serub. Be grateful that I am including you in my plans…"

Arakiel growled and threw a sidelong glare at Abtren, whose face went grim. Nyx scowled at both of them, her eyes shifting from brown back to midnight black. Bronson stood at a distance from the Synod, but even at his vantage point he could read the body language. Nyx spoke up.

"*We are grateful*, High King. We are grateful to be in Candor again, and we are grateful to serve your…" She paused, her black eyes flashing like unsheathed weapons. "…your Dominion."

Seam smiled but said nothing. Her outright showcase of loyalty did nothing more than confirm his suspicions. In any instant the outcast divines would turn on him like a pack of wolves, but as long as he held the Keys, none of it mattered.

"Bronson." Seam's voice lifted with excitement. "You brought the supplies, yes?"

Bronson's right hand shook in a rapid burst of nervousness. "Yes, sir. They are held in the caravan awaiting your command."

"Good. Release them, and have them line up. It is time for a full display of my power."

Bronson nodded and threw a hand signal up to a soldier standing guard outside the titan. A whistle blew and the long line of transports opened their massive storage chambers.

Seam's eyes flew over the multitude of Baggers that emptied out into the desert. Nearly two thousand Baggers filled the desert floor, their faces a mixture of confusion and dread. Those expecting work were able to quickly recognize that there was no mining or constructions waiting for them in this cursed place. Seam stepped toward the three Serubs and pointed to the mass of Baggers.

"I have kept you well fed for months. It is now time that you earn your keep."

The Three said nothing, but the heat of the desert seemed to dissipate in an instant. Bronson felt a cold chill envelope him, and he took a step back away from the King and his puppets.

Seam stretched his hand out toward the crowd. "*I know what you are capable of. I know what you can do.* Even with only three of you, you can *and will* create my desire."

Arakiel's voice boomed over the dunes. "**What is it that the Keeper of the Keys would ask of us?**" He sneered at the King as he lowered his gaze to Seam's level. "**For he need only to ask, and it shall be done.**"

"Provide me an army, Arakiel." Seam's face twisted with a swell of insanity. "A willing and loyal army! *Push out all their essences, and leave me the frames.*"

Arakiel nodded and glanced over to his sisters. Abtren nodded, and Nyx's face grew into a cruel smile.

Seam walked toward her and laid his hand on her pale, cold face. "Nyx...I want you to show me your skills as an architect. Build me a masterpiece. Do not hold back in what you can create."

Nyx's eyes delved into the deepest black that Seam had ever seen, and her face *changed* before him, its likeness like that of a hawk. The monster breathed heavily, enraptured and intoxicated with desire at the High King's request. She spoke, her voice like a hundred men, as the clear desert sky grew black with rippling thunderclouds, bringing with it a rush of sudden darkness.

"I will make them strong for you, Keeper. I will build you an army that will shake the foundations of Candor."

Bronson collapsed from the realization of Seam's plan with the Baggers and from the terrible sight of the Serubs' transformations. His body quaked with both fear and remorse.

Seam stood like a statue. From the edge of darkness, he could see the other two creatures he controlled. A ravenous wolf and a powerful lion, all monstrous assemblages of animal and human. The hawkish monstrosity that was once a beautiful woman looked at him and somehow smiled.

Peace comes at such a high price. It will continue to cost. It will always cost...

Arakiel knelt and placed a hand into the sand. A low, inaudible pulse pushed out from him, rippling through the ground. The Serub's frame appeared to swell as he drew in a continuous breath. Arakiel's eyes rolled back into his skull, revealing the smoky whites that hid behind his blood red pupils. The desert continued to quake as shockwaves pushed out from Arakiel and swept toward the helpless Baggers assembled in the valley below.

As the waves of sand swelled and rolled toward the crowd, many turned to run, but Abtren stepped forward, raising her hands. A wall of flames surrounded the Baggers. Seam smiled as he watched them screaming, attempting to find some escape. Men and women alike, surrounded by flames, with no choice but to await their new fate. *Their new purpose. His purpose.*

Arakiel's wave of energy flashed through the walls of flame and swept over the Baggers. The screaming ceased and Abtren's walls of flame disappeared beneath the desert floor. The thousands of once panicked men and women stood like ashen pillars. No one moved, no one blinked. They simply stood, waiting.

Nyx let out a loud screech and began to hover above the ground. She looked to Seam as she pointed her palms at the fresh new army. "**Remember. It will cost.**"

Seam nodded. She focused back onto the swarm of bodies and smiled. Her powers had no visible display, accompanied by no tremors or thunderclaps. However, within moments the entire field of bodies came alive with rage, their frames reverberating with an invisible energy. The men and women each made small movements, turning to face the High King, and every hollowed eye held the unmistakable look of rage.

The husks of what had once been Baggers stood still for a moment before stampeding up the dune toward Seam. The sound of the mass running thundered and shook the ground. The Serubs' new creations had one purpose and goal, to overthrow the king.

Seam grit his teeth and leapt, taking hold of Nyx, grasping around her legs in mid-flight. His rage held her as a lightning bolt of energy shot through his arm, rattling his body. The keys locked in his arm grew hot with unholy fire. Seam felt an overwhelming instinct to close his eyes, as Nyx screamed. He slammed his eyes shut and focused. The physical touch allowed him to feel Nyx's mind and within he found the others. In that strange dark place, the keys bridged through the Serub and into the hive. He could feel them, *all of them*. Nyx's voice cut through his mind as a surge of electric current coursed over his entire body. "**What are you doing, you fool? Let go! You cannot control them!**"

An epiphany struck Seam and he opened his eyes. *I can control them. Just as I can control you.* It was inexplicable but Seam could feel the control, the unseen mechanisms that puppeteered the hive mind of the hollow bodies rushing toward him. He forced himself to think beyond the pain hammering through his veins. His vision went black, changed, and then opened anew. Spinning views sprouted in Seam's mind, slowing and locking into place. From this altered perspective he could see himself, he could see Nyx, and through a splintered web of viewpoints, he could see through the eyes of each and every man and woman swarming up the hill. Nyx screamed once again.

"What are you doing?! Stop!"

Seam pulled himself close to Nyx and spoke through clenched teeth.

"You hold no power over me, you false god."

CHAPTER TEN

The captive was surrounded by impenetrable darkness from all sides. He could not make out where he began and where the midnight ended. It was as if there were no limits, no borders, nothing to separate him from the dark water that held him in an immovable stasis. He was part of the void.

His senses were a maze unto themselves, with inputs to his mind that made no sense; scrambled, disjointed, and nauseating. He could taste the blackness and hear the salty brine that enveloped him. Underneath the titanic weight of the water that pinned him down, his mind was drowning with questions. Questions that had at one point been self-evident and obvious, but now were as murky as the depths that pressed in on him.

Where am I?
How long have I been here?
Who am I?

There were no answers. The questions bubbled in his mind and the darkness swallowed them without a single response. The questions were his only possession, and what little energy remained within him, he used to keep them in the forefront of his consciousness. He knew that to quit asking questions was to give into the darkness. *He could not give in to the dark, he could not join the void, he could not become nothingness.* The emptiness of the place pressed in on him like an endless horizon, a titanic weight threatening to absorb him if *he would only give in*. He did not know how much longer he could keep his silent resistance. Whatever this place was, it went on forever. An eternity for fighting against the dark, fighting only to ask the questions that seemed so vital to his existence. So he kept fighting.

An eon went by, and then something changed. A sensation stirred within the depths. He opened his eyes to be greeted by a familiar wall of black, but he felt something moving. The water around him shook and stirred until he heard a thunderous eruption of voices screaming, howling for mercy.

A rush of movement swept in behind him, filling his mind with untold fear. The thought of sharing this space with *another* was no comfort. He panicked. His eyes strained to see, to see something other than the inky gloom that had kept him imprisoned for so long. A shift in the water brought forth *the other*. Massive and moving with amazing speed, the large serpentine body circled around him. There was no light except for the dark glow of a pair of massive eyes with pupils slit like a cat's. In that dim light, he could barely make out the full figure of the beast, the enormity of its body, accompanied by long rows of black, sharp teeth. Silver scales covering *the other* came into view as the circling beast closed in tighter and tighter, constricting the space between him and it with its terrible presence. A low, steady voice called out through the deep, unencumbered by the waters.

"Who are you?" The question wrapped around him tighter than the depths, causing him to struggle with his very existence. The being continued to ask in a threatening yet playful manner. **"I have seen you before. She knows who you are but won't tell me."**

The circling stopped and the creature's eye pushed closer toward him, never blinking.

"You were the first to disturb my depths in a very long time and now more follow you." The eye rolled up and down, scanning him like a curious predator, slightly amused at the small life before him. **"No matter. I will learn your secrets in time."**

With a snap of the creature's jaws silence returned and the monstrous beast disappeared, merging with the darkness. There were no more visions of that terrible eye and the feeling of its presence dissipated in the depths of the water much to the relief of the captive.

More time passed and the captive fought the urge to give in and disappear, melting into the nothingness around him. The unexpected visitor had at least interrupted the torture of solitude for a moment, but the emptiness pressed in harder on him than ever before. After countless unknown increments of eternity passed, the waters stirred again.

His spirit quickened with the changes, and he felt something other than water press in on him. He felt the sensation of being pulled higher and higher to a surface he never knew existed.

A sloop sailed through the dark waters, towing long lines of netting behind its stern, churning the depths of the ink-black ocean. Long oars ceased their rowing and were pulled into a locked position as a stifling hot wind filled the dirty patch-worked sail.

A horrible voice rang out over the water. "You feel that, File? Wind! WIND! A new crop of them must have just came through! By the Beast's name, what luck!" The man, if one could call him that, was the culmination of an eternity of beatings. Long, thick scars marred his face and body. He crawled to the ship's brig on all fours, wheezing with ragged pain, as if whatever lungs he possessed could only provide him with the minimum air to keep moving.

The imp made his way toward the impressive warden of the cursed vessel. The warden sneered at his underling, who cackled maniacally in the darkness, and cursed, reaching beneath soiled garments to pull out a single match. He lit it, the fire illuminating a face that could only be framed within a nightmare. It bore one ever-open white eye that streamed a never-ending river of brine. Where the other eye once resided there was nothing more than a hollow cavern. The tall horror of a man responded to his crewmate, his pipe clenched between a small collection of sharp black teeth.

"Ye think I'm a fool, Rank? I can read the signs, just as you can." With his one good eye, File spied the lines dragging behind the sloop. *Something was moving down there.*

"Check the nets, Rank. Check them!"

Rank looked down behind the churning ship, obeying his captain's orders. His jaw dropped at what he saw. "File...by the Beast...it looks like we *got something*!"

File shot back, his mouth muttering through his pipe, "Hoist them up, Rank! Time to see what we got." As File spoke, long ribbons of noxious smoke filled the air, forming a hazy fog that hung around the thin outcrop of Rank's soiled and matted hair. He barked at his counterpart, issuing orders as they flung their bodies against the taut, wet ropes.

Hours went by as the two hoisted the nets that had long combed the depths with no success. File locked the first half of the nets in place and dug around the dirty, stinking webs of rigging, looking for their prize. His talon-like fingers probed through them, piercing the webbing like long, white knives. There was little value to what he found; rotten carcasses of dead seabirds, bones, blankets of rotting detritus, and seaweeds.

"Gods—and here I thought we be graced by *something fresh*." Rank growled at the catch like a starving animal and kicked at the nets with frustration.

File shot him a sidelong glance with his one eye and spat on the deck. "We still got another hour of rigging below us. Quit moaning and wasting time or you'll see my whip. Put your back into it! I don't want no more time wasted on yer words."

Rank sneered, "We've got all the time in the world, File. You know that."

The captive was pulled to the surface, breaching the impregnable barrier between the midnight waters and the air above, but despite being plucked from the depths he could not move freely. He was tangled in a web, completely unable to support himself. A dense, sunless place full of fog replaced the midnight he had known for so long. Despite the additional light, it was hard to make out what was happening or what was holding him above the sea.

He reached out and felt the webbing that surrounded him. *What is this called?* A pinprick of recollection shot across the amnesia that had long fogged his mind. *Net.* It was a net. A net was pulling him up from the depths.

But where? And who? Other questions pummeled him. *How is it I never drowned?*

The answer barely mattered to him anymore. Wherever he was going, the captive thought that it had to be better than his prison below the water. It was a relief to know that there was more to this place than the water, the darkness, and the circling nothingness that sought to swallow him with each passing moment. A strange feeling trickled into him as he was slowly pulled from his watery prison. It felt light, airy, and full of possibility.

What was this feeling called before? His memory began to turn over, and it engaged with the emotion. The captive felt his mouth move and the word came out. "Hope."

Through the thick netting the captive caught glimpses of what was dragging him from above. It took a while before remembering what a boat was. The tattered sail and the long oars dipping into the murky waters all brought back the memories of boats. The captive tried to focus on whoever was struggling to pull him in, the man slumped over the black sloop, yanking at the massive webbing.

The waves slapped up and down, splashing over the net and making it nearly impossible to catch too many details of who was onboard. That was until the captive spied a pale white monster of a man crawl over the hull on all four limbs, his face as ragged as the sails of the ship. He rasped for breath as he tugged at the net's towline and scurried back over the edge of the ship.

His voice was faintly audible. "This one has something! Heavier than the last."

The last of the netting lay on the sloop's deck, a stinking heap of raggedness strewn across the worn wooden planks. Both Rank and File probed the netting, cursing as they methodically scoured over their paltry catch.

Rank pulled up a large blanket of tangled rope and jumped back. Below him was something he had not seen in a millennium. The essence shone in the darkness, its white light glowing with pure substance.

"*Gods*!" he screamed at File. "FILE! An essence! AN ESSENCE! After all these turns, we got a fresh essence!"

File blew a long draw of smoke into Rank's cavernous face. "Well, what did you expect, you idiot? You saw the waters turn, just as I!" File leaned down to inspect the catch, his white, moist eye gleaming in the dark. "By all the hells, I didn't think today would bring us this. Yer right. It's an essence, and a fresh one at that."

Rank's horribly worn and ragged face could not hold back his twisted excitement. "It's just been so long…since we've caught one." His eyes flashed toward his captain. "We might find favor with the Master again."

File's long, sharp claws flashed, running fresh, deep trenches across Rank's face. "*Don't speak about the Master*. Don't you *dare* start that talk. I've only got one good eye left, and I aim to keep it!"

Rank whimpered and covered his face as a flow of black blood wetted the rigging on the decks. File spat on the ground and pointed. "Go get me the *dust*. We got to make this catch whole again."

Rank nodded and whispered a hollow confirmation, still holding back the flow of black blood that poured from his flayed face. "Aye."

The captive's essence laid there, motionless as fear swelled with him. Despite being freed from the water's captivity; he was unable to move. The will to move was present, but he was limited in this form, so he lay motionless; paralyzed.

A shocking truth ran through his mind. *I don't have a body.* The smaller of the two fiend-faced creatures reemerged from below deck and crawled toward him, craning its horrible head from side to side as it licked at its sharp, yellowed fangs. The creature named Rank had two large, bulbous eyes the color of dawn, and they glowed in the gloom like torchlight. The owl-like eyes hovered over him, examining him with a horrible lust. It ran its long, jagged fingers over him, but still he could feel nothing.

"*I said get the dust!*" screamed File. The sound of a whip lit across the deck and Rank scurried away from the catch toward the underbelly of the sloop, grumbling and cursing loudly as he dipped down below. "What's all this concern with time, captain? We ain't wasting nothing."

The captive lay still, waiting for whatever might come next. His mind searched desperately for something. Clarity shook through him.

A name. I once had a name.

He strained to search within for an answer but none came. If he could only look at himself. If he could only catch a glimpse of who he was, then perhaps the memories would flow. No answers came, and he lay there helpless and paralyzed on the deck of the filthy boat, despondent.

Rank returned to the deck with a small jar of what appeared to be mud. *Dust. He had called it dust.* He dipped his talon-like fingers into the dirty jar. Shoveling out the contents, File's vile fingers ran them liberally across the captive.

File screamed, shouting curses. "Easy with it, Rank! It's hard to come by! We'll need more of it, yet, if these wind's tales are true."

The nameless catch of Rank and File jolted on the ship's deck with an electric current. His mind exploded with vitality, and he felt himself move again.

What is that sensation? I can feel! I can feel again.

The feeling grew like a fire, a spark across tinder, until it grew with a fierce heat.

"ARGHHHH!" He screamed out, his mind shocked at the sound of his own voice. Pain. The memory of the word returned as Rank scratched his muddy claws over the surface of his extremities, finishing, finally, with his face. Rank paused and squinted his bulbous yellow eyes at him, his vile face smattered with concern.

"File! Ain't never seen an essence wear a necklace, have you?" He reached for the necklace that hung around the captive's neck.

It did not take long to remember how to move. The mud had not only brought with it a fiery furnace of pain but also the freedom of a living, yet crude body. His hand shot up and grasped Rank's thin wrist and words tumbled from his lips.

"Don't touch. It's not yours to take."

Rank screeched and jumped back, crashing into File. File shoved the lesser being to the side, nearly sending him overboard as he stormed forward.

"We do as we please on this boat, cur." His one good eye went to the necklace and his scarred face froze with fear. He paused, licked his lips with a long black tongue, and took a step back, lifting his one good eye toward the darkened sky. "I don't know why you bear *that* here. We have no need for baubles in this place and *he*," File pointed to the etching on the necklace, "he certainly cannot help you here." File paused, his face looking like a man who had to make a grave decision. "Keep it *Nameless*...for now."

The captive's mind filled with questions. *He? Nameless?* He stood, enjoying the new freedom of movement. He looked down and realized that he was naked except for a small silver necklace around his neck. He stared at the symbol etched on the pendant, causing his mind to whirr with new energy. New realizations of what had just happened exploded in his consciousness. *I have a body.* He had somehow been without a body all this time. The *dust* the imp had rubbed on him had crudely restored him. Now he could move again. He could smell the dank air and feel the slippery planks that made up the ship's deck below him.

Rank threw a dirty heap of rags toward him and spat, "Put these on, Nameless. Welcome aboard *The Hunt*. She's not much to look at, but she's the only home you can have on this sea." He took a few steps back and kicked open a large wooden hatch.

The creature smiled, his mouth full of sharp black teeth. "Saving your little life, Nameless, does have its costs. That dust don't come cheap. You'll have to work off your debt to Rank and me before we set you free. *It's the least you can do.*"

The dark innards of the sloop revealed a lower deck filled with multiple rows of long, narrow benches. A crowd of haggard men and women bearing crude, dust-formed bodies were stationed on the benches, manning long oars. File peered into the hellish space and smiled. "Time to join your kin, Nameless. Down you go."

An electric crack ran out and Nameless felt a seething pain run across his back. He turned to find Rank standing behind him, his yellow eyes full of sickening glee, a long leather whip flying out from his hands.

"Get down! Get down below!"

Nameless had no choice. He wanted to fight, but for the first time he realized how much smaller he was compared to his captors. Even the once imp-like File seemed to have taken a new form, towering over him like a giant, cracking the biting whip at his heels.

Nameless plunged beneath the deck through a cloud of stench that made him want to vomit. Rank followed, leaving File high above. Long, rusted rivers of chains soon fell over Nameless' body, locking tightly around his ankles and wrists. Rank set him on an innermost seat in the middle of the rowing hoard, a mob of misery. Rank's horrible laughter echoed in the darkness.

"When we give the signal, you slugs, put your backs into it! Row!" Rank's whip cracked out and the miserable bodies beneath began their motion. "Row like the Beast is upon you!" Nameless' hands were slammed onto the long, smooth oar before him, and Rank's clawed fingers gripped his face, drawing him toward the yellow eyes of his new Master.

"I'm talking to you, too, fresh catch. *It's time you pay your debt.* Row, because it is the only thing that will set you free. If you give us any lip, we will be sure to take them off or sew them shut. Do I make myself clear?"

Nameless' head nodded, shaking with fright.

"Good, fresh catch. Welcome to the Sea of Souls. You'll be rowing here until your debt is paid. NOW ROW!"

Nameless put his hands on the oar and joined the others for fear of the whip, joining the dust-formed bodies who rowed of the cursed *Hunt* in that dark, dank place.

CHAPTER ELEVEN

Grift rummaged through the supplies in the back of one of the many trucks parked along the edge of the tent city. The trucks had been parked, waiting for dawn's first light to pull out of town and make their voyage to Henshaw. Thanks to the commotion caused by the swarming medical teams, Grift went unnoticed as he stocked up. He did not know what the town of Henshaw would be like, but if Cotswold and Tindler were any indication of what the border towns had become, he had no reason to hold out much hope.

Grift inspected his new wares and grabbed a bag of saline solution before slipping between the rows of white tents. Queen Aleigha's brief visit had proven useful. He had procured a few meds for Rose, a supply of field rations, a small emergency tent, and more importantly a secured datalink. He jumped as a hand fell on his shoulder. Smoke poured from Ewing's pipe like a flare, and the embers highlighted his face in a worrisome way.

"You got everything you need?" Ewing muttered as his eyes wandered across the crowd surrounding them.

Grift tightened the drawstrings over his shoulders and adjusted his pack. "Aye, Ewing. I've got enough. Enough to make for the border."

"What about Rose?" Grift's eyes wandered behind Ewing to the large green medical truck holding Rose, Eva, and Adley. The two women had not left her side and continued to toil over her as she slept under the truck's canopy. Rot fixed himself beneath her cot and refused to move. She would have looked almost peaceful had it not been for her rapid, shallow breathing. Each short breath filled Eva's eyes with more concern.

"Eva says we have to hurry. She won't last much longer with the few supplies she has. I did at least grab a few extra supplies. Might buy us a couple extra hours, maybe even a day if we stretch it."

Ewing shook his head, despondent. "Then don't waste any time in Henshaw. Make for the border as quickly as you can." Ewing turned and looked at Grift with a grim face. "The queen charged Rend Brinkley to command this mission, so if you get in any *trouble*, know you've got an ally watching over you. He will be most useful should anyone recognize your face."

"Rend? How did you manage that, Ewing?" Grift said with a wry smile.

"I hardly know, Grift. I just keep moving, hoping for the best. I'm afraid it will not be enough to prevent what is coming, but I'm not going to stop." Ewing's voice cut short. After a few moments, he carefully weighed his words. "I never thought I'd see you again, Shepherd, truth be known. I...did not know what I was doing when I sent Kull with Wael. I thought he would be in good hands."

Ewing's voice broke like an avalanche. "Oh, Aleph above. I was a fool." His eyes brimmed with tears and his voice trembled. "I was wrong. I will never forgive myself. You know how much..."

Grift gripped Ewing's shoulders. "Not another word, Arthur." He embraced his friend, doing his best to remain composed. "I'll contact you as soon as we get into Preost. We should be there in three days if we don't run into any problems. Are you sure you can spare Adley?"

"She's itching to get out of Lotte, Grift. Either that or she's tired of me." Ewing chuckled as he wiped a tear from his eye.

A swell of engines roared and the lights of the vehicles flipped on, casting amber light in the darkness.

"Probably both," laughed Grift. "Thank you." Grift leaned in toward his friend and embraced him. "For everything, Arthur. We will see a better day."

"Aye, in this world or the next, Grift. Take care and good luck." Ewing turned and sauntered away. He turned one final time and called, "Oh, and thanks for taking that beast. Tell the monk he owes me a thousand credits. Dog eats more than a family of four and smells worse than hot garbage."

Grift laughed and called back, "I'm sure Wael is good for it! I'll deliver the message." Grift held up his hand to his friend and Ewing did the same before disappearing into the darkness outside the threshold of the headlights.

"You've got operatives in Elum, as well?" Grift shook his head in unbelief.

"We even have a small set of agents in Zenith, though far fewer than when the city was being built. In Zenith I'm afraid our leadership seems to be fading."

Grift nodded. "Bronson?"

Adley's expression fell flat as she looked out the back of the truck. "Him more than any other. I can't put my finger on it, but he's changed, Grift."

Grift exhaled and shifted in his seat as he looked down over Rose. "We all have, Adley."

Adley nodded. "Some by choice and others by destiny. I like to think some of us have changed for the better."

The words shook Grift. For so long he regarded Adley as a child. Now, here he was learning about the resistance forces that were popping up all over Candor, much due to her influence. A harrowing thought pierced his mind. *You thought of Kull in the same way.* Grift's face flickered with pain as Adley continued, "Lotte, if you can believe it, serves as a large base for the continent's discontent. We're lucky compared to the other Realms."

"Because of the queen?"

"Exactly. Aleigha still holds a lot of power and sway within Lotte and even Zenith. And so far, she has kept Seam's eyes occupied as we continue to build up our forces."

Grift bristled at the sound of referring to King Camden's wife so casually, but he let it go.

"What of the Groganlands? I haven't had any connection these last few days."

Adley paused, her face discontent. "We haven't penetrated that Realm yet. Not in any official capacity. The Realm is in an uproar, and the Reds are less concerned with Seam as they are with Hosp. If Hosp can be overthrown, then perhaps we can turn the Reds' attention toward the Jackal of Zenith."

Grift's eyebrows raised. "Jackal? Resistance word?"

Adley cocked her head as Grift explained. "Same word Rend Brinkley used when he picked me up in Cotswold."

Adley nodded. "It's our code word for Seam. Our way of testing who is our ally and who is not within mixed company. Of course, it works best when you're not specific. Jackal of Zenith is not exactly covert." She smiled and Grift nodded.

The truck bed exploded with a harrowing fit of shaking, causing Grift's teeth to rattle in his skull. His eyes shot over to Eva sitting next to Rose, who lay strapped in her cot. Eva spoke calmly. "She's still stable. Nothing's changed. Couple bumps will be okay."

Grift's eyes lingered on the shell of what had been his wife. *She's still your Rose, Grift.* All of it was almost too much to process. The sickness of his beloved seemed to overflow and seep into his soul. He had lost so much over the past few months, but it felt as if he had lost Rose years ago. Even during her best times, she was a shade of the woman he had married so many years ago during the summer solstice.

His love for her had never diminished, but when he was away on patrol, the reality of her sickness had been temporarily alleviated. A dark voice spoke in his mind. *This is what you left Kull to deal with, you fool. You left your son to do your job.*

Grift shifted in his seat, his eyes locked on Rose as the guilt constricted around him. Another voice fluttered in his mind, commanding his attention.

Stop. The one word fell over his mind and felt as audible as a cymbal crashing in his ears. He closed his eyes and did his best not to torture himself.

Okay, Rose. I'll stop.

A voice crackled over the radios fixed in the trucks. "Approximately two hours to arrival. Check supplies and prioritize deployment."

The voice continued on with a checklist of supplies, listing one item after another. As the instructor droned on, Grift allowed himself to tear his eyes away from Rose and drift off to sleep.

Grift's dreams offered no solace. As he closed his eyes and the vision of his emaciated wife faded, it was replaced with the face of Kull. All Grift could see was Kull standing with a knife to Seam's neck. The last vision of Kull is what had haunted Grift's sleep ever since he left him to die in Zenith, but this dream was different.

Kull's face was that of his childhood. He was a boy and he was scared. His eyes begged Grift to save him, but Grift could not move. He was frozen, forced to watch as Seam overtook his son, wetting his dark ebony blade with his son's blood. Every night the dream played out with some new variation or change, but the end was always the same. Kull was dead and Grift was stuck, unable to move.

Stop.

Rose's voice cut through the nightmare. Grift tried to spin around but was stuck in place. He could not see her but soon he felt her tender arms wrap around his waist and her cheek press into his back.

"He made his choice. His choice was to save you. Stop torturing yourself. Let him go, let him make the choice. *It was for all of us.*"

The warmth of Rose's embrace melted the icy dreamscape and lifted the weight pressing on Grift's chest. For the first time in years, Grift felt like he could breathe. He tried to turn but was still frozen in place.

He spoke, his voice echoing in the dream. "I want to see you, Rose. Please just let me see you. It has been so long…"

Rose's arms loosened and her fingers ran down Grift's spine. "Not yet, beloved. But soon."

A violent jolt rattled Grift from his dream. He looked down and realized he was holding the cold, thin hand of his dear wife. He kissed her frigid skin and whispered to her. "Soon. You will be well soon. I promise."

The convoy began to slow. Grift peered out the side of the truck and jerked back into the bed of the truck.

"Adley." Grift pulled close to Adley and looked back over his shoulder. "I thought this was a medical mission. This city has hardly been touched."

Adley gathered her medical satchel and threw it over her shoulder as she responded. "This stop has multiple purposes. Medical support is only one of them."

Grift climbed from the truck and stepped out as men and women started yanking crates from the truck beds and laying them out on the street. Grift knelt over one of the crates marked with a large red cross labeled 'saline.' Grift slipped the lid open and peered inside. There were no bags of fluid. Instead, lying inside were numerous rifles stacked on top of one another. Grift slammed the lid shut and looked over to Adley.

He nodded at the container and shot an inquisitive glance to Adley. His lips mouthed the word, "Why?"

Adley made her way to Grift's side and leaned in close to his ear as she whispered, her eyes grave. "You can't fight a jackal with words alone."

Grift ran his fingers across the lid of the box and looked back over to the truck holding Rose. "We need to move soon."

"I know." Adley nodded in agreement. "The southern side of the city is a bit less occupied. Once we make this delivery we should be able to slip away without any notice."

Grift squinted into the sun as it began its descent below the horizon. "How long until you are ready? We don't have much daylight."

"Give me an hour and I should be able to get these affairs settled. I need to meet with a few of the local leaders."

Grift pulled himself up into the back of Rose's truck. His face did little to hide his exhaustion. Despite finally being reunited with Rose, he couldn't settle into his surroundings. Maybe it was the strangeness that accompanied being with Rose again, and not being with her all the same. *Something doesn't feel right.* Grift held to his instincts, but hid them from Adley. "We'll be ready as soon as you are, Adley."

The truck bed was quiet. A restless energy hung in the air as Eva checked Rose's vitals. She flashed Grift a quick smile. "She's still stable, dear." She patted Rose's small hand. "She's been a trooper."

"Eva. I can't ever say thank you enough for all you've done. I owe you more…"

Eva waved off the thanks. "You all are like family, Grift. Rose would've done as much or more for me. She helped me deal with my own mother's sickness, remember?"

A flash of memory. Before Kull, before her own sickness. Images of an empty house and a lonely few weeks were all Grift could recall of the time Rose went to help Eva with her dying mother.

'She's on the threshold. She will pass very soon.'

Grift had been gruff with her then, muttering selfish statements under his breath in Rose's presence; veiled selfishness that didn't express his real longing for his home life to return to his version of normalcy. Rose had chosen not to engage with this attitude, making herself busy preparing a pot of beans for her husband so he could eat during her absence. Rose was always like that, good to know when to stand up to his stupidity and when to let him stew in it so he could eventually come around.

The memory made Grift shake his head, wincing at his own pride. "No, Eva, I had quite forgotten that. Rose was always the better part of me." He shot a sidelong glance at her, the frame that somehow still carried her on this plane of existence. "I'd trade anything I had to make her well." His eyes lingered on his wife, memories washing in and out like the tide. He laughed, a small whisper laugh, glancing into Eva's eyes. "It's a cruel joke that the better one of us is crippled and wasting away. I wish it were me...Aleph, I wish it were me."

Eva's crooked hands gently slipped over his. Her voice was firm but sincere. "Grift, we don't get to choose what the journey holds when we join fates with one another." Eva smiled and whispered, "You and Rose have something strong, even now." Her light brown eyes stared deep into Grift's. "Don't give up now. She's still counting on you."

Grift nodded, allowing Eva's words to sink in. There was nothing he could say. The darkness in Grift's mind cracked and shook under her words, and for the first time he understood that Eva had more healing gifts than herbs and poultices.

The moment gave way as the crew rushed out of the truck, beginning their work around the convoy, setting up medical tents, escorting supplies to different areas of the small town, and gathering up the injured. With Rot following at his heels, Grift pulled out a long sled from beneath the truck. He examined the ropes tied to it and buckled them to a harness. He slipped it around his arms and let out some slack in the lines until he was satisfied that the ride would be as smooth as possible for Rose. It wouldn't be the quickest way into Preost, but it would be the quietest.

He took a quilt and laid it out over the metal frame. Frustration fired in his mind at how paper-thin his plan was, but Grift focused on Eva's words. *She's still counting on you.* He dug into his pack and fished out the encrypted datalink provided by the queen. He skipped through several menus and opened a map of the surrounding area.

"Five miles." The words tumbled from his lips. "Going to need to drag her five miles until we hit the edge of Preost." Rot sat beside him, his head easily coming up toward his hip, and gave a thunderous bark as if to encourage him.

"Yes, at least I got you, big guy. You want to pull this thing?" Grift lovingly rubbed his hands around Rot's scarred face and ears as tendrils of drool wetted the ground and the beast closed his one good eye.

As Grift strapped down the last of the supplies, Rot began to growl. The dog that had nuzzled him disappeared as the growling, teeth-baring monster revealed itself once more, his one good eye fixed on the horizon. Soon Grift heard what Rot sensed; the sound of another approaching convoy rumbling with life, its engines echoing over the horizon. The hills north of Henshaw were spotted with numerous approaching transports, but there was something different about them. They weren't the same green government trucks used by the support teams from Vale. These convoys were jet black. Grift's mouth went dry and he felt his instincts surge with adrenaline. *Military transports*. Barreling in like a black, polished tidal wave waiting to sweep away everything in its path.

Grift flipped the datalink back open and tried to open a connection with Adley, screaming over the booming barks coming from Rot. "Adley! We have company! Please tell me these are trucks you were expecting."

Adley's voice flashed back over the datalink with rapid precision. "Get to Rose. We've been compromised."

The sound of approaching engines began to swell as Grift cut across several rows of tents. He leapt onto the tailgate and peered inside. Eva was oblivious to the new threat as she sat next to Rose, humming a soft song while holding her friend's hand.

"Eva! We have to go! *Now*." Eva jolted in her seat and Rot jumped into the back, growling like an engine, the hair on his back ridging up like a mountain range. Grift climbed on the back of the truck and peered out over the horizon. "Eva, strap her down. We aren't taking the sled. We don't have time. Make sure she is ready to move. We have to get out of here."

Eva's face clouded over with fright. "What is going on? Grift, I just got her unbuckled and ready for the sled." Eva eased to the edge of the truck bed and looked out. "What's going on?!"

Grift held his hands at Eva's shoulders and whispered, his eyes wide. "Seam and his army, Eva. They're here. We have to move. *Now*. Strap her in and hold on."

Eva scrambled to Rose's side and unwound several straps she had tucked under the cot. "Can you give me five minutes? I can make do, but she has to be secure."

"Just hurry!"

Grift scrambled back over to the crates lining the road and kicked the top off. He pulled out an automatic assault rifle and checked the clip and chamber. Empty. Grift cursed under his breath and threw open a few more crates before his eyes landed on the shimmering brass shells he was looking for. Grift loaded the clip and shoved several handfuls of magazines into his pack.

The datalink on Grift's wrist resounded with Adley's voice again. "Grift. Did you make it to the truck?"

Grift climbed into the truck's cockpit, hammering his hand over the ignition switch, the engine roaring to life. "Yes. I'm here. Where are you?!"

Adley shot back. "Don't worry about me! Go! Go now! I'll be fine, I have clearance, but you need to leave. They are pulling in now."

Grift revved the engine and screamed back to the bed of the truck. "Eva. Are we ready to roll?"

"Almost!"

His heart in his throat, Grift eyed the rearview mirrors and scanned the dirt streets that ran through Henshaw. It was clear, but Grift knew he was wasting time. "Eva, we've got to go now!"

As the words slipped through his lips, one of the military transports turned a corner to the north, putting their vehicle in plain sight.

Grift's foot hammered down on the gas as he screamed to the back. "Hold her down, Eva!"

The truck's tires spit gravel and dust as Grift leveled the accelerator. The old transport lurched forward, out and away from the city, but the black truck rocketed behind them in chase. Grift's teeth rattled in his head as his truck bounced over the rolling hills. *Aleph, please.*

The black military vehicle raced closer, chewing up the few precious meters between. Grift downshifted and punched the accelerator to the floor as he managed to pull up Adley on his datalink.

"Adley! Anything you all can do? This one's tailing me!"

The line was silent.

"Adley! Come on!" Grift punched the steering wheel and slammed the datalink shut. He peered back into the rearview mirror and his pursuer was within one truck length. Grift rolled down the driver's side window. A round of shots rang out and the windshield exploded into a thousand shards of glass. Holes ripped through the back of the truck's cabin and the driver's side door.

"No," he whispered to the shadows of his mind. He spoke to both them and the Dominion soldiers chasing him. Cold rage pumped through Grift's body, and without hesitation he moved. His rifle's barrel swung free outside the truck's cabin, and he unloaded several rounds in the direction of the truck behind him. The shots hit their mark, crimson clouds exploding over the shattered windshield, as the dark truck careened, crashing down the hillside.

Grift reloaded, and his eyes fell on the empty mirrors. "Eva!" he called out, praying for a response. None came, and he jerked the steering wheel, sending the truck swerving a full ninety-degree turn. He leapt out of the cabin and jumped into the back of the truck bed.

Eva was laid out over Rose, her chest a mottled patchwork of bright blood. Rot stood next to them barking madly. Grift's hands shook and his mind reeled to comprehend the scene. Rose lay beneath Eva's body and Grift's consciousness flew away like a caged bird. He sprinted past the barking dog and rolled Eva off Rose, his hands racing to check his friend's vitals. She was gone. Eva had died, protecting his precious Rose. Tears rolled down his cheeks as his eyes fell on Rose.

To his surprise, she met him with open eyes. Her face was transfigured in that moment. Her eyes were wide open, alert, and brimming with a life as wide as the horizon. He looked at her, lost and unbelieving at what he was seeing. Everything felt distant to him, as if all the world's purpose, beauty, and power were located in this one horrible moment of space and time; a nexus of tragic purpose.

"Rose," he stammered, his mind firing but unable to form the words.

"You have to keep fighting, Grift," she whispered to him, her words a grim, titanic force.

His mouth went dry. He had no words for this.

"He'll never stop, Grift. He'll never stop," she stammered, her voice looping with an unending mantra of delusion. The crisp white sheet covering her began to pool with her blood, and Grift grabbed her hand, stroking it softly as hot tears streamed down his face.

"I'll stop him, Rose. I won't let him win," he said, trying to comfort her as best he knew how. She stopped and turned, her eyes as bright as dawn's daylight.

"You can't stop *him*, Grift. *He can't be stopped.*" Her mouth closed and the bright light within her blew out, releasing her from her crippled, mortal frame.

Grift held her cooling hand and felt her presence disappear. *She's gone.* He stood as a landslide of emotions threatened to buckle him. Trembling, his hand found the rifle strapped on his back.

Pressing the butt of the weapon against his shoulder, he stepped out from the cover of the green convoy, the war dog running point in front of him. They had both shed their civility for what would come next.

CHAPTER TWELVE

Willyn took in a ragged breath in the darkness, bracing herself for what was coming. A sickly sweet smell rose within the cold air permeating the gloom of the chamber. Her dizzy eyes swirled around in an effort to reorient herself. Her brain felt like it had been scrambled, but the pain of her fall was easing.

What happened? I fell. Yes. I fell...down a pit. Willyn's mind began putting together the loose details of the room, trying to remember what significance they held. The end of the rope dangled at her feet, its end dancing on the cold stone floor. It brushed against a pale hand that lay broken on a heap. Her eyes lingered there for a moment, trying to make sense of the image.

Oh no.

That wasn't her hand. Her eyes adjusted with the darkness, and she forced her hands down to the floor. It gave way from her, absorbing her body's force as she pushed herself up. Her flesh recoiled at the sensation. She looked down at the new horrors lying beneath her.

Bodies littered the floor, a ghastly collage of stiff and destroyed human life. The floor was littered with them, the emptied shells of both Red and Bagger laborers, disposed as if they were nothing but trash.

These are the miners that disappeared. The boy had warned her of this. *The boy. Legion's Teeth.* Her mind slowly turned over the details when a voice whispered in the darkness.

"Do you know how long it has been since I last feasted on the blood of man?"

Aleph above. She remembered now, everything that had transpired in the Eastern shaft. Her heart froze in her chest as the monster in the mirror continued to mutter. Slowly she turned her head only to be met with horrible green eyes shedding an eerie light over the large chamber. Her chest tightened as she wheezed for breath, her hands clumsily searching for her mask.

"I was very surprised when my benefactor above began dropping me these morsels. I didn't know what was happening, you see. I can't hear my siblings very clearly in these depths. *Whispers in the dark.* The mountain...it shields me. For eons I became ravenous...nearly losing my mind down here. It is so very lonely to be forgotten. Forgotten by the world, forgotten by my kin."

The Serub's voice was like a song, and Willyn did her best not to be caught up in it, for something in it wanted to draw her up, as if her soul could be lapped up in just his words. "**My surprise was great when I heard the rumblings in the mountain. Once the seal was open and the first few sacrifices dropped in, it was good to know that I had not been forgotten. You have my thanks, child.**"

Willyn's blue eyes locked with the green ones that shone in the dark and she remained silent. The Serub stepped closer to the mirror's edge. "**I see that you are not like the others. Your hands are covered in blood, a most useful ally for me and my kin on Candor.**"

Willyn's mind quaked at the words. She stared down at her hands. No blood lay on them. *What was the Serub talking about?*

The owner of the green eyes laughed, his voice filling the room, his laughter shaking what felt to be the whole mountain. Willyn stepped forward and words left her mouth.

"What is your name, Serub?"

Willyn's voice sounded like a child's in the darkness, the words weak and impotent in the presence of the divine. He sneered, but relented from some unspoken offense.

His voice rumbled like a hurricane, forcing Willyn to cover her ears as the mountain quaked with power. "**I am Bastion, defender of my kin and their claim on Candor.**"

As Bastion's announcement echoed down through the mineshaft, Willyn noticed the rope dangling at her feet. Bastion approached the edge of his glass prison as he, too, gazed upwards to the opening in the ceiling of the chamber.

His head was shaved and he bore a chiseled face, his body decked in an intricate set of ancient armor. Two swords were sheathed by his side, and if Willyn had not known she would have sworn she was looking at some mimicked form of the Mastermonk.

"Well, go on," the Serub spoke, his deep voice echoing in the dark. **"You've found me, learned my name, and tended to my needs. Pull me out from this pit. I take it you are the Keeper?"**

A memory, like a bird, fluttered in the rafters of her mind. *Deceive him. Deceive him and secure the mirror for yourself.*

Willyn nodded and stood to meet Bastion's emerald eyes. "I am only a servant of the Keeper." She pulled at the rope and glanced up, shaking with fear that the Serub would not buy the ruse. "I will be back. I need to make preparations, but you will soon be released." The words came and for a moment she feared she would be found out.

Bastion nodded, his eyes radiating with anticipation.

Relief poured over her as she left the chamber, climbing hand over hand up the rope, up toward the jagged opening carved out by the jackhammers. She pulled herself up the height of the secret chamber, her mind racing, full of questions.

Who had dropped the rope? Her mind danced through the crooked hallways of memory until she found something she remembered. *Viga.* Viga had nearly killed her, and she braced herself for another fight. As she eclipsed the chamber opening, her nose caught the burning smell of gunpowder. Silently she waited, her eyes trying to penetrate through the settling dust that still hung like a thick cloud in the darkness. A black mass lay on the ground five feet away from her.

Viga. His chest was riddled with holes and his eyes were open and hollow. She leaned down, sheathing her dagger in her robes just as the cold muzzle of a pistol was placed directly on her temple.

"Easy. Move away." The voice was familiar, but Willyn dared not make any sudden movements. "Stand up. Walk slow."

"Why the Eastern tunnels? Why?" The voice. She knew this voice.

"Your mask? Gone? Strange things, you see now, yes? Eastern shafts of the Teeth, no good for the mind." The cadence was the singsong, cobbled mishmash of the common tongue.

"Bri," she whispered, her heart filling with relief. She glanced down and saw the body of Viga riddled with bullet wounds. *The four shots.* Willyn swallowed. Bri was still holding the pistol against her, and her mind spun hard to make sense of it all. She braced herself for what might be coming.

"You must...be easy now." To her surprise, Bri did not lower his weapon from her head. The mask that covered his face was fogged, blurring the outline of his dark face and thick braided mustache.

"What are you doing, Bri?" Willyn had so longed for a friendly face, but the darkness of this place was beginning to crumble around her. *Why does he have a gun to my head?*

"I ask you same question." An audible click echoed through the shaft as Bri pulled back the hammer of his pistol. "You...you are not doing what Monk said."

Willyn whispered to him, throwing a wary glance at the opening in the floor that led to the Serub's pit. "Be quiet. Not here. I can explain."

"I heard you talk with the demon. You are...how you say... planning things with him?" He shoved the muzzle further, brushing it against her midnight dyed hair. Bri's eyes were sharp, unyielding, and though he struggled to handle the common language, his resolve did not diminish. "Monk...monk would not bless these things."

Willyn stared at Bri and whispered the only thing she knew to say. "The Serub..."

Bri cut her off. "Do not speak that name, child. *Demon.*"

Willyn stammered, "The...the *demon* is convinced I am his ally. I am nothing of the sort, but we must get the mirror before…"

Marching footsteps echoed down the dark hallways, and Willyn stared into Bri's eyes. "There is not time for this, Bri. *You must trust me.* Seam and Hosp are after this mirror and we have to stop them. We have to take this mirror out and hide the demon from them. I am your friend!"

Bri blinked and his pistol lowered for a fraction of a second. "I will...believe story now, but know this. I will talk with monk."

"And he will tell you that my story is true."

The footsteps grew louder and Willyn envisioned rows of Dominion forces plunging into the Eastern shafts armed to the teeth. She picked up Viga's pistol, pushing past Bri, her heart still hammering in her chest. She sprung for Viga's body and reloaded the weapon with a fresh clip. They were trapped and out of time. It would come down to a fight.

Bri looked at Willyn with pity and rested a giant hand on her shoulder. "Easy. Easy now, little one. These that come are my brothers, and they are set to remove the demon. We hide his glass deeper in... secret tunnels."

"Secret tunnels? Wait...you knew?" Willyn glanced past Bri toward the sound of the oncoming mob. "You knew why I was here."

Bri nodded and smiled. "Yes. Monk told me you came to help destroy demon. For that I will help. We hide again."

"In your tunnels?" Willyn kept her eyes locked on the passage beyond Bri's broad shoulders.

"Yes. Tunnels hidden from eyes of our Masters." He cut his sharp eyes toward her. "Like you. The Realm people do not know all of the Bagger..." he paused, weighing his word choice, "tricks. We crafty people. Know how to survive. Know much that Realm people do not."

"I see." Willyn held tightly to Viga's pistol as the sound of footsteps echoed down the tunnels. Soon the bright lights of headlamps turned the corner as ten miners marched, greeting Bri in the Bagger tongue.

"Trey! Yaq me dell, no?" A short Bagger approached Bri, pointing at Willyn, his face painted with concern.

Bri nodded, responded, and turned toward her. "He say you need mask. Has one for you."

Willyn nodded, loosened her grip on Viga's pistol, and graciously accepted the mask from a dirty satchel. The miner rallied around her, connecting the hose to a small ventilator. She felt the air rush through her face and she inhaled. In an instant, her head exploded with sharp pain.

"Arghh...what's happening?" It felt as if her brain had been set on fire, and tears streamed out her eyes, fogging up her mask.

Bri hammered his hand on her back and explained, his words disjointed. "It is air here. Kills, but does slow. Dulls brain and kills you." He pointed to the ventilator, shaking his head. "Real air—real air does not do this. Shows you how the mine air kills." He held his hands up to his head, accentuating every detail. "The hurt, it will pass."

The pain did slowly dull, and Willyn was thankful for her newfound companions. The miners approached the opening in the shaft and looked back at Bri. Their fear was obvious.

The lead miner called out, his voice dulled by the rubber mask. "Ach tey dela-ray mondtru tere?"

Bri nodded and responded, pointing his finger down the opening in the floor. "Frick. Getta don munt. Nere cantak do mir."

The miner nodded and pointed to a young Bagger near him. He whistled and pointed for him to run back up the shaft. The boy, much younger than any of them, took off like a flash.

Bri glanced down at Willyn and patted her on the back. "You must go. We hide demon now."

Willyn furrowed her brow and dug in her heels. "I'm not leaving. I have to know where he is so I can report back to Wael."

Bri laughed and shook his head. "*So you no trust me now.* Silly. We need trust."

The giant was difficult to read, but Willyn was happy to no longer have his pistol on her skull. She turned and looked down the shaft leading back to the main complex. "What is the boy doing?"

"Look out. He watch for us good. Fast. He will warn us if we need him."

Willyn turned as the Baggers dropped themselves into the secret chamber. A chorus of loud curses spilled from the pit below as the Baggers met the demon in the dark. The curses and shouting evaporated, giving over to wild screams as the men climbed over one another to pull themselves back up from dark hole. Bri grunted and barked at one of the men lying on the ground, panting for breath.

"Qet tey do?"

The Bagger, his face as white as a sheet, mumbled an answer. Bri dipped his head and softly answered the man, placing his hand on the miner's shoulder. Bri looked back at Willyn and nodded toward the pit. "Demon is liar. Has tricks." He tapped his head with two sausage-sized fingers. "Men's mind not clear, he lies to them with pictures."

Bri pulled a thick, black canvas from his bag and jumped into the pit. Bastion's voice echoed up from the chamber. "**Where is the one who fed me?** "

Willyn yelled down into the darkness. "I am here. We have to move you discreetly. There are many who wish to harm you. We will make sure you are transported safely. Don't mind the laborers. They will be dealt with."

Willyn dared to peer over into the pit. Green eyes pressed up against the mirror's edge, and Willyn saw for an instant the face of a rabid boar looking up at her. Memories of hunting such creatures flashed in her mind. Memories of Hagan.

"You are trying my patience."

The voice from the mirror spoke and Willyn sneered. Something within her awakened, something that had fallen asleep ever since she had been alone in the cavern. Her mouth lit with words, "You are trying mine!" She turned her attention to Bri, her face twisted with frustration.

"Let's get the mirror out of here. I am done with this."

Bri nodded and yelled out, his voice booming through the caverns. He held up a dark piece of glass and put it up to the mask's faceplate. It covered the faceplate entirely. Willyn watched Bri instruct the men, doing her best to follow. Bri then took large rubber gloves, gloves that Willyn knew were used to deaden electric currents, and put them on. All the men in his crew stood alert and followed his instructions.

Bri turned to Willyn, his face barely visible through the darkened faceplate. "Mask hide our eyes from demon. Demon's eyes…" His fingers pointed to where his eyes would be behind the mask. "Weapons. Important…not let them see ours. Don't let them see ours…we okay. The gloves…the gloves keep us safe when we move glass."

"Interesting." Willyn was impressed, and she watched the crew plunge back down into the depths to begin their work again. Bastion screamed, his voice booming through the caverns, but this time the Baggers moved with authority. They hoisted the mirror from its cavern and wrapped it with the thick canvas. Willyn was careful to shield her eyes as Bastion paced the width of the mirror like a predator. He was desperate to distract the crew, screaming and roaring, his voice like thunderclaps. Several of the men unstrapped poles that had been on their back and used them to create a gurney to carry the mirror. As soon as they wrapped up the mirror entirely, the din created by the Serub ceased.

Bri walked up to the wrapped mirror, took off his mask and gloves, and motioned to the others to do the same. The crew stood there, their faces somber, their mouths silent. The mirror was placed on the shaft's floor, and Bri spoke his native tongue, the words lost on Willyn's ears. He untied a small satchel from his belt and scattered a fine white powder over the covered mirror. Willyn knew what it was in an instant: salt.

Bri closed his eyes and extended his hand. The dirty miners mirrored the giant's movements, and Willyn felt her heart beat deep in her chest. She had never seen such devotion or reverence on the part of the Baggers and her eyes went wide with anticipation.

Bri's voice boomed in the hall, "Que tell doray, Que tell doray, Tell Uld Bohs restran, und Kuening Aleph es restran."

The crew chanted with their leader and dropped to their knees. The shaft was silent.

The Baggers stood and whispered the prayer's end, "Selah."

Willyn stood, her mind and heart swirling with a strange feeling. It was as if a warm wind had blown through the chamber, and she felt chills ride up and down her spine. Bri stood and pointed to the crew. Without a word, he began to lead the brigade deeper into the mountain, carrying the mirror with them. Willyn followed as the crew turned down one dark corner of mineshaft that Willyn had failed to notice. Her mind swirled with the implications of Bri's sudden ceremony with the mirror. *What did it mean?*

One of the lead miners sent a sharp whistle up the shaft. Like a dog, the young Bagger lookout sprinted back to rejoin the crew. The miners were in much better spirits now, and Willyn noticed it just in the way they walked. It was not long before they began to tell jokes and sing songs.

The crew journeyed for what felt like a long distance, but the mountain halls within Legion's Teeth were so disorienting that Willyn could not be sure how far they had come. They stopped every couple of turns to inspect the route, Bri leaning down, inspecting when the path would diverge. Everything looked the same to Willyn and she soon surrendered to the fact she could not make her way back on her own.

"Keep your eye on him," Willyn whispered to herself as she eyed Bri. "Without him we will never get this thing back and protected."

The team stopped in a small hallway that was carved just wide enough for two men to make it through shoulder to shoulder. Bri examined the walls and nodded.

"This. This will be very good." He pointed at a crack in the wall with his headlamp. He turned to the Baggers and pointed at the crack. "In."

The men positioned the mirror and slid it into the mountain wall. Bri gathered the men and his face fell solemn. "Nit don vong. Nit."

The men all placed their closed fists over their hearts and shouted in unison, "Nit don vong."

Willyn sat across the table from Bri as he guzzled his third bowl of beef stew and fifth beer. She shook her head as he leaned back and belched before wiping at his thick, wet mustache. The man seemed so content and relaxed, but all Willyn could think of was the mirror. Despite the dizzying hour-long trek into the heart of the mountain, Willyn could not help but worry over the men helping Bri, or that Bri himself might have some ulterior motive.

"Bri." Willyn's voice was sharp. "What was that prayer you led back there? What did it mean?"

Bri looked up at her, his light brown eyes distant. Willyn thought that perhaps the food and drink had slowed his mind, but Bri spoke and the world began to fade away.

"There is much you Realm people...you do not know. We Baggers, we have strange beliefs. Strange history. We were Rihtian, long ago. Before war."

"The Great War?"

Bri nodded. "My people...we were..." His eyes searched for the word in his mind. "*Deceive*."

"Deceived," Willyn corrected. Bri nodded, his long mustache moving up with a slight smile. "We the children of old Rihts. They fell under Aleph followers."

Willyn cocked her head, entranced in the deep cadence and rolling timbre of the man's voice, despite his straining grasp of the common tongue. For the first time she realized she had only heard her people's side of this history.

Bri continued, "Landless, Riht destroyed, my ancestors search for a new...*purpose* in desert." Bri's eyes cut across the roughly hewn table, and he leaned in toward her. "My peoples' gods...*deceived* us. Darkness, death, blood. All ruined. No land. No gods. No home to go."

Willyn had pressed up on the edge of her bench, completely silent. "What happened?"

"*He came.*" Bri took a giant gulp of his last beer, put down the tankard, and belched.

"Who?" Willyn's eyes stared at the intricate ravens tattooed on Bri's arm, the size of her thigh.

Bri shook his head, his eyes distant. "The...six."

"Sixth?" Willyn guessed.

"Yes, yes. *Sixth.* A Serub, not *demon* like those in glass like those we worshipped. *This is good Serub.* Fallen, but still good." Bri shook his head. "He came to my people and spoke to them. Told them future. Told them to go deeper in desert. To make peace with Aleph."

"Aleph?" The name of the divine fell off her tongue before she could stop it.

"Aye. This not easy. We told to curse Aleph. Taught to curse him, but...the *sixth* he came and help. Said Aleph who sent him to help us. Sent him to us, to find *a new way* in the desert."

Willyn took a bite of bread and chewed it thoughtfully. "What did he tell your people to do?"

"The sixth lead us to...toto de rusim." Bri broke into his Bagger language, straining to utilize the limits of his knowledge. "Restrain?"

"What?" Willyn had no idea what the Bagger word meant.

"To change." Bri searched for the definition. "To better."

"Restore?"

Bri slapped the table, which groaned under the giant's force, his booming laughter filling the chamber. "Aye! This is it. Be *restore* says *sixth*. Ride the rails, he say. 'Serve brothers and sisters in Realms. Work your restore out,'" Bri spoke, his face overcome with emotion, "and Aleph will give you new home. Make you mighty again."

A solemn silence grew between them. Willyn shook her head, taking everything in.

"So that is why the Baggers ride the rails?" She sat stunned, taking a small sip from her drink. "And the prayer over the...demon? You never told me. What did it mean?"

"We Baggers...we believe strange things, different from Realm people." He shrugged. "Our prayers was for demon in glass. Maybe he can restores too like six."

Willyn shook her head, her eyes wide, her skin pin-pricked with strange energy. She did not know if she could believe everything she heard. She would not have believed in the Serubs, but her experiences had shattered her original thoughts on faith and religion. With all she had encountered over the past few months, she knew there had to be something to all of it. She threw a mischievous glance at her companion. "And what would our friend the Mastermonk think of this?"

"Oh," Bri smiled broadly. "The monk and I have much common, little one." He held a monstrous hand over his barrel chest. "I am priest of my people, too. My...clothes, my words, my skin." He showed off the tattoo of the ravens and arrows. "...they different, but we are same in spirit. *Same in purpose*. Monk is good friend. He follows the One; the same as I."

Willyn nodded and sighed. "The One will need to help me soon." Her eyes cut over to him. "I have to meet with Rander, Bri. We need the Reds' support. Maybe the One can help me tame that beast."

Bri nodded and ran his finger along the rim of his soup dish. "Yes. But that not easy." He popped the greasy finger in his mouth and looked over Willyn's shoulder. "But we will try."

Willyn stared at him, trying to get a read on him. "We have to figure out what we are doing. Viga was down in the Eastern shafts trying to dig that thing out for Seam. Once Seam finds out he is dead they will either storm this place or do something worse. We have to make sure Rander does not side with the Dominion. We have to..."

The sound of marching filled through the mountain halls, cutting Willyn off. All talking ceased within the mess hall as a massive swell of Red soldiers poured into the cavern with weapons drawn. Willyn cursed under her breath and her eyes widened as a man stepped forward. He could only be Rander. *Viga,* she thought. *They found Viga.*

Rander's voice ripped through the hollow room.

"Everyone silent. NOW!"

The room fell quiet as Rander raised his voice. "There are traitors here. My loyal guardsman Viga was shot down, his body pulled out from the Eastern shafts. *Who here knows anything about Viga?"*

The Baggers and Reds in the common area all shared worried glances. No one moved or spoke. The entire congregation of bodies was mute.

Something within Willyn pushed her forward. She glanced over at Bri, whose eyes were locked onto her. Willyn whispered to him, "Now?"

Bri nodded.

The nod encouraged her and soon Willyn found herself stepping into the circle that had formed between Rander and his Red bodyguards. Her voice filled the silence and commanded all eyes on her. "I did it. I killed Viga in the Eastern Shafts. He was allied with Seam Panderean and that snake, Hospsadda Gran." She stepped on top of a table and shouted out, "Reds, hear me! I am Willyn Kara!"

With that one statement, the room erupted into chaos. A massive fight broke out and Rander screamed to his men, "Seize her!"

Willyn fired a shot into the air as Bri crumpled those who dared approach her. She leveled her pistol toward Rander's face and screamed, "You will not touch your Sar!"

Rander's men stopped in their tracks and turned questioning gazes back to their leader. He stormed toward Willyn and pulled out his own pistol, unfazed by her drawn weapon. He threw back the hammer on the revolver, leveling it at Willyn's chest.

"Stand down!" shouted Willyn. A mad rage of adrenaline coursed through her veins as she hurled her pistol at Rander's feet. "Put down your gun and face me! I am the same Sar you swear to serve. Here I am in the flesh, and yet you deny my reign. *Now stand down!*"

For a moment, Willyn could see Rander waver in his resolve. He lowered his pistol and threw it to the side. He stepped within an inch of her face and spoke, loud enough for the whole room to hear.

"If you are the Sar then no doubt you will meet me in the dueling ring. Prove to me your martial prowess. Show me your combat training. Any Sar worth their mettle would not shrink back from a fight to the death." Rander cut her a glance. "Or are you what I fear, a dirty Bagger with dreams of glory? I would hate to have another Bagger sully up my boots."

Willyn's lungs heaved with rage. "I gladly accept your challenge, fool. I will rip you into shreds, and all the Reds will see me for who I am."

Rander laughed and the Reds screamed with delight.

Bri whispered in her ear, "You sure this okay? Monk said we must unite the Reds, not fight leader."

Willyn threw a sly glance at the giant Bagger. "Bri, there is much you don't know about Grogans."

CHAPTER THIRTEEN

Seam sat with his eyes closed, his head bent forward as the subtle motion of the titan carrying him pressed on toward Hangman's Pass. By all accounts, it looked as if the High King had fallen asleep, but it was a charade, just a secret game that Seam played trying to induce his body toward a state of rest. If only he put his body in the right position and mimicked the motions of what he most desired, perhaps then he could drift off, leaving Candor for just a little while.

Yet the dark horizon of dreams ever eluded him. Instead of darkness, all Seam could see were the *others*, the hive mind of newly made morels that rode behind him, crafted by the dark architect he had enslaved. Seam sat up, his face worn and his mind full of bitterness.

If this is the cost of power, so be it. He assured himself that he was not tired, and that much was true. He had never felt such energy in all his life. Yet, something within him cried for release, for rest, if not from his body, from his mind.

In an effort to distract himself, he stood up and inspected the metallic chamber of the Grogan titan. It was an impressive war machine, a physical expression of Seam's growing respect and appreciation for the Grogans since the truce that had been brokered between his nation and Hosp's. The Grogans were such a hardy people, and their technology in warfare knew no equal. Over the months since beginning his rule in Zenith, Seam had taken to assimilating many of the Grogan practices. He abandoned the production of Lotte's military vehicles in favor of adopting the Grogan rooks and titans. He also abandoned his regal dress of Lotte for the Spartan uniform of his allies in Rhuddenhall.

Rhuddenhall. A curious thought flickered across the High King's mind. *You could quell the Reds, murder Hosp, and secure the mantle of Sar for yourself.* The thought oscillated in his mind, and he weighed it carefully. It was an interesting idea; one he had danced with many times over.

Yes, his inner voice pressed, *but now you are actually heading to the Groganlands with an army. An army that cannot be stopped.* Seam stood, his lips pursed as his mind sought clarity. His army, the multitude, had added to his perpetual state of consciousness. The keys had more power, by far, than he once supposed. These strange objects extended further than just merely leashing the false gods. He now knew that he could absorb their power as his own.

Since unlocking Nyx he had felt this, a burst of new influence, a rapid energy soaring through him, yet he did not know how to wield it. His actions against Nyx in the desert were made under an impulse, a powerful act of survival that forced his mind to make the connection to *the others*. It was as if the Keys had directed him to his newfound power. He had kept his rabid dogs in check. The Serubs themselves seemed perplexed that he could link with the Bagger husks, championing them all into submission. He knew that the possibility of this power existed, but he didn't know if he could actually control them all until now. *Yes, now you know the truth. You can check the Serubs into submission and control untold armies with your thoughts.*

Seam glanced up to the dark corner in the back of the titan. There, stowed with the supplies and weapons, stood the shadow, rigid and still in the darkness.

The body of his enemy had long healed from its wounds and stood with open, vacant eyes. The shell of Kull Shepherd served as the High King's secret training ground for his newfound abilities, confirming the immense powers that the Keys actually bestowed upon him. At first the living, soulless body of Grift Shepherd's son served as some sort of sick trophy, a cold, tangible reminder of what he could and would do to anyone who dared to oppose him.

This was before he realized he could make him move. The oddness of standing by a living corpse did not keep Seam's inquisitive mind away. There was something magnetic about being near the morel form of his fallen enemy. Something that was confirming and intoxicating. The High King felt drawn to Kull's shell in a similar way that he had felt drawn to the forbidden tomes he stole from the royal archives. It was an emotion that felt like a well-worn path that he had walked down long ago. *Destiny.* It was destiny, and it made his body shake with excitement and secret longing. Something about the vacant body of Kull Shepherd was full of *purpose,* and even though this mystery eluded him for many months, he could feel the weight of power orbiting it. Then one night, he looked at the silent, mute body and spoke to it.

"Stand here." With his arm brandishing the Keys of Candor, he pointed and the morel servant obeyed without question. He closed his eyes, and like a child learning to use his voice for the first time, Seam's mind reached out and found another vessel that he could control.

For weeks, he tested and honed his abilities with Grift Shepherd's son, realizing his full potential. Only weeks later he controlled an army of newly created morels. On the periphery of his vision, he could feel their perspectives, their visions shifting into his mind, the kaleidoscopic mass of the hive-mind riding behind him in the convoy. Thankfully, with none of these new powers were there voices to contend with. No additional mindscapes to sort through, no psychic strain. Yet every time he closed his eyes and attempted to feign the rest he so sorely desired, all he could see were the viewpoints of thousands of vacant eyes that filled his dark transports, waiting to wage war in the Groganlands.

It was more than Seam could truly comprehend. If he could mimic the abilities and even supplant Nyx's powers, what other secrets did her kin have to offer? This new mystery tantalized him, but his thoughts were clouded with images of the restless deities and their continual attempts to overpower, seduce, and defeat him. It made his mind fill with rage and a fire burn behind his eyes. "They won't stop," he whispered to himself. "And as I unlock the remaining two they will continue to strive for power. *My pow*er."

Seam clenched his eyes shut and marveled at his ability to observe and control the thousands of husks tucked away within his convoy. He smiled and thought to himself, his mind as fractured as the vision he saw behind closed eyes. *They may try, but I will be waiting. I will drain them down to the dregs. I will crush them under my boots and smear them across the lands they once ruled.* He ground his teeth. *I am the Lord of Candor.*

Seam stood silent, searching the depths of his mind, plunging down in his memories in an effort to remember the details of the ancient forbidden scriptures he had poured over what felt like eons ago. *There has to be something I am forgetting. Something I've overlooked.* There had to be an answer to keep the Serubs in check, something that only the Keeper of the Keys could do to remain in power and keep the deities at bay. Lost in thought, the datalink on his wrist blinked with life. He flicked open the screen and glanced down at the young face staring back at him.

"My High King. I have news to report on Grift Shepherd."

The name Shepherd stood up the hairs on Seam's neck. "Speak, Reuben. Is he still alive?"

Reuben glanced over his shoulder before addressing the High King. "I am uncertain, sire. He was caught attempting to flee from Henshaw. The last communication I received was that he had taken out one of our armored personnel carriers but that his vehicle was disabled in the firefight."

Queen Aleigha's scout had made a most excellent spy for Seam. "Did you notify Cyric or one of the others?"

"The bounty hunters? No sir. I thought you would like..."

Seam ground his teeth and hissed, "So you are bothering me to tell me you *don't know* if this terrorist is dead and that you have not notified the hunters?"

The young man dipped his head and swallowed before stammering out an answer. "No, sir. I am actually contacting you about the queen. I was simply providing a brief on Shepherd."

Seam sat forward and cocked his neck to the side. "What about my mother?"

Reuben paused as he weighed his words. He stared at the High King and whispered, "Sire, she was behind the fight in Henshaw. She is arming an active resistance, trying to help Shepherd and other sympathizers."

Seam bristled at the words and leaned into the screen, his bloodshot eyes glowing with the light of the diodes. "Reuben, you understand the cost that will be inflicted if the words you are speaking are false? I will happily cut out your lying tongue if you are trying to deceive me."

Reuben stared at the king, unwavering, as if the words that his king had just said were a commentary of the weather. "I understand very well what I am telling you, sir. I heard her speak with Shepherd. She met with him in the industrial district only days ago. A resistance cell has set up shop, busily planning their strategy. I heard it all. They had planned to take over Henshaw and set up a base on the borders of Preost." Reuben was shaking, but he refused to break his eyes away from Seam.

The thought of his own mother betraying him twisted in the pit of Seam's stomach like a viper. The poisonous accusation gave birth to a strong rage and Seam could feel his blood boil beneath his skin.

"Reuben."

"Sir?"

"I want proof, and whether you provide evidence or not I want you and my mother in Zenith within twenty-four hours. Do you understand?"

The words trembled from Reuben's lips. "Yes, my lord."

Seam held the datalink open as he spat one more sentence, "And bring me definitive news on Shepherd. No excuses."

Seam snapped his datalink shut, his face painted with rage. He ran up to the cockpit of the titan. Two Dominion drivers sat with their hands on the controls observing the barren desert filling the horizon before them.

"How much longer until we are at the Pass?"

The co-pilot, startled by the High King's sudden presence, pulled up a map on one of the titan's screens. Seam stared at the blue topographic map. The blue desert was filled with a long line of red convoy vehicles.

"By my estimate, sire, we will be there in a matter of hours."

"Speed it up, soldiers. I am growing restless."

"Of course, sir." The soldiers glanced at each other and put their hands on the thruster. Both pushed at the device, and Seam felt the huge hovercraft pitch forward. The pilot called over his datalink, "Convoy, increase thrust. Match point speed."

Twenty affirmatives chanted over the datalink and Seam smiled, his eyes full of malice.

I'm coming, Hosp.

Hosp stood, shrouded underneath the shade cast by the thick outcrop of red stone that soared above him. Hangman's Pass had long been empty, but all that had changed since the Red Rebellion. It had been so long since the Grogans had needed to hang their enemies on the borders of their territory, but these were dark days. Hundreds of Red rebel bodies swung in the hot desert wind, suspended by the rusted chains hammered into the rock ages ago. Hosp raised his face up to them and smiled, his gray eyes shining beneath the dark shade of the Pass. The carrion birds had come to feast on his enemies. They filled the arch, shrieking and shaking the chains of those Hosp had slaughtered.

Let the High King see my work and fear. Hosp was under no illusion that Seam had underestimated him. In fact, he had meticulously counted on Seam to believe that he actually needed his help. *Let him underestimate me,* Hosp thought to himself. *He is bringing my strongest weapon and has no clue.* He knew that it would only be a matter of time before the fool would make a fatal mistake.

A voice interrupted Hosp's thoughts at he glanced up at his defeated foes hanging overhead. "Sir. The men are in position."

Hosp smiled and welcomed the news. "Very good. Ensure they understand that they are not to move until I give the signal."

"Yes, sir." The commander tightened his stance and lifted his head. "We will wait for your command."

Hosp looked back overhead at Hangman's Pass and sneered, his cold gray eyes glazing over. "High King Seam will soon learn that I am no lap dog and that my Realm bows to no one."

The sun dipped beneath the horizon as Seam's convoy arrived at Hangman's Pass. The red rock burned with the glow of the setting sun as deep black shadows draped over the canyon pass. Seam glanced out of the titan cockpit at the silhouettes swaying from the rock overhead. A single armored personnel carrier was waiting in the center of the cannon. The black vehicle was nearly lost in the shadows settling at the bottom of the gorge.

Seam darted to the back of the titan and opened the heavy iron door locking the rear compartment. Inside, Abtren and Arakiel sat in silence over the withered body of Nyx. Seam had sapped much of her former strength after she completed her *modifications* to his morel army. She had to be punished for her display of defiance; there was no other recourse. Her two celestial kin offered no acknowledgement of Seam as he entered the chamber. All he got were several piercing gazes that threatened to tear holes through him.

Pouting like children. When will they ever understand the new reality? Seam glanced down at Nyx and spoke. "Oh...why the long faces? Do not fret, my friends." He leaned down, leveling his eyes with the gods that so many men feared, daring not to mention their names louder than a muted whisper. His eyes were bold weapons, daring to peer within their horrific eyes, unashamed and unafraid. "Nyx will soon be restored. I give you my solemn oath.

There will be enough blood for the three of you shortly, but for now, I need you to come with me."

Arakiel growled and stood, his lips curling up to reveal a row of jagged white fangs. **"I will not rest until I grind you into dust, King of Candor."**

Seam leaned his head back to gaze at the immortal being who stood three heads taller than him. Any normal man would have been petrified, but Seam held his ground. "I thought I had made this clear, Arakiel. I thought I had made everything so abundantly clear..."

His wrist bearing the Mastermonk's gauntlet shot out like a viper, ratcheting down on Arakiel's arm. The Keys locked in place burned with hot white fire as Seam's grip crumpled the illuminated flesh of the immortal. Arakiel's arm ignited and the god screamed in the chamber as flames swallowed him. Arakiel stood in Seam's grip, his voice booming like an avalanche as he screamed. Seam stared at the burning god in his clutches, feeling the energy surge within him like a waterfall. *It felt so good to take what was rightfully his.*

The High King spoke, his voice resounding over the chaos. "I will not relent until you and all of your cursed kin submit to me. YOU ARE BOUND."

Finally, Seam let go of Arakiel, throwing him to the floor of the titan across from his withered sister.

Seam's eyes stared at Abtren, daring her to speak, waiting for a shred of resistance to show on her face. *"What say you, Abtren the Defiler? Do you want to test my resolve? Or will I feast on another Serub today?"*

Abtren's mouth hung open in disbelief. She fell to her knees, her hands fluttering over her ruined brother and sister. "Please...Keeper of the Keys. Please...have mercy on us." She stood, her beautiful face marred with fear as she spoke. "Mercy. Mercy on us. We yield."

Gods who ask for mercy? "You will do much more than that." Seam spat. "Get up. Now."

Abtren stood, but her face was hesitant. Seam did not relent. "Leave your useless siblings here. They have an eternity to think on their choices. You would be wise not to follow their steps." Seam's eyes were filled with rage as he looked over the two he had siphoned. "Besides, we are going to meet your most beloved acolyte today. Hosp…"

Abtren's eyes grew wide. "King Seam, you should know that Hosp means to betray you. He would have the Keys for himself."

Seam cut a horrid glance at the Serub and laughed. "What is one more betrayer, Abtren? Did you think I did not already know of his plans?" He held up his gauntlet, the light of the Keys locked within slowly beginning to fade. "If he wants them, let him come and take them."

Seam stepped out of the titan into the twilight painted desert. Abtren followed him and the two made their way to the armored personnel carrier parked underneath the Pass. A team of five soldiers surrounded the two as Hosp exited his transport and walked toward them, holding up his hand in a sign of peace. Even in the fading heat the Surrogator insisted on keeping his face hooded, shrouded in black. Despite his dress, Seam could still see that his ally's eyes were locked on Abtren, dripping with lust and devotion.

Hosp stopped and bowed before them, his hands resting across his chest. "Thank you for coming, High King Seam. Your assistance with the Red rebellion is most appreciated." Hosp chuckled as he nodded his head upward toward the bodies swinging in the wind. "As you can see I am making progress, but the Red contingent continues to swell in the mountains and we need a bigger knife to cut them out." He then turned to face Abtren and kneeled. "Your presence, my lady. I have no words. I have long awaited your return."

Abtren said nothing, but her face blossomed with pride. Hosp's clear obsession with the Serubs disgusted Seam on a level that surprised even him. He stepped closer to his *ally*, his presence causing Hosp to stand back to his feet and face him. The High

King's mind clouded with anger. *Let him adore the blood drinkers. Let the fool worship these dogs on my leash.* Hosp's devotion kept him in check, and for Seam, that was enough, or so he told himself. Yet something deep within his mind, something past his rote rationalization was incensed at Hosp's devotion for the Five.

Seam looked up at the canyon ridge and examined the sheer rock walls. "So tell me, Hosp. Why are we meeting here if the trouble is within Legion's Teeth?" He stared up, glancing at the mass of dead rebels swaying in the hot wind. "Do you think I am impressed by this?" Seam turned his back to Hosp and scanned the top of the canyon. "Tell me, *friend*. Do you have some other reason for meeting me here?"

Hosp swallowed hard and turned his glance to Abtren, searching her eyes for answers. Abtren's voice rang within Hosp's mind. *This is not the time.*

Seam sauntered and placed his hand on Abtren's shoulder, turning again to face Hosp. The High King's casual attitude toward Abtren made Hosp bristle, and Seam smiled as he saw the offense light like a fire in his colleague's eyes. "You seem...tense, Hosp. Is there something *bothering* you, Surrogator? You still haven't told me why you have brought me out here."

A twitch revealed itself on Hosp's pale face as his eyes darted across the ridgeline. He kept staring at Abtren but she would not hold his eye contact. Hosp relented, looked back at Seam, and held up his hand, the echo of his scream filling the canyon. "NOW!"

"**No, you fool!**" Abtren yelled, her face incensed with rage.

A bullet ripped through Seam's shoulder as a barrage of gunshots erupted along the canyon ridge. The five soldiers that stood around the king and Abtren dropped, their bodies ruined in the bullet storm. Seam stumbled backward, his hold on Abtren unyielding. In one swift motion, he threw both of them inside the titan as bullets ricocheted off the mammoth vehicle's armor. Hosp darted for cover inside his own transport.

Seam yelled to the drivers. "Fire on the ridge of the canyon. NOW."

"Yes, sir," the voices called back and the titan shook in recoil as the giant cannon unleashed a torrent force toward the incoming fire. The ridgeline erupted with fire and smoke.

"Oh, Hosp. You have forced my hand." Seam stood talking to himself in a voice of mocking pity. *"Now you will truly see who I am."* Seam closed his eyes and fought through the pain searing through his arm and up his neck. *Focus.* His mind searched and he found them. The thousands of eyes waiting on him. ***It's time to fight.***

Hosp peered out from his carrier as it backed away from the explosive shots of Seam's titan. He prayed that his snipers still held their ground. He glanced back at the convoy and saw Seam's transports open up. Hosp screamed over his datalink. "Ground troops are entering the pass. Drop the mortars on my signal!" Hosp got a confirmation from one of his generals, and his eyes turned back to the army coming out of the transport. They were unlike anything he had ever seen. "What is that?"

Clad in black Dominion armor yet unarmed, they moved like a swarm of locusts, bodies flooding from the vehicles like a surging tidal wave. Soon they were stampeding toward him and Hosp's mouth went dry. Seam's titan did not relent from its assault, sending rocks crashing down from overhead, filling the canyon with a thick haze of smoke and red dust. Hosp sat paralyzed in his vehicle as Seam stepped out of the fog, his shoulder already healed.

"This ends now, Hosp," Seam whispered.

A swarm of black clad bodies rushed through the canyon, climbing over one another. They made their way up the sides of the canyon, the throng rocketing its way toward the snipers overhead. The confused tangle of bodies frenzied up to the top like a swarm of bees. The remaining snipers tried desperately to pick them off one by one. The sound of their sniper rifles came to a quick stop. Hosp realized a horrible truth. Seam was in control of a morel hive.

"What is this!?" A panicked voice crackled over Hosp's datalink. "What are those things? Are those people? What the..."

Static flashed over the lines and the signal died.

"Stop." Seam's voice was swelling with pride as he spoke through the datalink. "Cease fire."

The titan's guns eased and came to rest as the din of noise died down. Hosp's armored transport was beginning to tear away. Seam chuckled as the worm tried to crawl to safety. His eyes narrowed and a sinister grin spread across his face. The whites of his eyes rolled up as he focused in again on the collective he controlled. "This will be fun."

Hosp glanced from one of the small windows cut in the side of his transport, trying to glimpse Seam's army. All he could make out was a swarm of black, a mass of bodies lining the canyon ridge. As the sun continued to set, their dark form was lost to the shadows.

"Go now!" Hosp screamed. "Get us out of here!" Stammering, he pulled up his datalink. "Fire the mortars. Fire them now!"

A regiment of rooks outside Hangman's Pass received the orders. The mortars extended out of the black hovercrafts, erupting in unison.

The engine of Hosp's transport fired to life. The tires spun, kicking up red rocks and a cloud of dust. Hosp glanced back out the window, only to find the shadows of the canyon wall pulsating and closing in on the transport. "Gods! How is this possible?" Hosp mumbled to himself.

The rocket fire from his rooks filled his ears and soon the canyon filled with fire, the impact pushing his military transport forward like a bullet in the chamber. Despite the firestorm, Seam's force did not relent. Even as they burned, the morels leapt onto and under Hosp's truck. They slammed into the vehicle like rabid animals, their faces horrid nightmares filling up the windshield of the transport. Their skin was still burning as they slammed their fists into the windshield and used their brutalized bodies to block the driver's sight. The sound of them threshing against the machine sent Hosp into a panic as he scanned the walls of his transport for some type of weapon.

His transport drummed with the sound of screams and snapping bones as the vehicle was covered by a multitude of Seam's undead army. Soon, the sound of them clawing against the vehicle's armor swelled as the vehicle began to rock from side to side.

The truck jolted to the left and made a hard jerking motion back to the right as the driver screamed back to Hosp. "I have lost all steering and brakes. Those things must have jammed up the wheel wells."

As soon as the words left his mouth, a massive force struck the left side of the transport and sent it tumbling end over end before smashing into the canyon wall. Hosp flipped inside the carrier like a rag doll before crashing face first into the truck's metal wall. Once the chaos had silenced and the truck came to rest on its side, Hosp wiped the fresh blood running from his broken face and shook his head, trying to gather his wits. A memory jostled out of his mind. He had handed Seam two of the Keys so many months ago so that he could make his sacrifice to Abtren. He had handed him this power, unaware of the cost. A tide of regret and storm of fear swelled within him.

"Come out, you worm." Seam's smirk was audible, hanging off his every word. "Quit hiding and come out NOW."

The doors on the back of the carrier were ripped from their hinges and a sea of shambling figures flooded into the transport bay, grabbing Hosp and dragging him to Seam's feet.

Hosp's entire body was seized with tremors as he fought to compose himself. He could not make sense of Seam's newfound power. Dumbfounded by his defeat, he shook with the realization that he was surrounded. Thousands of black clad bodies lined the canyon walls, standing at attention, while several dozen others made a tight circle around Seam and Hosp, constricting any escape. They wore the faces of men, women, and children, but all humanity had been purged from their eyes. Like feral dogs, they growled in service to the High King.

Seam slowly stepped forward before throwing his foot into Hosp's face. Seam smiled as his heavy boot cracked against Hosp's jaw.

"Get up." Seam's voice was cold. "Get up and look at me."

Blood poured from Hosp's opened lip and cheek, pooling on the red rock floor. The Surrogator fought to stand and face Seam, but his body would not cooperate. As he tried to straighten his knees Seam's fist smashed across Hosp's face, crumpling him again to the canyon floor.

"I said GET UP."

Hosp scurried back several feet, trying to distance himself enough to stand without being assaulted, but as he tried to stand, Seam kicked his legs out from under him. Hosp reached out, head bowed as he crawled toward Seam and tried to pull himself up using Seam's leg as a brace. Seam's knee hammered into his nose, sending him to the rock floor again.

Two of the morels darted in to pick Hosp up from the ground and force him close to the king. The Surrogator's legs wobbled beneath him, unable to support his weight as Seam strolled forward. He clasped Hosp's face in his hands and forced the Surrogator to look him in the eyes. Hosp's face was swollen and bloody, his skin taking on deep purple and black tones.

"Look at me, you fool. Did you think that you could dare challenge *me*? Your precious *gods* serve me. Soon your beloved Realm will be mine, and all of Candor will be mine. Did you honestly think that a few mortar rounds could quell me? A few snipers?"

Seam turned Hosp's face to look toward the thousands of morels lining the canyon walls.

"And tell me, *Hosp*, are you able to command a legion with nothing more than your thoughts?" Seam shoved Hosp's face to the side. "You worship bound gods, nightmares who serve only me."

"Pl... please. Mercy...High King." Hosp's words shook from his bloody mouth. "I will serve you fully."

Seam growled at the request. "No. There will be no mercy. After all, Hosp, we both realize that Candor in its new unity will not tolerate *sedition*. But you are right, Hosp." Hosp's bloodied face broke with a pinprick of hope as he stared at Seam, his life hanging in the balance. Seam smiled, his eyes like graves. "*You will serve me fully, Hosp. You will do exactly as I say from now on. Welcome to my legion.*"

Hosp screamed as he felt his consciousness being ripped from him, the thundering force somehow being channeled from Seam's extended hand. The darkness edged around his vision before finally caving in over him as everything went mute and disappeared.

Abtren quietly watched from a safe distance as Seam dispatched Hosp's consciousness, surrounded by his new multitude of soldiers. Never in her eternity of existence did she feel so powerless. Arakiel and Nyx slowly exited the transport, their eyes full of scorn. Nyx was the first to speak, baring a haggard mouth full of fangs.

"**Your plan has failed us**, *dear sister.*" Nyx's face flowed from her human disguise into her true, hawk-faced form, her full eyes filled to the brim with midnight. The hawk beast lumbered over to the closest fallen body. In one swift motion, she plunged her beak, the sound of ribs cracking through the desert wind. She stood over him, lapping up the crimson drink that she most treasured. Arakiel, wearing the face of a lion did the same without a word, tearing through the body of another fallen soldier to feed, and Abtren stood watching her kin feast.

Refreshed, Nyx stood, her hawkish face fading but her eyes remaining the color of dead stars. She then turned on her brother,

her voice no less threatening. "**And you, *mighty* brother. You too have failed us.**"

Arakiel stood, his face again that of a warrior as he cut his red eyes at her. His hand struck Nyx, sending her to the desert floor. "I will not hear such talks from you, Nyx. Not to the one who so clearly clamors for the High King's favor."

Nyx screeched at him, "I mean to live, Arakiel! For too long have I been sapped to the dregs. *I will not fall back to that again, brother.* If I have to garner the favor of him, I will, so long as I get my food. I do not see the point of challenging someone you cannot defeat."

Arakiel stood, towering over her, threatening to fall over her in one sudden, swift motion. "*How dare you. I would push you to the darkest ends…*"

Nyx interrupted, spitting her words at him, "Except you can't, mighty Serub. You are *bound*. You can't lead us anywhere. *Not anymore.*"

Arakiel growled with rage and threw up his iron staff, but Abtren cut him off. "ENOUGH." Her eyes filled with a collage of colors and her figure shone like the sun, full of terrible beauty. "Fighting between ourselves will get us nowhere."

Nyx laughed and slanted her horrible eyes toward her fair sister. "So what would you suggest, *Abtren?* Find another worshiper to contest the High King?" She stood up and put her face an inch away from her sister's. "In case you haven't noticed, Candor has changed. Not many worship the Old Ones anymore. The smell of this place, the stink of those worshiping…"

"Don't say his name." Abtren cut her off, her eyes raging with fire. "You think I don't see that, Nyx?" She glanced over to Seam. "Hosp is gone. Seam has learned how to *push*, mimicking even your power, Arakiel."

Arakiel stood, his face a chiseled scowl, shaking his head with disbelief. Abtren looked at Nyx and Arakiel, her beautiful face full of fear. There was only one answer left for them.

"Only Bastion and Isphet remain." She cut her eyes to Arakiel. "You say that Bastion is in Legion's Teeth?"

Arakiel nodded, the scowl growing with each second. Abtren continued, "We must get Seam to free Bastion, but you must tell us, Arakiel. Where did they put Isphet?"

Arakiel shook his head with rage, his voice rumbling like an earthquake. "**We will not release Isphet. We strove too hard to keep him checked.**"

Nyx shoved her brother with all her might. "You are useless! What option do we have!? Your leadership has left us bound to this sniveling king." She cut her eyes at Abtren and back to Arakiel. "Abtren's right, Isphet is our only way to break this enslavement. He has grown in power, even as he has been locked in his mirror. *He has found something.* We must get Seam to unleash him as soon as Bastion is freed."

Arakiel growled and paced around his sisters like a panther. "Have you forgotten, dear sisters, what Isphet will do to you? He does not care about power, control, or security! He does not care about empire or might! Have you forgotten that it was he who deceived us to go back to Aether in the first place? To collaborate with the betrayer and seek to overthrow…"

Abtren screamed, "Don't say his name!"

"**Aleph!**" Arakiel screamed. "I will not let you forget his name. Isphet brought us all back to *him.* Even if Isphet does free us from Seam, what then? Would you have us go from one slave master to another? *You have not thought about this.* Seam is mortal. His body and soul will fail in time. No mortal can exist forever on this plane. It might be years, but once his body fails him, we will be free. Free to rule Candor again. Free from both Isphet and Aleph."

Abtren and Nyx writhed under the name and bared their fangs at their brother. Arakiel's countenance was like a storm, and the horizon rumbled with black clouds, masking his voice from Seam's earshot. "**We will free Bastion, and we will wait. Seam will fall in time, and then…then we will be free. Do not mention Isphet to me again.**"

Arakiel left his sisters standing in the desert, retreating to the titan as thunderclouds rumbled on the desert's horizon.

CHAPTER FOURTEEN

Nameless panted, gasping for air as he rowed with the other forgotten souls below the deck of *The Hunt*. Misery, pain, and the whip were his only companions in the shadows of that hold. The reek of the place was colossal. Hundreds of crude, dust-formed bodies were chained together in neat order to fill each narrow bench. The rows of ever-moving, never-resting oarsmen moaned through the endless night. There was no stopping, no breaks, and no reprieve. Nameless' back and hands ached with exhaustion, not having stopped his labor since being chained. Time had no meaning below the deck of the cursed vessel, for moments felt like both seconds and eons, as if the entire universe was caught in the rhythm of the oars slapping the dark water.

Desperate, Nameless threw his eyes to his brothers and sisters in chains, seeking some glimmer of hope, some thread of connection, but none gave him notice. In the darkness, he could barely see them, even the prisoner next to him somehow felt distant, like a shadow on his periphery.

What little he could see were his fingers grasped on the oar and the yellow, horrible eyes of Rank who patrolled through the hold, whipping any who dared to pause. There was something strange about his hands. Nameless glanced, searching for Rank's eyes, but he was gone. He let go of the oar and held his hands mere inches from his eyes. His flesh, if you could call it that, felt crude, worn, and dry. *Crumbling.* The word filled Nameless' mind as he realized his body was the consistency of cracked clay. The powerful substance Rank and File put on him gave him a solid form, but it was horribly flawed and broken.

Pain threw across his back, and Nameless felt sharp talons gore his back. He screamed and his hands flew out for the oars.

"Take your hands off again, runt, and I'll take out an eye. *Make you look like Master File.* I'll let you in on a litt'l secret. You don't need 'em peepers to row."

Rank leaned down and laughed over Nameless, his breath smelling like a shallow grave. "You looking for answers here in the dark, fresh catch? You'll find none here. *There are none to be had.* The only way you'll ever be free from us is if you row. So ROW!"

The crack of the whip sent Nameless into a frenzy of rowing, causing Rank to cackle, his yellow eyes glowing like embers in the darkness. "That's more like it, Nameless. You can keep that eye, for now."

Nameless thought about his situation, trying desperately to orient himself in his current hell. A horrible cloud of darkness fell over him as he felt completely trapped in the gloom.

Whatever debt I have to pay is too great. You will never be free. The thoughts raced through his mind and Nameless knew that they were true. The darkness, the stench of defecation and never-ending labor, the gnawing pain within his gut told him there was little hope of any change. So Nameless grew numb, conceding to the rhythm of the oars, and his mind disengaged and dimmed. He had almost given in to the dark completely when *The Hunt's* hull shuddered with a thunderous crash.

File screamed from above, cursing. "RANK! Get up here now!" The yellow eyes of the whip bearer darted through the darkness as Rank threw the hatch back violently.

"What was that!? What was that!?"

Nameless blinked, his hands screaming as he lifted them off the splintered oar. He ran his hand on his face as another ear-splitting shudder ran through the ship, the timber moaning under strain.

A small trinket bounced on Nameless' chest and he glanced down at it. The small rune was etched in the metal, just like the memory in the periphery of his mind. There was something special about the bauble he wore, as Master File had called it, but the significance was entirely lost. All he knew is that whatever it was that hung on his neck, it had caused both of his Masters to appear fearful, if even for only an instant.

Rank and File cursed above the deck, exchanging harried commands to one another.

"Run aground? How in all the hells could we run aground! In the Sea of Souls?"

Rank quipped, trying to be reassuring, "We can shove off, can't we, File? Nothing stopping us from shoving off, is there?"

"GET DOWN THERE!" File hollered, his voice thundering over the hold's hatch. "Get down there, now, and shove us off this rock!"

There was that, at least. Nameless knew that there was something in this world that the Masters feared. He had seen it when they had laid their terrible eyes on his amulet. He could hear it in their voices now. The Masters of *The Hunt* were afraid. There was something that they feared here in the dark waters. If that were true, then there was something more *than this.* It was a revelation for Nameless, a sudden spark of hope within that dark place.

A hollow *thump* across *The Hunt's* bow announced that Rank had dropped off onto whatever object they had rammed. Through the splintered timbers, Nameless could hear the whip bearer moan as he pushed against the ship.

"HURRY, you dolt! We can't stay here! We've got to keep moving!"

Rank screamed back at File, "You think I don't know that, File?! I'm giving it all that I've got." Another more forceful THUMP knocked through the ship's hull, and Nameless felt the vessel bounce with new buoyancy.

He did it. We've shoved off. Nameless felt his heart sink. The rowing would begin again. The unexpected reprieve brought him much clarity, and his eyes filled with tears at the thought of losing his new revelation to the monotony of rowing.

They fear something. Don't forget. They fear something that is here.

The hatch overhead flew back open and a dripping wet Rank slid through the door and gnashed his teeth as his eyes flew across the slaves.

"Row, you worms." Rank's whip cracked against the floor. "Like the Beast is upon you, ROW!"

Nameless flinched beneath the pain of his crumbling hands as he once again pushed and pulled the oar. The ship bobbed in the waves, and Nameless felt the ocean sliding below his feet. File kicked the hatch shut overhead and the crew was once again enveloped in darkness.

Nameless lost himself with each weary stroke in the shadowy depths of *The Hunt*. Despite those few moments of running aground, his existence was one continuous torment, crudely threaded together with the bite of the whip, as they churned the black water, their low moaning filling the hull.

After endless days of nothing but rowing, darkness and pain, something unexpected happened. The floor groaned beneath Nameless' feet. The boat began to pitch forward, and the timbers groaned under some unseen pressure. An explosive force slammed into the ship, nearly sending the vessel over on itself. The hull of the boat shook under a rhythmic constriction, and Nameless' mind filled with fear.

"RANK!" File's voice was laced with panic.

The one-eyed sailor's voice broke through the shadows as the hatch flew open overhead. The ruined face spoke in a shrill whisper, "Rank. *He* is here. Hurry now!"

The boards of the hull creaked as if the visitor File announced could squeeze around the entire vessel. The boards moaned and popped under what Nameless could only imagine was a massive weight. Whatever was doing this was huge, and Nameless stood, placing his hands over the coarse beams of the hull. In the dark, his fingers felt timber akin to a bow fully drawn, and he knew that in any instant the only home he knew in this cursed world would come crumbling down on top of him. The sea would gladly swallow him once again.

Rank sprinted toward the hatch, forgetting to shut it behind him. Nameless' eyes adjusted to the murky green light that poured from above, penetrating the darkness. As his eyes adjusted, he listened, trying to decipher what had called his captors to attention.

He. It was a person of some sort, but who? A titanic voice bellowed out like a thunderclap, shaking the cabin, and Nameless had his question answered.

"**Rank and File,**" the beast growled showcasing no goodwill in its voice. "**You half-blood crossbreeds have been left to your own devices for long enough. It is time you make good on your oaths.**"

Rank blubbered, his sobs filling the silence between the beast's monstrous words. File spoke, his voice the sound of a cockroach. "Magnificent one, only name your price and it is yours."

Fear swallowed Nameless like a cloud of fog with the words. "**I long to feed.**" The voice; Nameless had heard the voice before. Images flashed in his mind of the moment before Rank and File pulled him from the depths. *What had he seen in the depths?* His mind scrambled for the answer as if recalling a distant dream. *A colossal serpent.* Piercing memories of the worm flashed in his mind. Rows of fangs and piercing, glowing eyes. The thought of the monster made him shake, fear constricting around him tighter than the chains that locked him to the oar. Down in the depths that thing had circled him, coiling around him in the dark, filling the void with questions. "**Who are you?**"

Nameless heard Rank and File squabble overhead, bickering to decide an appropriate sacrifice. "I will bring you our strongest oarsman," stammered Rank.

File shot out, enraged. "No! That one is nearly wasted. Don't insult the Magnificent One with that garbage," spat Rank. "Bring him out someone fresh."

The two continued to bicker and curse until the serpent's voice rattled the ship, booming over the sea. "**SILENCE. Bring me what is mine.**"

The sound of Rank's feet thumped overhead as he approached the chamber below. Nameless squinted in the darkness attempting to make out the faces of the fellow captives. Their faces lay blank like a slate; no fear or anxiety could be found. Each and every slave sat in a stupor that did not reflect the thundering panic within Nameless own chest. Perhaps they prayed to be sacrificed, allowing their torture to finally draw to a close.

As Rank's footsteps got closer, Nameless gripped his oar and pulled with all his strength. His voice rang over all of the others, "ROW!"

The small ship creaked as his paddle splashed, slicing through the black waters. Nameless called again, unrelenting as Rank came down through the open hatch and locked his horrid, puss-colored eyes onto him. "I said row. ROW!"

The crumbling shell of a man sitting next to Nameless took hold of the long oar and joined in, rowing in unison with each stroke Nameless made. The other captives joined in, each pressing at their oar, pushing the boat forward.

Rank dropped into the cramped room and his whip flashed from side to side, ripping into his drivers' backs. Nameless screamed as the gnarled whip dug into his flesh, but the punishment only made the oarsmen rally with newfound strength. They were rowing with a frenzied pace as Rank filled the hold with cursing. Each crack of his whip only sent the crew into a more tumultuous pace.

A massive blow slammed across the ship and nearly rolled it on its side. Another shot to the ship's hull sent Rank tumbling into the wooden wall, yelping as he smashed his hollow face against its timbers. Rank's yellow eyes cut to Nameless as he bore his dagger teeth and hissed. *"You! I know it was you!"*

As Rank lunged for Nameless, another deafening collision rocked the ship, knocking him back as the beast outside bellowed. **"I WILL CRUSH YOU ALL. YOU CANNOT HIDE!"**

Nameless plunged his oar deep within the murky waters and fought to push harder with each stroke. *Just keep rowing!* He threw himself into each stroke, but soon Rank was on top of him, his claws ripping into him, clamoring for the locks on his ankles and wrists.

Rank's claws reached for Nameless' arms and legs, unlocking his shackles before he was jolted into the air by another cascading blow from the outside, the ship nearly buckling from the force. Nameless was free from his chains but was helpless against Rank, who pinned him down before shouting out. "I have your sacrifice, mighty one!"

The other slaves continued to row, but the water tossing the boat from side to side was lost to the uneasy suspension of the serpent's coils that gripped around the vessel, causing the ancient timbers to creak and groan under the pressure.

Rank's jagged fingers plunged into Nameless' flesh as he rushed him above deck, only to face the colossal horror above. The beast towered over the ship as the stench of hot death filled the open air. Nameless stooped to his knees, covering his mouth, desperate to relieve himself from the reeking smell. Despite the noxious odor, he was completely absorbed in the creature's magnificence. Scales that had looked as black as midnight in the dark waters gleaned crimson in the open air, the color of blood covering the beast like a royal cloak. Burning yellow eyes pierced him, hammering Nameless down to the floorboards of the deck. The beast's massive jowls moved, revealing a cavernous maw of fangs, a bed of knives that could skewer a city.

"Fresh catch, I see." The beast's eyes flitted back to Rank and File as its long black tongue flitted out in the air. "**His essence is strong. Intact.**"

"Yes...my lord. Freshest one on *The Hunt*. Hasn't yet begun to fade. We've been saving him for you."

The beast growled and flashed his yellow eyes toward File. "**Lies. Don't dare lie to me, File. I can see them before they leave your mouth.**"

The serpent's mouth opened wide and a flow of hot, frothing saliva rolled out. The spew hit the deck and burned through the wood, causing a fog of smoke to fill the air.

"**You are much more than a meal to me, little one. You are the proof that my cursed kin still have some worth after all. Now** that most of them are free, I had expected much more, but *you*...you are the first that they have sent to me in a very long time. What was your name on the other side? My sisters...they won't tell me."

Nameless' heart slowly fell from his mouth and he whispered the only answer he knew. "I don't remember."

The dragon roared with laughter and flashed a cruel smile over the black chopping waters of the sea. **"Of course you don't, silly for me to forget how this works."** The beast cocked his head and muttered, *"No matter, you'll do just the same."*

The monster drew close to Nameless and inspected him again. He blew a puff of hot air from his nostrils as he jerked back. **"Your charm is intriguing. I've never noticed an essence carrying any symbol before."** Nameless noticed a moment of hesitation cross the dragon's face, as if he were pondering something grave. It spoke, its voice booming over the expanse, **"I am Lord of this Realm and soon you will feed my power."**

The beast opened his monstrous jaws, revealing ten rows of dagger teeth lining the way to his cavernous throat. Trails of golden saliva dripped from the man-sized fangs. A crimson light swelled from the serpent's belly and pushed from its mouth. The light moved like a vapor and swept toward Nameless.

Rank and File retreated from the ship's deck as the radiant haze covered their vessel. Nameless was locked in place as the biting smog enveloped him. The crimson glow continued to swell into a blinding eclipse of red. The color of blood filled Nameless' vision as an overwhelming pain crept over his skin. The feeling of thousands of stinging insects covered every inch of his being. Each tiny bite gave way to the intense pressure of exploding boils as Nameless crumpled to his knees beneath the searing agony.

The pain of the non-stop rowing and Rank's whip held no comparison to the terror enveloping every inch of Nameless' body. He opened his mouth to scream but no sound escaped. Instead, the glowing nightmare began to rip at the roof of his mouth, sending bolts of white-hot pain to the top of his skull.

"Enjoy the pain *my essence*. This is the most enjoyable part." The leviathan's voice swallowed Nameless and shook him from inside. **"You belong to me now."**

The vibrant crimson light began to fade to black, but the pain continued to swell and Nameless felt his body separate cell by cell. Nameless could feel himself being pulled asunder like a tattered rug being pulled apart one string at a time. The crimson light burned like a white-hot flame, consuming him as the dragon breathed him in.

Then, a small drop of relief, followed by another splashed against Nameless. The serpent growled as the small drops of rain grew into a downpour that suddenly rushed against Nameless, washing his skin of the boils devouring him. A tempest rose over the black waters and waves smashed against *The Hunt*, sending Nameless reeling to the ship's side.

"No!" the beast snapped. "Impossible."

The waves billowed and the rain intensified, splashing over Nameless who fought to open his eyes. He grasped the ship's hull as wave after wave assaulted *The Hunt*. The dragon whipped back and forth and coiled around the ship, trying to hold it in place, but the waves continued to grow, rising and falling like liquid mountains. Lightning flashed over the horizon with bolts striking down around the ship.

The serpent fought to contain his prize as a bolt of electricity snapped across the waters and shattered over his scales. The beast let out a roar before diving beneath the black waters, escaping the growing storm. The ship continued to toss and turn in the storm before striking something solid. The boat let out a CRACK as its hull surrendered to the onslaught and buckled, snapping from bow to stern.

Nameless lost hold of the boat and slipped into the tumbling rip tide. He kept his eyes closed as he rolled head over toe and side to side. He did not fight to right himself as the waters roared around him. He was as helpless fighting the ocean as he was standing up to the dragon just moments earlier. Soon the flurry subsided and Nameless felt himself being carried on a swift current. The ocean's waves gave way to an intentional pulling as if he were caught in the flow of a river.

Time slipped by without notice as the waters dutifully carried Nameless along before he felt himself washed onto something soft, yet solid. The waters receded and Nameless reached down, grasping the ground between his fingers. The wet sand pressed between his fingers and toes as he scrambled to his feet. He opened his eyes wide, realizing that the murky, green light and black waters had all but disappeared.

I'm somewhere else.

An empty shore of porcelain-white sand stretched out before him with a bright, white light emanating from the horizon. Nameless stood to his feet and stumbled toward the empty horizon, trying to find some landmark to help gather his bearings. The beach inexplicably stretched in all directions, a desert of white sand. Nameless dropped his head and let out a sigh. First, he was trapped in a black abyss beneath the waters and now he was just as trapped amidst an endless ocean of sand.

Nameless shook his head and began walking, turning to his left, strolling across the beach. He tried to shield his eyes from the bright light pressing in over the horizon. After a few minutes, he noticed a small black dot on the horizon that continued to grow with each step. *What is that?* Nameless fought his sluggish limbs and took off into a sprint toward the small speck. With each step, it became apparent that the black dot was a person, a woman. The sand underfoot fought any progress Nameless hoped to make, but he pressed on before standing face-to-face with a beautiful young woman wrapped in a flowing gown.

The woman was gorgeous, with smooth olive-colored skin and blonde hair cascading over her shoulders. Her eyes were gentle and compassionate as Nameless approached. Her lips pressed into a broad smile and she opened her arms.

Nameless stopped and took a step back, waiting for some terrible surprise and more pain. The woman was so familiar and so inviting, but after surviving his ordeal, Nameless would welcome no more violent surprises.

The distance between the two held until the woman took a soft step forward and tilted her head to the side as she offered her hand.

"Do you not know me?" Her words were as soft as silk and as comforting as a summer breeze. Nameless shook his head and turned his shoulder to the woman, sheltering himself from her advance. "I have waited so long to see you."

Nameless took a step back and examined the young face smiling back at him. It was familiar and welcoming yet foreign at the same time. Her eyes glistened with tears as she spoke. "Kull, it is me. Rose. I'm your mother."

CHAPTER FIFTEEN

The bloodstained hills of Lotte cried out behind Grift and Rot as they sprinted into Henshaw. As Seam's forces slowly poured into the border town, Grift decided that it was time to go down fighting. His eyes locked on the armored vehicles forming a perimeter at the northern border of Henshaw and his finger lay heavy on the trigger of his assault rifle. His battle instincts moved him forward as Rot lumbered next to him, baring fangs and letting out a steady growl like rolling thunder. Grift could feel hot, damp blood clinging to his shirt. *Rose's blood.* It unhinged him and he felt his heart sinking into a black chasm, but he refused to let that happen. These men, *this Dominion,* had robbed him of everything and he would not let grief slow him.

No more. There would be no more running. There would be no mercy. Grift would repay them for all the death he had suffered; the death of a son, a wife, and even of his own soul. Grift's vision locked in on the men clad in black and gold, but his focus was interrupted as Adley sprinted toward him, panting from the town's edge.

"*Stop!* There are too many of them, Grift!"

Adley's call for caution fell on deaf ears as Grift pressed forward. Adley snagged his sleeve and tried to pull him off course, but Grift yanked himself free. "Take your own advice, Adley. I'm not running."

"Stop!" Adley shouted. Her face burned with hot anger, but her eyes were wide with fear. She hammered a hard fist on his shoulder, her voice enraged. *"You can't die like this."*

Grift stopped for a moment and pointed a finger toward the eastern skyline. "My son died fighting, Adley. I plan to do the same. Seam and all his forces be damned."

Adley grabbed his arm again, wrenching him to look her in the eye. The words fired out from her mouth like bullets. "He fought to free you. So you could KEEP FIGHTING. Don't throw your life away. *You have more to do*. Kull would not want this."

Grift shoved her away and screamed, his face painted with fury. "All I had to fight for just died. She died on that hill." Grift spat as he pointed to the wreckage of the burning transport. He ran his hands through his hair and cursed. "Now you go. You run."

Adley opened her mouth to speak as an eruption tore through the city. A Dominion rook careened around a narrow corner of a red brick building and rocketed toward their position. "Hide!" screamed Grift as he shoved Adley through the open door of a nearby abandoned home. Grift and Rot slipped around the corner as a maelstrom of hot lead licked at their heels. Dirt and rocks leapt in the air as the gunner refused to release the trigger.

Grift's emotions vanished as his mind shifted into survival mode. He quickly scanned the small alleyway on the side of the home as he heard the rook roar toward them. He whistled and pointed at a pile of debris leaning against the hovel, his eyes flicking up to the roofline. Rot read the command and leapt over the rubble, using it as a stepping stone path that led up to the roof. Grift nodded, his mind running over the plan he was making up as he went along. He continued circling the building, careful to listen to the vibrations of the rook's engine. He could only estimate where the war machine was. Carefully, he held a small shaving mirror out of the doorway.

As if triggering a trap, the mirror released another firestorm. The rook's mini-gun roared, releasing a torrent of bullets that barely missed Grift as they ripped through the outer wall. He put his back to the rough brick wall of the building and cursed. *Well, you know where it is*. Picking up a worn brick, he glanced out up over the broken window that faced the other side of the alley, hidden from the rook's guns. Grift chucked the brick out the doorway, causing the gunner to react. As the Dominion soldier opened fire, Grift hunkered down and glanced through the broken window, reading the position of the war machine. The Dominion hovercraft stopped firing and strafed between the alleyways, watching for Grift's escape. He jumped into a sprint, kicking in the back door of the home where he had thrown Adley for cover. He ran toward the front of the building, calling out for her.

"Stay down, Adley. This will be over soon." She was huddled in a corner behind an overturned table, loading her pistol. The rook swept by the window as it anticipated him to try again for the building's corner. Grift stepped out of the open front door and unloaded his rifle's magazine into the less armored rear compartment of the rook. Sparks danced into the air, flying from the machine as its engine sputtered. The hovercraft reeled askew before spinning and smashing into the ground. The vehicle's crash kicked up a cloud of dirt that filled the street. Shortly after its violent landing, the cockpit flew open. When Grift heard the Dominion gunner exit, he let out a whistle. Before the pilot could square his shoulders and aim, Rot was already on top of him, latching onto him with his massive jaws. The soldier didn't even have a chance to scream before it was all over.

"Good boy," called Grift. "Now come on."

The screaming engines of oncoming rooks echoed in the streets as the warrior and his dog slipped back into the house. Adley stood by the back door and spoke, her voice grave. "We have to get somewhere more secure, Grift."

"I already told you I'm not running," said Grift as he glanced out the open door, his eyes wide at the sound of more Dominion forces flowing into Henshaw.

"It's too late for that now, but we need to at least take a more defensive position and fight as long as possible." Adley chambered a round in her pistol. "Let's make for the town hall. It's the most fortified building in Henshaw."

Grift realized that Adley was right. Of the border towns of Lotte, Henshaw's town hall was set apart in its appearance. Five stories tall and covered by a tall brick wall, it resembled a small fortress. Adley spoke, confident in the decision. "We have a weapons cache there."

Grift nodded. It was as good a plan as any. Adley peered down the alleyway running behind the small house. A large abandoned factory hid them from the Dominion forces that continued to crest down the valley from the north. Adley brought up her datalink, which projected a map of Henshaw's buildings. Red dots indicated the movements of Dominion forces.

"How did you manage that?" Grift was impressed that the resistance had established scanners in the city. Adley pointed to a narrow, windy street that stretched to a small courtyard adjacent to the town hall.

"No time to explain, Grift. Let's go!" Adley said as she sprinted into the alley. Grift followed close on her heels with Rot rambling by their sides. There were no sirens or voices barking over loud speakers. The only sound the Dominion made was the gunfire erupting on the northern outskirt of the town. The tempest that was swelling in Grift's chest exploded as white-hot fury flew over his skin and flushed every inch of his body. The Dominion was not content to take his son or his wife. They would never stop. They would gorge themselves again, and they were bent on creating another field of carnage in Henshaw.

Screams rang out as citizens began to flood the streets and run for cover, but a new noise joined the din. Engines were rumbling as armored transports and rooks circled the town, moving closer to Grift and Adley's position.

The sound bounced off the alley walls, making it difficult to pinpoint, but at least four rooks were tearing their way straight through the streets, and they were coming fast. Adley brought up her datalink, staring as red dots rushed toward their position.

"Adley!" Grift screamed, pulling her attention off the screen. "We have to split up. They want me, not you. We can flank them!"

The two slowed as they approached the small courtyard between the factory warehouse sheltering them and the town hall. "No way, Grift. This pistol won't do anything for me now."

Grift glanced out across the small plaza. Everything was clear for the moment, so he nodded for them to run for the courtyard.

Grift took point and he rushed through the iron gate in the brick border wall of the government building. Rot and Adley followed him as he splintered the frame of the thick door of the town hall, forcing his way into the old government building. The sound of the rooks was unmistakable. High-pitched acceleration echoed off the tight corridors of Henshaw's narrow roads. Grift knew the truth in an instant; they had been spotted and now they were charging. As Adley and Rot ducked into the threshold, another blistering round of machine gun fire erupted, decimating the red brick wall of the town hall.

"Upstairs!" Grift yelled. "Get as close to the center of the structure as possible!"

Adley shook her head. "The cache is down the hall, ground floor! There is a weapon that I need. We can't leave it."

"No time," ordered Grift. "Come on." A harrowing explosion hit the building, and Adley followed as the structure shook.

The two sprinted down the wide hallway of the aged building and sliced around a corner leading to an old wooden staircase. As Grift ran up the creaking risers, Adley pushed further down the hallway. Another explosion went off, accompanied by shattering glass and splintering boards. The brick retaining wall around the complex was destroyed. With the wall down, the rooks outside unhinged their restraint and unleashed a torrent of bullets in the front of the town hall. Grift turned around, realizing that Adley had not followed.

"Adley!" screamed Grift. There was no response, causing Grift's heart to race. "Adley!" Again, no answer, just the earsplitting hammering of destruction below.

Aleph, no. Grift felt like his mind might snap as he screamed at the top of his lungs and punched the old plaster wall in front of him. *She can't be...* The wall cracked under his rage. Again and again he drove his fists through the wall as the roar of the bullets continued below him. As long as they fired, he could not get to her. The gunfire continued and the building creaked, shifted, and moaned under the assault until a fireball rocked the structure's foundation and sent Grift reeling into a corner of the stairwell.

Grift jumped to his feet and crested the second story landing, kicking a door in and running to a corner window. He popped his head around the window frame in time to see the red tail of a rocket flying from one of the rooks into the foyer below. The explosion was even more potent than the one before, and the floorboards beneath Grift's feet sagged after the force of the second blast.

This place won't hold for long, thought Grift as he checked his rifle's magazine. *So much for a more secure location.*

He swept by the window and leveled his rifle on the nearest rook, ripping off ten rounds as he flashed past the opening. The four rooks continued to cover the building in a blanket of lead as two armored transports pulled up behind the position. Grift took five more shots on the closest rook, but they seemed unfazed to his counter attack.

The wall between Grift and the rooks began to sag as the weight-bearing wall beneath him was chewed up by the fifty-caliber chain gun fire. Grift pressed into the window again and held down the trigger, sweeping across one of the armored transports and a nearby rook. The rook ceased its machine gun fired and slid back as its rear-mounted cannon rose to aim at the second story.

A rocket roared into sight and exploded into the rook. The black hovercraft erupted into a titanic fireball of black metal and red flame. The force of the blast sent the machine reeling, crashing into the windshield of the armored carrier positioned behind it. Both went up in flames, engulfing the Dominion forces within the transport in a furnace of twisted metal.

"Adley!" Grift yelled out.

The attack seemed to stun the Dominion forces outside as the three remaining rooks ceased fire. The sound of footsteps ricocheted up the stairwell as Adley called out for Grift. "Third floor!"

Grift turned for the stairwell, relief filling his heart. As he turned, the wall behind him erupted. Scattered bricks, boards, and fire surrounded him as he slammed into an inner brick wall. Grift's ears rang with an unbearable electric buzz and his vision swept in and out. A black ring of darkness shaded his sight, threatening to swallow him. He blinked, his breath bound in his chest as the darkness grew. As the shadows rolled in like the sea, a familiar face flashed before him: Rose. Her face was beautiful, free of pain. Grift tried to reach for her but his vision would not stop sliding in and out focus.

As his consciousness kicked back in, Grift barely had time to question the flashes of mirage he saw. He tried to lift his head, but a dull pain weighed on his entire body like an iron anchor, making every motion brutally difficult. He reached out and fought to drag himself toward the door leading to the stairs. He pulled himself over broken glass and jagged wood as he fought to follow Adley. She flashed into the room with a rocket launcher slung over her shoulder and a rifle strapped to her back. She hoisted him from underneath his shoulder, jerking him up toward the stairs.

"Come on, Grift. You've got to help me out a little. Come on, you can do this!" Adley shouted as she pulled. Rot trailed behind her, whining, the stub of what had once been his tail hunkered down with worry. Adley pushed the dog away from Grift and realized that the machine gun fire had stopped. She set Grift down and glanced through one of the second story windows. A long brigade of Dominion troops was lining up, setting to storm into the town hall. *Aleph above.* Her mind filled with fear, but she did not hesitate to rip the pin from one of the grenades she pulled from the cache. She lobbed it toward the marching soldiers. As the grenade landed with a thud, Adley reached down and pulled Grift up again, managing to maneuver him up into the stairwell. The blast of the grenade went off as soon as they had taken their first step on the stairs.

"Can you move, Grift?" Adley's voice was stern and laced with fear as she helped him slowly up the stairs.

"Yeah," Grift said with his eyes pinched shut. He nodded his head. "Yeah, I think so."

Grift shook his head with his eyes still closed tight as he grasped at his head. "Ears won't stop ringing."

Adley sat him down and reached into her satchel. She fished out a syringe that she loaded and plunged into Grift's leg. The drug flashed through Grift's veins like a cold bolt of lightning, sweeping away the darkness from his vision and dulling the pain pressing on his joints.

Adley broke the silence and handed Grift a new rifle. "Come on. We need to get to the top floor. We don't have much time."

"We'll be sitting ducks up there, Adley," Grift countered.

"You'll see."

Grift fought his wobbling legs and stumbled up the stairs behind her. He knew he had no choice. With each Dominion strike, the stairs shook under their feet, threatening to cave in. Grift fought to focus, following Adley as they hurried up the stairs.

"We need to get to the fifth floor," Adley called as they sprinted. "If I go down, don't stop. On the top of the building you will see a console. It is Predecessor make."

Grift blinked as he lumbered behind her. "Predecessor?" *Aleph above.* "What is it?" Everything in Candor with a few minor exceptions came from the technology left by the Predecessors. Railcars, rooks, and the datalinks all had their origin in this ancient technology. If what Adley was telling him was true, then there could be no limits to what rested on the fifth floor.

Adley gave Grift a knowing look. "Ewing. Ever since you told him about the true nature of Seam's power he sent out an all call to his network of associates." A thunderous blast hit the building, forcing Adley and Grift to pause in their ascent. It felt as if the building was swaying beneath them, and Grift kneeled down on the steps as Rot yelped at the echo of the blast. The building shook and mercifully settled. Adley continued, "One of his contacts said that he had discovered something from the Predecessors, a weapon of tremendous power. Found it deep in a mineshaft in Lotte."

Grift reached out and grabbed Adley's arm, forcing her to stop climbing. "What does it do, Adley?"

She recoiled for a moment, her face determined. "It's going to save us, Grift. We're out of options now."

Grift said nothing, but followed her as she ran up the final staircase. On the top floor, there, as she had described, was the console. Next to it, connected by a long, thick wire was a canister. Adley approached the canister when her datalink chirped with life.

"Adley? Adley—status report now!" The gruff voice bellowing on the other end of the line was unmistakable. Ewing roared again over the datalink as the sound of mortars fell all around them. With each shot, Grift could feel the building sway as if one more shot would topple the entire structure.

"Grift." Adley looked at him and pointed. "Get yourself on here with Rot now." She pointed to a small metal platform attached to the base of the console. Adley slung her pack onto the ground and fished out a small black box as Grift and Rot made their way to the platform. Her fingers fumbled at the combination lock on its face before popping the small safe open. She pulled out a key that looked like a computer chip and slid it into the console, causing it to blink on with power.

Adley flicked a switch and the console whirled with life, displaying images and runes from a bygone age. A few seconds went by and Adley pressed down on one of the runes on the console's screen. Instantly, a large, translucent shield bubbled over them all, causing Rot to pant in full panic. Grift's eyes opened wide.

"What are you doing, Adley? What's happening?" Ewing's anger was still resonating over the open datalink channel when Adley whispered to him, "We are going to live to fight another day."

She slammed her thumb onto a green rune before her. The canister on the outside of the transparent purple shield opened and a smaller cylinder rose up out of the device. Inside the device Grift could see what looked like small black beads or pearls lined in neat little rows within the smallest canister. Grift quickly counted fifteen. Adley threw her hands down on the small screen behind the bubble shield and the black pearls were dispensed from the host, dropping out onto the ground, clanking like small balls of iron.

A screen enveloped the shield, and Grift realized he was seeing a heat map of Henshaw. Adley threw up her hands and gestured, marking the three remaining rooks, the transport, and the Dominion troops that were quickly surrounding the building. The figures became enveloped in red, and the projected screen flashed with a box filled with the runic language. Despite not being able to read the characters, Grift knew that Adley was being asked for confirmation. She flicked her wrists onto the affirmative, and Grift stood with his mouth agape.

The metallic spheres shot out from the floor and seared through the walls of the structure in a flash. Grift watched the screen. The spheres were colored in a yellow pattern over the display. They flew around the building like hornets protecting their nest before coming into formation, one behind the other. The projectiles arched up high in the sky at an uncalculated speed before swooping down to tear through the marching soldiers, ripping through them like dominoes. Grift stared blankly as he saw thirty soldiers go down in seconds, their heat signatures slowly beginning to cool on the screen.

The three rooks veered back, hammering down on their thrusters to back away from the flying weapons that were pitching back up into the air for another pass. On the screen, each of the rooks took shots at the formation of pearls flying through the air, before unleashing their taze nets in quick succession. The nets hit and covered them, binding the formation, causing them to fall to the ground. The black pearls split, and then split again. What had once been fifteen projectiles were now sixty smaller but no less deadly weapons. The mass tore through the nets that had briefly bound them and then congealed into one huge sphere. The sphere rocketed toward the first rook like a boulder, crushing the war machine.

Grift glanced at Adley and whispered, "Did you know that it could do this?"

Adley said nothing and crossed her arms, engrossed in the devastating display. The sphere that had crushed the rook divided in mid-air into two and flew at the two remaining rooks that were retreating. The Predecessors weapons ripped through them like a hot knife in butter, only to turn and slam through the last remaining Dominion transport.

Grift shook his head and swallowed as he realized that the Predecessor's weapon had leveled a small army in less than a minute. He knelt down, his face transfixed on the screen as the enemies Adley had painted with red on the display were now the mottled purple color of everything else. Adley brought up a menu and motioned her hands. The weapons fractured into the original denomination of fifteen and landed back within the canister. The lid shut, and the console powered off.

Speechless, Grift sat down on the platform, his hand resting on Rot's panting head. He had never seen anything like it in all his years of serving Lotte as guardsmen. Even the horrors of the Serubs had not showcased such an effective and powerful weapon. *Aleph above. This could turn the war. We might actually have a chance.*

Ewing's voice crackled over Adley's datalink again.

"Adley. Please come in, girl. Please."

Adley held her datalink to her face and responded. "We're here, Ewing."

"Aleph above, girl, what happened down there?" Grift looked at her, wondering what she would say. Her response surprised him.

"We've lost Henshaw, Ewing. We need to pull our forces into Preost. HQ has been compromised."

CHAPTER SIXTEEN

Willyn took her first step onto the dark, sandy floor of the arena. Grogan cities were known throughout all of Candor for their marvelous, sweeping amphitheaters. The glorious structures filled the entire Realm, serving as the nexus for all Grogan life, centers for both entertainment and justice. All disputes that could not be settled civilly between two parties were settled in the arena, often to the death. There were no courts in the Groganlands, with the exception of the Sar's.

Other Realms cringed at such practices, calling it barbarism, but to Willyn, the arena served as a symbol of peace and unity for her people, threatening those who could not make amends with their fellow brother or sister with the swift and public display of martial judgment. It kept her people strong and unified, which was more than she could say about the other Realms.

Legion's Teeth was no different from the other Grogan cities, other than the fact that its arena had been completely carved out from an open cave in the depths of the mountain range. Huge electric lights illuminated the large carved bowl of the stone colosseum. The entire city had poured into the gigantic subterranean chamber, and the crowd shook the mountain with its excitement.

As Willyn stepped further inside the sandy circle, the crowd erupted with cheers. The lights poured over her, enveloping her with a blinding intensity. All she wore was the light linen clothes Wael had provided her. The bright illumination forced her to shield her eyes. She tied her faux raven hair back and glanced at the arena's end.

Rander was there, wearing a pair of military pants, but otherwise shirtless. The Red leader's body was a testament to his prowess as a warrior. Long scars left their mark over mountains of muscle, and though the man was small in stature for a Grogan, he lacked no strength. He strutted into the arena and spoke, his boisterous voice causing the crowd of Grogans and Baggers to hush.

"Legion's Teeth. Today we fight to avenge the loss of Viga, my honorable guardsman." He pointed to Willyn and screamed, "The murderer stands before you, her own words accusing her of the crime."

A colossal wave of curses and insults flew through the air at Willyn, but her face remained stoic, as hard as flint.

"This would have been enough for me to kill her on the spot, but then this murderer threatened my own life and had the audacity to claim that she is the Sar." He spat onto the dirt floor. "Bagger scum. How dare you?" The crowd erupted with praise, and he turned to face them. "So, my brothers. My sisters. Today you will see us practice our ancient custom. Let this fraud prove her claims, and may Aleph have mercy on me if I am wrong."

The crowd began to chant Rander's name in unison, causing the whole dome to echo. He looked at Willyn and spoke, "Do you have any last words, *Sar?*"

Willyn lifted her head and spoke, her voice ringing out over the chanting crowd. "Grogans, I have traveled far and wide to get back to you. After Hagan...died, I knew that there would be many who would try to claim the Sardom from my family. Hospadda Gran, the snake of the Grogan council, poisoned my brother and effectively banished me from my homeland. My brother died in dishonor, but I have returned to avenge his death. You, the Reds, swear fealty to me. Now let me prove to you who I am."

A chorus of boos echoed from the arena walls as the crowd hissed with disapproval. Willyn looked out into the crowd and caught a glimpse of Bri's face. The giant sat solemnly with his head bowed, a look of concern painted on his face as he wrung his hands. Willyn took in a deep breath and locked her eyes on Rander.

A voice roared over the loudspeakers, silencing the dome. *May Aleph's justice be granted today.* A low pulse of sound buzzed over the loudspeaker, indicating that the fight would begin.

Focus, Willyn. Willyn continued to draw in deep breaths and could feel her heart slowing. *Focus on your mark.* She stalked forward and gauged Rander's reach. Though he was stout and built like an anvil, his arms were compact and his legs offered him no clear advantage other than sheer power.

Willyn bounced from side to side as she edged closer to Rander. He lumbered forward with his cold blue eyes focused her. Willyn had seen this face before, the cold brutality that falls on a person ready to take another's life. Rander charged toward her. He dipped his head as he attempted to tackle Willyn, but she was able to slip to her left and land a quick kick at Rander's knee. The blow was hardly enough to cause Rander to notice as he stumbled past her, catching himself before tumbling to the arena floor under his own weight.

He cursed as he pulled himself from the floor, grabbing a handful of sand. He spun on his heels and threw a fistful into Willyn's eyes. "Bagger witch," he shouted as he threw his knuckles into the bridge of Willyn's nose. The shot sent Willyn reeling and she fell back, landing on her elbows. A warm gush of blood flowed from her nose and she fought to see through the sand that was burning and scratching her eyes.

Rander lunged for her, but Willyn rolled to her right and scurried to her feet as she continued to swipe at her eyes. The sand was unbearable and her face welled with tears, trying to clear her vision. In the confusion she could feel him coming. Rander charged again, ready to pin Willyn and end the fight. As he pushed forward, Willyn dropped to the ground and shot her right foot into the air, connecting with Rander's chin. The force of the collision threw them both back in opposite directions. Willyn rolled back head over heels as Rander crumpled and fell on his back.

Willyn used the slight separation to wipe her eyes clean before popping back to her feet. Her nose continued to drip red, hot blood, soaking her linen shirt. Rander scrambled to his feet and took a wide swing. As Willyn sidestepped the blow, she grasped his left wrist and used her opposite arm to slam an elbow into the back of Rander's neck. She used the force of the shot to spin Rander to the ground, where she straddled over her foe and landed three punches to his face as she used her left arm to lock and close in on his throat.

A heavy elbow slammed into Willyn's side, colliding with her kidney. The blow knocked the breath from her, but she harnessed the pain to ratchet down on her foe, continuing to constrict his windpipe and hammer at his face with her free hand. Rander's massive hands grasped for Willyn, clamping around her waist and hurling her to the side. She tumbled through the dirt, landing face down in the middle of the arena. Her face had become an unrecognizable mixture of blood, sand, and bruises as she pushed herself back to her feet and spit blood and dirt from her lips.

Rander squared back up and wiped at his swollen cheek. "You can't win, you little piece of trash. I am going to crush you," he roared. The crowd erupted with cheers. The arena had grown to a feverish pitch over the scuffle. With each counter and every new blow, the din grew louder.

Willyn slowly backed her way to the arena wall as Rander stalked her. He had the look of a hungry dog as he mimicked her movements and mocked her retreat. As her back pressed against the concrete wall, a spark lit in Rander's eye. She had nowhere to run. A fist slammed into her stomach like a sledgehammer and another followed, crashing against her ear. The sound of the crowd was lost to a constant ringing as Willyn covered and blocked the next punch and slid to the side.

As Rander reared back for another heavy blow, Willyn sent a lightning quick kick to the side of his knee. A loud pop announced the disjointing of his kneecap and Willyn followed with another kick to the same leg. Rander buckled and stumbled to the ground, landing on the disabled leg. He screamed as Willyn stomped on the back of his broken joint. Willyn stepped back before leveling another heavy kick to the side of Rander's head.

The brute crumpled and wilted into a worthless husk. Rander panted and wheezed as Willyn scrambled to lock his arms behind his back. She wrenched at his arms and used all her weight to pin him into place as she shouted into his ear, careful to focus all her weight and strength on the broken joint of her enemy.

"Tell them who I am, Rander."

Rander spit and grunted his response. "Bagger trash."

Willyn whipped her head back and head-butted Rander in the back of his skull while tightening her grip on his arms. Rander's writhing stopped with the blow, but he puffed and grunted beneath Willyn's weight.

"Tell them who I am," she commanded. "NOW!"

Rander made one final push and wrenched himself free from Willyn, hurling her to the side. He fished into his pockets and drew out a blade. He took three lazy swipes while hobbling on one leg. Willyn buffeted the attempts, ripping the knife from Rander's grasp before plunging it into his one good leg.

Rander howled as he fell to the dirt and grasped at his new wound. Willyn locked one of his arms behind him while holding Rander's own knife to his throat.

"Tell them who I AM!" Willyn shouted as she pressed the blade to the side of Rander's neck.

"You'll have to kill me first, Bagger filth."

Clarity buoyed in her mind, and she spoke. "I can tell I am fighting with a true Grogan. Very well." She slung the blade into the ground and wrenched her arm around Rander's neck. Using her legs, she stood, as Rander's injured legs flopped uselessly in the sand. He desperately kicked his legs, trying to find leverage against the constricting hold, but she would not give in. His face turned red, and then crimson, only to settle into a deep purple. Willyn released her grip for a half second, and Rander took a whisper of a breath.

"Tell them who I am, Rander." Willyn spoke softly into his ear.

Rander's eyes cut her down and he whispered, "Never."

"Very well." Willyn wrenched her hold across his throat, shutting off all the air to his brain. He struggled, flopping like a mouse in the coils of a serpent. She held him in that painful place, straddling his consciousness with the darkness that threatened to swallow him, only allowing him to gasp for breath in brief, terribly short microseconds.

"Tell them, Rander. You know who I am. I have bested you. Surely you do not want to die today. We are allies, you and I." Willyn did not honestly know if that was true, but something within her told her to stay a killing blow. Willyn's heart quickened as she knew there was little time to waste. She either had to kill Rander or risk being viewed as weak.

Rander refused. The crowd was booming, the sound like a roaring avalanche. She ratcheted down on him once more and whispered softly into Rander's purple ears. "I'm only going to ask you one more time. The choice to save your life is in your hands. Tell them who I am, Rander."

She stared at his eyes riddled with the red dots of broken blood vessels. His head bobbed with a nod and immediately Willyn released him. He flopped out onto the ground, wheezing for breath as Willyn pulled the knife out from the ground. She pointed the blade out to him as he wheezed, slowly lifting himself up from the sandy arena floor.

"Tell them, Rander. Tell them who I am."

Rander looked up and the crowd hushed, waiting to see what would happen next.

Rander opened his mouth and his voice cracked over the multitude. "She is Willyn. Sar of the Groganlands."

Willyn screamed at him, a wave of sheer passion sweeping over her. "LOUDER. SAY SO ALL CAN HEAR!"

Rander nodded and slowly stood. His voice thundered, broken but powerful. "REDS, BEHOLD. THE SAR, WILLYN KARA, SISTER OF HAGAN THE GREAT, HAS RETURNED TO US."

The mountain range of Legion's Teeth quaked in celebration. The chorus of screams and praise could be heard from the deep mountain caverns for miles around, filling the forests like some invisible chorus of joy.

The Sar had returned to the Groganlands.

Willyn immediately ordered Rander to receive medical attention. She refused the medics until they assisted him. As the team put Rander on a gurney, she was overcome with the realization that she would need him. He had nearly defeated her, and the mission of rallying the Reds would have been compromised. She was thankful for the realization that keeping Rander alive would be worth more to her in the long run than if she had killed him. This man, despite his failure to best her, had somehow controlled the raging mobs of the Grogan people in her absence, crafting their rage into a useful and sharp weapon against Hosp and his Surrogate supporters. This was no small feat. Rander had done much in her absence to keep the fires of resistance burning hot against Hosp's forces. She limped off the arena floor as a second team of nurses and doctors washed over her, putting her on a rolling gurney. A fleet of examiners surrounded her, inspecting her body for any critical damage.

A young man spoke over the others to her directly as he scanned her with his eyenocular. "Madam Sar, all I can see is that you've got a broken nose and a few cracked ribs. I'm not seeing any more internal damage that needs assistance." He held a light in her eyes, inspecting her pupils. "And perhaps a mild concussion. We'll give you a boost to expedite the healing." The doctor took out a syringe and drove the long needle into Willyn's arm. She could barely feel it, and in an instant, the pain that had enveloped her body subsided. She ran her scraped hands through her hair and sighed, but she still felt rattled as if someone had scrambled her insides. The doctor spoke, his voice serious, "You are going to need to take it easy. The boost should help heal the broken bones in a matter of days, but you'll need to rest."

"Understood, soldier. Thank you," said Willyn. The doctor stood, staring at her. He whispered to her with awe in his voice. "I knew it was you before the fight. You might not know this, but there had been rumors that you had arrived only a few days ago. We all thought it was a tale, but something about it felt real. When we saw you on the arena floor, we knew you had returned. We thank Aleph you are back."

Willyn flicked a curly lock of raven hair and smiled. "My disguise didn't do that much, I take it?"

"No, madam, but it got you to us again, and for that we're thankful."

The doctor bowed reverently and instructed the others to leave her. Willyn eased up to a sitting position on the gurney. They had rolled her into one of the holding pins outside the arena. There, standing in the corner, was Bri, who had somehow snuck into the room with the medical team.

"You did well, little one. You have great spirit. Great strength."

"Thank you, Bri. Do you have my datalink?"

Bri extended the tech toward her, the device looking dwarfed in his gigantic hand. She picked it up and booted up the screen. She looked at the giant sharing the room with her. "It's time we contact Wael." Bri said nothing but nodded in agreement.

Willyn punched in the coding for Wael's secure line and waited. The screen regularly flashed the words 'connection pending' for several minutes before finally changing to 'connection failed.' Willyn grumbled and tossed the datalink to the side before looking up at Bri.

"When was the last you heard from him?"

Bri scrunched up his nose and glanced at the ceiling. "Um. Long time. We were on train."

"That's what I was afraid of," said Willyn as she rose to her feet. "I have another idea." Willyn reached down to pick up her datalink and punched several words into the machine. A newsfeed flashed up, revealing if there was any article or chatter related to Wael or Grift.

There was nothing on the feeds about Wael. It was as if his presence had been completely scrubbed from the datalink networks. There also were hardly any mentions of Preost, though that was not so surprising.

Willyn scrolled through the different bits of information before finding a military feed referencing Grift. He had been spotted in Lotte, and there was a lot of chatter around troops mobilizing toward his position. Several feeds discussed the bounties on his head. Another proposed that Willyn might be with him. The bounty had grown significantly since her escape from the Spire; up to nearly two million credits. Willyn sneered as she read through the posts.

Let them think I am in Lotte. It serves me well for now.

Flickers of worry regarding Grift danced in her head, but Willyn shoved those feelings away and allowed herself to breathe in a deep sigh of relief. Her time in the Teeth had worn her down. She was exhausted. A thought rumbled back to the front of her mind. *Bastion.* The thought of the demon in his glass cage sent Willyn's heart into a flurry. Everything in her wanted to leave him buried under the mountain, hidden away by Bri, but her mind had put together the truth. The mirror would not be safe in the long term. Soon, Seam and Hosp would hear of her rise to power, and they would come looking for her. More importantly, they would come looking for the mirror. It had to disappear completely.

The thought of diving back into the heart of Legion's Teeth caused a sweeping anxiety to fly over her. She waved for Bri to come closer before speaking in a hushed voice. "How quickly can we move the glass?"

Bri shrunk back and tilted his head to the side with a questioning look. His expression was a mixture of concern and disbelief. "Move? The demon stays."

Willyn limped toward Bri and shook her head. "No, Bri. It has to move. Far away."

"It is in good hiding. No one knows the tunnels." Bri's voice was stern.

"Have you not seen the other Realms, Bri?" quizzed Willyn. "Hosp and Seam will tear these mountains down to locate that mirror. They don't care what stands in their way. I trust you and I know it is well hidden, but it is *too close* to its original location. We need to move it far away."

Bri examined Willyn through squinted eyes before letting out a deep sigh. "This is right. The monk said the same." Bri leaned down and placed his lips next to Willyn's ear. "We will get mirror tomorrow night."

Willyn studied Bri's eyes and nodded, placing her hand on the giant's shoulder. "Thank you, Bri. I could not have done this without your help." She limped to her cot and examined the battle fatigues set out for her. "Can I have a few minutes, Bri? I need to gather myself."

Bri nodded silently and slipped from the door. He was already gone as Willyn let her hair down. The room was quiet. Willyn sat on the cot and closed her eyes, drawing in a deep breath of cool air. All she could hear was the buzzing of the light overhead. Silence had the habit of unnerving her. The thought of the quiet made her think of her time locked away in the dank prisons of Elum, but *this*. This silence was welcome. She took in another refreshing breath and examined her clothes.

She dressed, allowing herself to unwind. Soon she would step out and announce her place as the next Sar. It had been a long and horrible journey for her, one that, if she had the choice, she would have never taken. Her thoughts drifted over all that had transpired when a voice cascaded in her mind. It was the same voice that had haunted her for months. *Hagan.*

"Fight for me." The words repeated until Willyn opened her eyes and jumped to her feet. She turned, scanning the corners of her small room, but she was alone. The voice and presence of her brother had felt so real. It felt like he was there with her in the room. She thought on the words and whispered a response into

the silence of her surroundings. "I fight for you every day, Hagan."

Willyn hurried to the pile of clothes laid out for her and flipped through what few belongings she had brought with her. There, underneath a few extra pairs of clothes, was Hagan's hunting knife. She lifted the blade and examined it again, thinking of the last wild boar hunt she took with her brother before he was poisoned. As she peered down the blade, a small note fell from its sheath. Willyn carefully unfolded the note and studied the words neatly scribbled on it. "Rendezvous - Rhuddenhall - 5th district. Cortez Landing. 1100 - Novem month"

The words in plain black ink burned in Willyn's mind. The note had been planted by someone since her fight with Rander. It had not been there before. She studied the dagger, turning the blade over in her hands, trying to make sense of the note. Everything inside quaked with dark suspicions. *This is a trap. It has to be.*

The one thing that would not stop gnawing at her was the location. When they were younger, Cortez Landing was the place she and Hagan would retreat to when they wanted to slip from their royal spotlight. High above the sparsely populated fifth district of Rhuddenhall, they would sit at the landing, overlooking the manufacturing plants below. The two had spent many nights peering down at the smokestacks and bright yellow lights burning below their secret space.

No one knew the significance of that place. *No one except for Hagan.*

Willyn folded the note and slid it back in the sheath, trying to cover up the suspicions swelling in her mind that maybe, somehow Hagan survived and was in hiding, waiting for her help.

"It's a trap," Willyn whispered to herself. "Don't let your guard down." She slipped the hunting knife into her utility belt and paced back down the hallway. She had a throne to reclaim and a Realm to unite.

Bri was waiting for her, his presence never too far away. He leaned in, whispering his dialect, blunt but melodic. "Rander. You should see him, no? Make an ally. We will need them."

Willyn nodded. Ever since Bri had rescued her from Viga, Willyn had developed such deep respect for Bri. He seemed to keep her in a consistent state of awe. "You are very wise."

He shook his head and spoke. "I'm just reminding you of the things you know."

Rander lay on the sagging military cot, but struggled to his elbows upon Willyn and Bri's entrance into the room. He winced at the slightest movement. "You should have killed me back there. You had every opportunity."

"Why would I waste the life of a man who kept the fires of rebellion burning during my exile?" Despite the words leaving her lips, she still did not fully trust him. *Trust or not...you need him,* she thought.

Rander's face mirrored her own. "You are the Sar. There can be no doubt. You proved that fact on the arena floor, but you haven't explained yourself yet."

"What have I not explained?"

"Viga." Rander sat up further in the cot, speaking through gritted teeth. "You killed Viga in the shafts. Why?"

Bri's deep voice broke. "I killed this man." Rander threw a sidelong glance at Bri, his eyes intense and questioning. Bri continued, "I killed him. He betrayed Reds. He betrayed Grogan people. Allied with the jackal king."

"I don't know who you are, but I didn't ask you for an answer." Rander coughed and turned his gaze to Willyn. "Is it true? Did he kill him?"

"Everything he said is true," Willyn deadpanned. "The man was a traitor."

Rander shook his head. "What proof do you have?"

Willyn tried to examine Rander's eyes as he searched her for answers. She wanted to find someone to trust, but there was nothing about Rander that helped reassure her suspicions that he might be as crooked as Viga.

"I overheard him in the tunnels. He was trying to unearth a weapon for Seam." Willyn stared down the doubt on Rander's face. "Viga was the one murdering those Baggers in the tunnels, and he would have murdered me too had Bri not stopped him."

"What weapon?" inquired Rander. "I've never heard word of any weapon buried in the mountain. How can I trust you?"

Willyn stood and straightened her back. "You can trust me because I am your Sar." The words landed like an iron weight. "And as Sar, I have one devotion and that is to the Groganlands. If you doubt that then you doubt this Realm and I have no use for you."

Rander clicked his tongue and let out a whistle. "My apologies. I have grown accustomed to my place of power and trust does not come easy." He paused, trying to find the words. Finally, he spoke, his eyes held high with strong, Grogan pride. "I will question you no further. You have my loyalty, my Sar. I am at your service."

The tone was subdued and assuring. Willyn felt the fingers of doubt releasing in her mind, but she knew Rander would still have to prove himself before she gave him any *real* information. Willyn feigned a smile and nodded. "You are correct. Trust does not come easy for those of us burdened with the mantle of ruling the Groganlands."

Willyn paced the cement floor for a moment before addressing Rander again. "What was your plan? This rebellion? What was your objective?"

Rander slipped back down into the cot and laid his head back. "Isn't that obvious? Take back Rhuddenhall and disband the Council. You were a missing piece of all that, too. Now that you're back, we won't need to worry with a blood feud."

The thought of a blood feud sent chills over Willyn's skin. Visions of tribal chaos and war filled her mind. Without an established leader, the Grogan clans would each vie for power, each grasping desperately for the blood-soaked mantle of Sar. The Sardom had been established to keep the peace amongst the warring tribes, but the fears of a blood feud had not entered Willyn's mind. She shook off the brief barrage of images and spoke. "I will see to it there is no more war within this Realm. Enough Grogan blood has been spilled over Hosp and the Council's treachery. We need to move on Rhuddenhall quickly."

Rander shook his head. "We will be able to move more quickly than you think." He sat back up in the cot and motioned for one of the nurses. "Get me a wheelchair. We need to get out of here."

"But, sir, um...we have orders to..." Rander flipped a bedside tray, spilling gauze, IVs, and syringes on the floor.

"I did not ask you for your orders. I gave you *my* orders." Rander hissed through clenched teeth as he grasped at his broken knee. "Now get me a chair."

"Yes, sir," the medic mumbled as he ran from the room.

Rander tried to smile through the pain of his legs and nodded toward the door. "We have access to Rhuddenhall's datalinks and broadcasts. Soon the Sar shall return to her rightful place."

The screens in the central plaza of Rhuddenhall went dark. All of the datalinks within the Grogan borders dropped signal, and any radio broadcasts were scrambled to nothing but a static buzz. Soon the screens all flickered to life with Rander standing with a cane in the forefront of the picture.

"Grogans. I have an urgent message for you. For too long we have been warring, killing one another. Our loyalties have been divided over the past months. I stand, a proud Red, swearing my allegiance to our rightful Sar, Willyn Kara. Hospadda Gran and the Council moved like a serpent and struck at our Realm's heart with poisonous treachery. They killed our glorious Sar, Hagan, murdering him in cold blood, only so they could sweep in uncontested. You have heard that Willyn was Hagan's murderer, but I stand today and declare that this is a lie. A murderer runs and hides, but our leader has done no such thing. She was driven from us, exiled, but despite the threat of death, she has returned. She has returned to her Realm."

Rander stepped to the side to reveal Willyn standing in front of a cement wall, draped with the crimson Grogan banner; wolf and lion locked in conflict. Her jet-black hair had been dyed back to its fiery color. It was the only thing she insisted on before the broadcast. Her newly restored locks fell over her shoulders like a mantle of flames. She stared into the camera, proud, her face still bruised and splattered with specks of dried blood, chiseled in defiance.

She spoke, her face filling the datalink screens. "My brothers and sisters, I have returned to call you to arms. We have been betrayed at the hands of our trusted Council and their chief leader, Hospadda Gran. I have been accused of murder. Murder of my own brother. Any true Grogan knows that there is no bond stronger than that of blood. If we don't have family, then we have nothing. My family was ripped from me, murdered for political gain, but I am not empty-handed or empty-hearted. I have a family. *I have you.* I am calling out to you now to join me in fighting for our proud Realm. We have been killing one another for months, and I stand proudly before you, accepting the mantle of Sar to lead this Realm. I beg of you to end any loyalty to the Council and to Hospadda Gran. They have betrayed you and left you to fight one another while Seam Panderean expands his new kingdom in Zenith. Do not be fooled. Seam Panderean will stop at nothing but to restrain our people under his banner, under his rule. Hosp has bowed to a dog viler than himself and has partnered with a man who murdered his own father to ascend to power. On my honor, this is true. I was held captive in Zenith as Hosp pushed for my execution, but I was able to escape. Now I vow to fight for the Groganlands. I vow to fight for you! To restore that which was lost and reclaim our heritage and our honor."

The screens went black once again. A hush fell over Rhuddenhall before a chant rang through the streets, in the alleyways and the tenement houses. "Kara! Kara! Kara!"

CHAPTER SEVENTEEN

A torrential downpour of rain and hail hammered down on the metallic shell of the titan sheltering Seam and the Synod. Arakiel sat across from Seam as the High King flipped through topographical maps on his datalink. He looked up from the red and green lines and spoke. "Arakiel. Where is Bastion? I know we are close."

"Not as close as you may think," growled Arakiel. The Serub's threatening voice was barely audible over the din caused by the maelstrom raging outside. "He is not in the Red city. He has been buried beneath the mountain. Within Legion's Teeth."

Seam scrolled over the dipping lines until a blanket of sharp pinnacles were illuminated beneath his fingertips. The holding area of the titan was dim, but Arakiel could make out a smile as it crept across Seam's face. "Tell me again, Arakiel. How is it that you know where each of your kindred is buried?"

Arakiel stood from his seat and was silent for a moment before providing a brief answer. "I listened."

"You listened?"

Arakiel nodded. "Yes. I listened before each was locked away. They called out to me. They all call out to me."

"Fair enough," quipped Seam. "Now, let's go find your brother. I've been waiting long enough."

Seam slipped from the cargo bay and stepped into the cockpit. Waves of rain and hail ran down the portholes, making it impossible to see the red rock walls surrounding the hover tank.

"Change of destination, captain. Plot a new course for Legion's Teeth."

The captain leaned forward and tried to glance through the porthole. "With all due respect, sir, we can't see a thing. We're likely to run this convoy right into the cliff walls. We're barely moving as it is."

"I don't want excuses." Seam's voice was flush with frustration. "I want us in Legion's Teeth by tomorrow."

The captain dipped his head and glanced back out the window. "Yes, sir."

The stench of alcohol wafted through the air, and the echoes of shouting and music could be heard through the floor. Wael closed his eyes behind the blindfold wrapped around his face and tried to concentrate. The room holding him was dark, but warm. His hands were bound, but he could feel the old wooden floors beneath him and the thin, dingy curtains hanging behind him. From the sound of the rustic Elumite music and smell of spirits, Wael deduced he must be above a bar or brothel. Each was common enough throughout Elum.

The journey to find the Sixth had not been easy. After sending Willyn and Grift out of Preost, Wael had spent a full day in prayer. He did not sleep and no substance touched his lips during that day, yet despite his intentional silence and rigorous focus, Aleph did not speak to him. The One did not provide any guidance, no clues as to where the sixth Serub was hiding. A spark of disappointment and doubt had threatened to light within the Mastermonk, but he extinguished it with a skill that only came from rigorous decades of discipline. *Aleph had not abandoned him. Aleph had never abandoned him.*

Long ago, the Mastermonk had learned a valuable secret. Hope was a discipline. After his chants had ceased and his incense was burned down to ashes, Wael stepped out of Taluum with no true direction, his mind completely devoid of any real insight into where the Sixth could be found. Yet his hope remained, and it pushed him out into the wilderness.

He had spoken to his associates before departing, instructing them in their tasks to keep the Realm's priorities in place. This was no small task for his protégés, but his instruction was largely a courteous formality, as the Mastermonk's closest protégés had long ago learned how to manage Preost in his absence. Wael left them in the night, after sharing a small prayer with his trusted advisors. He took only his staff and a small satchel and disappeared, blending with the chorus of night animals that surrounded the hidden fortress. The other monks had seen their master go many times before, but never had Wael left with such a weight on his shoulders. Finding the Sixth divine was not like brokering peace during a time of war. His present challenge, the conflict with Seam, Hosp, and the Five, was completely different. With the exception of what Aleph could or would do, the Sixth Celestial was the only path that Wael knew to take. A path that had led him straight into a bounty hunter's trap.

Seam sat staring at the wasteland rolling by the porthole as his long caravan of titans, rooks, and transports made the slow trek to the mountain range of Legion's Teeth. He couldn't help thinking how odd it was for a thunderstorm to break over this arid bit of borderland that sat between Riht and the Groganlands. Hosp stood rigidly next to the High King, at least by all appearances. None but he and the Serubs knew that it was all an illusion. The Surrogator's soul had been sent into whatever dark abyss would dare take it, and Seam sat chuckling to himself as he thought on his meteoric rise in power. *Each and every day brings me new abilities, new gifts.* Soon there would be nothing left to check him. All of Candor would soon quake under him and no puppet government in the Groganlands would be needed. *You can claim the Sardom and finally leash the furious Grogans.* He glanced at the empty, rigid body of his old, worthless ally.

As the hours dragged on, Seam excused himself into his private chamber. The empty body of Hosp followed like an orbiting moon, silently pulled by the High King's presence. He closed the door and extended his hand toward Hosp, testing his powers on the malleable body. Somehow, the High King found it easier to control Hosp than the body of Kull. He was surprised at this revelation, but he could not argue at the truth of his experience. It was as if there was some buffer in his ability to connect with Kull's body. A buffer that did not exist with the baggers he had enslaved nor with the body of Hosp who stood before him.

This is strange. Very strange. Hosp's body mimicked his every thought, whereas Kull's body had only obeyed with his utmost concentration. He would have given this more thought, but he quickly assumed that this was linked to the incredible surge of power he had gained inexplicably over the last few weeks.

He extended his hand outward to Hosp, focusing his energy, concentrating on the body before him as he had with Kull. A masterful feeling of capability fell over him as his arm bearing the brace of keys surged with a warm, encouraging energy. Suddenly, without warning he felt a wave crash over him and he tumbled underneath a colossal current. He opened his eyes and saw *himself* staring at *himself*. His brain panicked in an effort to understand what had just happened. He cursed, but the voice filling his chamber was not his own. *The voice was Hosp's.*

Seam looked down and saw the hands of the Surrogator filling his vision. Somehow, he had projected his very own essence into the empty body of Hosp. Panic shifted into glee as his jaw dropped at the newfound ability. He could not believe that the Keys would allow such a possibility. Suddenly, an onslaught of memories merged with his own consciousness, as if a titanic memory dump from Hosp's brain was reconfiguring itself with Seam's essence. Memories flashed by Seam's eyes like holographs, and Seam stood transfixed.

A desert dune stood in his mind, with the cursed sun blazing overhead. The fiery orb was oppressive, its hot light

hammering down on him. He looked down and saw the hands of a child, his hands, and heard a rumbling behind him. He turned, knowing that the small backwater town filled with small adobe dwellings was Intryll. The distant rumbling was now close, too close. He turned back toward the dune and ran to its summit, his little legs straining to push him forward.

Then he saw them. A fleet of black shadows, Grogan rooks flying through the desert. A raid. As he turned screaming, he heard the machine guns begin to whirl and the rockets explode. Then there was only blackness.

Another memory, another place. He stood next to a woman, her face marred with hot tears streaming from red, tired eyes. He reached out to her, his hands now the size of a man's, but the woman pushed him away, cursing him. He stepped away from her to better see the mob of people gathered in the starless, desert night.

Two enormous bonfires burned, casting long billows of red light over the crowd of Rihtians huddled around them. A small child stood between the two fires, bound. She looked out over the people, staring at him, clamoring for him to see her, crying out for him with a shrill voice. A thought fell through Seam's mind; a horrible mind-numbing realization. 'That is my daughter.' The truth of the scene fell over him like a ton of bricks, but Seam could feel that she was not the true focus of this memory. Behind the girl stood a huge earthen pillar, decorated by an elaborate mosaic, a collage of shining tiles. No. Not tiles, but something else. Seam strained to see what it was, ignoring the cries from the girl. Broken glass. The mosaic was made of broken glass that reflected the nightmarish red firelight out into the desert air.

Mirrors. A mosaic of broken mirrors. From a distance Seam heard chanting, low and ominous, yet building. A parade of five dark-clad figures snaked their way out of the shadows, joining the crowds who surrounded the scene. They walked in a row as the Rihtians clamored to give them a wide berth. The figures were draped in black, but bore stark white masks of animal skulls. Upon closer inspection, Seam could see that they wore a wicked collage of bones, draped over the strangers like cloaks, each rattling as they walked.

The desert witches had arrived.

The ceremony began. All were silent except for the wails of the small child bound between the flames. The crimson light of the fires seemed to grow with new energy, their light reflecting off the broken mirrors and giving the crowd a nightmarish hue. The five desert witches undulated like twisted puppets in the red light, kicking up sand and throwing handfuls of ash into the desert wind. They danced like dervishes, causing all the people gathered to shake with palpable fear. Their moaning chant rose with each turn of their dance, with each spin of their skull masks, circling around the girl like the coils of a snake, until finally they stopped. Four of the witches knelt down, bowing toward the shattered obelisk. In the middle of the circle stood their leader, a warlock known only to the people as Dyrn.

More shade than man, Dyrn stood tall, wearing the skull of a stag crowned with giant white antlers that threatened to scrape away the midnight sky. He walked with grim purpose toward the sobbing girl who threw herself against her chains. Dyrn unsheathed a dagger of bone and stood before Hosp's daughter, running his dirty, long-nailed fingers on her face, tenderly pushing away her tears. He turned around and screamed, his deep guttural voice echoing off his bone mask as he pointed directly at Hosp.

"Remember this day, Hospsadda. Remember the day you gave your all to the true gods. Remember the power and life you have bought for your people. We will be once again spared by their coming wrath, spared by their coming rule because of this sacrifice. Your sacrifice. You have secured your place in their coming kingdom."

Hosp stared at the warlock's eyes behind the mask of bone. They were the color of blood.

Dyrn turned, chanting a low, undulating prayer that grew into a din of howls and screams. The sound of Dyrn's voice echoing in the night made Seam's consciousness recoil. The dagger bone was lifted above the warlock's head. He held it there for only an instant and he screamed with horrific finality, "FROM DEATH COMES LIFE!"

The broken mirrors flashed in an instant with the horrible faces of the Five, each smiling with unholy delight. Seam felt Hosp's own emotions mimic the faces of the Five in the broken mirrors. He was pleased with what he had seen. The memory faded and Seam felt swept again to another place.

The beautiful face of Vashti faced his own, and Seam felt Hosp's fist tighten with rage. The Crossroads. Hosp had been with Vashti at the Crossroads. Vashti stood, her face bent in a scowl.

Vashti sneered widely, her teeth like white pearls, shining against her luscious dark skin. "There is nothing to worry about, Hospadda. My father does not suspect anything...."

Hosp's thin, weasel-like voice echoed in the musty sanctuary commanding his young protégé. "You must take every precaution. It is imperative that you remain discreet.

You did not listen to me. You've been away from Preost for too long, and now our plans hang by a thread."

Vashti growled, "I will not go back to Taluum, Hospsadda. My mistress needs me." "

Hosp cut her off, "It is time to focus, Vashti. The plan is already set into motion and I can't have the Mastermonk suspecting anything. He's already on high alert. The young Panderean has snuffed out Camden's life. You must be more careful.

"What did you tell him? What did you tell Seam?" Vashti's eyes narrowed with the question.

Seam felt Hosp's body tense as he whispered, "I have convinced him that he will be the Keeper."

Vashti roared, her voice echoing over the abandoned chamber. "What?!"

Hosp held out his hand to silence her. Seam felt Hosp's face bear a twisted, cruel smile. "Yes, Vashti. He will be the Keeper. It is to our benefit that the new High King gather all the Keys of Candor. He already will have one, and soon he will have two. That is once he gathers the one protected by his Captain of the Guard. I will see that he gains the Groganlands Key once Hagan is disposed of."

Vashti pulled away from Hosp her voice as sharp as a razor. "How could you do this? The plan was that I would gather my father's brace, and pay Filip off." She turned away from him running her fingers through her hair. "This was not our plan, Hosp. She stared back, her eyes threatening. "Why do you shrug away your rightful place? Why will you not be the Keeper?"

Hosp stared at her, but his mind grew distant. "Because Seam is the only one who can unite the Realms under one banner. He comes to the table with many advantages. First, he is of a royal lineage. Second, he is young, charismatic, and charming."

Vashti sighed, frustration washing over her face. Hosp's voice grew more determined, challenging her attitude as he spoke. "The most important thing, Vashti, is that he is malleable. He has been easy to manipulate. He killed his own father with only an empty promise."

Vashti interrupted, "And why would you give him the Keys? You are handing the most powerful weapons in the world to a fool. Don't you understand how dangerous that is?"

Hosp took a step closer to his apprentice, and Seam could feel the cold anger running through him. Hosp spoke, his voice as cold as ice. "Vashti, don't you dare question me. Seam will unite the other Realms, and I will bring the Groganlands under his banner. He will do all the hard work for me."

Vashti spat at him, "Is this who you really are?" Seam could see her shake with rage. "Content to be the High King's lapdog?"

In an instant, Seam felt Hosp tackle her, slamming her arms back to the stone ground. Hosp screamed, "I AM NO DOG." Disgusted, he stood over her, his voice growling in the dark. "You are short-sighted. Seam has no idea the power that he will wield. It will take time, but I know much that you don't, young one. Seam will push the limits of the Keys too far. It is only a matter of time. It will happen in an instant, and that, Vashti, is when I will strike."

Vashti struggled, unable to break away from Hosp's grip, her face flushed. "What? What do you mean? How will you do this?"

Hosp laughed at her and whispered, "He will gain too much confidence in his powers. He will test his limits and lose control of his own body. And that is when I will strike."

Seam's consciousness panicked within the memory, the truth of his sudden weakness revealed. He screamed, trying to push through Hosp's detailed recollections, trying to re-establish control over the Surrogator's body so somehow he could push his way back to his own. Hosp was not waiting to strike; instead there were much more powerful foes waiting for this moment. Mind-numbing fear washed over him when he felt the thunderous crash against the titan's walls and heard Arakiel scream for his kin.

"Abtren! Nyx! Get in there! NOW!"

Seam felt the vehicle carrying him crumble like a cardboard box. The three Celestial nightmares did not hesitate to rip through the thick steel walls, their blood red eyes fixed on the Keys latched on the arm of Seam's unguarded body. They howled with an otherworldly blood lust and for the first time in months, Seam felt fear. With all his might he focused, channeling his energy, extending the Surrogator's hand toward his own abandoned body. He would only have seconds before everything he had built would crumble.

Seam cursed himself as he fought to forge a connection with his abandoned body. He forced Hosp's palm open and channeled his entire focus back to his own flesh and blood. *Please. Please don't let me die like this.*

The steel walls surrounding Seam gave way like paper in seconds as Arakiel ripped a large section of the wall free. Abtren and Nyx joined him, howling like a pack of wild hyenas. Arakiel seemed to swell and grow as he pushed himself through the wall. With no Keys to check them, the Serubs bolted toward Seam's unguarded body with unbridled rage. Seam focused one more time, trying to find his way back. *Aleph! Don't let me die like this!*

Arakiel slammed into Seam's rigid frame, tackling his body to the floor. The Serub chief drew back his massive hand and swung for Seam's skull. It came down like a hammer, only to be grasped by the king's hand. Seam's eyes flew open as he snapped forward and clamped down on Arakiel's fist, absorbing the god's power once again. Seam's eyes mimicked his enemy's, turning blood red, only to fade back into their natural color. The High King stood, wrenching Arakiel to his knees, his face a mask of rage.

"How dare you?" A rush of power swept from Arakiel's bones and flooded Seam's veins.

Arakiel pulled himself free, snatching himself back and scrambling for the room's edge. Seam stood to his feet, incensed. "I have had enough of this!" Seam sneered at Nyx and Abtren as they shrunk back into the adjacent room of the titan liked whipped dogs.

Seam stood over Arakiel before kneeling and piercing him with his eyes. "Tell me, you so-called god. Why should I allow you to live?"

Arakiel spat on the floor between them. "You speak of things you cannot possibly understand, mortal. Tell me, did your heart twist in your chest when you saw me coming for you?" A horrible rolling laughter spilled out of Arakiel, and the god's eyes pierced through him as he continued, "I have all the time in the world, High King. You can never kill me and you know it. A thousand years is but a day, and a day is but a thousand years. Even with your precious Keys, you've shown yourself to have weaknesses. You are capable of mistakes. There will be more. You will err, and we...we will strike. So punish me, cruel Keeper. Drain my powers again. Make me feel the pain only you can inflict. **It is only a mere shadow of the fate that awaits you, Keeper.** You cannot hide behind those cursed Keys forever."

The words sent a jolt through Seam. He retaliated in an instant, grasping Arakiel's throat and choking his laughter through clinched teeth. "When I am finished with you, you will wish you could die."

Arakiel opened his mouth to scream, but all that came was laughter. Cursed, defiant laughter. It rattled the titan as it rumbled through the canyon pass. It made Seam furious as he fought to pull as much energy from Arakiel as his body would allow. Soon the mocking laughs were barely audible, weak, crisp whispers escaping from the fragile frame of the cursed god. He dropped

Arakiel onto the steel floor of the titan like a tattered rag and spat on him. He stood over Arakiel and slammed his steel boot into the god's small frame only to then pick him up and hurl the crumpled mass through the destroyed, concave wall clawed out by the Serubs. Nyx and Abtren lingered in the shadows, wary of their raging master. Arakiel let out a soft whimper as he crashed at his kin's feet, but he still bore a twisted, insane smile. Seam's nostrils flared and his eyes met with Abtren and Nyx's, his face mottled with hate. "Remember this before you test me again."

Seam stepped back into the cockpit, his mind boiling, full of fury. He could not believe his own stupidity. His reckless experiment had nearly cost him everything. All of it, his kingdom, his power was nearly destroyed in an instant. Seam sat there, his mind a mixture of fear and unmistakable relief. He was so caught up in his thoughts he barely noticed the chirping of his datalink. Grateful for the distraction, he flipped open the screen to meet a face he had not seen in a long time. *Cyric.* The hunter smiled, his stubbled face glowing with pride. "I believe you owe me one million credits, High King."

Seam's cocked his head. "So you have him? The Mastermonk?"

The camera panned from Cyric's smiling face to reveal Wael blindfolded and bound in the corner of a dark, wood-paneled room. Cyric's face reappeared and his smile grew wider. "So, High King. We had a deal. When do I get my money?"

"As soon as he is delivered to the Spire. Alive."

Seam snapped the datalink shut, ready to rid himself of the mercenary. *At least Cyric is loyal to me as long as he is paid.* The thought of having the Mastermonk in his possession was a victory, but it did not shake the empty void Seam felt within. He thought on the Arakiel's words, and those of Hosp. *What if they are right?* Seam took in a deep breath. He held the warm air in his chest and slowly exhaled it. His mind felt like a tempest of buzzing bees, painfully alive with too many thoughts. *If only I could sleep.* Sleep was the only thing his power could not give him, and the only thing that he wanted more than all the gold and glory in the world.

The Serubs had nearly bested him, but fate, it seemed, had other plans. The thought of releasing two more of the cursed creatures from their mirrors gave him much to consider. For the first time in his ascension, he realized a horrible truth. There was no one who could guide him, advise him, or help him. *You are alone in this journey. Completely alone.*

A rough hand grasped Wael's arm and jerked him to his feet. "Come on, monk. Time for me to get paid."

A rope slipped around Wael's throat and he could feel a vibration of energy swelling within its fibers. *Taze rope.* Wael cleared his throat as he took a few steps behind Cyric.

"Now, don't make me fry your pretty little brains out, monk. Seam asked for you alive and I do my best to keep my clients happy. I don't want to watch your eyes boil out your head."

Wael nodded behind his blindfold as he dutifully followed his captor. Cryic had been an unfortunate and unexpected roadblock in the monk's search for the Sixth. Wael had guessed that there would be hunters, and he had carefully instructed Grift to stay out of the cities or towns where he would be seen and travel through the wilderness. Willyn would stay concealed deep within the throngs of Baggers on her way to the Groganlands. Wael had followed suit, keeping his journey on the outskirts of civilization, choosing the desolate, crooked paths to conduct his search for the Exile. *Someone has betrayed you, Wael.* The thought entered the monk's mind and he shuddered at the thought. Someone in Taluum was allied with the Dominion. That could be the only possibility.

Unfortunate. No one within the entire Alephian Order could be trusted now. Wael's mind ran circles around the thoughts, as he heard Cyric open a beer and sit down next to him, his breath tainted with the bitter Elum brew.

"I'm not taking any chances after the fight you put up. Most trouble I've ever had out of a mark, but I have to give you credit, you do know how to use that staff. Too bad for you I had to sell it." Cyric looked back at Wael and smirked. "Staff or not, I wager you'll be dead soon. I'm sure you won't miss it."

Wael paused, weighing out his response. "You're a very skilled hunter, Cyric. The best in all of Candor, I would suppose...but listen to me. Listen to what I have to say."

Cyric chugged the remainder of the beer and tugged on the taze rope, pulling Wael down to the ground, still tied to the chair. "I wouldn't waste your words, monk. One million credits is too good a bounty for me to reconsider, even if you are a holy man."

Wael spoke through the pain, his voice filling the room. "Seam is not what you suppose. His ambitions have gone too far. He has unlocked our common enemy."

"The Serubs?" Cyric laughed. "I see and know much more than you could guess, monk. I know exactly what Seam is doing, and he's playing a dangerous game. I aim to make the most of this chaos. It's good for business."

"You must listen to me, Cyric. This is not a game!"

"You're wrong there, preacher. All of this is a game." Cyric's voice went dark, growling in the gloom. "One big, cosmic game made up of pawns and kings. The game you're playing, Wael, you can't win. It's rigged, stacked against you. I don't like your odds at all, my friend. That's enough talk. It's time to collect my credits." Wael tasted a dirty gag come across his mouth.

An old worn jeep sat with its back hatch open on the dirt road behind the tavern Cyric had used as his temporary hideout. He loaded Wael into the trunk and snapped the tailgate shut. Wael could feel the engine fire to life as it spun off, beginning the slow journey to Zenith.

The vehicle bounced along, its busted suspension pummeling through the rough gravel and dirt roads for what seemed like an eternity. Wael felt the heat of the day give way to the coming dusk, and to his surprise, the jeep slowed down. The engine shut off, and Wael heard Cyric come around to the back.

"Time for a break, monk. I've got some bread and water for you. If you scream, I'll gag you and we'll be back on the road again, got it? I don't have time for foolishness."

Wael nodded and Cyric removed the dirty rag from his mouth. Wael felt a small loaf of bread fall in his hands, followed by a canteen of water. He worked his sore jaws and rubbed at his cheek. He was happy to have water pass through his dry and chapped lips. He coughed as the liquid relieved him and he spoke to his captor with genuine thanks. "Thank you." Then he tore into the stale, dry bread.

After eating, he tuned his ears for any clues. He could hear the lonely calls of the owls, echoing over the trees. *We are on the border of Riht, just before the desert passes.* He spoke, hoping to gain something from his captor more than food and water. "How far out are we, Cyric?"

The bounty hunter laughed and threw a sidelong glance at the monk in the dark. "Are you counting the last remaining days of freedom?"

Wael smiled and stared at him behind the blindfold. "I am free at all times, Cyric. I simply wondered how many days I have to pray for you and the High King. I don't want to waste time."

Cyric coughed and grunted. Wael could feel the hunter wanting to make some comeback, but in the end he said nothing. The only sound that accompanied him was the scratch of a match flick followed by the repugnant smell of a stale cigarette. After a long pause, Cyric grumbled, his voice reluctant, "It's time we keep moving, monk." A firm rope fell across Wael's arms, tightening around his wrists to the point of pain.

"That's not necessary, Cyric. I'm not going to run away." The words came out of Wael almost unconsciously, but the Mastermonk knew that he was exactly where he needed to be. He could feel it in his bones. He whispered a silent prayer of thanks.

"You're worth too much to me, Wael. I'm not taking any chances." Cyric tightened the harsh rope around him and led him back to the jeep.

Wael's voice whispered in the night, not in fear but in jarring confidence. "You don't have to do this. There is nothing stopping you from letting me free."

Wael could see Cryic cringe in his mind's eye, only to feel the dirty rage come across his mouth.

"No more sermons, holy man."

The jeep roared again with life, and Wael felt the tires spin beneath him. Despite the violent rumbles and quaking of the derelict vehicle, Wael relaxed and the darkness of a deep sleep soon enveloped him.

Wael woke to the sound of Cyric slamming on the brakes. Pain eclipsed over his face as he slammed in the back of the jeep, and he gasped behind the gag, trying to remember where he was. The sound of Cyric's horn filled the air, and Wael could hear him cursing at someone standing in the road.

"Hey! You! Move it or I'll run you over!"

Cyric laid into the horn one more time before Wael felt the front of the car being lifted from the ground. The dark world around him began to spin and Cyric screamed out a torrent of curses as the sound of gunshots filled the air.

The world stopped spinning, and Wael's head collided again, only this time against the back of the jeep. He felt the truck lurch forward while its engine roared with life. Cyric was slamming on the gas. Suddenly, the vehicle lost its connection to the earth and spun in the air. *What is happening?* The vehicle erupted with an explosive crash, rolling in a chorus of shattering glass and crunching, moaning metal.

Wael tried to brace himself as the small vehicle tumbled multiple times, but it was impossible due to his bindings. The sounds of the crumpling car mixed with the sound of snapping tree limbs before the car made one final crash and came to rest on its side. Wael heard Cyric kick open the door and bolt for cover in the woods. There was no chase as the hunter retreated deeper into the dense forest, his rapid footsteps crunching through the foliage.

The car was silent for several minutes and Wael waited, still tied in the cargo hold. A dreadful conclusion entered his mind. *Another hunter. It has to be.* He kicked at the trunk lid, but it shuddered under the hard brace of a deadbolt. After a few seconds, Wael heard the sound of the trunk lid being ripped from its hinges.

Light flooded the trunk as Wael tried to find a way to peer from behind his blindfold. A hand pulled the fabric from his eyes and untied the taze rope around his neck.

Wael blinked and focused in on a familiar face, his mind struggling to comprehend who he was seeing. There, nearly eclipsed in the noonday sun, was the face of someone he had longed to find, one thought dead by many: Luken. He smiled and reached into the trunk.

"I understand you've been looking for me, Wael."

Wael's mouth opened wide as Luken loosed his gag. Wael's heart hammered in his chest. He could find no words as relief washed over him. The Exile, the Sixth of the Celestials, had revealed himself.

CHAPTER EIGHTEEN

"Kull."

The name landed with a thud against Nameless' ears. The sound of the name was distant, yet recognizable.

Nameless dug his toes into the fine, white sand and stared at the beautiful woman in front of him. Her blonde hair shone like a river of gold, cascading over her shoulders. Her cool blue eyes sparkled like sapphires, and her face looked as if it had never bore a single worry.

The woman had a name too. *Rose*. She claimed to be his mother, a term that his mind strained to remember the significance of. Yet, in the woman's presence, Nameless felt small thoughts beginning to trickle into his memory, causing his body to tremble.

A collage of faces sped through his mind, each one calling him by his name. *"Kull."* The faces flashed by him too quickly for him to recognize them, but the reality of his name hit him like a thunderbolt. His name was Kull. *He was Kull.*

After surrendering to the name, he turned to face the woman. She was radiant and her presence brought a feeling unlike any other. *Peace*. Yes, that was the feeling, though far weightier than the word he remembered from the other side. It was as if everything was in a state of serene safety and perfection.

"Kull. It's me." Rose reached out a soft hand and touched his cheek. She smiled as she held her hand to his face. "Your spirit has grown so strong, son. So strong, and so brave. That day you left me, when Cotswold was burning, I knew we would see each other again." A gentle smile grew across her face. "I love you."

"I love you too, mom." The words escaped from Kull's lips before he could register them in his mind. He reached out and embraced his mother. "I...I've missed you."

"I've missed you too." Rose gently kissed Kull's head and repeated the tender words. "I missed you too."

Kull stepped back and looked down at his crumbling, coarse skin. His *covering* was nothing like that of his mother's. Her body was in a state of perfection. As he gazed down at his own crumbling frame, he realized that he was broken. He glanced from his own cracking, breaking skin to his mother. The look on his face surrendered his thoughts, and fear grew on his face.

"We are here for very different reasons, Kull." Rose's answer was as gentle as the breeze blowing over the coast. It comforted him. "That is why we are different now."

Kull glanced back out over the black waters that crashed against the shore behind him. His eyes met with his mother's again. Rose nodded softly and continued, "I am thankful I was able to meet you here, before you begin."

"Begin?" The question rolled out of his mouth before he could stop it. "What are you talking about?"

Rose lowered her gaze on her son, her voice loving, but serious. "You are here for a very special purpose, Kull. One that was not intended by those who sent you." A smile grew over Rose's countenance. "I am so proud of you. You never gave up. At every moment, you continued to fight. You never lost hope, even when you were trapped out in the Sea of Souls."

"I don't understand," stammered Kull. Questions orbited around his mind with growing ferocity. "Where *are we?*"

His mother stared at him, her face like dawn's coming. "You will soon find out, my son. I am not permitted to say anymore." Rose turned and motioned her hand toward the horizon. "Now...follow me."

Kull obliged and followed Rose as she walked toward the horizon. Nothing changed at the horizon's edge, but the Sea of Souls disappeared into a tiny black blot behind them. Rose and Kull continued to press forward. The sound of the crashing waves retreated into a vacuum of pure silence. There was no noise in that space, no texture, only a bright, consuming light. Light, Rose, and Kull, nothing more. The two ventured onward and Kull tried to unearth more memories of his mother. They were few and far between, but Kull treasured each small image that passed through his consciousness as they walked.

A song came to his mind, and with it the memory of his mother cooking. Rose was exuberant in her singing as she baked for her son and her husband, Grift. *Grift.* The name of Kull's father exploded in his mind, joining the chorus of his mother's song.

> *His guiding hands they pull me through,*
> *This pain, this pause for me and you,*
> *Reason hidden and locked away,*
> *Grows our patience for each new day.*

Kull found himself humming the tune as they marched. Rose looked back and smiled. "You always did love music." Her voice felt distant though she was only feet away. The empty space they paced through distorted even the sound of her voice.

Their march finally ended, and Rose stopped to face Kull. She smiled again and kissed Kull on the cheek before hugging him tightly and stepping back. A small tear rolled down her cheek.

"This is where we must say goodbye for now." She smiled and wiped the small drop from her cheek. "Thank you, Kull." With her final words, Rose vanished, disappearing into the bright light that surrounded them.

Fear grew in Kull's heart and he screamed, "Wait! Where are you going?" The question was too late. She was gone, but Kull knew he was not alone. He turned, and behind him, a vast mountain appeared. The shift in scenery caused Kull to close his eyes and open them again, only to find he was now standing on solid ground. The pillar's base was surrounded by a thick canopy of huge, strong trees that stood proudly before him like soldiers standing at attention.

Kull shook his head, expecting the scene to disappear like a mirage, but nothing changed. The enormous oaks and evergreen trees swayed in the cool wind of this new place, bowing only to the foot of a great, gray stone mountain that pierced the sky with its summit.

"What do I do now?" Kull cried out. "Why did you leave me?"

There was no answer, only the sound of wind rustling through the thick branches of the surrounding trees. Kull turned and looked into the dense forest behind him, but the trees were so close together that it made it impossible to find any path to follow. He looked back to the mountain and gazed up the side of the colossal formation.

There, standing about a hundred yards away, was a man. Kull could not make out his face, but he saw his figure in the distance. Dressed in simple gray robes, the man silently motioned for Kull to follow him. Kull waved for him and called out, "Hey! Wait!" The lonesome stranger did not answer, but turned and began climbing up a thin, winding trail leading up toward the gigantic mountain's summit.

Kull ran his hands through his hair and groaned. *What is this place?* The chill, crisp mountain air gave no answers. There was no other option or path; he had to follow.

At the onset, the path toward the rock face was sheer but manageable enough. Kull felt his legs burn as he started up the arching, tree-covered base of the pinnacle. His breath could not keep up with the thin air, and soon he realized that the journey up would be much more difficult than he ever supposed. After what felt like hours, Kull stopped to catch his breath, leaning against a tall thin pine.

He glanced down from his position. He saw a thick, impenetrable forest that covered the land like a robe. His eyes trailed upwards toward the mountain's peak. He was at the edge of the tree line but the sharp summit still towered over him, thousands of feet in the air, revealing his true lack of progress.

I've barely made a dent in this.

A low, mournful howl echoed off the peak, and Kull's eyes went wide with fear. The call descended into a high-pitched laugh, ringing like a vicious siren. The hollow tone came from far below him, near the base of the tree line as far as he could tell. Kull was shocked when he heard the call answered by another to his left. Another cackled, far from the other side of mountain, an insane scream of unknown origin that made his heart seize with fear.

Kull didn't wait to find out what was shrieking below, but he could feel the sounds pressing closer. He forced himself, wheezing through his ragged breaths, to climb further up the mountain. His eyes scanned the mountainside for the man in the gray robes, but he was nowhere to be found.

Another cry erupted, this time much closer, coming from the thinning tree line below. Kull turned around, his eyes locking on a nightmarish creature that lurked below. The beast was unlike any Kull had ever seen. Its skin had a black sheen, like polished obsidian, and it possessed a collection of long limbs. The animal's front extremities were equipped with three fingers, each knuckled up in fists on the ground, while its back feet had three long toes with sharp claws. A long black tail swished behind the being, and Kull stood transfixed, straining his eyes for a better look. The beast possessed a beak of some sort and a long, cropped mane of needles that ran down to the center of its back. Four pairs of eyes were mounted in its skull, and all of them stared up to the mountain peak in Kull's direction.

Kull crouched to the ground, his body frozen with fear as two additional beasts flanked the original monster. The three shadow creatures stood on their hind legs and cocked their heads to the side as they examined Kull's hiding place. The first of the three creatures sniffed at the air until he snapped his head back to the ground, locked on Kull's scent. The trio let out a shrieking chorus and leapt up the mountainside like a pack of horrific panthers.

As the animals gave chase, Kull sprang from his crevice and sprinted up the perilous path. He stumbled with every other step as loose stones slipped and rolled beneath his feet. The brutal terrain ripped at his brittle feet, splintering them with sharp pain.

Kull glanced over his shoulder, trying to determine how much space was still between him and the pack of dog-like creatures.

The beasts flashed across the trail with lightning quickness, flashing from ledge to ledge. Their movement was so swift that Kull swore they were not running, but were skipping through the air to their next foothold. He turned and saw one of the creatures disappear in the thin air, only to reappear fifteen feet up the mountain. *Aleph above, save me.*

Fear strangled Kull like a rope. "Help!" Kull screamed out, hoping for the robed stranger to reemerge. "Where did you go? Help!"

Kull's lungs and legs burned as he continued to weave up the thin trail, pressing through the pain that was escalating throughout his body. He could hear the creatures closing in on him, but he dared not look back. The trail grew smaller as Kull pressed on. He glanced up and decided to try to leap and pull himself up to a ledge a couple feet overhead instead of weaving his way up the small path. Kull leapt, his fingers searching madly for a finger hold. He found it and pressed himself against the ledge to pull himself up. A wave of exhaustion tried to sweep over him, but he squared his shoulders and leapt for the next ledge. His hands trembled as he grasped the cold, gray stone, but as he pulled himself up the mountain the earth slipped and crumbled beneath his hands.

Kull felt himself fall, head over heels, freefalling in the wide open air before colliding against the hard rock trail beneath him. He slid about twenty feet down before thudding against a thick, open ledge. The impact felt as if it shattered every bone in Kull's body. He fought to raise himself back to his feet.

"Help!" Everything within him was electrified with pain. His thoughts went back to Rose, his mother, the only person he had truly met here on the other side. *Why did you leave me?*

Hot tears swelled and ran down Kull's cheek as he stared up at the mountain summit, hoping for the robed stranger, his mother, for anyone. As he raised himself up on one knee, the ground beneath him shook as one of the monsters pounced onto the ledge right beside him. The spikes lining the beast's spine bristled as it stalked forward only feet away. It opened its mouth, and to Kull's horror, the beast's jaws unhinged and disconnected, baring four layers of razor sharp teeth. It howled out for its counterparts, the sound like a large bird screeching.

Kull could hear the other two monsters clawing their way up the mountain, following the alpha's call. Kull was transfixed by the four eyes of the monster that pinned him down, white orbs surrounding a sliver of midnight, but he forced himself back to his feet to take a step back from his hunter. His foot nearly slipped off the cliff behind him. He was trapped, teetering between the chasm and the dog-beast with its layers of teeth and long, sharp claws. He examined the path inching back toward the top of the mountain. There was a thin grove of trees scattered across the trail leading away from the alpha who was inching towards him, its maw dripping with black bile.

Kull heard the other two bounding up the rocks, chittering like birds. They were close. If he waited, there would be no more chances.

You've got to run. The thought propelled Kull as he buried his fear and barreled for the trees, sprinting past the creature in a flash. The beast howled and shot after him in hot pursuit. Kull's lungs were on fire as he made it to the young saplings, but he did not stop. He weaved between the trees, ignoring the overwhelming exhaustion that was sweeping over his trembling body. Terror and adrenaline fueled his sprint between the trees. He darted between them, before doubling back and slicing between the thinnest openings he could find. The obsidian stalker charged, smashing through the young grove as if it was only twigs. It roared and swiped a massive paw for Kull, slamming against his chest with a thunderous thud that sent him hurdling across the ground toward the mountain's edge.

Kull's breath was gone, and his will was broken. Desperately, he sucked in for air as a low chorus of growls and chirps approached him. The three lurkers were together and the pack prowled near his broken body. The alpha beast lurched forward as

Kull scrambled back to his feet. *Don't go down like this. Go down fighting.* There were no more escapes. No more paths. The kill would be swift. Kull felt the resignation of death approach with each step of the obsidian hunter, but he inched back further to the edge of the cliff. The monster let out a tremendous roar, which the other two echoed, filling the valley with their thunderous call. A simple thought exploded in Kull's mind as he looked away from them and out over the forest below.

JUMP.

The two additional fiends leapt over the alpha, landing inches from Kull. Their white, cat eyes locked on him and they snapped their massive jaws.

Kull made his decision. He stepped back and took a running leap over the edge of the mountain. A feeling of suspension overtook him, similar to the aura that had surrounded him while buried beneath the surface of the Sea of Souls. Kull flailed his hands as he tumbled through the cold air, waiting for the feeling of a free fall to overtake him before the coming collision that would finally end his nightmare.

Yet the feeling of falling never came. Kull could see the ground below screaming toward him and he closed his eyes before uttering a desperate prayer. "*Aleph. Help me.*"

Something collided against Kull's body, and he thought he had hit the ground until he felt himself being pulled through the air. He opened his eyes only to realize that he was in the powerful grip of the alpha creature, who had teleported, snatching him from his death. The beast lunged from ledge to ledge and let loose a roaring howl, holding Kull as if he were one of its young. The two other beasts flanked it on each side as the three raced up the mountain with uncanny ease. Kull's mind fought to compute the swift movements and insane speed made by his captors, but he did not struggle.

The three beasts clicked and whined at one another, chirping with excitement as Kull kept his eyelids clenched shut, refusing to witness his own slaughter. The alpha dropped Kull to the ground and then all went silent. The silent void reminded Kull of his mother leading him through the light. He forced his eyes open and there was no blinding light, just more gray stone. Kull lay still, afraid to make any sudden movement this close to the beasts. Slowly, he continued to peer above him. The gray stone grew upward, its texture slowly morphing into a new substance. *What is that?* Kull stared, his mind unable to understand how rock could take on the appearance of fabric. Burying his fear, he lifted his head only to realize that the stone texture and color melded into the robe of the stranger he had seen earlier.

The stranger smiled, his full face shrouded in the stone colored robe. "You have a strong spirit, young one. Foolish, but brave."

Kull slumped over, struggling to hold his head up to the gaze of the stranger standing over him. Kull's brittle and broken body was wilting from his journey and the thought of moving any more was too painful. The three beasts circled Kull and proceeded to sit behind the robed man. Kull pushed himself back from the creatures, trying to place as much distance between them as he could.

"I see you still don't trust my guardians. Kala, Amser, and Ido would have destroyed you if I had wished it, but they are loyal." The stranger slipped past Kull and looked out over the ledge. "You have no reason to fear them."

Kull shuddered at the look of the foul beasts, distrusting of the robed man's statement. "Who are you?" Kull turned his gaze to look on the man, still feeling uneasy about turning his back on the obsidian guardians.

The man turned and knelt in front of Kull, pulling back his hood. The man's sharp eyes pierced into him, the color of silver daggers. His olive-skinned face was radiant, bearing features of someone both aged and young, his long, dark hair held back in a tight ponytail. His countenance was kind, but knowing, and the smile he bore was both subtle and radiant. He spoke, and his voice caused Kull's heart to quicken inside of him.

"You know me, Kull Shepherd of Cotswold. *I am no stranger to you.* I am here to help you, once again." He paused and leaned forward, leveling his eyes on him, causing Kull to shudder with an uncontrollable mixture of fear and awe. "I am your friend, Kull. You have no need to fear."

Kull dropped his eyes from the man's gaze and his voice broke in exhaustion. "*I don't know you. I've never met you.*" Anger and sorrow overcame him as he whispered, "I don't know where I am, much less who I am!" He glanced back at the stranger. "I just want to rest." He glanced down at his body. The flesh that he possessed was cracking and breaking, withering like dry clay in the desert sun. "*Please. I am so tired.*"

Without a word, the stranger stooped down to pull Kull to his feet and spoke. "Now is not the time to rest, Kull. There is much to be done, and much to discuss. Your rest will come soon enough." The man turned and paced back up the mountain trail. "Now. Follow me. We are nearly to our destination." The man flicked his hands in the air and the three obsidian guardians scrambled back down the mountain, leaving Kull alone with him on the narrow path.

A dull fire swelled in Kull's feet and legs, but he pushed himself on, following his new guide. Something in the way this man walked caused a memory to flourish in his mind like a mirage. The pain radiating from his legs reminded him of another time. The image filled his mind of a desert as he watched the robed man climb above him, charting the way for him. The man's pace, stature, and clothing swayed like that of a dark-skinned monk who had led him once through a desert in some other world. Kull tried to focus in on the image, on the monk. *What was his name?* He remembered he had been injured, his leg...it had been badly crushed. *But how? Why?* Pieces of memory flashed in his mind but refused to click into place.

The guide stopped at an opening in the mountain wall and motioned for Kull. "Here we are, Kull. Come on in."

Kull followed, sliding himself behind his guide into the small cave. A fire was burning on the floor. A spit of meat sizzled splendidly above the flames. A few scant belongings hung on the walls: a satchel, a bedroll, and a book. The smell of the savory meat was intoxicating, causing Kull's mouth to water uncontrollably. Suddenly, for the first time in what felt like eons, Kull realized he was hungry. He had not eaten since he found himself in the Sea of Souls, and now everything within him was starving for the food cooking over the fire.

The stranger wrapped a quilted blanket around Kull's shoulders and spoke. "Sit down, Kull. You have come a long way."

Kull pulled the blanket tight around his shoulders and shivered as a cold breeze pushed through the cave. The temperature continued to plummet, forcing Kull to huddle beside the fire, smelling the large slab of meat the stranger kept turning over the flames.

"Tell me, Kull, why are you here?" The hooded man sat right across the fire from Kull. The flames cast dancing shadows on his face, making it difficult to read his expression. "Why are you here?" The man repeated as he opened a clay bottle and handed it to him, motioning for him to drink.

Kull put the bottle to his lips, and the rich, earthy taste of sweet wine poured into his mouth. The drink warmed him from within, loosened his aching muscles, and made his mind relax. He managed a fumbling answer, awaiting some explanation. "I don't know. I don't know why any of this is happening." Kull huddled beneath the blanket, still tasting the wine in his mouth. He squinted his eyes across the fire, trying to read the man's face. "Do you know where we are?"

"I do." The answer was quick and resolute. "But I still have some more questions for you." The man's eyes narrowed. He took back the flask of wine. Slowly, the man produced an iron prong and shoved it deep within the coals of the fire. There, covered in the coals, was a covered iron pan. Using the prong, he pulled the container from the coals and removed the lid. Inside, Kull saw a beautiful, freshly baked loaf of bread. "You must be hungry," said the stranger, carefully slicing the hot, steaming bread. "Taste and eat." Kull did not hesitate, as an explosion of flavor hit his mouth. The stranger's question filled the cave. "Why should I help you, Kull?"

Kull shook his head as he devoured the large slice of bread. He spoke, his mouth still full. "I...I don't know?"

The small loaf of bread was soon gone, but Kull's stomach continued to growl as he eyed the roasting meat. The man's gaze did not relent. He still expected an answer. Frustrated, Kull spoke. "I really don't know." The man's eyes continued to bore into him, begging him for an impossible explanation. Kull fought to focus on his question. He thought of his time covered by the black waters of the Sea of Souls and remembered his torturous captivity on *The Hunt*. Then his mind turned to the three deadly beasts that threatened to kill him on the robed man's mountain pass. He stared through the darkness at the stranger whose silver eyes glistened in the firelight. "What choice do I have? The real question is will you help me? How do I know that I can trust you? How do I know you aren't like everything else I've encountered?"

The man continued to turn the spit, rotating the meat over the fire. "I am not like *anyone else* here, Kull." He was silent for a moment, his eyes lost in thought. "And yes, I am going to help you."

A strong breeze pushed into the cave and Kull huddled closer to the fire, trying to prevent his body from quaking in the frigid cold.

"The night is setting in." He glanced outside the entrance into the darkening sky. "It gets cold on the mountaintop at night." The stranger unhooked the satchel from his back and unfurled a leather skin. He hooked it over the cave's entrance. Instantly, Kull felt relief and was thankful. The makeshift door was just enough to trap the heat from the fire inside the small cave. "This should keep you warm enough."

"Thank you." Kull didn't know what else to say and the words felt so inadequate.

The man smiled and gingerly picked up the spit from the fire. He sliced the meat with his knife, layering thin slices of it onto two wooden plates. "You need to eat." He handed the plate over to Kull, and without hesitation, Kull began eating the delicious meal. The stranger soon filled his own plate and together the two ate in silence.

After eating, Kull felt his eyes begin to tremble with the weight of pure exhaustion. The stranger laughed and pointed to the empty bed roll. "Lie down. Rest. We will continue tomorrow."

Kull mumbled, "What about you?"

The stranger waved away the question and pointed to the bed. "Lay down. We will talk more tomorrow."

Kull did not protest, though doubts still lingered in his mind. He laid his head down on the thin bed roll and had barely closed his eyes when the whole world faded away.

When Kull woke, sunlight was pouring in from the mouth of the cave. The skin door had been rolled back and there was another small loaf of bread next to the warm embers of the previous night's fire. He rubbed his eyes and sat up. He took a deep breath of the cool mountain air and reached for the bread. As he ate, he felt refreshed and rejuvenated. He stood up and walked outside. The forest below was quiet, and it no longer seemed to be as threatening as it had the day before. The stranger was nowhere to be seen, but Kull heard the rhythmic sound of an axe hitting lumber in the distance.

Kull hiked down the mountain path toward the sound. There, standing in the cool air below, was the stranger, naked from the waist up chopping firewood. A huge oak tree on the edge of the forest had fallen, its gigantic trunk and branches lay spread across the small mountain plain. The stranger was slowly whittling the tree down into firewood, arranged in a large, orderly stack. Kull stood perplexed at the man's bare appearance. On his light brown skin was an intricate array of strange runes written in his flesh. The markings covered his entire chest, back, and arms with dark patterns of flourishing ink. Kull stared at the unintelligible words and symbols that were arranged in a magnificent pattern, filling Kull with a mixture of both awe and fear. It certainly was not what he expected to see, and something within Kull wondered if he should turn away from the stranger, but he couldn't force his gaze away. So he stood there, silently watching the man as he labored, adding to the large pile of chopped wood with firm, swift strokes of the axe.

"Good morning," the stranger said, his silver eyes trailing up to Kull's. "Come closer. I'd like your company."

Kull's heart jumped in his chest as he buried his inclination to hide. He came down the mountain path, careful not to stumble over the large stones that lined it. He spoke, his voice nervous, trying to fill the silence.

"Do you need some help?" It was all Kull knew to say.
The stranger smiled, wiping his brow. "I'd welcome it, though I've made much progress since you've been asleep."

Kull couldn't help but smile. "I didn't mean to sleep so long..."

Without a word, Kull joined him, picking up a spare axe and stooping to place a heavy log on the chopping block.

"Lift it with your knees." Kull took the stranger's directions and hoisted the log up. "We've got more to chop, so save your strength. The key is to let the axe do the work for you. Your job is to swing the axe, and the axe's job is to split the wood. You don't split the wood, the axe does. Do you understand?"

"I understand." Kull took his first swing of the axe and clipped the outer edge of the log, knocking it off the chopping block.

The stranger laughed and smiled. Kull put the axe down, embarrassed. He ran to the fallen log and hoisted it back on the chopping block. The stranger continued to split the wood as Kull positioned to take his second swing.

Kull focused on the swing and allowed gravity to do the rest. The axe head fell through the log and split it with a satisfying crack. Kull smiled, but instead of praise he heard the stranger speak.

"Split them into fours. That way we can get them up the mountain easier."

"Up the mountain?" The thought of carrying the large load of wood up the trail was dreadful.

The stranger's silver eyes connected with Kull's. "Do you know a better way to bring firewood up the mountain?"

The question was earnest, but Kull could not help but shake his head while cursing his own stupidity. The stranger smiled. "Yes. Split it into fours so we can haul the wood."

Kull nodded, and the two worked for hours splitting the timber. Kull fell into the rhythm of the task, placing the large logs on the block, swinging the heavy axe, and allowing the weight of the axe to split the wood. Sweat poured from Kull's body, and as he placed the last log onto the chopping block, he looked at his hands.

The flesh that had been crumbling, falling, and breaking down had changed somehow. *Healed.* His fingers had been crumbling apart only a day ago, whittling down like dry clay. The dust that Rank and File had put on him on *The Hunt* had all but failed him when the stranger's guardians set after him on the mountain pass. Now, Kull looked at his fingers with amazement. They were whole again and stronger. Not completely healed, but much better, even after a hard day of work. He pondered this and swung the axe one last time. The last piece split with a satisfying crack.

Kull cast his eyes over to the stranger. "Done."

The tattooed man nodded, flashing a broad smile. "Not quite yet. We've got to get the wood back up the mountain, remember?"

Kull wiped his brow and shrugged. "Yeah, I almost forgot."

The man stooped down and pulled up a pack frame dressed with loose bindings. Kull only had to look at it to understand its purpose. The man strapped the pack onto Kull, loading the pack with the freshly hewn lumber.

"I have to tell you, it is nice to have your help here, Kull. I haven't had any help in a long time."

"How long have you been up here on the mountain?" A flash of realization washed over him. "And where is *here*, exactly?"

"These are good questions." The man wiped his brow, his long black hair curling in his sweat. He picked up his own pack, which was loaded with lumber. "The short answer is that I've been here as long as I can remember. I've been many places, of course, but this...this is a favorite place."

The two began to climb the thin trail, and Kull was thankful for the cool breeze blowing through the darkening twilight. The pack was heavy, weighing down over his aching shoulders. As the sky darkened overhead, a blanket of starlight blossomed in the air and Kull felt himself overcome with a magnificent awe. It felt like all of the stars were on display just for him.

"You didn't answer my second question," Kull quipped.

"Oh?"

"What is this place called?" Somehow, Kull could feel the man's smile in the dark.

"Oh, yes. That. I call it *Mir*."

"Mir." Kull let the sound of the place roll off his tongue. He liked the name.

The two found themselves again inside the cave, and the man settled into stoking the fire. Bread and wine were once again procured, and the man opened up a large pot and held it out for Kull to inspect.

"What's this?"

"This, Kull Shepherd, is what we will be working on tomorrow."

Kull looked down into the clay vessel to see a thick, golden liquid sloshing in the pot. He dipped his bread in it and brought it to his mouth. Sweetness exploded in his mouth like a thunderclap and Kull remembered the word. *Honey.* Kull ate and drank so much that night that his aching body could not resist the coming of sleep.

It had been a good day.

CHAPTER NINETEEN

Clouds of dust and ash drifted in the air as Grift inched out over the edge of Henshaw's battered town hall, inspecting the damage. The building creaked and moaned under his feet, making it a wonder that it had not collapsed during the assault. Even from his vantage point, Grift could see gaping holes missing from the side of the building where it had endured artillery bombardment.

Grift ran his fingers through his peppered hair and left his hand on top of his skull as he tried to gather his thoughts. Bodies and charred hulls of destroyed rooks were strewn about the brick buildings as if they were a toddler's playthings. He took in a deep breath and scanned the slaughtered mounds of townsfolk below. Nothing living was left. Nothing.

The Dominion forces had butchered most, if not all, of the remaining inhabitants, and the weapon Adley unleashed had destroyed an entire platoon of Seam's soldiers in seconds. Grift glanced back at Adley in disbelief.

"What is that thing?" Grift stammered as he pointed at the machine. "And how did you know how to work it?"

Adley kept dialing commands into her datalink as Grift addressed her, her eyes focused on the screen.

"Adley." Grift's voice grew. "*Adley!*" She glanced up, annoyed by the distraction. "What is that?"

Adley looked up from her datalink and shook her head. "We don't know what it is, exactly. Predecessor tech, for sure, but we can't tell how old. Like I said, we found it in an abandoned mineshaft."

"Where? Where did you find it?"

"Near the Crossroads..." Adley's voice trailed off, grim at the mere mention of that place. "Once we figured out what it could do we knew it could turn the tide of the war. We just did not plan to have to use it so early."

"But how did you know how to use it? That thing is covered in ancient glyphs. I know you can't read it."

Adley shut the datalink on her wrist and ran her hand over the machine's control panel. "No. I can't, but a number of the monks can. They still keep a codex that is able to translate some of the Predecessor's runes. They knew enough to boot up the machine. Once you get past a few commands, the system is pretty intuitive. The monks worked for weeks on this thing before we got it..."

"But how?" Grift sat next to Rot as the dog panted and slobbered on the ground next to him. "Who commissioned it? Who released it? Since when did monks peddle weapons?" The thought of Preost being involved in the weapons trade didn't sit right with Grift as he inquired.

"The queen and Wael have..." Adley was cut short as her datalink chirped. Ewing's voice bellowed from the device. "Adley! Got word that a convoy is headed your way from Preost. Should be there in minutes and they have the Mastermonk with them."

"Wael?" Grift jumped to his feet and stood behind Adley, looking over her shoulder. *"Where has he been, Ewing?"*

"Wouldn't believe me if I told you, Grift. I will let him tell his story when he gets there." Ewing read Grift's face and assured him. "Don't worry, Grift. He's fine and he said he has a weapon of his own. He didn't give me any specifics." Ewing fidgeted with a pipe on the other end of the screen and puffed a cloud of smoke as he continued, "Maybe we stand a chance after all."

Grift looked down and rubbed at Rot's grimy fur. "Hear that, boy?" He looked out over the golden horizon, trying to spot the transport, his heart light for a mere moment. As he scanned the horizon, his gaze fell on the burning remains of the truck that held his precious wife. His chest went empty and his breath escaped him, leaving him heaving for air, trembling with distress as he relived the last terrible moments of her life.

He slipped to the edge of the roof line and gripped the waist-high wall surrounding the roof. He wrung his hands on the rough, red brick as he fought to catch his breath, to control the panic that shook him at his core. The episode came over him without warning, the inescapable truth of his loss crushing him from the inside. *Wael may have found what he was looking for, but I've lost everything.* Tears streamed from Grift's eyes as he looked to the sky and quietly muttered his painful inquiry. "Why, Aleph? What did I do to deserve this? Why me?"

"Grift." Adley's voice sliced through the fog of despair that had surrounded Grift and threatened to suffocate him. "Grift. Are you ready? I need help getting this thing unhooked and ready to move."

"Yeah." Grift wiped at his eyes and paced toward the machine, his hands still shaking. "What do you need me to do?"

A single truck barreled over the hills toward what was left of Henshaw. It slowed as it passed the wreckage on the town's perimeter and proceeded to pull up to the bottom of the town hall. Grift peered down on the truck and glanced over to Adley. "I hope this is them. If not, we tore this machine apart about fifteen minutes too soon."

Rot let out a long howl and sprinted for the steps, disappearing into the smoky building's innards. Grift could not help but laugh. "Well, Rot knows who it is. Looks like we're okay."

Adley snatched up several pieces of the weapon and nodded for the staircase. "Let's see if we can even get down the steps."

Grift picked up several more of the remaining components and followed. Adley nimbly maneuvered down the five flights of steps, leaping over charred sections that had been blown away. Once the two reached the second floor, the staircase disappeared into a large, smoldering void. The ground floor was nothing more than ash and char, a burned out hull where the steps once were.

Grift looked back up the staircase. "Well, we can always jump down, but this will make it a lot more difficult getting the bigger pieces down."

Adley nodded and squatted as she examined the drop off stretching out a few inches from her feet. "I guess we can make a few trips and just pass it down to Wael. Maybe he has some help with him." A timber broke loose and dropped from the third story, flashing by Adley.

Grift pulled her back from the falling wreckage. "I don't know that those stairs can handle a few more trips." Grift squinted and tried to focus on the stairs rising over him. "This entire building has been beaten into a pulp."

"Maybe I can help." *The voice.* It was...familiar. It was a voice Grift knew before his world had been torn apart. He looked down through the smoke-filled first story only to see Luken emerge from the gloom.

"Wha...what?" Grift sputtered, pushing back from the ledge. "Ha...how? *It's not possible.*"

Adley glanced at Grift as the color fell from his face, leaving him as white as the ashen walls surrounding them. "Grift. What's wrong? He's here with Wael." She pointed, her face twisted with confusion. "Look. Wael is right behind him with Rot."

Grift pointed at Luken and screamed, "You're dead! I saw you die!"

Luken's mischievous grin stretched over his lips and he chuckled. "I'm afraid there is a lot to tell you, friend."

Grift stammered and gripped the top of his head. "Impossible! How? Where were you? What happened?" He stared at Luken and then turned to Wael, his face demanding an answer. "How?"

Wael stepped forward and spoke up. "Grift. We don't have time to explain right now, but you know who Luken is now. He is the Sixth. The Exile has been found. We will have time to explain the details later, but now we have to get to Taluum as quickly as possible."

Thoughts crashed through Grift's mind as he digested the fact that Luken was standing in front of him, breathing and well. Luken leapt from the first floor and landed next to Grift, causing both Adley and Grift to gasp.

Grift pushed away from Luken and recoiled from his outstretched hand. "Who are you?"

Luken's eyes softened as he grinned. "We don't have much time now, Grift. You have to trust me."

Grift shook his head and reluctantly took Luken's hand. He looked back to Wael, searching for answers. "Wael?"

Wael nodded and glanced out of the building before turning back to Grift. "We don't have long, Grift. They are coming."

Adley adjusted the large piece of machinery tucked under her arm and gestured toward Luken to help. "Grift, I have no idea what's going on or how this guy can jump one story in the air, but I don't care at this point. We don't have long. We need to get the rest of the machine down."

Luken glanced at the weapon component tucked under Adley's arm and cocked his head. "Where did you get that?" His eyes flew from Grift to Adley, searching for answers.

"It's Predecessor tech—" Adley stammered.

"I know what it *is*, but *where* did you get it?" Luken's voice was sharp, edged with concern.

"Lotte. It was found in a mine near the Crossroads."

Luken's countenance dropped and he turned to look at Wael, his face heavy with some unspoken secret shared between him and the monk.

Grift spoke. "If it wasn't for this thing, we would have died. Seam's forces had us pinned down. Adley used the weapon as a last resort."

Luken nodded and muttered, "I've heard that before."

Adley spoke, turning her attention to Wael. "Ewing can give you more details, Wael, but the machine needs to be transported to Taluum. If it fell into Seam's hands…" Her voice trailed off.

"We need help. There's too much up there for one person to carry."

Luken cut in, "I will help you get the pieces down. You both need to get to the truck with Wael. We need to hurry. We intercepted an emergency broadcast in route. Your little show of power has already made some waves, and reinforcements are on the way."

Grift shook the cobwebs from his mind and focused on the task at hand. His eyes cut between Wael and Luken as he struggled to process Luken's reappearance. "How far out are they?"

"Not sure," said Luken as he started up the steps. "They weren't saying too much, but I know there are a lot of them." Luken pointed at the weapon component. "Get that thing to the truck. I am right behind you. I'll gather the rest."

Grift and Adley carefully made their way down to the bottom floor. Rot playfully danced around his master, bounding up and down, shaking his rotten nub of a tail. Wael's deep, booming voice filled the room, and he stooped down to allow the beast to pelt him with powerful licks and nuzzles. Wael fell to the dirty floor, delighted to be reunited with Rot.

"You missed me, didn't you? I missed you too, dear one." Rot howled in answer and nuzzled his massive head into the monk's chest, happily panting.

Grift couldn't help but smile at the exchange, but still his heart felt empty. Suddenly, his face went pale. *You can't leave her. You can't leave them.*

"Wael," Grift whispered to the Mastermonk. Wael pushed away Rot's advances and stood.

"Grift?" The question was an invitation, and Grift's whole body thought it might explode.

"Rose...she's dead. She and Eva were killed in the attack."

The Mastermonk wasted no time. "Take me to their bodies."

Grift nodded and led the monk to the burned out convoy. He came as close as ten feet, but he could go no further. Fresh sobs constricted around him as he fell to his knees. Wael stooped down with him and whispered into his friend's ear.

"There are no words for such a loss, Grift. You have suffered much, and much has been taken away from you. May I bless her?"

Grift nodded, his eyes bloodshot. "And Eva. Aleph knows she wouldn't have made it this long without Eva."

The Mastermonk nodded solemnly. "I will bless Eva as well." Wael stepped into the convoy and removed from his satchel two white linen robes. Grift moaned, still on his knees, as Wael wrapped them both and hoisted them from the wreckage. As he laid out the covered bodies, he spoke, his voice echoing over the field, filling it with the prayer language known only to the monks of the Order. The prayer crescendoed and suddenly halted, falling into the common tongue.

"Aleph, Lord of all, these two we commit to you, into your watch. Into your goodness and peace." Wael turned to face Grift, his eyes filled with resolute purpose.

"What is your first task, Grift Shepherd? For those you have lost? For Rose. For Eva…for Kull?"

The mention of his son's name made Grift almost black out. Grift peered behind him, desperate and destroyed by the death that cloaked him like a casket. Adley and Luken were behind him, standing ten yards away, their heads bowed. Adley fell to her knees, her face marred with sorrow as she finally confronted Rose and Eva's death. The sight of their covered bodies overcame her senses and twisted a sour knot in her throat.

Wael walked up to Grift and placed his hands on Grift's head, his low voice cracking with pain. *"What is your first task, Grift?"*

Grift knew the words. He had heard them at every funeral he had ever been to. His lips moved and his voice whispered across the plain, "To bear the dead to their final resting place. To hold them in my heart and to carry on their lives through my own."

Wael nodded and spoke again, his voice so low that only Grift could hear. "What is the task for your people?" His eyes turned to look at Adley.

"To submit my will to their betterment. Thinking always of their welfare before my own." Grift choked on the words, but they came. They came filled with hope and dread for the last and final question.

Wael kneeled down, his large brown eyes blazing into Grift's, demanding that he look into them. "There is only one more question, Grift."

"I know."

"What is your duty to Aleph?"

Grift's body crumpled on the freshly torn earth. He ran his fingers through the dirt and grime, screaming, releasing all the grief and rage that stormed within him. He hit the ground like a madman and cursed with abandon. *I will not say the words. I will not say them, damn me to hell. He took them from me.*

The monk would not relent, kneeling like a stone statue, unmovable. "What is your duty to Aleph, Grift Shepherd of Lotte?"

Grift rose from his knees and stared at Wael. Anger and rage rolled through him like a hurricane and all he wanted to do was slam his fist into the monk's face for asking the question, for mentioning the name of Aleph. His mind whirled with chaotic energy, roaring with malice. Everything within him wanted to rebel. Wanted to shirk the duty to the god who had cursed him and allowed everything to be stolen from him.

Yet his mouth moved and the words came, if only in a whimper as his heart refused betrayal. "To honor He, above all else."

Wael closed his eyes, and Grift noticed the Mastermonk's face was streaked with fresh tears. He stood and extended his hands out across the valley, the sing-song language of the monks booming over the plain. The common tongue came and Wael blessed them.

"In this great loss, it is my prayer that Aleph may bless us all. Bless us all in our loss. In our defeat. Bless these, our loved ones, who have died. We commit them, Aleph, to you. Eva. Rose. Kull.

To them we give freely, and with open arms, as you so freely give to us. They are yours again in your hands, in your vision. Until the *true* Keeper comes to lead us into your restoration, Aleph, we ask for your peace. Your peace. *Selah.*"

Dizziness swept over Grift and his head felt light as he forced himself to breathe. The monk had been so quick, so decisive in leading the traditional ceremony, that Grift had no time to prepare himself. The mention of Kull's name had nearly destroyed him, a fresh wound in his tortured soul. The sight of his beloved covered in a sheet, lying on the ground lifeless and dead ripped the air from his lungs. The realization of his loss was paralyzing. His legs felt like lead and his chest was hollow. The thought of standing was impossible as he dropped his head and wept.

Wael placed his hand on the top of Grift's head and murmured a blessing between each painful sob. Wael stooped and settled on his knees in front of Grift and then wrapped his arms around him as Grift let out shuddering moans. The two sat in the green field, embraced in sorrow as Adley and Luken watched from a distance.

Adley turned to Luken and wiped a tear from her face. She took in a deep breath and whispered, "Let's give them some more time."

"I'm afraid we don't have long." Luken's countenance fell. "The Dominion is coming."

Adley turned and motioned for Luken. "Then let's get the truck and make sure we are ready to move out. Grift just needs some time. Let's at least give him what time we can spare."

Luken nodded and followed Adley and Rot to the truck. Adley hopped into the back, counting the pieces of the Predecessor weapon.

"It's all there." Luken's voice was short. "Quit worrying about that thing. It is all in there. Now let's move." Luken peered over the edge of the truck. "Is there room back there? No way we leave without Rose and Eva. Make room."

Adley adjusted the cargo area and hopped out from the truck bed. As she exited, she paused to examine the streets. Dominion soldiers were strewn about, mingled with the wreckage of burned out rooks and shattered buildings. Rubble and debris littered the street from the town hall's assault. Adley examined the stronghold that had protected her and Grift. Ten-foot sections were missing from the brick walls and smoke was still billowing out its windows and shattered walls. Countless bullet holes covered the brick facade like stars covering a clear midnight sky.

"Surprised the old thing didn't give out and fall in," said Luken as he hopped in the driver's seat of the truck. "Looks like you have someone looking out after you."

"You're telling me." Adley spoke under her breath as she climbed into the truck cabin. Rot followed her, lying down in the in the truck bed, exhausted.

As Luken fired the truck engine, a datalink on the truck's dash began to beep. Luken threw the truck into gear and groaned as he motioned for Adley to answer the device.

Adley accessed the message and read it to Luken. "Zone four breached. Convoy is approaching."

"How far out?" Luken glanced nervously in the mirrors of the truck.

Adley read the flashing screen, her face filling with fear. "ETA to visual contact three minutes."

Luken punched the steering wheel and shook his head. "They just passed the last outpost. You have any weapons?"

"No. We used all the ammunition we had defending the town hall. You didn't bring any?" Adley peered through a porthole to the cargo bay. "We don't have time. How could you not bring any weapons?"

"No time to worry about that now," Luken scolded. "We just have to go. We have three minutes."

The truck's tires spit gravel and dirt into a cloud as it sped through the littered streets and rumbled out over the hills, approaching Grift and Wael. The two were looking over the petite figures covered in white linen as the truck approached. Luken skidded to a halt ten feet from the pair and hopped out of the driver's seat.

"Grift. We don't have much time. Three minutes. There is another convoy coming. It just cleared the last outpost. We need to go. Now." Luken's words were soft but carried urgency in their tone. "I'm so sorry, but we have to go now."

Grift nodded and staggered toward the two figures lying in the grass. Luken jogged in front of Grift and put his hand on Grift's chest. "Let me get her for you, Grift. In your shape right now..."

Grift smacked Luken's hand away and growled, "Don't touch her." He knelt down to gently lift his lost love and carried her to the truck. Luken followed behind with Eva's small frame wrapped in white cloth.

The truck spun out from Henshaw, making its way to Preost, leaving only dust in its wake.

The Mastermonk and Grift Shepherd? Cyric lowered his binoculars and shook his head, marveling at his good luck. *Lose one mark only to gain two.* There was still time to make good on his promise to Seam. If he could bag both the monk and Grift, he could double his pay. He got into the truck, smiling to himself.

Losing Wael had been unexpected. The variable he could not have foreseen was the monk's ally, the enigma who picked up and tossed jeeps like they were toys. Cyric rolled a cigarette and put it to his lips. It took everything within him not to pursue the truck that was speeding away in the distance. He thought back to the man who had nearly killed him by lobbing his jeep into the forest. *Can't say I've ever seen someone do that.*

Cyric flicked a match, held it to his cigarette, and took a long draw. He held it for a few seconds, allowing it to slowly release from his lungs. He savored the flavor of the drag and thought about how he would need to proceed moving forward. As long as the freak with inhuman strength was around, the job would be difficult. Not impossible, but very difficult.

Slowly, he drove through what had been Henshaw, examining the scene. The scattered bodies of Dominion soldiers surprised him further. There was more to this than one strong man. He counted through the carnage as one might figure sums in grade school. *Three rooks. Over twenty soldiers.* It didn't sit right to Cyric. Grift had something else with him to do this type of damage.

Cyric ran his car down the town's street, his eyes focusing on anything that could give him clues. He swerved his truck around and stepped out, his boot grinding against the gray gravel street. He approached four Dominion soldiers, reaching down to flip one of the corpses.

The man had only recently died. His body was cooling, but still warm. There was little blood, which was perplexing. Then Cyric saw it. A single hole had cleared through the man's chest, right where his heart was. The hole was about the circumference of a large coin, but it ran clear through, cauterizing the wound as the projectile shot through with medical precision.

Cyric dropped the body and flicked his cigarette out of his mouth. *Aleph above. Predecessor tech.* He stood, his head shaking silently, weighing the situation. He sprinted to the back of his truck, making a call over his datalink.

The black screen flickered with life, filled by a scarred, ugly face.

"Cyric?" The man spoke through clenched teeth as he scowled at the screen.

"Parker, we need to talk."

CHAPTER TWENTY

"We have to go to Rhuddenhall." Willyn's voice was firm as she paced the small command room perched in the rafters of Legion's Teeth. "We just got word that the capital building has been cleared and the streets are open. No one has heard from Hosp in days and everyone in the Realm knows I have returned. Seam will catch wind soon if he doesn't already know by now."

Bri folded his tattooed arms and shook his head. "Not good to go now. Much danger."

"Bri. You're wise and you saved my life, but you have to trust me." Willyn squared her shoulders and stared up at Bri. "The people of the Groganlands need me. My people, they are ready to fight. This is what we needed."

The words ricocheted from Bri as he pursed his lips and continued shaking his head. Willyn slammed her fist on the old oak table between them. "We need them, Bri. How else will we fight Seam and his forces? *Who else will fight the Dominion?* We can't sit here cowering in this mountain."

"I don't like it." Bri loosed his arms and rubbed at his forehead. "What about demon? That is main job."

Willyn nodded and paced to a plywood wall that had a tattered, yellowing map of Candor pinned to it. She scanned the lines of the mountain range stretching between their current stronghold and Rhuddenhall. She ran her fingers over the map and pointed at one of its depressions.

"Here." Willyn leaned in to examine the map. "This is the quickest way to the capital. We pack everyone in and we make the journey down the Serpent's Backbone. We can be there in less than five hours."

Bri stepped toward the map and squinted at the path that snaked its way from Legion's Teeth to Rhuddenhall. The path held multiple pitches and bends but it was wide. The hair on Bri's neck and arms stood on end as he thought of the massive convoy making the passage.

"Is there cover?" Bri rubbed at the bushy mustache, weaving his hands over its intricate braids, nervously.

Willyn shook her head and gathered a few papers from the office table. "No. That is why we have to move *now.*" She stepped over to Bri and grasped his forearm. "Bri. *Please trust me.* This is my homeland and these are my people. We have to gather them now if we are to stand any chance. As soon as Seam hears about what has happened he will send his legions into the Red City and burn it to the ground."

Deep thoughts wrinkled the giant's face, but he finally nodded as Willyn sighed in relief. She continued. "I need you and your men to retrieve the mirror, but please be discreet. I will have a rook ready for it to be loaded by the time you get back."

"Will it be marked? How do we know which one?"

"No." Willyn made her way for the door. "I don't want anyone knowing there is anything special in that rook, not even the driver. I will meet you in the docking bay and assign a rook to the task before we instruct pilots to load in. Understood?"

Bri nodded, but his face was pained with concern.

Willyn stood in the silence of the docking station. Only the sound of her footsteps interrupted the silence as she paced between the few rows of midnight black rooks the Reds had managed to seize. The machines gleamed beneath the overhead work lights, and the hangar smelled strongly of fuel. The machines brought a calm peace over Willyn as she walked among them. She could feel their engines throttle as she imagined them roaring to life.

"It's been too long," she whispered to herself. The noise of shuffling feet disrupted her concentration. She turned to find Bri and one other man carrying the mirror, still wrapped tight under its covering.

As Willyn opened her mouth to speak, Bri shook his head and placed his finger over his lips. He pointed at the mirror and tapped his ear. Willyn acknowledged the warning and pointed at an open rook. The men lowered the mirror into the cargo hold and sealed the door.

"It will be safe?" Bri's eyes carried his concern and did little to hide his fear as he spoke in hushed tones. "Who will drive it?"

Willyn waved off Bri's assistant and pulled Bri to the side. She whispered as they moved away from the rook. "I can't tell you, Bri." She glanced back at the rook. "I can't tell anyone. Not now. If anyone knows, then there is the chance of it falling into Seam's hands."

Bri frowned and tugged at his beard. "We need to hide it fast in the Red city."

"We will, Bri. We will hide it and then get it to Wael as fast as possible." Willyn squeezed Bri's hand. "And I will make sure you stay with it until it is secure."

Bri grinned at the offer. "Thank you."

The docking station that had laid silent an hour earlier was filled with the rumbling growl of rook engines and humming transports as they cranked to life. The cement box of a room pulsed with the vibrations of the machines. The roar of the room rattled Willyn's rib cage as she stood over the vehicles on a suspended catwalk.

Willyn paced down the thin metal riser as her voice called out over the loudspeakers, cutting through the chaos. At the sound of her voice, the engines were throttled back and all eyes turned toward the Sar.

"This is our time, fellow Grogans! We will hide no longer! Hosp's lies and the murderous members of our once proud

Council will never threaten us again! Our families have been murdered, our houses burned, our way of life shaken to its very foundations! Those seeking to disembowel our proud realm called us traitors! *Traitors!* I do not accept this. You, my brothers and sisters, are not traitors; you are warriors, patriots. Be proud, for today we will take our Realm back or die fighting."

Shouts went up, truck horns blasted through the air, and the men and women below her all threw their fists in the air, pumping their knuckles skyward five times. Willyn held up her fist and bowed her head, her red hair cascading over her face and shoulders. She pulled the long river of crimson back, donned her helmet, and leaned over the railing. "Ride. Do not stop. We ride to our deaths if that be Aleph's will. We stop for nothing!"

Willyn jogged down the metal staircase, leapt into the last remaining rook, and fired the engine to life. The rooks echoed the call, screaming with energy. She smiled as her helmet flashed her machine's diagnostics on her visor. Her rook lifted from the ground, swelling with energy as it hovered in place waiting for the bay doors to open.

The thirty-foot doors slid open and the midday sun slashed through the holding bay. The Red vehicles flooded through the opening with mechanical precision. Each machine fell in line in an ordered formation, swarming at breakneck speeds down the mountain. They were like a hive of angry hornets spilling into the valley below.

The Serpent's Spine soon came on the horizon. Willyn muted her microphone and listened as her commanders reported in. "Raven five on point. Rear guard, call in."

"Fox company calling in. Command, please report."

Willyn flipped her microphone back to life and answered. "Red Command in place. All companies proceed."

"Sir. We have a call from one of our insiders. They are moving." Seam opened a map on his datalink as his driver continued. "A large convoy of Red insurgents is on the move, streaming out of Legion's Teeth. It seems that they are making their way to Rhuddenhall."

Seam cursed and spun the map with his fingers as he examined his current position. "Push their coordinates to my datalink."

"Yes, sir."

Seam's map filled with red dots flowing between the green mountains. He ran his finger across the display and smiled before calling back to the driver. Why would the Reds leave their fortress in Legion's Teeth? The question rolled in his mind, until suddenly he realized it. *The mirror. The Reds were moving it to Rhuddenhall.* Seam laughed at his good luck.

"Fate smiles on me once again. They have left their mountain fortress and we are close enough to intercept them in route. Double your speed and set for mark 10-75 in grid G." Seam smiled as he pinched his eyelids shut. He drew in a deep breath before standing and pacing over to the figure standing in the corner.

Hosp's body stood alert, yet lifeless. Seam smirked at the frail frame in front of him before commanding the empty body to attention with his thoughts. "You will finally be of some use to me, you wretched worm. I wish you could feel what is about to happen."

Seam walked to the room holding the Serubs, as Hosp trailed close behind. As the High King stepped into the room, he was greeted with sneers of disdain from the three weakened deities. Their eyes spoke for them, and they snarled at their captor.

"It is about time we free your brother, Bastion. I need your strength. It is time for you all to prepare for this fight." Seam stepped to the side as Hosp's husk paced into the room and stood just a few feet from Arakiel. Seam smiled as he turned to walk away, leaving Hosp's body behind. "Enjoy your meal."

***

Willyn felt her heart thumping in her chest as she stormed down the wide mountain pass. It had been many months since she had lost herself within the cockpit of a rook. Here she was finally back in her element; at peace, at home. *When was the last time you rode?* Her hand vibrated over the two steering bars, and her memory trailed back. *Elum. You rode to Elum, hunting for Grift.* Images flew through her mind of Filip Darian storming from his glass palace, nearly naked if not for his thin silk robe. He had been drinking, of course. *When did that man not drink?* Darian's eyes were red from the booze, his face flushed in a stunning mixture of rage and brandy.

He's dead now. The thought fell in her mind like an anchor and brought her no glee. Under Filip's rule, Elum had kept to its word in all treaties and deals it had with the Groganlands. Filip might have been a drunk, but he was an honest drunk. Honest and loyal.

"More than I can say about the filth that killed him."

A mechanic voice came over the speakers in her helmet. "Come again, Red Command?"

Willyn jumped, her consciousness rejoining the mission at hand. *Focus Willyn.* "Nothing."

Another voice cut in over the coms. "My Sar." The rolling growl was easily placed. *Rander.* "We've got some disturbance on the radar. Something big is heading our way. You will have visual once you and the men are at the end of the pass."

Willyn looked outside the cockpit, the arid mountains flying by her. "Send me whatever you see, Rander." Instantly, in the left corner of her helmet a small map appeared. The Grogan forces were colored in red, careening down the green topographic mountains at full speed. Ten miles ahead was an enormous amorphous smear of yellow, undulating like wasps dancing on a nest.

Willyn felt her stomach seize. The bright streak of yellow was huge. Her headset filled with questions stemming from her soldiers.

A nervous soldier broke through the communication feed. "What the hell is that?"

"Command, do you have a visual?"

"Easy, soldiers." Willyn's voice thundered over the coms with brute force. "Steady yourselves." Her mind searched for the right words. "These are Dominion forces. They have brought the fight to us."

Silence overtook the com channel. The void of fear was palpable, and Willyn fought to find the words to say when a low melody slowly rolled over the emptiness, filling the coms. Willyn's breath seized within her as the hair on her neck stood up.

"To die a good death is great, my friends. All for all. For the Groganlands." One by one, the others joined the chorus. The ancient war song rang out over the thunderous sound of the rook motors roaring as the war party barreled down the Serpent's Spine toward a fight that Willyn knew she could not win. She screamed, her voice filling the coms, pushing her thrusters forward with an explosive pride. *Go down fighting.* "Let's give them hell, boys! Let's take back what is ours!"

The Synod let themselves into the chamber where Seam sat on his royal seat, a knowing smile etched on the High King's face.

"My dear friends, you look so...*refreshed*."

Arakiel, Abtren, and Nyx glided into the room, their eyes like open tombs. Arakiel did not waste his breath. "We are ready. What would you have us do, Keeper?"

Seam stood and walked toward them, unfazed by the slaughter he witnessed over the security feeds. The Serubs fought over Hosp's carcass like a pack of ravenous lions – there was no decency and no restraint as they gorged themselves. His mind was clear, somehow summoning an ability to filter out the horrors that the Serubs could rend, able to look past the mutilation and the reek of death that befell Hosp. He would study them meticulously, he promised himself, even if it took a thousand slaughters for one clue at how to keep them in check. *Watch them, study them, find their weaknesses.*

"Well, Keeper? What is your command?" Arakiel's crimson eyes burned with new energy, stirring Seam out of his daydream.

He stood from his seat, self-assured, willing to step among the den of lions as if they were kittens. Seam held up the bracer that bore the Keys of Candor and spoke, his voice echoing through the chamber.

"It is time, my Synod. We will rout the Grogans, and I will claim the Sardom."

The three barely showed any emotion. The Serubs did not care anymore for keeping up the charade, and would no longer play games. There was no point, for each had tried to openly strike him down and had failed. They had taken off their masks, unable or unwilling to mince the reality of what Seam had unlocked from the glass prisons.

Abtren was the first to look at him directly, her eyes filling with unholy, purple fire. A long black tongue snaked out, licking her plump lips, and she smiled. Seam noticed that Hosp's blood was still smeared across her white serrated teeth. "I'm *starving*, Seam. Is there something more to eat?" It was not so much a question as it was a demand. Abtren stood and roared at him, the purple flames within her eyes alight with new fury.

Arakiel pulled out a broken bloody femur from his robes. He held it up toward the High King, smiling as if to offer him a bite, before siphoning out the marrow within. He turned and locked his dead eyes on Seam, his voice in agreement, "This...this...is not enough."

Nyx crooned, stepping from the shadows, her dead black eyes vibrating with a sick excitement. She crawled on the floor like a spider. She cocked her head up toward him and whispered, barely audible, "You've brought me something, haven't you? Something sweet? Something... *young?*"

Seam's face was set like stone. *He was in control.* No matter what they did, *he was always in control.* He reminded himself of his power as he tried to chase away the doubts clawing at the back of his mind.

"I'm glad to see you are ready for more, my Synod. Don't worry, there will be much more for you to eat. I know what debts I must pay. The Reds are coming down from the Serpent's Spine as we speak. We will be waiting for them there. You will have plenty to choose from. Have who you would like, my friends. But know this. You have one task and one task alone..."

The three stared at Seam as he pointed toward the front of the titan. "You will call for Bastion. The Reds are moving, undoubtedly with his mirror. We must find it!"

The three Serubs snarled at their master and shared quick glances with one another before nodding.

"We will find him, Keeper," Arakiel muttered.

A bead of sweat slipped down Willyn's forehead and stung her eye. She blinked and focused on the mass of yellow objects that were locked on a collision course with her army. It did not take any fancy calculations to understand her faction was outmatched. Willyn coached herself as she made final approach. *Wait for a visual, Willyn. We don't know what type of firepower they are carrying.*

"Raven company, report." Willyn flipped a switch and her visor split her companies by color, the black spot of Raven was positioned only seconds from enemy contact as they led the pack down Serpent's Spine.

"Visual confirmed, command. Four heavies, two dozen lights, and ah maybe a dozen, no two dozen transports."

"Transports?" Willyn ran a check on her weapon's system. "Are they armed transports?"

"Negative command. Civilian."

What? Civilian transports? Willyn ran scenarios through her mind before laying out commands. "Fox unit, break from rear guard and climb. Get some elevation. Red command, stay on me. Phoenix, decrease speed and make for Rhuddenhall. Be ready to reverse course on my command." She paused, her mind weighing her options. "Raven unit...light 'em up."

A chuckle came over the com as Raven leader called in. "Yes, sir!"

Willyn's rook sliced around a jagged red rock in time to catch Raven unit opening their firepower. Two of Seam's own rooks at the point of their procession exploded in a fiery crash as the Reds fired hundreds of rounds through them.

"Woo!" Raven leader's cheer rang over the comm. "Don't let up, boys!"

One of the Dominion titans unleashed a cannon blast that sent several Red rooks spiraling out of control, their steel frames crumpling in a fiery explosion. The black hovercrafts smashed into the sheer red rock walls sending clouds of red dust and fire across the canyon floor.

"Spread formation, Raven!" Willyn screamed. "Don't cluster or those titans will take you all out at once." Willyn scanned her visor, waiting for the brown dots of Fox unit to crest the top of the canyon. "Fox unit, pick it up!" Willyn called. "We need you to drop in and concentrate fire on the rear units."

"Thirty seconds ETA, Command." Fox leader called in over the datalink as another titan thundered with life, its blast obliterating a Red rook while grazing another, forcing it to break formation.

"Make it twenty seconds, Fox company," Willyn barked through the microphone as she pushed her own rook forward. "Red unit on me, let's clean this up."

Willyn sped through the canyon, deftly sweeping past the downed rooks and fallen stones littering her path. Ten rooks with red stripes running down their side followed closely behind. The jagged canyon walls flashed by as Willyn flipped on her heavy weaponry. "Command Three and Five. Mortars with me on the lead titan. Everyone else, spray their perimeter units."

"Yes, sir!" her company called in unison.

Willyn watched as the meter ticked up as her mortar cannon heated. "How soon, Three? Five?" The two confirmed they had no more than five seconds to ready their guns. "On me, guys. Let's blow their point wide open. Raven, cut down the middle once there is an opening." The rook flashed an alert that her mortar was ready. "Lock and fire...now!"

The three fired on the hulking titan leading Seam's company. The first landed three feet wide, spraying red dust and rocks against the hovering menace. Debris rolled down the shimmering black hull of the tank, but the blast had no effect. As the smoke from the first shot began to clear, Willyn's round smashed into the front of the titan, lifting it from the ground as the outer hull peeled back. Almost simultaneously, the third round hammered into the colossus, rolling it to its side, sliding it into several Dominion rooks flanking it.

"Again!" screamed Willyn. The three unleashed another round of artillery fire and all three met their mark, turning the titan into a fiery cloud of shredded steel. Cheers rang out over the com as Raven company sped through the opening and fired on the surrounding rooks. Bullets and light rockets flashed across the canyon as the Reds and Dominion traded casualties.

Seam watched from his titan as the Red forces pressed closer to his titan and the rear of his formation. "Synod. It is time to end this."

Seam called to the driver. "Drop the rear cargo bay doors."

"Yes, sir. Right away." The driver's voice quivered as he answered.

Seam shouted into his datalink. "Transports, stop all progress and open your doors. *Now!*"

Seam closed his eyes and drew in a deep breath as he opened the thousands of eyes waiting in the dark behind him. The swarm of morel bodies spilled from the sides of the formation. They leapt from the transports and slipped up both canyon walls, scaling the rocks, using one another like a human ladder, easily reaching the ridge and running toward the Red army's position below. Seam glanced through his hosts and observed the Serubs as they moved with the fray of puppeted flesh.

Seam smiled, a feeling of ecstasy sweeping over him. Soon, even the Sardom would be his. His army hung on the canyon walls like vultures, waiting for the right moment to strike.

"Sar Kara. Do you have visual? What is *that?*"

Three figures had exited the transports and were strolling toward the Red forces, unaffected by the chaos around them. Two women and one man. Willyn stared at them, her heart sinking with the recall of memory. *The Spire. The Fallen.* The face of one of them, one of the women she undoubtedly recognized. *Aleph, above. They're here. He actually brought them.* The three broke into a sprint toward Willyn's forces with wide, insane smiles.

One of the nearest Reds opened fire on the three, but the bullets melted into an invisible sphere that lit with fire upon impact. The Synod continued to press on until the largest figure, the man who stood a head taller than the women, thrust his hands in the direction of their attacker. The rook suddenly stopped its attack, turned, and opened fire on its nearest comrade.

"Raven nine. *What are you doing?*" Raven leader's voice cut through the airwaves, but there was no answer as the rogue unit destroyed his nearest partner and moved his guns onto the next.

"Stand down, Raven nine!" Number nine continued firing only to rip down another ally before Willyn screamed over the line.

"Take him down! Now!" Raven unit obeyed, surrounding their partner and cutting him down with their massive firepower. Willyn screamed out over the coms. "All units, concentrate all your fire on these three!" She pressed her finger on the datalink map over the three dots marked in blue. "Give them everything you got, and don't let up! Fire at will! Now!"

The remaining Raven and Red Command units turned in an instant, and the three were lit up like fireworks. Willyn kept her trigger finger engaged as the ripping sound of heavy machine gun fire thundered through the valley. "Keep shooting! Don't let them move an inch! The orb of fire that surrounded them grew brighter, forcing Willyn to squint and shield her eyes. She screamed over the lines, "Don't let up! Whatever you do, don't let up!"

Seam outstretched his arm, his mind extended beyond his body, deep within the hoard of morels he controlled. He was careful to focus, computing the thousands of perceptions belonging to the soulless, who clung to the walls of the canyon; silently waiting for his command. In the kaleidoscope of views within the hive mind, he could see the Serubs marching toward the line of rooks, easily deflecting the firepower focused on them. The Reds unleashed all they had, and the Serubs' shield erupted with a blinding light.

Nyx's voice called out. "*Unleash them now!*" In seconds, the wave of morels rushed into the valley like a tsunami. The Serubs had distracted their enemies long enough. Walls of bodies swarmed into the fray, roaring with unnatural life. Two thousand mouths opened and screamed in unison with the High King's voice.

"FIND THE MIRROR. KILL THE REDS! KILL THEM ALL!"

The deafening scream of the Reds' firepower filled the valley, and Willyn let up from the trigger. *Something has shifted.* She couldn't explain it, but she knew to trust her instincts. Her heart froze in her chest as she scanned her datalink. It took only a second to read the map. Her company of fifteen rooks were positioned against the three Serubs in a firm line. The Serubs stood alone in the empty valley, while Seam's other vehicles were marked in a line of yellow. Fox and Phoenix company continued to fill in from behind.

Willyn tried to convince herself that the odds were in her favor. Then she heard it; *a roaring scream*. Her cockpit sounded with an alarm and her map projected thousands of green dots flooding into the canyon. The mass stampeded into the fray at an unnatural speed akin to a herd of wild animals, their formation a living wedge, coming down on the Reds like an axe. She realized she had seen this same manic movement before. *Tunnel 1AAE.*

The memory cut her focus to shreds as images of her proud men running to their death to defend her filled her mind. She tried to scream over the com, but the words were too late.

The wave of bodies tore through their formation, and the rooks adjacent to Willyn somersaulted into the air, flipping over the rush of enemies. The bodies clung to the vehicles like locusts, slamming their hands and heads into the machines, willfully breaking their bodies to claw out the protected pilots. Willyn's forces desperately tried to pivot their fire to hold the surge back, but the horde was too great. The first rook in formation was covered and dismantled in seconds. The radio lines filled with screams as the pilots met their end under the swarm.

Willyn engaged her thrusters, and pulled herself out of the fray as she barked commands. "All units, pull back. Fox and Phoenix units, deliver your full payload! *Now!*" A booming chorus of mortars erupted from Fox and Phoenix company, and half the valley was filled with a hellish blaze; a firewall that reached fifty feet into the air. The wall of the shambling bodies twisted like dead insects in an inferno, but for each one that fell there was another to take its place. The remaining Reds formed a phalanx of machines, lobbing explosives up and over the front guard of rooks while the units in front kept their chain-guns blazing.

Aleph, there are too many of them. Willyn's mind searched for solutions, when her com lit up with a familiar voice.

"Get out of here, little one!"

Her heart slammed in her chest. *Bri.*

An open bed transport pulled next to Willyn's rook. Bri stood in the back with a mounted fifty-caliber deck gun. Bri's weapon blazed as he called out to her, his jumbled language barely audible over the roar of mortar and gunfire. "Did you not hear me? Get out. You must get to the Red City!"

"I'm not leaving them, Bri, not like this!" she screamed.

Despite the shockwave of sudden force, the Reds were regaining some control. The morels drifted back, but the margins of containment were painfully thin. Arakiel the Defiler charged, barreling toward them like a freight train, his light linen robes blazing in the hot desert wind. He carried only a heavy staff. No matter how many rounds the Reds unleashed, Arakiel could not be stopped. He madly swung his staff as he burst through their formation with sheer rage. His eyes blazed like burning rubies as he slammed his weapon through the machines, vaulting himself over the front line and into the middle of the force. He ripped through the companies in seconds, tearing five of their rooks to shreds with his bare hands.

He's breaking up the formation. He's breaking us down. Willyn's datalink chirped chaotically as she witnessed the orderly formation crumble under the single Serub's hands. Suddenly, two other points in the formation began to disintegrate. *The other Serubs are flanking us. Aleph, help us!* Willyn's eyes darted from one side of the formation to the other, trying to locate the others.

The goddess with midnight black eyes stood over the rooks on a pedestal formed out of the living bodies. Like a conductor of a symphony, her hands extended as mobs of the soulless rushed, forming themselves into huge weapons. Willyn's jaw dropped as she saw a school of the monsters morph themselves into a war hammer for the Serub to wield. The Serub swept her minions up and down, pummeling her enemies to the sound of crunching bones and broken bodies. With each swing, the hammer healed itself anew with more of the mindless, only to be crushed against the Reds' rooks, again and again.

The Serub Willyn recognized from the Spire was far less exotic in her movements, but the speed at which she operated was horrific. She leapt over the fray and tore out Red pilots one by one from their machines, throwing them like rag dolls or ripping their bodies like paper. The gore of her work filled the air with a fine red mist. Each kill the Serubs made emboldened and strengthened them.

Bri's voice cut through the fog of war as he yelled over the com. "Willyn. You must go. Make for the Red City! Take the mirror and go!"

Willyn's heart slammed into her throat. *He knows. He knows I have it.* Bri had not fallen for her ruse. Willyn knew that there was little time. She would either die here or fight another day. She barked over the coms, "*All units scramble to Rhuddenhall! I repeat! Scramble!*" The phalanx crumbled and the rooks broke from their formation, thundering out of the valley. The morels that remained gave a furious chase, but the Serubs held their ground. Willyn swept her rook and turned for retreat, but her machine shuttered under a shocking blow. Willyn fired the engines, only to be greeted with the grinding sound of the mechanics sucking in dirt and swiftly dying.

The roof of the cockpit peeled back and Arakiel stood over the wreckage, peering down at Willyn as if she were a bird in a cage. He snarled as he smiled, his eyes burning with an unnatural fury. His voice shook Willyn's entire frame.

"**You. You have him.**" Arakiel stretched his arms to the side and let out a cry that filled the canyon. Nyx and Abtren focused their attention on Arakiel as he announced the discovery of Bastion's mirror. The Serub flashed his dagger fangs as he moved to rip Willyn from the cockpit. In one swift motion he snatched her from her seat and hurled the helmet from her head. He lifted her in the air and spat as he screamed.

"You dare try and hide our brother from us? You dare attack the divine and think you can live? You will pay for your sins, you worthless insect!"

A flash of immense heat and light burst in front of Willyn and her skin was singed with a sharp pain. The unknown impact jarred her from Arakiel's grasp and she fell, thudding against the hull of her rook and rolling in the dirt. Stunned, she struggled to her feet, only to hear Bri's voice.

"Run, little one! Run!"

Bri stood, fixed on the back of the truck as it barreled toward Arakiel. Bri's deck gun rattled his giant frame as it slung fifty caliber rounds into Arakiel. A rook swept next to Willyn and she was snatched into its cargo hold. Willyn screamed for Bri to turn around, but her cries fell on deaf ears. Arakiel charged Bri, ignoring the bullets slamming into him. The Serub leapt on the bed of the truck and slammed his iron staff across Bri's back. The mighty Bagger warrior fell to the earth, his back caving with a deafening crack.

Willyn opened her mouth to scream. A choking cry tried to escape, but her body refused to give in to the storm roaring within. Bri fell to the ground in a broken heap, his size shrinking in her vision as the rook rocketed her away from the battlefield. She had failed him, and she had failed her mission. An overwhelming rush of grief crippled her. She slammed her fist against the cockpit, cursing her life and all that she had ever loved.

CHAPTER TWENTY-ONE

Seam kicked at a charred corpse that littered the canyon floor as he walked toward the rook holding his next prize. The rust colored stone of the canyon was spattered with the crimson carnage showcasing his brief encounter with the Red forces. Burned and twisted rooks joined dismembered, bullet-riddled bodies, a quilted patchwork of hell on earth. The rancid smell of burned flesh wafted in the air, filling Seam's nostrils. The smell of victory was not sweet, but it was glorious.

"Let me keep them." Nyx's body was spread across a pile of ravaged cadavers, like a spider guarding its catch. Her black eyes glistened with desire as she glanced up at Seam. "These will make an excellent supply for you, Keeper. You've seen what *they* can do." She threw her sable eyes toward the hoard of Seam's idle warriors. "You can do so much more, High King. You can accomplish so much more than you even realize." She glanced down on the bodies of those dead beneath her. "With these supplies, your army can be strengthened, improved." She stared at him, her eyes reflecting the smoke that filled the battlefield. "Just say the word, my lord."

Seam turned up his nose at the site of Nyx digging through the numerous bodies of his fallen enemies. He spoke, turning his eyes from the sight, quelling the wave of nausea that threatened to come over him. "Fine. But I don't want to see or smell them until they are ready."

Nyx licked her lips and smiled as she closed her eyes and pulled in a deep breath. She exhaled and in one motion, the bodies beneath her rose to shambling life. Morels began lining in formation, stowing themselves within the transports, while a remnant of the hollow soldiers drug the remains of bodies too damaged to be puppeted. Nyx ensured nothing was left behind.

Seam stepped past the lines of morels as they set to their work, moving closer to Willyn's rook. Arakiel was standing next to the machine speaking in the ancient tongue to Bastion, his voice painted with pride and authority.

"Te alek man zeth..." Arakiel snarled as Seam stepped around the shredded rook and peered at Bastion locked in the glass prison.

Seam smiled, confident. "I take it your brother is telling you what a gracious master I am." Bastion's eyes did not sway from the High King. The green glowing orbs radiated like bewitched marbles, and they followed Seam's every move, reading him with untold curiosity. Bastion's face remained stoic as Seam crossed his arms and leaned over the cargo hold. "I welcome you to a new Candor, Bastion."

Bastion glanced at Arakiel, his face searching for approval. Arakiel nodded, and Bastion spoke. "I understand your ways, Seam Panderean. Your power. Count me along with the rest of my kin at your side. I only ask for one thing."

"Name it." Seam growled as he prepared for yet another proposal from the Serubs. The cost was always the same, and Seam would pay that price no matter how high the cost.

"I will spare you flowery speech. I want to feed, to kill. Not one, not two. But *thousands*." Bastion's voice held a strange tenor, a voice that seemed to surround the High King from all sides. The pair of hollow green eyes blazed behind the glass. "Make no mistake. If you try to curb my desires, I will turn against you."

Seam's lips curled into a thin smile and his eyes narrowed as he nodded. "Your brother and sisters have already named the same price, Bastion. I am happy to pay it. There will be much opportunity for us. So bring your fear and destruction. Fear breeds order. I will ensure that there is enough fodder to keep your trough full."

The High King pointed to the mirror and snapped his fingers at Arakiel, causing the massive warrior to bristle with curtailed rage. Seam's voice was tinged with impatience. "Lift him from this wreck and bring him to the titan. Now, where is the last mirror, Arakiel?"

Bastion's voice bellowed, interrupting the exchange. "Keeper. Please...it is time to release me. There is something that I must do." Seam paused, his mind weighing the veiled answer of the god in the glass.

The High King felt the presence of Abtren pressing in behind him. He turned and looked at her, his face full of questions. Abtren nodded, an answer for his hesitation. "It is time. Release our brother, Keeper. He will serve you well." The Synod gathered closely around Seam, pressing in on him, their countenances filled with an emotion that the High King had not witnessed before. *They are hopeful.* Seam stood silent, weighing what this meant in his mind.

"Very well. I now release you, Bastion. Join my Synod. Join my Dominion."

He extended his right hand, bearing the Keys of Candor, and reached into the glass. It gave way like water, and Bastion grabbed his hand. In one swift motion, Bastion exited the mirror, shielding his green eyes in the desert sun.

The Synod gathered around him, and Seam stood aghast as they embraced him. Bastion's release marked something unspoken between the family of divines, though Seam did not understand its significance.

Bastion openly hugged his sisters and bowed reverently toward his elder brother who, in turn, embraced him. For the first time, Seam looked at the beings who were always on the edge to kill him in a new light, and it confounded him.

"As much as I do cherish this, there is much to be done. Bastion, you are now released, so do what you must."

Bastion turned to the Keeper of the Keys and bowed his head in reverence. "Gladly." Bastion stepped toward the High King, and for the first time Seam noticed the growing fangs that protruded from his face, razor sharp protrusions extending from the face like tusks.

Seam braced himself for an attack, his heart hammering in his chest. He screamed, his voice full of rage, "Come at me and fall like the rest of your kin! I do not fear your kind."

Yet to Seam's surprise, Bastion strode by him, sprinting for a large body lying twenty yards away. Bastion stooped to pick the carcass up and smirked as he realized the man was not yet dead.

Bastion's voice struck out over the desert plain. "Priest of the Landless. Did you think you would leave this world so easily?" He held up the body of the large tattooed warrior. The man's legs dangled loosely beneath him, and Seam's mouth went dry as the Serub's physical size expanded, his frame growing to gigantic proportions, dwarfing the man he held within his hand.

Bastion spoke, his booming voice becoming almost tender. "You...and your people surprise me, Rihtian. You deny the very gods you served for generations? Why do you betray us?"

Bri forced his swollen eyelids open, painfully turning his head to face Seam, his voice trembling, barely above a whisper. Even across the waste, Seam was struck at how bright the Bagger's eyes were. "You can stop this. You hold Keys. Put them all back in mirror. Stop this. New start."

Bastion laughed and turned to face his siblings. Arakiel, Nyx, and Abtren howled like beasts, but Seam felt a shift in the air radiating from the Synod. *Fear.*

The priest spoke, his voice calling out over the throng of laughing Celestials. The voice of the broken priest took on a new intonation, a new cadence of pure and absolute authority.

"Seam Panderean, hear now the words of Aleph, the last words that I will ever speak. You know the truth about these you have unlocked, and you know the truth about *me.* Your destiny hangs by your choice; your very kingdom hangs by your choice. So choose now. **My will for you will be accomplished and my peace will reign over Candor.**"

The Serubs went silent and pounced onto the priest, tearing his body to shreds like a pack of ravenous lions. Seam could barely register what was happening as his mind grappled with Bri's final words.

'Peace. My peace will reign over Candor.'

The words clawed at the inside of Seam's chest. The word peace felt so cheap. There would never be peace, but there would finally be order which he would see to himself.

Seam watched as the Serubs gorged themselves on the flesh of the Bagger priest. The earthly remains of the man were gone in mere seconds. They turned and faced him, their faces covered with the blood of the seer. There was no joy in this kill. Unlike his private viewing of Hosp's final demise, an unsettled nervousness clouded his thoughts and tainted his recent victory as he watched his celestial pets gorge themselves.

Abtren stepped forward, her eyes full of dancing, mesmerizing light. "Well, what is your answer, High King? Do you seek our enemy's counsel now, or do you claim your place as the Lord and Master of Candor?"

Seam glared at them, staring at the rabid dogs he had released on the world. Heavy thoughts clouded his mind, but he spoke without pause. "There is one more mirror, Abtren. One more of your cursed kin to release. I will see this task through." He turned to face Arakiel.

"Where is it, Arakiel? Where is Isphet's mirror?"

Arakiel's lips were pursed, but he spoke with little dissention. "The last mirror is one you must consider carefully, High King. Isphet has been growing in power for weeks now, by means that I cannot see. I warn you...he will be less *agreeable* to your lead than we have been."

Seam turned and walked toward the Synod and stared into their terrible eyes, feeling no fear. "*Less agreeable?* Well, that gives me much to think about, Arakiel." He held up the bracer that bore the keys, his eyes locking on the Serub chief. "A shame that I will have to train Isphet like the rest of you. Will you dogs never learn? Now tell me, where is the last mirror?"

Arakiel growled, and the others in the Synod bristled at the insult. "Preost, Keeper. The monks have Isphet locked in their forest monastery, if it still exists."

Seam nodded, his eyes widening. "Taluum." He could hardly believe it. They had been hiding the last cursed god under Aleph's own sanctuary. "Very well. *Let's finish this.* We will rendezvous in Zenith and gather more forces. Then, we make for Preost." Seam turned away, stomping through the desert, his mind still clouded by the last words of the Bagger priest.

Peace.

Bronson sat over a table covered in empty bottles and the chalky remains of broken pills. He fought to steady his trembling hands, shaking as if hypothermia was overtaking him. He was sweating so profusely that it looked like he was baking in the heat of the desert sun. A sharp pain spiked in his stomach, and he fought to remember the last time he had eaten. Unsteady hands cupped the last few pills strewn on the table and he chewed them whole as he sat back, trying to ignore the pain searing in his gut.

The consistent, throbbing dagger of pain in his stomach caused Bronson to curse, wiping the bottles and drugs from the table. He screamed, his hoarse throat trembling and tattered. Screaming, medicating, drinking, nothing would shrink the devil that had taken residence deep inside.

He got up, pacing toward his bookcase. His hands fumbled past several books before landing on an overturned, dust-covered picture. Hot tears rolled down Bronson's cheeks as he grasped the picture and fought the desire to throw it as far from himself as possible.

"I can't." Bronson choked on his words. "I can't do this anymore. I can't let you see me like this."

He turned the photograph over and stared at the bright, smiling faces of his family. The children he prayed to receive for so long stared back at him, unaware of their father's private sins. He had fought to protect them the only way he knew how: sacrificing other lives to save theirs. Sobs overtook him as he clutched the small frame to his chest and collapsed to the floor. His tears smeared the polished floor as he balled up over the image. *They are beautiful. So pure.*

"Please forgive me." Bronson could barely choke out his plea. "I did all this to protect you. I am a fool. I know you would not want this." His eyes fell over the faces of his family.

Gods. Their eyes.

What had been the blue and brown eyes of his daughters and wife were now just hollow black voids, deep pits that swirled to some dark hellish place.

They are taking my mind. The Serubs won't rest until they destroy everything. They're taking my body. They're taking my mind. Soon...they will take them. My family. He stood and threw the picture, shattering the faces of his loved ones against the marble floor. His soul broke with the sound of the glass shattering, releasing a flood of misery that caused him to wail without control. He laid on the floor, a broken shell of the man he once was. He could have stayed there if not for the datalink that chirped with life. The chime was unique. *Seam.*

"No more." A resolve quickened in Bronson's soul as he composed himself. "This has to end. *You* have to end."

Bronson wiped his face and opened his datalink. His heart stopped as his eyes fell over Seam. The High King spoke, his voice thin and tinny over the small speaker. "Bronson. I will be arriving within twenty-four hours. Ready the guard and assemble a full military force. We are heading for Preost. Make the appropriate preparations."

"Preost, my lord?" Bronson tried to steady his trembling fists.

"The monks hold the last treasure that I seek."

Bronson nodded, fearing to hold eye contact with the king. "Anything else, my lord?"

"Yes. Check in with our mercenaries. I want a report on the targets. Let them know if they can't locate and capture within seventy-two hours all deals are off. I'll just have to do it myself."

"Yes, sir." Bronson dipped his head again and began to close the datalink before he was interrupted by his master.

"And Bronson. Clean yourself up. You look terrible. If you can't handle your affairs and this post, then I have no reason for you." The hollow eyes on the screen nailed him in his place. "Don't put me in that position, Bronson. There always needs to be a reason."

Bronson nodded without a word before terminating his connection. He wiped his calloused palm across his face and tried to breathe as he started to pull up Cyric's channel. His finger hovered over the final confirmation. He could not force himself to comply. He swiped away the protocol, only to pull a new channel up again.

His datalink blinked and chirped as Bronson waited, staring down into the glare of the small machine's screen, trying to avoid eye contact with his own reflection. The screen lit up and Adley's face greeted Bronson. The sight of his secret ally brought a bit of momentary relief to him, and he sighed as he saluted her.

"*Adley*. I am glad to see you." Bronson took in a deep breath and checked his office doors. "Is everything okay?"

Adley shook her head and responded. "Bronson, is this a secured line? Why are you contacting me?"

"I have news. It can't wait." Bronson checked the line source and nodded. "And yes, this line is secure. How are your efforts in Lotte going?"

"I don't really know. We have secured some new weapons and our numbers are growing, but we are losing ground. Seam's forces just destroyed Henshaw. If not for the...*tech*, we would have died." Bronson's eyes grew at Adley's aside. She continued, "We need help, Captain. What is the news of the resistance in Zenith? Have you taken any ground?"

Bronson swallowed hard, trying to ignore the fact that he had completely failed to connect with any cells of resistors in Zenith while playing the errand boy to Seam. He cleared his throat and tried to change the subject.

"Grift? How is Grift?" Bronson's hands shook as he mentioned his old friend, threatening to drop his datalink onto the cold floor below. "Is he okay?"

Adley's countenance dropped and she whispered over the line. "Not good." She leaned in and whispered, "Rose is dead. They killed her in Henshaw, too. He's on the edge. It's not good."

The two sat in silence on the line when Adley spoke up again. "You said you had news?"

"Yes." Bronson shook his head, nodding. "But it's not good. Seam has secured another mirror. He is making for Zenith as we speak, but his eye is set on Preost. He says that the last mirror is there. Is that true?"

Adley's eyes went distant, and her lips tightened. She nodded, her face washed in disappointment. "Was Willyn...?"

"Killed? I don't know." Bronson stared at the floor. "Seam mentioned nothing of her. I just know Seam got what he wanted. She was going for the mirror too, wasn't she?"

Bronson continued, "He also wanted me to round up the mercenaries."

Adley ran her fingers through her hair and took a deep breath. "That's okay. We intercepted the merc chasing Wael. The Mastermonk is secure."

"That's not the issue," blurted Bronson. "He is about to call all the hunters off. It won't matter anymore, Adley, if Seam can get his hands on the last mirror. He knows that nothing can stop him. He's not worried about Wael or Grift any longer."

Adley cursed under her breath. "How much time do we have?"

"Seventy-two hours." Bronson's answer was quick, certain. "He will be here within the day and I have a feeling he won't waste any time moving on his last target."

Adley leaned in and spoke, her voice barely above a whisper. "Bronson. Gather who you can. We are going to need as much help as possible. We don't have time to waste. Thanks for checking in."

The datalink went blank and Bronson stood in the shadows of his room hunched over his datalink. He stared at its blank screen, allowing himself to finally glimpse at his pale, sunken face. He no longer recognized the ghost staring back at him, the loose skin hanging from his frame and dark black bags beneath his eyes. In mere months, he had wasted into a living corpse, a shroud of death fitting for the dead soul that hid within his body.

Bronson paced to the bookcase and snatched up his pistol. He stepped over the broken glass littering the floor and flipped over the picture. His family's eyes were normal again, thank Aleph. He spoke to them, his voice trembling, "I'm sorry. I won't fail again. I promise."

Seam's convoy barreled through the streets of Zenith as if they were part of a triumphant parade within the metropolis. Soldiers and citizens gathered to witness the procession, stopping to salute the brigade as it passed by, traveling to the black, shining Spire that stood proudly within the city center. The rooks accompanying the convoy swept from front to back of the formation while the transports barreled over the freshly poured asphalt streets. The desert heat pounded on the proud city as it simmered in the midday sun.

Seam growled, staring at his datalink. Bronson had quit responding to his calls. Cursing under his breath, he snapped the datalink shut and leapt from the titan as it came to rest underneath the shadow of the Spire.

"The worthless old drunk, he probably finally offed himself..." Begrudgingly, the High King contacted another aid. A cherub-faced young man answered the call immediately.

"My king?" The advisor saluted and held, waiting for the order.

"Open up a universal broadcast." Seam began to shut his datalink connection as the assistant stammered a follow-up question.

"Is tomorrow morning the best time?" The self-assured follower smiled as he waited for a response.

"Now, you fool." Seam slammed the line shut and opened the back of the titan.

Every screen in Candor lit up as an alarm screeched over each of the datalink screens. From smoky taverns to city squares, men and women gathered around the transmission filling every screen on the continent. The insignia of the Dominion, the black and gold shield surrounded by burning flames, held the screen for several minutes before cutting to the High King standing on a stage with the Synod standing behind him. Arakiel, Abtren, Nyx, and Bastion towered behind the High King, covered with long black robes trimmed with golden threads, their faces covered by cowls draped over their heads. Seam's chest was wrapped in golden silk, and his long brown hair flowed over his shoulders, blending with the black cape hanging from his broad frame.

He stepped forward and stared into the cameras. "Candor. The time has come to stand united. For months, we have worked together to unite, binding the deep wounds of our infighting, rebuilding the five Realms into the splendid nation we have always longed to be."

Seam glanced behind him at the Synod and continued. "Yet there are those among us who would destroy us, wolves in sheep skins. These have sown strife and fighting between us and despite my best efforts to unite the last of mankind on this world, their tactics are working. Terrorists continue to destroy our unification, our attempts to establish a secure and long-lasting peace with a never-ending chain of violence." Seam paused, his face somber. "It brings me great pains to report to you that rebels in the Groganlands have unleashed a vicious coup within the Realm, and have succeeded in assassinating the Surrogator, Hospsadda Gran, our ally. Because of this, to all my loyal Grogan allies: I now stand not just as your Sar, but as the High King of Candor. We are all one, and I will die uniting us if necessary! The contingent, identified only as the Reds, will stop at nothing to try to weaken our resolve; our Dominion."

Seam stepped closer to the camera, crowding the screen. "I want to make myself very clear, Candor. This Dominion will not be opposed. It will not be challenged. If any man, woman, or child makes an attempt to create discord within our continent, they will be dealt with swiftly. Rebellion and resistance will not be tolerated, for peace and security must be enforced at all times." Again, Seam paused, his eyes never blinking. "It is my duty as High King to protect us all from this growing threat of rebellious upstarts, these wolves who would threaten our flock. They come for blood, but I come for justice and order, and I will not flinch in my resolve."

Seam cleared his throat as a map of Candor came up on the screen. "Intelligence has been gathered around the rebel factions that have been meeting in secret within our Realms. Rest assured, all of the cells of rebels have been identified and will be extinguished swiftly. Yet, to my dismay, it has wounded me to learn that the trusted Convent Order housed within the Forest Realm of Preost has been fanning the flames of insurgency against the Dominion. My friends, though it might be hard to believe, the monks want only to see our Dominion crumble. Undoubtedly, they seek my own death. I have evidence today that the Alephian Order has aided the Reds multiple times within the Groganlands. Rest assured, they are aiding other conspirators. Because of these crimes, I have no choice but to declare war on the Realm of Preost, only so I can extinguish the flames of rebellion. Tomorrow, the Forest Realm will rejoin our Dominion and our nation as a conquered province." Seam held up his fist, as his voice swelled behind a crescendo of powerful, swelling music. "For a new tomorrow. For a lasting peace. For unity."

CHAPTER TWENTY-TWO

The sound of songbirds woke Kull from a deep sleep. Slowly he yawned, stretching as he sat up on the edge of his small cot, enjoying the melodic rise and fall of the birds' chorus. Bright, yellow sunlight flowed through the opening of the cave. Kull expected to step out and descend the mountain to cut more wood, but as he stepped from the mouth of the cave, his feet sunk into hot, soft sand.

Kull spun on his heels, his eyes wide with confusion. The cave opening was still behind him, but the lush mountain range had disappeared. Instead, he was surrounded by rolling sand dunes. The amber, windswept dunes simmered with a dry heat. Kull pressed out over the hills, searching for the stranger that had sheltered him. As he slogged through the soft sand, his mind pondered on his host. The man was impossible to understand, from his tattoo-covered skin to the guardian beasts he kept. Everything about him was at odds, much like this ever-shifting place called *Mir*.

What is his name? The questions plagued Kull's thoughts as he pressed on, pushing himself up a massive dune.

"Kull!" The stranger's familiar voice called out from behind him. "Come help me with this!"

Kull turned and blinked, trying to discern how he passed without noticing the man. The stranger was no more than twenty feet away. He stood with a shovel in one hand and a bucket in the other. He held out the shovel and offered it to Kull.

"Ready to dig today?"

Kull looked at the sand beneath his feet and kicked at the golden granules. "I thought we were gathering honey or cutting wood."

"The plan has changed, friend."

Kull nodded, squinting under the blazing morning sun. "What are we digging for?"

The stranger lifted the bucket and smiled. "Water."

Kull grimaced, trying to comprehend as he stared up at the blazing sun. "Out here? Water?"

The stranger handed over the long-handled shovel to Kull and nodded, his bright eyes covered under the cowl of robe. "Yes. Out here."

The two went to work on the sand, scooping it away one shovel at a time, tossing it to the side. The deeper they dug, the harder the work became as the hole caved in from its sides, erasing their progress. The sun stretched higher in the sky and soaked the two in an immense, consuming heat. Kull could feel sweat dripping from his entire body as he fought to move the shifting sand.

Kull's host scooped dirt silently, never breaking a sweat. Kull paused and leaned on the handle of his shovel, panting. "I've been meaning to ask you, sir." He wiped away the sweat pouring from his brow. "What is your name?"

The stranger continued to dig, but glanced up from his work. "You don't know?"

Kull shook his head and dipped his shovel back into the sand. "No, sir. Never thought to ask. Been too busy I guess."

The man smiled and bobbed his head as he chuckled. "Busy indeed. You've been a great help to me here, Kull. Do not worry. You'll remember my name soon enough."

Kull furrowed his brow. The promise of "soon enough" did little to quell Kull's curiosity. Instead, he decided to focus on the task at hand: digging. Silence settled over the two as they continued to dig deeper into the desert, searching for water. The hole grew around the men as they struck deeper and deeper into the ground. After a while, Kull marveled at their progress. His mouth dropped open as he realized they had created a small crater and the rim of the hole was several feet over their head.

"How long have we been digging?" Kull scanned the hole, turning in a full circle.

"How long?" The stranger shrugged. "I haven't really kept up with the time."

Kull wrung the sweat from his shirt and stopped to think that despite the heat and effort he was not fatigued. Then he saw his hands. They were whole, no longer ragged tatters of broken flesh, but whole and healthy. Kull stared at the fresh, smooth skin of his hands and stared back up at the sun. The elder smiled at him and they both continued shoveling.

A strong wind swept over the dunes and swirled in the pit. Kull felt the sands shift, and he glanced at his companion. "Are we safe here?" A river of loose sand slid down the sides of the pit.

"No, but we must find water." Outside the crater, the wind picked up until the steepest wall of the crater broke free, releasing a rush of sand that threatened to bury them. It crashed down around Kull and the sound of the rushing wave of sand unhinged a new memory within his mind. The memory flooded Kull's vision like the sand that collapsed over him.

He was still in a pit of sand, tool in hand, tasked with the duty to dig. However, he was not alone. He was surrounded by hundreds of baggers. *Baggers. Yes. That's what they were called.* The beleaguered servants were bent over, broken and beaten down by the heat as they tried not to wither from exhaustion. They were being forced to work until they died. Their dirty faces and tattered clothing blended in with the sandy soil that surrounded them like a tomb. Kull continued shoveling and scanned the crowd. A woman shrieked and was soon joined with a chorus of cries.

Kull looked down and was greeted by the hollow stare of a dirty skull resting at his feet. The truth of the place hit him like a lightning bolt. The whole crew was digging through a pit of bones. The sand had long since disappeared and morphed into the chalky grime of brittle bone. The baggers sank into the skeletal void, gurgling and screaming as they drowned in the broken pit of death, leaving Kull alone at the center of the cursed crater. The bones rattled, as a thousand skulls pushed through the sandy walls of the crater and gathered into a great serpent.

The beast rose thirty feet in the air and glared down at Kull, its thousand faces each flashing him a hollow smile. The monster snapped its jaws and circled Kull, tightening its cold, hard coils around him. The thousands of skulls all opened their mouths and a chorus of screams washed over him, thundering in his ears. **"Know this, young one. You are dead, and you are Mine."**

The bone coils hinged over him, closing in on his body tighter and tighter until Kull felt the air being pushed out of his lungs. He lifted his shovel and slammed its blade into the ground at his feet. "Never!"

Kull's scream shattered the memory. The coils of bone exploded and evaporated like a mirage.

Kull screamed, kicking up sheets of sand. He blinked madly, unable to tell where he was and what he was doing until the stranger's gaze leveled on him. Kull exhaled a trembling breath and stabbed the shovel between them, fighting to gather his composure after the terrifying vision. He took heaving breaths as a bubbling noise filled his ears. He stared behind his host as he witnessed a stream of water flowing out and around the shovel's blade. The water level grew with great speed, quickly covering over Kull's toes. Every scrap of energy he had felt was depleted. The memory, the horror of remembering the labor camp and the death that once surrounded him was exhausting. *Death. Gods...*

"Kull." The hooded man's voice was calm. "Take deep breaths. You are okay. I am here."

"Is it true?" Kull's question landed between heavy breaths. "I'm dead, aren't I?"

Kull's guide placed a strong hand on his shoulder and smiled. "Do you feel dead?"

Kull took a deep breath and felt his heart beat. He looked up to the sun blazing above him and felt the comforting grip of the elder's hand on his shoulder. "No."

"Then there is your answer. You are very much alive."

The stranger looked down at the water that was up to their calves and smiled. "Now help me." He handed Kull a bucket. "Good job. You found our water."

Kull dipped the bucket into the clear, cool water, relishing the feeling of it surrounding him. The water smelled crisp and sweet, its presence and aroma intoxicating. Kull felt as if he had drunk gallons of it just by looking at it. He shouldered the overflowing bucket and climbed up the side of the crater. The ground rumbled beneath his feet as Kull crested the pit's edge. The small pool of water at the base rushed behind him, only to fill the entire void before surging forward, chasing at Kull's heels.

Kull scanned the crater for his guide but he had disappeared. The ground shook with a new violence that caused Kull to stumble. He straightened himself, securing his pail of water and sprinted for the horizon. Kull had nothing more than memory guiding him as he tried to remember which direction led to the cave. The dry, soft sand underfoot became wet and viscous, and the shallow waters grew behind Kull, roaring with unnatural life as the pool developed into waves that smashed behind him as he ran.

With each step, the water grew with raging fury and crashed to the sides of Kull, splashing dirt and water in his face, threatening to cut him off. The crystal clear water transformed, darkening as it grew more chaotic. Kull wiped his face clear and sprinted with all he had, his hands gripping the pail the elder had given him. A wave swelled several meters behind him, threatening to crest over him entirely as the sound of thunderclouds crescendoed in the air.

The desire to look back tempted Kull as he fought to free himself from the pursuit of the flood, but he kept his eyes locked on the horizon.

"Come on. It can't be that far." Kull screamed as he sprinted. "Where is the cave?" He glanced around him and screamed, "*Where are you?!*"

As the words left his lips, the black wave broke and crashed down on top of Kull. The water hit like an onyx sledgehammer, leveling Kull with its fury and throwing him across the ground. Kull wrapped his arms around the bucket and balled up as the waters swept around him, enveloping him in a void of turbulent darkness. Kull flipped end over end and smashed against the sandy soil time and time again. He kicked and tried to catch his footing, but he could find no foothold. He was surrounded, the water was too much for him to fight, and he was helplessly consumed by its assault. Fear choked him as he realized that this was no normal water. It was the dreaded *Sea*. The Sea of Souls was breaking into Mir. It was after him.

"YOU ARE DEAD. YOU ARE MINE."

The voice of an untold memory filled his mind as the waters constricted around him with an incalculable weight. Kull felt the waters shift as a massive force passed by him. Something was in this tempest, something familiar and threatening. Amidst the panic, Kull whispered a simple prayer within his mind. *Aleph, please.*

Kull kept himself balled around the wooden pail and tried to brace himself as he tumbled through the deepening waters. In an instant, his body crashed against solid rock. He reached out and clamored for the surface, forcing himself up the rock face. Finally, the waters rolled back as Kull gasped for breath, lifting himself out of the water, up onto the rocky crags. He had made it; he had found the cave. He staggered to his feet and felt a shadow fall over him. The stranger stood before him.

"Kull, get inside the cave." The man's voice was calm, yet stern. "We are not alone."

Kull had barely stumbled past the threshold of the cave when he saw it. Cresting out of the water was the immense serpent, the leviathan that had nearly brought down *The Hunt* and all who were trapped onboard. The beast emerged from the inky depths, its long, thick coils lapping up on the furthest rock from the cave's mouth. The beast's scales shimmered as the black water dripped from them. His long snout was lined with jagged fangs, and sharp spines protruded from the flesh of his back. Kull shrunk back, retreating as far from the beast as possible. The dark, churning water had swallowed nearly everything in Mir, and the sea had turned the mountain into a tiny island, the summit being the only bit of land remaining.

Spider webs of lightning lit up the sky, and a symphony of thunder sounded. The serpent's eyes bent down and locked on Kull, burning red with rage, as hot steam flared from its nostrils. A ragged maw of teeth lined the strong jaws of the behemoth's massive head, and Kull felt like all he could do was scream, but no words would dare come out from his mouth.

The beast sneered at the stranger who stood in front of the cave's entrance, blocking Kull within. "*You.* **You are out of bounds. The boy is mine by right.**" The sound of the beast's voice made Kull's body go cold with fear, as his mind filled with thoughts of throwing himself into the sea and giving himself over to his pursuer. *Anything to make the voice stop.*

"Are you sure of this, Ma'et?"

The serpent roared, his mouth filling with golden venom. Kull shuddered as long fangs fell from the cavernous mouth and dripped with amber death. **"Do not call me *that*. That is no longer my name. It never was. Not since you abandoned us."**

Lightning crashed in the sky as the stranger walked to the giant beast, indifferent to its showcase of power. He leveled his gaze on its crimson eyes, standing only feet from the venom that poured out of its mouth. The golden bile pooled at the man's feet. The beast recoiled from the man's presence, slithering deeper into the black waters.

"Abandoned you? Is that what I did? That's not what I remember." The stranger shook his head, his face bearing an unknown puzzle in his mind. "You...you and those that followed you…" The stranger's face ignited with the memory. "You left me here alone. There is still so much work to be done."

"**I did not come here to revisit** *our history*." The snake growled, the sound of it rumbling over the island like an avalanche. "**I haven't much time. Give him to me. He is mine.**"

Lightning flashed and Kull stared out to the surrounding sea that filled the horizon. The lightning illuminated numerous bodies within the dark waters for an instant. They were bound, chained below the surface of the Sea, bobbing like submerged buoys anchored below the black depths. The serpent's red eyes locked onto Kull's and it laughed.

"**The boy himself knows this to be true. He belongs in the Sea. With the others, just as you have willed it for millennia.**" The leviathan sneered at the man, as its massive jaws spewed venom, curses, and rage. "**Have you not told him yet? Have you not revealed your master plan to this little soul?**"

The viper cut his eyes to Kull. "**Of course not. You never show your true intent. You offer these morsels false hope and grace only to cast them all into the darkness. Into my Sea.**"

The stranger glanced at Kull, his face stern and stoic. "*Ma'et*, I have never forgotten those in the Sea, just like I haven't forgotten your true name. The boy…he is not under your care anymore. He is under mine. I've claimed him for myself, though I must thank you for bringing him to the other side."

The beast thrashed in the water and slammed his tail against the rocks to the side of Kull's guardian. The blow rattled the ground and shook the walls of the cave, causing a small landslide of debris to break free, threatening to seal the cave.

"**Save your thanks for one who does not hate you. GIVE ME THE BOY NOW!**"

The man waded into the murky waters and stood within feet of the leviathan towering over him. He folded his arms and sighed. "*No*. You have your answer. Now leave us."

The serpent bellowed and lifted higher into the air, swelling to a monumental size. It spouted smoke from its lips as it rose into the darkening sky, roaring with fury. It whipped its tail with hurricane force and hammered it against the black waves. **"You have stolen from me for the last time. Why are you hiding this small soul?** *Does he know what you intend of him? Does he know your cruelty? Your indifference? Your lies?* **I know who you are!"**

"All this time, and still you don't know me." The stranger sighed as he turned his back to his adversary and walked toward the mouth of the cave.

"I know you all too well, A..."

"Do not speak my name." The stranger spun on his heels in an instant and held an open palm toward the serpent. "Leave us, Ma'et. *Now.* Do not come back."

The serpent growled and snapped his razor sharp teeth together, releasing a thunderclap. He turned from the high place, swimming on the surface, whipping his massive frame from side to side. Soon his gigantic body disappeared beneath the midnight waves, but his head still towered over the dark water's surface. **"Fine. Waste your time and steal a single soul. Soon he will be of no difference to me. I will have my revenge against you. My agents will soon fill the Sea full of the Forgotten, and I will gorge on them for an eternity. There will be nothing you can do, so enjoy your victory today. The boy you stole from me will soon be forgotten. An afterthought."**

The stranger smiled and turned back to the beast. "No, Ma'et. You will never forget him."

The serpent paused, his crimson eyes flickering with an instant of surprise. Or was it fear? Kull couldn't tell, but his mind swirled at the conversation he had just heard. The beast huffed as it disappeared into the Sea and soon the monster was out of sight, descending beneath the dreadful waters. The black water followed, rolling back and receding, transforming the island back into a mountaintop, causing Kull's mouth to drop as everything was suddenly put back in place. Mir was restored again, its tall pine trees swaying proudly in the wind, lining the rocky mountain that now jutted up in the sky. A breeze rustled through the trees as songbirds returned to their singing, joining a chorus of song. It was as if nothing had ever interrupted their melody.

Kull's eyes turned to the man, finally understanding the truth as his mouth tried to find the words. "You're him. *You are him.*" Kull's eyes grew wide and he fell to his knees, trembling.

"Who?"

Kull stammered, chasing the idea that darted off in his mind like rabbit from the brush. "How could you not be *him*? I mean...you must be. You are."

The man's hands grasped around his, and his eyes flared with a power that Kull could not comprehend. "I am."

"Aleph," Kull's lips said the name, and his body seized with both fear and awe. His heart hammered wildly in his chest and stole his breath away. The whole world felt as if it were melting away, and Kull thought he might lose himself in the gaze of the Divine.

Kull's body trembled as he hid his eyes. "What do you want with *me?*"

CHAPTER TWENTY-THREE

Grift peered through the muddy windshield of the truck carrying him and his few allies to the safety of Preost. Luken sat at the truck's wheel, dutifully maneuvering the clumsy vehicle over the rough dirt road. Grift had been silent since the group escaped Henshaw, his pained gaze fixed on the oncoming forested terrain. His face was as cold as a statue's. Grift glanced back into the covered bed of the truck at the two miniscule bodies neatly wrapped in white linen.

Emotions rushed in with each heartbeat, a dreadful reminder that he was still alive in his own living hell while the curtain of death hung between him and his loved ones. Rage stung his veins as he balled his fists and clenched his teeth, but the anger eventually shifted into a flood of complete indifference. He took a deep breath, hoping to fill his hollow chest, but there was no relief. Sorrow, instead, filled the void.

Tears broke free from the corners of his eyes as he tried to shield his face from Adley sitting across from him. The kaleidoscope of emotions twisted and churned inside of him, tossing his battered soul like a helpless toy boat in an oceanic hurricane. Grift turned his face from his wife's body and fought to focus on something different, anything. He leaned into the cockpit again and tried to discern how far they were from Preost's border.

"I'm sorry," Luken whispered as Grift eased into the driver's compartment. The soft whisper thudded against Grift's ears like a mallet. Grift fought the urge to recoil into the cargo bed and drew in a deep breath. He exhaled and a new calm broke over his soul as he stared at his old friend. He wanted to reject the apology and spit in the Serub's face, but his heart refused. The words were sincere and he knew it. He didn't want them to be real, but they were.

"Why, Luken?" The words escaped from Grift's lips as he pinched his eyes shut. "Why are you...sorry?"

Luken sighed and dropped his head. "I'm sorry for all your loss, Grift. I'm sorry for your pain." He paused and forced out the words. "And I'm sorry I was not there to help you save her."

Grift grimaced at the mention of Rose but buried the torrent of rolling chaos within. Hot tears streamed from Grift's eyes. He wiped them away and spoke, his voice and countenance grim. "Me too, Luken. I can't speak of this now. We need to get into the forest."

Luken nodded and exhaled, saying nothing. Grift focused in on this person, his friend, whose true nature and origin had eluded them all. Grift tried to force himself back to his seat, but the questions clawing within pulled him to Luken's side and Grift finally let the words slip from his mind, sharp and barbed.

"Where were you? How could you leave us to all this, Luken?"

"Grift, you saw what happened to me on that ship."

"Yeah, that's why I'm asking the question. You were dead, but now...you're here." Grift ignored the uncomfortable expression painted on Wael's face. "And now I learn that you are one of *them*. One of the Serubs. *How do we know we can trust you?*"

The question surprised even Grift, and Wael put a hand on him, whispering, "Grift..."

Luken's face drifted, his face looking like he was recalling a long-forgotten memory. "It's alright, Wael. It's a fair question." He glanced up at Grift through the rearview mirror and spoke plainly. "I was a Serub, but please don't call me that again. Yes, I am different from you and your friends, but being hurled into the Endless Ocean via grenade does a number on anyone, even on me. As far as trusting me, Grift, I would hope that our friendship would be enough..."

"My son is dead, Luken. My wife is dead." Anger drew Grift's face back into a snarl. "My home is destroyed and my town is burned to the ground. Why? Because of Seam and his affinity for *your kind*." He threw his hands up in the air with mock reverence, his voice laced with sarcasm. "*The gods*. What wonders *the gods* have worked. What kind of god are you that you can't take a grenade?" Grift's voice broke, giving over to the dark fire within him. "Everything around you *dies*! My family has taken the lion's share of punishment from your kind, and now for all we know Willyn is dead too! *How many more people are you not going to be able to save?*"

The mention of Willyn's name cut at Luken. He shifted in his seat and cleared his throat before choking out his words. "Listen to me, Grift. There's a lot you don't understand, which I don't know how to explain to you."

"Well, why don't you give it a try? Or are you afraid that a mortal can't understand?"

Wael spoke, his voice trying to balance the conflict. "Grift... please."

Luken chimed in, "I wanted to be there. Do you actually think I didn't want to help you, to help Rose, to help Kull?" Luken cleared his throat again before continuing. "To help Willyn? Once I healed enough to be functional again I knew to reappear too soon would cause more problems, more chaos. Eventually I knew I had to come out of hiding."

Grift tilted his neck to the side and tried to get a good glimpse at Luken as the man-god leveled his gaze back on the horizon. "Chaos and confusion? *Well, that sounds really bad, Luken.* What changed your divine mind? What was finally so important?"

The vehicle was silent as Luken squinted into the setting sun, obviously hurt from his friend's barbs.

"What was it, Luken? *You at least owe me that much.*" Grift growled as he stood in the back of the truck's cockpit. "WHY? Why now?"

"I could hear *them* speaking, Grift, and I didn't like what they were saying. They always call out to one another." Luken struck the dash and wrung his hands over the steering wheel. "There were only two who never spoke." Luken stared at Grift, his eyes weary. "Me and the only one that is left in the mirror. Isphet is hiding something. He has tapped into some power...I can't explain it, but I can feel it. It is worse than any power a Serub could wield. A power I can't even begin to understand. Isphet...Isphet can't be released."

"What about the others?" asked Adley from the backseat. "What about them? Can you still hear them?" She glanced up from the datalink that she had been fumbling with since escaping Henshaw.

Luken's expression sank. "They've gone silent since their release, which worries me more than ever."

"You still haven't explained why you stayed hidden for so long, Luken." Grift would not relent.

Luken spat back, "Don't you get it, Grift? Haven't you put the pieces together yet?" Luken stared at Grift, his gaze flashing between him and the Mastermonk. His voice went grim, but it was full of authority. "I am just as vulnerable to the Keys as the rest!"

Luken slammed the brakes down on the truck and turned to face Grift. He pointed out into the distance and spoke through clenched teeth. "For me to just reappear would be to invite Seam to put me under his foot and use me to rip people that I love apart. People like you, Grift!" A tear rolled down Luken's cheek as he looked past Grift into the cargo hold and his eyes landed on Rose's body. "For all you know, had I come back earlier it would have been my own hands that took Rose from you. Present or absent I am cursed, my friend."

The words knocked the breath from Grift's chest. He sat back into his seat and glanced at Luken with pity in his eyes. "I'm sorry, Luken, but that still doesn't answer why you returned. Why now?"

Luken wiped his cheek and returned to the driver's seat. "I had to try. Too much pain. Too much death. I couldn't take it anymore, Grift. I could feel them killing, gorging themselves. And if I can feel it, Isphet can too. I had to at least try, regardless of the result."

"So Seam can control you too?" Adley searched Wael's face as she questioned Luken.

Luken put the truck back in gear and eased the gas pedal to the floor. "You've been warned. Just know I am on your side, no matter what happens." Luken glanced at Wael and Grift in the rearview mirror. The smudged glass revealed the creases next to his eyes softening. "I am not like the rest. I promise. I made my choice."

Adley's datalink blinked and her eyes widened as she examined the text on the shimmering screen. "Oh, this is good! I've been doing some research on the feeds. Looking for the signal level that the Dominion troops are utilizing for military coms. From the dark feeds, there is speculation that many of the ground troops' frequencies can be accessed from analog receptors for voice communication. Their feeds are shielded from datalink use, though." She reached for the ancient radio overhead and dialed a knob through channels of static. As the radio screeched and squealed, she smiled. "Let's see if these dark feed guys are right." Minutes of pure static went by until the sounds began to coalesce into recognizable forms and patterns. The shadows of speech began to form, and the truck went silent with anticipation. Adley slowed the knob as voices came together, undulating over the static in rapid bursts of static correspondence.

"Setting down in three..." The voices broke out before sputtering back over the radio. "Ten units..." Adley tweaked the knob, but the signal refused to settle. "Seventy-eight percent border locked."

Grift leaned forward further as the voices dropped in and out on the airwaves.

"King Seam..." A burst of static interrupted the signal again before the final words drifted through the cabin. "Ten hours until siege."

Adley checked her datalink and gazed up at Wael. "How far are we from Preost? Taluum?"

Luken peered over his shoulder to answer. "Almost two hours to the Preost border. Eight hours at least to Taluum."

Grift grumbled as he ran numbers through his head. "We aren't getting any help. Not with the window of time that we have." He spat and cursed under his breath. "So much for safety in Taluum."

Adley looked out her window and bit at her thumbnail before speaking back up. "What about our forces in Zenith? What about Willyn and the Reds? Can they converge? Rout Seam's forces from behind? Maybe buy us some time? If the Grogans rush into Zenith, it might cause Seam to pull back his forces."

Wael nodded in agreement. "It is worth the chance, though I don't want their lives sacrificed. We need to get into contact with the Reds. We could request they attack Zenith to draw Seam's forces back." Wael glanced out in space and his lips offered a silent prayer before continuing. "Perhaps Willyn has survived Seam's assault on Bastion's mirror. We can pray for as much. If she has survived and holds control, we can supply word to her once Seam draws out of Preost so the Reds could fall back."

Grift barely stifled the laughter that rose from his mouth. "HA! Grogans fall back? Once they have a chance to level Zenith they aren't going anywhere."

Wael spoke, his voice grave. "We have to find out the fate of our sister in the Groganlands. If Willyn is well and has garnered her people's support, then we will need her to move quickly. Seam is moving toward Taluum as we speak. If Willyn is compromised..." The word lay heavy in Wael's mouth, and he grimaced as if it tasted sour. "Then we will have to make a plea to what Red resistance is left. Either way, we need the Grogans." Wael glanced at Luken, whose face was as pale as a sheet. The monk reached out and placed his giant hand on his shoulder. "We still don't know that she is dead." The monk glanced back, his eyes scanning the lot of them. "We need to reach out to the Grogans and garner their support...and whatever other resistances there are in the other Realms. We need them, too. We will need everyone's support if we are to hold Seam back from the final mirror."

Adley shook her head as she dialed into her datalink. "I don't know, Wael. I've been trying to establish contact with her for a couple days now and there's been no response." Adley flipped through several screens, but each registered a negative response. "She's off the grid."

Wael glanced up as a wall of evergreen trees grew in the distance. He sighed and nodded. "We need to hurry then. We don't have much time to get ready. Adley, once we arrive let's try one more time to reach out to Willyn and the Red resistance. I have reached out to my friend Bri who accompanied her." The monk's face pursed in hard lines. "I've gotten no response either."

The truck lumbered toward the tree line with no military presence in sight. "What percentage border control did they claim on that call, Luken?" Grift asked as he leaned in to scan the horizon.

"Seventy-eight percent." Luken kept his eyes fixed on the tree line, his pupils darting from side to side, scanning for any sign of a siege.

"We can't be that lucky. This doesn't feel right," Grift said as he reached for his rifle. He shook his head and sat back down. "Nothing feels right anymore."

As the transport passed beyond the tree line and pressed on for Taluum, shadows and silence filled the cabin.

After an hour of driving, Luken slammed on the brakes, sending the truck into a lurch. Rot let out a few short barks as Grift, Adley, and Wael braced themselves.

"Why are we stopping?" Grift shouted as he climbed back into the front of the truck. "What is going..."

Grift's mouth dropped open as he looked on at the mass of bodies huddling in front of the truck. A large mob of men, women, and children covered in tattered clothing tried to slowly slink off the path Luken had been following.

"Baggers..." Grift scrunched his face as he tried to get a good look at the few individuals in front of the truck's headlights. "What are they doing here?"

Wael opened his door and whistled for Rot to follow. "Let me speak with them."

"I'm coming with you," said Grift as he followed Wael from the truck and leapt onto the dirt road below.

"Baku!" Wael let out a loud but welcoming yell, holding his hand up with the sign of peace. "Baku! You are safe friends."

A middle-aged man approached with shaking, open palms outstretched. "Baku?" He kept his head bowed and cowered in Wael's presence.

Wael placed a hand on the man's shoulder and spoke with tenderness. "Yes. Baku. I am a friend." Wael looked over the man's shoulder and offered a smile to the small party behind him. "Can anyone of you speak the common tongue?"

A young girl stepped forward, her blonde head nodding in the glow of the headlights. Her yellow eyes were wide with fear, but she moved toward Wael, her face covered with a strong dignity. Her miniscule frame was covered only in dirt and a large patchwork of handmade clothes.

Wael stooped down to one knee as Rot panted at his heel, with his tongue hanging from his open mouth. The girl chuckled at the sight of the slobbering mutt, and she timidly reached out to rub Rot's wet muzzle. The one-eyed beast gladly accepted the attention, and he whined with joy as the girl began to scratch him with no fear.

Wael smiled and addressed the young girl in a gentle tone. "Why are you here, young one?"

The girl paused, and Grift knew she was trying to assemble the few words of common she knew. "The king man. Took everyone."

Grift knelt next to Wael. "The king man? What do you mean he took everyone?"

Tears welled in the girl's eyes as the Bagger man with her wrapped his arms around her shoulders. "Put to train. Everyone leave."

"How did you get away?" Grift spoke and shared a troubled glance with the Mastermonk.

"No go to desert for work! No one come back. All leave on train. We not go!" The girl twisted her foot in the dirt and sunk into the older bagger's arms.

"It's okay, we will not hurt you. You are not in trouble." Grift reached out his hand and smiled. "I am glad you did not go. Why did you come here?"

The man holding the girl fumbled to piece together an answer. "Hide. Need safe. King bad."

The girl nodded. "Baggers keep leaving. No reason. Not many now."

Wael stepped to the truck with Grift and they huddled at the driver's side window. Luken leaned out. "What's going on?"

"The girl says they are running from Seam. Baggers keep leaving or disappearing. They are seeking asylum."

Luken's face went blank. He took in a short breath before blinking and shaking his head in disbelief. "Arakiel and Nyx."

"What, Luken?" Wael drew in closer. "What did you say?"

Luken rubbed at his face and furrowed his brow. "I am afraid Seam is trying to satisfy their appetite, Wael."

Adley leaned in from the back of the truck and interrupted. "I don't think we can take them to Taluum. If Taluum is Seam's target, there's no way they will be safe."

Wael nodded. He spoke in the Bagger tongue, gesturing to the people with large sweeping gestures, mimicking the movements and sounds that Grift had seen from the bagger people many times in Lotte. Wael turned and looked at Grift and Adley. "What supplies do we have?"

Adley spoke. "Not much. Except for the Predecessor technology, we've got a few rifles, a week's worth of rations, and a few tents." Wael circled around the back of the truck and opened the tailgate.

"Give everything to them. I've told them to make for the coast, for Elum. They are going to need any supplies we can give them."

Grift cut in, his face fearful. "The weapons too?"

"The weapons too. They need to protect themselves…"

Luken nodded, his face filling the rearview mirror, glazed with fear. "Seam will *not* be marching into Taluum with a normal army. These baggers need to get out of here as quick as they can."

Grift stared at Wael, his eyes searching. Adley spoke what he was thinking. "What's coming then?"

Luken throttled the engine of the truck and shook his head. "Not here. Not in front of them. We need to give them what they need and move."

The party handed out all that they could spare and moved out without a goodbye. The truck roared away through the thick forest, leaving the Baggers glowing red with the light of their taillights. Despite all he had been through and all that he knew, Grift spoke a silent prayer for the poor people shambling through the forest, with no aim other than to survive. *Aleph, have mercy.*

Wael turned and faced Adley behind him. "How far are we from the border, Adley?"

She opened the datalink, scanning the screen that lighted her face in the coming darkness. "From my position, we're only a half-hour out…maybe more."

The monk nodded, and he looked at Luken and Grift. "We need to go on foot. We can't take the chance that Dominion forces will be waiting for us as we get nearer to the border. We can find other transportation once we get inside Preost."

Luken shook his head. "No, we have to press through. You've got to keep the truck, or you'll never make it in time."

Grift glanced at Adley, his mind weighing the options. "Could we use the Predecessor tech again?"

Adley shook her head, biting her lip. "Maybe, but there is no telling if it would be ready for when Seam's forces push in."

Wael cut in. "We will use that technology only when we have no other choice." The monk glanced at Luken. "Do you have any alternatives, Luken?"

"We take our chances. I say we push through for the border. If there are Dominion forces, I will take care of them, but you all...you must make for Taluum. You must raise the alarm for all those still loyal to you, Wael."

Wael nodded, his face grim. "So be it."

It was the slowest half hour that Grift had ever lived through. In his lap he grasped his rifle, shouldering it with its safety off, ready for whatever was coming. The horizon line of trees was upon them, marking the border into Preost, and Luken shut off the lights as the truck drove through pure darkness.

"Keep your eyes peeled and keep that datalink screen shut, Adley." Luken peered at the wall of trees that covered the horizon like a thick, black blanket as the truck crossed the threshold into the holy Realm. Its engine echoed off the tall, thick trunks of the ancient grove, as a symphony of nightlife buzzed, howled, and called deep within the darkness. Grift leaned forward and whispered, "Can you see, Luken?"

"Well enough. Just be ready."

The truck rolled down the dirt road, and Grift felt the land beneath him turn upward. The military convoy swung slowly around the bends carved into the earth, as the starlight above was choked away by the reaching arms of the thickening trees. Wael rolled down the window and breathed in the cool air of his home. Even in the dark, Grift could see Wael smile, his ivory teeth filling his face with joy.

As they rounded the bend, Luken slammed on the brakes. Just beyond them on the pass, the hot white glow of artificial light filled the valley. Luken immediately cut the engine as the truck lurched to a stop.

"Up ahead, do you see them?" Luken's words came as staccato whispers.

Adley pulled up her binoculars and focused them on the camp below. "I've got a visual. Black and gold colors on the convoys. Dominion forces, for sure. I'd guess from the convoys alone, at least twenty are down there." Adley stared as Grift, Wael, and Luken listened to the dull roar of the chirping nightlife. A low growl began to grow in Rot's throat, joining the chorus.

"Rot." Wael's control over the beast was instant, but the dog let out a gruff whine of protest.

"What else do you see down there, Adley?" Grift questioned. Adley stared through the binoculars, but shook her head. "There's a small fire and two convoys, but no visual on patrol movement. They might be down for the night…"

The forest exploded with her words, and Grift lifted his rifle up to the white cascading flash that filled the night sky. Wael shielded his eyes, and shouted out orders. "Get out of the car, everyone! Now!"

A second flash of light followed the next as Grift, Luken, Wael and Adley poured out of the truck in a panic. Grift's body hit the cold ground next to the monk as they both stared down into the outcropping below them. Grift squinted his eyes, trying to make out the unfolding scene.

The small campfire that had only provided a faint red light within the forest erupted, as a third hot flash of light trailed twenty feet into the air. Grift heard screams coming from the grotto below.

"Wael. What the hell is that?" Grift yelled with wide eyes.

Wael stared into the light. "Aleph above. The Desolate…in all my years. The Desolate have reawakened."

An excruciating heat fell over the company as a new white-hot fire erupted. Luken rolled toward them and screamed over the roar of the flames. "Wael. I can't be here."

The monk stood up, his face full of otherworldly fear. "Stay with us, Luken. Trust me!" Wael took a step forward into the forest. The white fire intensified with each step. Grift called out to him, and Adley reached for his robes, but Wael pushed them away. Rot lurched, and Grift barely held the beast back as the monk strode out into the night of growing white fire. Wael reached deep within his robes and pulled out the rune of Aleph. He opened his mouth, his words lost in the growing roar of the ivory inferno.

Grift squinted his eyes, trying desperately to see past the blaze that swirled around Wael. The tall trees around him became dark black pillars, their features swallowed by the all-consuming light. Soon even the shadows of the trees disappeared into the brightness. He scrambled to locate Luken and Adley, but both had disappeared. Even Rot evaporated from his vision despite still feeling the massive beast shaking in his arms.

"All I see is fire. Hot, white fire." There was no pain, but the presence of the white fire somehow communicated that pain and death were only a breath away from them. Grift's entire body shook as his hands ratcheted on the dog that he could no longer see, his only tangible evidence that he had not yet died.

Grift heard a voice clamor over the roar of the flames. It was the ancient tongue of the Preost monks. *Wael*. A chilling cool swept over Grift and black darkness filled his vision. Grift screamed, his fingers clawing into Rot who howled beneath him. "WAEL?! WAEL?!"

"Peace. Peace, Grift. Hold still. You will see again soon. Just wait." The inky black vision lingered, but Grift's eyes filled with pinpricks of detail that slowly formed shadows of shapes he recognized. "What...what happened, Wael?" Grift's hands trembled and he loosed his hands from Rot's fur, reaching out to the shape he knew was Wael. The white flames caused him to fear for more than just losing his life. It was as if those flames could rend through his world and consume everything it desired for its fuel.

Grift blinked and realized that there were tears streaming down his face. Adley hugged him tightly. Luken stood, his face like a white sheet, shaking his head in disbelief.

Wael was amongst them all, his face full of awe and joy. "My friends, we will not protect Preost alone. The forest and its protectors are with us."

Adley stood, her voice still trembling. "What was that, Wael?"

Wael stood, glancing at Luken, who shirked away from them, his face still confounded with untold emotions.

"They are some of the oldest servants of Aleph. My order has only had scant records of their existence. Primeval elements of pure being, pure life."

"The Desolate," Luken spoke, his eyes full of fear. "They that could rend all this world into ash in seconds, if Aleph willed it. Unfallen, pure, and vicious protectors of those they love."

"Love?" Grift balked, still rubbing his face, wiping away tears that still flowed from his eyes.

Luken nodded as Wael spoke, his voice near a whisper. "There is not much time. We must make for the Taluum. It's enough to know that the Desolate are at work again. I spoke with them as much as I could. They...spoke. They were alarmed by your presence, Luken."

Luken nodded and whispered, "Thank you, Wael, for vouching for me. I wasn't ready to leave Candor. Not that way, at least."

Wael nodded, his eyes distant and calculating. Adley broke in.

"What about the Dominion forces?"

Grift turned, the feeling of a distant dream returning to his brain. *It felt like another lifetime ago.* He stared down into the grotto of the thick wood and ran down to the small camp, Rot trailing at his heels.

Piles of ash in neat heaps were scattered across the camp, surrounded by crumpled Dominion uniforms.

"They're gone." Grift stood wide-eyed as Rot sniffed the piles, his nose covered in white soot.

The Mastermonk walked through the camp and stared at the embers of the campfire. "We must move. Seam is not the only one who is protected by gods."

Grift stood, lost in thought as he stared at the piles of ash scattered across the campsite. His mind was tossed in a torrent of thoughts. In one day, his understanding of Candor was shattered as the heavens made Candor their new battlefield.

Luken called, "Grift. We need to move!"

Grift nodded and walked away, unable to disengage with the feeling of the hot white fire threatening to crush him beneath its power and heat.

CHAPTER TWENTY-FOUR

Willyn tried to catch her breath as she stepped over the ash-covered bodies that littered her once-proud capital square. Destruction spread across the grounds, with the remains of men, women, and even children scattered among the smoldering debris. No one was spared in the violence that had transpired. The city of Rhuddenhall had become a furnace of destruction, burning through all who stood in the way of Hosp's domination.

"Where's Hosp?" A flame of hatred spit through her veins like a raging fever as she mentioned the man's name. If he was alive, she would see to it that he would be publically executed for his crimes. If he was dead, then Willyn would cut his body into quarters and send them to the far edges of Candor. Either way, she would have her revenge.

"We don't know his location, my Sar. Red forces cleared the entire government complex, but the Surrogator was absent. Our last intel placed him on a convoy headed toward the Spire. However, during his last broadcast, Seam claimed Hosp was murdered by Reds, but we never had the pleasure of taking him out." The young captain held a stern face as he addressed Willyn. He glanced down at a datalink and typed a few commands. "Do you wish for me to send out a recon unit?"

"No, I will do it myself." Willyn turned her wrist up, ready to type the command on her datalink. She stared at it in disbelief. The device was dead, its screen a spider web of glass with the deep graze of a stray bullet roaring through it. She blinked, realizing how lucky she was to be alive.

"My Sar, I will get you a replacement datalink." The young commander held out his hand as Willyn unlocked hers from her wrist and handed it to him.

"Thank you," Willyn muttered as she stared out over the fiery square and took in a deep breath, rubbing her wrist. The smell of burned flesh stung her nostrils, incensing her taste for revenge. *Look what he has done to us. Look what they have done to us.* Never in her life had she seen her Realm in such turmoil. A sudden realization fell over her, causing her to gasp as her eyes stared absentmindedly at the charred, stiff bodies in the streets. "He killed him. Of course *he* did." Willyn furrowed her brow as a scowl set on her face.

The captain fought to hide a puzzled look and typed at his datapad again. "Pardon, my Sar?"

Willyn stepped toward the Sar's Hall and waved off the soldier. "That is all for now, captain. Please ready me with a new datalink feed, and for Aleph's sake, get some men on clean-up out here. Honor the fallen, all of them. I will not have my brothers and sisters rotting in the streets."

As Willyn paced up the high red stairs that led into the grand entrance of the Sar's Hall, the captain jogged for Willyn and cleared his throat. "My Sar! What of them?"

Willyn turned and sighed, her eyes stinging in the smoky wind, exhaustion sweeping over her. "Who?" she asked, her voice weak.

"The baggers." The captain pointed at the small group of baggers that had traveled with the remnant from Legion's Teeth. "Should we put them to work?"

"*No.*" The words snapped from Willyn's lips. "Give them refuge, food, and clothing. Make them welcome."

Confusion twisted the officer's face. He swallowed and leaned in, his eyes trying to reason with her. "But they're Baggers. Shouldn't they assist?"

Willyn tore into him. "*Did you not hear me, captain*? I made myself clear. Take them in. They are not *just* Baggers. They are our guests. *That is a direct order.*" Willyn clenched her hands into fists until her knuckles were white as she thought back on Bri and his last moments, saving her life.

"Yes, ma'am. My apologies for my concern, but I admit I am hesitant to trust them since the army that attacked us in the Spine was mostly Baggers."

The peculiar announcement snagged Willyn's attention and rattled her core. "What did you say, captain?" Her tone dropped as she spoke.

"Um. Yes, ma'am. A few of the attackers were still onboard or stuck to the hoods of our transports. Once we were able to clear them off we successfully identified them. Baggers. All of them. Not sure where they got military training, but there's no denying they are fighting for Seam." He glanced back at the Baggers huddled at the edge of the square. "How can we know they aren't trying to abuse our trust?"

Willyn looked back to the baggers and thought of Bri. She sighed, her eyes leveling on the captain. "You are right in part, but the army Seam wielded was not of this world, captain. We have no reason to fear the Baggers who fought with us." She turned, her mind still heavy with the loss of Bri. "They are our guests. Make sure their every need is attended to."

The captain's head snapped back at full attention, and he flashed a hasty salute before skirting away. "Yes, my Sar."

In the twilight of the day, the city swelled with activity as the Reds scrambled to clear out the streets, collecting and covering the deceased. The bodies would be off the streets and buried before morning. Willyn trekked through the scramble and slipped into the cement hallways of her family's bunker-like hall, relieved. All the dead were laid to rest that night. *At least they can be at peace.* Her boots thumped down the empty gallery. Thick shadows of memory chased in her mind as she pressed toward the royal quarters. A thought crystallized in her mind as she unlatched the giant doors that led to the Sar's chambers.

Where is he? The thought was not rational, but it refused to budge from her mind. The hair on her arms was electric with energy. She swore she could feel him, his presence. It was as if he was in that very space. *Don't be a fool. He is dead and gone.*

Willyn threw open the doors as her brain contended with her emotions. Her lungs emptied as she crossed the threshold into the space that once hid her brother's condition from the outside world.

Nothing had changed. The room sat in the same state she had left it, just moments before leaving the Groganlands to chase after Grift Shepherd. As she stepped forward, her boot rolled off something, filling the empty hall with a rattling sound. She looked down to see her long-discarded javes scattered across the floor, their tips blunted from their impact so many months ago. As her eyes fell over her weapons, her mind swelled with the memories of chasing Grift in her family's hall. She had hated him them, wanting only to have him die for a crime he had never committed, playing the game that Hosp had arranged for her to play.

You were a fool, Willyn. She kicked the jave away and the memory with it, scanning the dark chambers. The empty bed that once held Hagan sat abandoned in the middle of the room. The linens were turned back and neatly folded. All the plastic lines and IVs still perched over the lush bedding, while the machines waited to be reattached, still blinking.

Where is he?! Again her mind screamed wanting to know the truth. "Where did they put you?" Willyn whispered as she ran her hands through her thick hair, biting back the scream that wanted to roar out of her, her mind full of pain. *How can I know he is dead, if I don't see him? I won't believe it if I don't see the body.*

A footstep echoed behind her and Willyn reacted. In one swift motion, she spun on her heels, releasing her side arm from its holster, leveling it on the sound. The dark room did not reveal its secrets.

She screamed, her mouth turning back with a sinister snarl. "Show yourself!" She cocked her weapon, the click echoing over the hall of stone pillars. "By the gods...show yourself!"

The outline of a man stood in the darkness, facing her. Willyn could hear heavy breathing, and her heart hammered in her chest.

"Step out into the light! Now!"

The stranger took a step into the dim light that shone from the night sky overhead. He coughed, his chest rattling and wheezing.

"Is this any way to treat your elder brother, *Lyn?*"

The pistol tumbled from her hands, and Willyn crumpled to the floor, her mouth wide, her brain seized with a storm of indescribable emotions. A potent concoction of grief, rage, and relief washed over her in that instant, causing her to stammer, her body paralyzed with fear and disbelief.

She could only release a thin whisper from her lips, her eyes wide. *"Hagan?"* She crumbled to the ground, refusing to fully embrace the madness she was seeing.

The gruff voice of her brother echoed in the chamber as he stepped forward. His crisp blue eyes locked onto hers, mirror images of her own. "Yes, Lyn. It's me, though I don't blame you if you doubted it." Willyn sobbed at the sound of hearing the diminutive name her brother had given her, that one that only he used.

Through the tears that streamed down her face, she stared at him, her eyes wide in the growing dark. His face was a collage of both the familiar and the uncanny. His whole composure was loose, aged, and obviously sickened. If it weren't for his eyes and his voice, she would not have recognized him. He walked slowly toward her and Willyn gasped at the sight of him moving with a cane. He held out his right hand, a silent gesture to embrace, but still she remained cautious, despite her tears. Her heart longed for the reunion but doubts clouded her mind as she studied her brother as he approached.

She stood up, her voice a torrent of grief and rage. "They told me that you were dead. They told me..."

"They were wrong." Hagan took a step forward and slowly leaned down to face her, his crisp blue eyes locking with hers. His ragged breathing stilled after a moment. "I am alive, though that is a miracle."

Willyn shook her head and embraced him. His body was painfully thin, and Willyn recoiled at how she felt only bone behind the thin clothes her brother wore. "How?"

Hagan nodded and stifled a weak laugh. "I have to admit I am not one hundred percent certain of how it happened."

"What do you mean? How is it even possible? Your condition...I mean you were in a coma!"

Hagan nodded and sighed. "I don't remember much, so I don't know what memories I can trust." Hagan labored for a breath and continued. "The first thing I remember is being cared for by a few baggers."

"Baggers?" Willyn craned her neck and inched closer to Hagan. "Why would baggers be caring for the Sar?"

"Ha. Well, that is the funny part. They said they pulled me from the trash heap. Apparently, I was thrown out to be eaten by the dogs. Left for dead, or believed to be dead. Some baggers were searching through the heaps when they found me. Luckily their gaze did not turn away and they took me in."

"Unbelievable..." Willyn paced toward an open window and stood in the blue moonlight that poured through the dark room, trying to calm the rage that threatened to boil over. "That snake actually threw you into the dump. The Sar, thrown out and left to rot with the trash!"

Hagan broke into a violent coughing spell. The familiar gurgling cough that Willyn had been tortured by for so long. She quickly turned back to Hagan and rushed to his side.

"You may be alive, Hagan, but you still aren't well." She felt his forehead. His skin was clammy and a fever burned beneath his skin.

"That is why I have remained hidden, Lyn. I am too weak to fight. I have been very careful not to let too many know of my survival. This Realm...is too fragile now after what Hosp has done." Hagan's chest heaved as he spoke over deep breaths. "Can you imagine? If they knew right now?" His eyes leveled on her. "I need you, Willyn. The Groganlands need you."

Hagan staggered to his feet and leaned on his cane. He took timid steps to an open window and stared out into the night. "Lyn. Tell me what you know of Seam Panderean. I never told you about our Order, but I fear what is happening. My key...the key I swore to protect is gone. Please tell me that Seam is rallying the others? Please tell me the other Keys are safe? Surely you know by now what I speak of."

Willyn's fist balled at the mention of the High King's name. "That jackal is destroying Candor one Realm at a time. He has them all." Willyn's crisp blue eyes locked with her brother's.

"*Gods...*" Hagan sat himself down, leaning over his cane.

Willyn's eyes brimmed as she spoke. "He has all of the Keys of Candor, Hagan. Now he is gathering and unlocking the ancient mirrors."

Hagan peered over his shoulder and furrowed his brow, his face full of worry. "Mirrors?"

"Yes." Willyn continued. "He is releasing the five ancient Kings. The Serubs. They serve him, and are at his beck and call." Her thoughts turned inward, her mind distant. "I'm lucky to even be here. I've never seen anything like the power they wield. It is unlike anything on Candor. Three of them attacked my army on the way to Rhuddenhall and nearly ripped it to shreds."

Hagan turned and faced Willyn, his thin, pale face twisted into an almost unrecognizable smile. His eyes sparkled with life as he spoke. "Then I think I know how to stop Seam. We need to get those Keys, Lyn."

The sound of footsteps interrupted the discussion. Willyn picked her pistol up off the ground and motioned for Hagan to hide.

"Who's there?" Willyn's voiced bounced off the walls and echoed in the chamber. She cocked her pistol and shouted again. "Your Sar commands you to identify yourself."

"My apologies, my Sar!" The captain who had consulted her on the Baggers earlier slipped into view as he crossed the chamber threshold. "I am coming to report your datalink is ready. We are ready to transmit."

The young man's eyes slipped past Willyn and his face dropped. Willyn flashed around but could find Hagan nowhere. She let out a sigh and turned back to the young officer. His eyes were locked onto the empty bed, and his face did little to hide his grief. "I am quite sorry, my Sar."

"Now is no time for apologies." Willyn stepped forward and put herself between the officer and Hagan's room. "I will be at the square shortly to address our Realm. Now please leave me. I need just a few moments."

"Yes, ma'am." The captain saluted and jogged from the room.

Willyn shut the heavy door behind him and scanned the shadows of the room. "Hagan, where are you?"

Hagan limped from one of the darker corners of the room and chuckled. "A bit closer call than I had hoped for. Now, you need to go. Our Realm needs you."

"I just don't want to leave you. Not like this. Not in your... *condition*." Willyn peered out the door and pulled herself back into the shadows of Hagan's quarters. "I need to know you are safe."

"Lyn. I survived this long on my own, but I am not alone anymore. There are others. Since Hosp's coup, I've been assembling a remnant of forces to protect me and keep the true knowledge of my survival a secret. *My shadow guard.* Even now, they are watching us. I kept trying to reach you, sending members of the guard to you, but you never responded." The authority in Hagan's voice returned as he chided her.

Guilt washed over her as she thought back to the messenger she had fought and killed in the back alleys of Zenith. All the signs, all the attempts that Hagan had made, she had refused to believe them. *You are so stupid*, she scolded herself. *You kept denying the truth while Hagan patiently waited for your return.*

"Where are you staying? How will I find you?" Willyn straightened her back and took in a deep breath. "I won't leave you. Not again."

Hagan staggered toward the door and fidgeted with the cane in his hand. "I will not be far, Lyn, but I'm afraid that I'll have to stay in hiding...even from you. You need to lead, and I will only be a distraction. Trust me when I say I will be fine and I will not be far. But you must go. I will reach out to you again soon, my Sar."

Willyn shook her head, her eyes wide with awe. "I am not the Sar, Hagan. Not with you here. *You know that.*"

He looked at her, his eyes full of wisdom. He spoke, his voice no longer frail, but triumphant and grand. "I know what our Realm needs, Willyn. They need you as their Sar, whether I am alive or not." He clasped her hands with his, his bony palm encasing hers. "I give the Sardom to you, freely, dear sister. Take what is rightfully yours and soon the Groganlands will forget these painful memories of treachery and defeat. We are of one accord, you and I. We make our moves together. Our next move is coming soon, a checkmate against our true enemy. The Grogans' revenge against Seam Panderean will be swift, and our armies will hammer through the *High King* until he breaks under them." He stared into her eyes, full of the fire that always burned within him. "There will be no mercy for Camden's son. We will claim his Keys for ourselves and secure our place once again within the land, Seam and his Serubs be damned for their deeds."

Willyn nodded and reached out to hug her brother one more time, still shaking with the realization that he was alive. She could not believe all that had just happened and she refused to relinquish her grip over his brittle frame until she had convinced herself that this was, in fact, not a dream. She looked at him with tears streaming from her eyes.

"I will fight for our people. I will make you proud, Hagan."

"You already have, Lyn. You already have."

The silence of Willyn's quarters wrapped around her as she fought to still her nerves. Emotions swirled in her like a tempest as she tried to allow her mind to come to grips with her new reality. *Hagan is alive. Hagan. Is. Alive.* The joy of Hagan's return mixed with the sorrow of Bri sacrificing himself for her. If not for Bri, she would have died not knowing the truth.

The truth. Despite what she had experienced, discord roared within her. Everything was a brutal mixture of pain and confusion. Unrelenting loss and unexpected gain fought one another within Willyn's mind. Since she had returned to the Groganlands, nothing had gone as she planned.

Her mind snapped back. *Wael. Grift.* Frantically, she flipped open the datalink on her desk and offered a quick prayer that the signal would be picked up. The connection beeped for a full minute. Willyn reached out to close down the datalink just as a voice came over the line.

"Willyn?" Wael's voice was hushed. "Willyn, is that you?"

"Yes, Wael. It's me." Everything within her wanted to tell Wael about her brother's return, but Wael quickly steered the conversation.

"I feared your death. What happened to your line?"

"It didn't survive the firefight we had with Seam. My forces barely made it to Rhuddenhall alive."

"Bri? What of him?" Wael's voice was full of dread and it crushed Willyn's spirit to answer.

"He's dead, Wael. He died..." Willyn fought back the guilt that surrounded her. She swallowed hard and continued. "He died saving me from Seam and his Serubs."

Wael muttered a soft prayer on the other end of the datalink. "He knew how important you are, Willyn. He knew Candor needed your leadership to survive. Is the mirror safe?"

"Wael. The mirror is gone. Seam and the other Serubs have it. Bastion is free by now."

A long pause filled the line, and Wael sighed. "We feared for you, but I am glad to hear that you are well. If Seam has the final mirror, then we are in grave danger. He will soon turn his eye to

Preost and will begin his advance. Preost does not have the defenses to withstand the attack that is coming."

Willyn put the pieces together. "What do you need me to do?"

"We need you to push into his territory. Break his focus. Establish an assault on Zenith, and force the High King to pull back. It may give us enough time to escape with the final mirror."

Willyn smiled and nodded. "It will be my pleasure to level that cursed city."

Willyn stood to the side of Rhuddenhall's main square and scanned the crowd that had gathered. Hot white light illuminated the square. Thousands of Grogans had poured into the space to hear Willyn give her first official address as Sar. What had once been a war zone was now filled by a curious and haggard sea of faces. Men and women strained to catch a glimpse of her, some perching on top of the burned out vehicles that had been left on the square, while others hung precariously from second and third floor windows.

The crowd was swelling with a contagious energy. A frantic pulse beat through the bodies huddled in the night. Was this hope or pride? Or just the energy that comes with an oncoming change? Willyn could not be sure, but she felt the energy all the same, and it was echoing through the streets of her Realm, like a heartbeat of great expectation. Willyn stepped under an awning and retreated beneath its shadows. As she slipped out of the public's eyesight she examined the most sacred object of her family's dynasty; the Helm of Rodnim. Somehow it had not been destroyed by Hosp's brief and turbulent reign.

Her family's ancient symbol of power rested in her hands, waiting for her to assume the mantle of Sar. It was the Warlord's crown, humble in its origins, but made sacred through scope and weight of her people's traditions. The golden helm was worn only by those who dared to write the Grogan history in blood and war, passing from one generation to the next. Given only to the strongest and most capable leader. To hold the helmet sent a scintillating charge down Willyn's arms, but she felt a tinge of guilt. Somewhere in the crowd, Hagan was watching. She knew that he was still the rightful Sar, despite what he had said to her.

"I will return this mantle to you again, Hagan, I swear." Willyn whispered under her breath as she turned the helmet over and examined its every inch. An hour went by as the people stood in the cool night listening to speeches from Red captains and lieutenants as they readied the crowd for Willyn's ascent, but Willyn stood like a statue, unable to present herself to the square. Her thoughts turned to the memory of her brother, who had so long ago given a roaring speech to those who would have him as their Sar. *What can I say that could ever match those words?* Her eyes read over the runes of Rodnim's helm and a strange clarity set in. She stayed still, her mind focusing in on the feeling of insight that fell over her there in that quiet place between her people and her destiny. She thought back to the selfish thoughts she once carried about her heritage, and how being Grogan meant that she would never lead a life of her own making, a life built on her own choices.

Now she was faced with a choice she never thought was hers to make, and everything in Candor hung in the balance of her decision. The balcony where she would appear stood high above the growing throng of the war-torn who continued to push into the square. She could hear them and feel them as they all poured within the Red City, waiting and hoping that she would be the answer to their prayers. Over the din, she heard a sound that shot over the crowd, a small but powerful sound. Willyn's eyes flung up and landed on the sight of a small bird, a scarlet cardinal who flitted past the balcony's edge, unafraid and unconcerned with the thousands that gathered below.

Willyn's heart hammered in her chest, and she whispered almost silently, "I've made it home, little red. Now I must take my place."

The small flame of a bird swished by and fired off its rapid pulsating song.

Willyn stood, holding the sacred helm by her side, and presented herself to the people with the first light of dawn.

The crowds of Grogans roared with a furious applause as Willyn stepped out holding the helm of Rodnim by her side. Dawn tore through the fading night, quick to cast its light over the scene so that all could behold the coming of the new Sar.

Willyn stood, her face gazing down upon all of her people, her hair blazing in the burning red color of the dawn. She wore only black fatigues, a mirror image of her brother's own ascension. Her voice cascaded over the crowd like a triumphant revelry.

"Today is a new day, my Grogans." The crowd stood to their feet and began chanting her family's name. "Kara, Kara, Kara!"

Willyn smiled with uncontrollable joy. She held up her hand and silenced them, but her face was gracious. Her speech boomed through the crowd, as makeshift video feeds began to blossom across the Red City like flowers, each focused squarely on her.

"Brothers and sisters. I don't have to waste words telling you we have been fighting against an unbelievable evil. There are men and women who wanted to tear down our proud Realm and use it as their own private army. We have survived terrible infighting, thanks to the Reds who stayed loyal to our people's legacy and to the mantle of the Sar."

The crowds boomed with earthshattering praise, and Willyn had to pause so the people could have their moment. She spoke as the roar died down and her voice was solemn. "I owe an enormous debt to the Reds, most of all to General Rander, who kept the fire of rebellion burning in my absence."

The crowd's praise boomed again, echoing over the promenade with new force as Willyn presented Rander to the people. Rander looked out over the crowds, his eyes distant, and solemnly saluted the Red soldiers in the crowd. Willyn and the rest of the Red corps mirrored the motion, until Rander dropped the salute and turned to Willyn, bowing with reverence. Willyn placed her hand on her ally's shoulder and brought him back to eye level. The two stood together as the crowd showered them with praise. Willyn turned and continued, "Our battle is far from over. There are still some of our own who blindly follow the lies of Seam Panderean and his bloodthirsty Dominion in Zenith. Seam knew that to secure Candor for himself, he would have to quell the Grogans. He has failed, and the insurrection of Hospsadda Gran is over."

The crowds broke into another chain of triumphant cheers of "KARA! KARA! KARA!" that washed over her words.

As the roar of the crowds receded, she continued, "To all Grogans who hear my voice. It is time to stop fighting one another. Hosp's control is over. Those who conspired against the Sar within the Grogan Council will be tried and punished by court martial." Willyn paused, her mind wrestling with what she would say next. "All Grogans, hear my voice. I will make this offer only once. To those who have betrayed your Realm and your Sar in service to the Surrogator, I offer a full and free pardon if you wish to rejoin my Realm. Put down your weapons to take up arms for the Sar once more. You have one day to turn yourselves over to my authorities. On my word, you will be accepted and treated as brothers and sisters. After tomorrow you will be counted under Seam's Dominion and be put down like the dog that you serve."

The crowds went silent, and Willyn shifted uncomfortably under the reaction of the people. She filled the void with sharp, penetrating words. "We will stand united once more, not out of fear or terror as Seam Panderean would have us, but out of hope. We, the Grogans, will ensure that there is freedom once more in Candor. So, let it be written that on this day, on the first day of my ascension, that I declare war on the Dominion of Seam Panderean. I declare war on the desert city of our ancient enemies, those that our ancestors once brought to justice. We will burn Zenith to the ground and bring a swift and upright judgment on our enemies once more!"

The crowds roared with hot fury and hit their chests in support.

"I also declare a full and equal protection of the Bagger race, who have long served as all of Candor's caretakers. No longer will you be a people without a land, without a home. No longer will you be oppressed by us or by any other Realm. Riht and all its holdings will be yours once more, and the Groganlands will take its place as your strong friend and ally. May it be written on this day that if one mistreats a Bagger, he is mistreating the Mighty Sar of the Groganlands! So join us, my Bagger brothers and sisters! Join us in recapturing your ancient homeland this day, so that we, the Grogans, may be the first to bless you. May all of Candor follow us in our example!"

The Baggers in the crowd shrieked with uncontrollable joy and fell to their knees in a mixture of awe and jubilation. Willyn could not hide the tears that streamed from her eyes, and she silently spoke within her mind, *For you, Bri.* She scanned the crowd's reaction, momentarily scared of this unexpected announcement, but soon she saw Grogans and Baggers embracing each other and rejoicing over their shared cause.

"We go to war, my Grogans. A war where victory cannot be assured. This may very well be the last days of our Realm and our people, but let us press on, hoisting up the mantle of our ancestors. We will not be ruled by fear, by treachery, or by death! Our lands and our people will not be the spoils of some fool's mad conquest! We fight and will die in our fight, if that is Aleph's will for us."

Willyn's voice rang out over the hushed crowds as she sung the war hymn of her people:

"To die a good death is great my friends, all for all. For the Groganlands!"

Willyn lifted the helm of Rodnim into the sky, the rising sun lighting the golden helmet into a crimson glow. The crowd erupted in a wild euphoria as the chant of "Kara" rang throughout the streets.

Willyn slid the gilded helm of Rodnim over her head and she spoke words that made a chill of dread and purpose shoot down her spine.

"So begins the reign of Sar Willyn, the First."

A cloud of joy erupted across everyone within the Red City. From miles around, the echoes of the cries could be heard, and the rest of Candor trembled as the news was broadcasted over every data feed on the continent.

A Sar had returned to Candor.

CHAPTER TWENTY-FIVE

Seam's eyes were locked on his datalink screen. *That whore. That cursed little whore.* The High King stood in his chamber as he witnessed Willyn Kara's speech pour out over the entire continent. *His continent.* He threw a table against the titan's wall in a fit of rage, the antique splintering under his strength. A relentless stream of curses left his frothing mouth as he shook with fury. He had not expected his decision to kill Hosp to lead to this.

The feed lasted only a few minutes, but it was enough to prompt swift action. The rolling tides of curses roared within Seam's mind as he called Bronson in Zenith. Bronson's answer never came. Seam ground his teeth together and dialed in for another advisor.

"My lord?"

Seam screamed over the datalink, "I don't know where Bronson is, but you need to cut the feed that is coming from the Groganlands! I want you to lock all transmissions if you have to!"

"Understood, sire." The young man's voice was taut with fearful attention, and Seam relaxed a little, if only for a moment.

"Give me a status report as soon as that feed is jammed. After you do that, turn your attention to Bronson and hunt him down. I want to know why he is not answering my calls."

"I'll have an update shortly, sire."

Seam clicked the feed off and fell back into his chair. He closed his eyes tight, holding his hand up to them. They burned incessantly, stinging behind his eyelids. Whether it was a side effect of not sleeping or the residual effects of the stress he was under, he didn't know, but it felt like his body was a growing reservoir of pain and aches. None of it was enough to stop him, but it was building and Seam didn't know how much more he could endure. He ticked off the things that he would have to do to prepare for a Grogan attack. The items came with surprising ease.

He would have to secure Zenith, locking it down with martial law. All baggers and Grogans outside the Dominion army would need to be rounded up and thrown into the work camps or slaughtered. The Grogans within the Dominion army would have to be monitored and questioned to ensure their loyalty. All of the rail lines that moved the people across the continent would need to be monitored for defectors. *A logistical nightmare.* Willyn had thrown a wrench into Seam's plans and it sent him scrambling into a frenzy. His mind worked to tally the number of forces he had in his possession. Was it enough to invade Preost for the final mirror and protect Zenith from a Grogan invasion? He knew the answer...no.

"This is a distraction."

The voice was audible, but Seam was alone. He opened his eyes, scanning the small chamber, scowling. Much to his surprise, the titan chamber vanished and he sat alone in a dark, featureless void. Before him stood a mirror, and he instantly recognized it; the last mirror of the Serubs. *Isphet.*

Within the glass stood a handsome man, whose face and features reminded him of someone, but he couldn't place who. Seam stood and took a bold step forward as he spoke. "A fancy trick, Serub. It must be very taxing for your strength to accomplish such a feat." The words came out of his mouth confidently, but Seam was shocked to see a Serub he had not unlocked demonstrating such strength. *Who has fed him?* The question ricocheted in his mind, causing it to fill with doubts.

The man in the glass smirked and chuckled. "Seam Panderean, High King of Candor. You'll soon find out that I am very *different* from those you employ."

"Don't you mean your kin?" Seam snapped back, disgruntled at this interruption of his time.

The man within the mirror spoke, his voice calm but painted with threats. *"They are not my kin.* Fallen servants who would seek to keep me locked away so they can hoard the spoils of your wars." The being came close to the edge of the mirror and threw Seam a huge, crooked smile. "I'll let you in on a little secret, Seam. The others...they fear me. They fear what I can do to them, the power that I wield."

"Then you must be Isphet; and yes, the others seem concerned about releasing you." Seam turned away from the pair of dark brown eyes that stared in the mirror, his voice full of condemnation. "I don't trust you. All you Serubs ever do is lie. I've learned not to believe a word that any of you say. Your kin might have brought me unimaginable powers, but I grow weary of the cost I have to pay, maintaining all of your cursed *needs*. At this point, I've got enough to deal with without sending an army into Preost to fetch your mirror."

Isphet paced up and down the edge of the glass, shaking his head with disbelief. "Well, High King, please allow me to impart to you some truth. I want you to listen and mark my words, so that you can see that I am different than those you call my kin. My words are not wasted, and *they are always true*." Seam stared at the handsome face, intrigued.

Isphet continued, "You know for you to reach your full potential, *your* destiny, you must unlock me. Besides, I require nothing from you once I am released. All I want is one thing. *Revenge."*

Seam threw up his hands and began to walk away. "I've heard all of this before. It's the same deal I've heard from your whole lot."

Isphet banged his hands on the glass, which cracked into a brutal spider web of force. **"I'm not finished speaking to you yet, Seam Panderean**," he said coolly as if addressing a small child. "I want revenge on those you have already unlocked..."

"What?" Seam's mouth fell open as he processed the words. "You would betray your own kin?"

"Absolutely. If you would allow me the chance to *deal* with them. To take them off your hands. I would be a most loyal servant to you, High King. Give me my revenge and I will have a thousand years of life on your cursed little rock. No more blood sacrifices, no more death to innocents." Seam grimaced under the words and Isphet laughed. "Yes... I know how you humans abhor the costs of sacrifice. Release me and I could spare you and your kingdom untold lives, and still secure your power on Candor."

"And what of Zenith? What of the Groganlands? What can you do that would guarantee my city's safety?"

The Serub nodded and smiled widely. "For all your power, you are a fool when it comes to your wielding of it. Deny Willyn the chance to incite a rebellion in the desert city. *Gather up those in question, and construct a new army of the mindless.* Send them out against the coming Grogan forces! Use the army you have now and make for Preost. *Spare no one.*"

Seam blinked and put his hands up to his eyes, nodding with sudden revelation. "Yes...you are quite right. I have not been well the last few days. I'm not thinking clearly."

Isphet smiled. "I understand. You are not the first mortal that I've dealt with. You all are so very...fragile."

Seam snarled at Isphet and spoke, his voice firm. "I will do as you say. As for what happens to the rest of your kin, I would gladly allow you to *deal* with them as you desire. As long as it buys me peace and security."

"It will buy you more than that, King Seam, I assure you." Isphet smiled, his brown eyes somehow glowing in the darkness. Suddenly, Seam recognized the man within the mirror. *It was himself.*

Seam opened his eyes and he was back within the confines of the titan's chambers. A chill ran down his spine. He put the datalink up to his mouth and spoke another command to his assistant.

"Round up all the Baggers and Grogan soldiers in Zenith. I have a use for them. Use your contacts if you need help with the logistics. Pay what is necessary but see that it's done."

"Understood, my lord."

Seam sat in his chair, the memory of Willyn's broadcast distant and foreign. Something new was happening and he could feel it all around him. The thought of only having to contain one Serub eased Seam's mind. If Isphet could deliver on his promise, he might finally be free of the Serubs' tiresome attempts at mutiny. He stood and made his way to the Serubs, who were locked away within the back chambers of the titan.

As the chamber door slid open, Seam could not hide his smile. He plodded into the room and tilted his head as he grinned at the four deities. "It is time for me to let my dogs off the leash. You have proven yourselves to be efficient enough." Seam strode deeper into the small cell. "Arakiel and Nyx. You will be going back to Zenith."

"Why are you dividing us?" Abtren snapped. "I go with them." Bastion stood silent in the corner, silently observing the king.

"No." Seam pointed a finger at Abtren. "You and Bastion will stay with me. I enjoyed your brutality in the Groganlands and it will serve me well in Preost."

"What do you want Nyx and me to do, Keeper?" Arakiel kept his eyes on the floor of the titan, scanning the rivets running down the floor beneath Seam's feet.

Seam stepped within inches of Arakiel and peered up at the Serub. "I want you to purge any Bagger or Grogan you find within an inch of Zenith. As you get to the city, they should all be gathered and ready for you to *process* them." Nyx's eyes went dark and a wide grin grew on her face. Seam continued, "Push them out and command them to protect Zenith until we return. The

Grogans have declared war on us and will be making their way to our city. Show them no mercy."

Arakiel's eyes flew open and a sinister spark twinkled within as he finally looked at Seam. "I am pleased that you would trust us to partake in this task."

Seam smiled and nodded. "Don't disappoint me. Zenith must remain safe from the Grogans. Do not let them through."

Arakiel smiled and laughed. "You will be pleased in our work, Keeper. I assure you of that."

Seam peered from the cockpit of the titan as the two rooks carrying Arakiel and Nyx screamed away from the convoy, throwing a plume of sandy dust in the air behind them. He reveled in satisfaction as he turned his attention to the tank's displays.

"How far are we from Preost's borders?"

"Two hours, sir. We've maintained a steady clip." The captain fidgeted in his chair. "Any commands, my lord?"

"None for now. Alert me once we have visual on the border or see any potential targets."

"Aye, sire."

Seam retreated to his small cabin and drew his door shut. He sunk down into his chair and covered his face with shaking hands. "Just one hour of sleep. That is all I need."

His body trembled, refusing to calm itself. He fought to quiet his mind but whenever he closed his eyes he was assaulted by dark visions. Memories that were not his own: faces and sounds all stemming from the power he drained from the Serubs and from the morel husks he commanded. All of *them* waited in the darkness, coiling around him like a cruel, ravished serpent. The mammoth burden of his powers weighed on his shoulders and pressed him into his chair, as if he were buried beneath the sea.

"All I desire is sleep."

The bracer itched at his arm, as if it beckoned him to remove it to find the rest he so desperately desired. The idea was tempting, but Seam knew the Serubs were waiting for any opportunity to steal the Keys away. He had to be aware, *connected*, at all times.

Seam sat with his hands over his face, trying to still his mind in hope that he could at last achieve some form of rest. As he sat, trying to ignore everything around him, a quiet voice spoke from within.

Gods don't sleep. The thought pricked Seam's mind and catapulted him to the edge of his seat. *Gods aren't weak.* A new voice, one that was fully Seam's, but new and powerful rang in his mind.

I don't sleep. I am not weak.

Seam stood and rubbed his hand on the bracer holding the Keys of Candor. He smiled as he examined the five relics that had granted him power known only to the gods. He drew in a deep, refreshing breath and smiled as he spoke softly to himself. "I am the Keeper. I am the one of destiny. I am...*divinity*."

He paced to a small mirror and examined his face. His dark skin was smooth and perfect, without blemish, but his eyes bore the dark shade of exhaustion. Seam pried his eyes open and stared himself down. "This exhaustion is the last of my humanity being leached from my body. It is the price I have to pay for my destiny."

Seam's datalink blinked and the titan's captain came over the line. "My king. We have arrived. I have no visual on any hostiles, but our reinforcements are standing by at the border ready to join our advance. We await your orders."

Seam smiled and walked to the captain's cabin. Staring through the cockpit, his eyes fell on the hundred-foot wall of tall pines that marked the border of Preost. Seam stared at the trees slowly rocking in the breeze. The border made the forest feel ancient and impenetrable.

"Have you located any roads or thoroughfares, captain?"

The captain furiously operated his datafeed on the console, which brought up a floating map of the territory, a thick swatch of green indicating the forest. There were no openings that could be seen. "I have been pinging some scouts that were sent in from Zenith weeks ago, but they are not getting back to me. It's as if they've completely disappeared. I fear they might have been compromised."

Seam growled, and the captain furiously began operating the titan's information console, his face despondent at the results.

"There are no roads here, sire. None that my maps indicate. The forest is just too thick."

Seam nodded and gritted his teeth, frustration growing on his face. "We have to find a way in, captain. Send out some probes. The monks have roads to Taluum. We just need to find them. We must proceed as if our scouts have been compromised."

"Aye, sire. I will release some probes." The captain pressed a button on the titan's console. Two white probes lifted from the machine and shot up above the tree canopy. The white spheres spun as the black shiny lenses covering their sides collected data from the canopy below.

The captain spoke, his voice hopeful. "We should have a better sense of the terrain in a few minutes." Seam stared in silence at the live feed channeling in from the two hovering devices, watching as the machines analyzed the variations in the forest's terrain. Everything was highlighted, from game trails, animal patterns, and breaks in the tree limbs. The probes moved with incredible speed, scanning miles of the forest border in mere minutes. Soon, an alarm sounded and the cameras leveled their gaze on a thin vein of what looked to be recent tracks leading into the forest.

"Sire, looks like we've found a trail." The captain zoomed in on the feed to a small dirt trail, camouflaged by the dense forest. There, on the sandy, red dirt of the trail, were the shallow signs of hoof and footprints leading into the woodlands.

Seam stared at the opening and cursed. "We'll never be able to get our titans through that."

The captain shook his head. "These are the only trails anywhere near us. Wide enough for a line of horses or pack-mules, but not much else. They are hard to find unless you know the terrain. I could have sworn this was the drop site provided by our intel, but I don't see it. There should be a road near here."

Seam nodded. "Can our rooks get through?"

"Yes, sir, but only one at a time, single file." The young man dropped his gaze from Seam and scanned the images still beaming in from the egg-like orbs hovering overhead. He ran his hands through his blonde hair and beamed as he pointed to the glowing screen. "Looks like the trail opens up in about one hundred meters. We have enough firepower to clear some of these trees and push through. Maybe from there we can locate a village and have them lead us into Taluum."

Seam stared at the captain and smiled. "A very good plan, captain. Very good indeed." Seam read the moniker pinned to the captain's uniform for the first time. "Captain Reed, which Realm do you hail from?"

"Lotte, sir. It is an honor and privilege to serve you." The captain saluted the High King, who quickly followed suit.

"Well met, kinsman. Call for all artillery to focus on blasting our way in and mobilize the troops. I want them all in formation by the hour's end, ready to march."

The officer nodded and saluted one more time. "Yes, sir."

Wael sat alone in the sanctuary of Taluum, his head bowed in the dim candlelight of the sacred place. His mind was a storm of frustration, refusing to focus during his meditation. Luken, Grift, Adley, and he had safely made their way into Preost and prepared in haste for the High King's invasion.

Wael opened his eyes and sighed. His mind whirred and clicked with an endless cycle of checklists. No matter how many times he went over what needed to be done, he feared he might have missed something. They had prepared in every way he knew how for a coming conflict, but none of his strategies comforted him.

Informing the other leaders in the Order had been easy enough, but the plans changed when Willyn had given him additional intel on what was heading their way. Seam was moving to Preost not just with titans and rooks, but also with a horde of vicious, newly made morels. Wael shuddered at the thought of fighting the creatures again and grieved at what it would mean for the Forest Enclave, whose only real defense was in the martial trainings of their Order. In addition, it did not even account for the fact that Seam would be guarded by the Serubs he had already unlocked.

Focus. Do not give into fear. Wael's own conscience checked him into further meditation over what was left to be done. *What else?* Adley had prepped the Predecessor technology as the last defense. Even though the technology made the Mastermonk uneasy, he had pressed in on the Resistance leaders to dig it up and reactivate it. His monks, his brothers had been essential for rebuilding the war machine, but he was at a loss on what choice he really had. How could he ever fight what was coming?

All of these things swirled within the Mastermonk's mind, but nothing was so troubling as what he had encountered on the border of his very own Realm. *The Desolate.* The Desolate had reawakened and Wael sat paralyzed at this new and unexpected turn of events. Their coming was a dreaded sign, a sign of Aleph's coming judgment. *Aleph has made his presence known again.*

Wael stood and walked slowly to a cabinet bearing the tomes of the monks who had gone before him, located just to the side of the main altar within the Sanctuary. The candlelight that burned from the seven lampstands barely cast enough light as he scanned the ancient manuscripts. Wael paused for a moment and fetched a small tome. He blew the dust off the book and read its title, *Signs in the Night*.

Carefully, he thumbed through the pages, scanning the dark, intricate text that swayed under the guiding of a forgotten hand, long ago.

> *Aleph's eyes are open, scanning, watching all*
> *Lofty hands, strong and steady, waiting for the call*
> *Exacting judgment, mighty; piercing through the fog*
> *Pitch black of night is vanquished; His power shown to all*
> *Watch the stars as they tumble, marvel as they fall*
> *White fury burning from the sky, obeying Master's call*
> *Desolate will awaken, shaking through the timbers,*
> *Their power known, their fury hot, burning with white embers,*
> *Listen faithful, listen; heed this warning song,*
> *Once Desolate awaken, judgment will soon fall.*

Wael's hand trembled as he closed the ancient book and kneeled to pray at the room's altar. His face rested on the cold timber floor as he tried to calm his soul, but it refused to be tamed. His heart slammed at the walls of his chest, growing with unrelenting pressure, squeezing out his breath. Tears fell and soaked into the wooden floor, adding to the stained altar as Wael moaned out in desperation. There were no spoken words, only the groaning of his soul as he pleaded with Aleph, who still remained silent.

Please, Aleph. My Lord. Help.

Pine trees buckled as mortars and cannon fire ripped through the forest. The twelve titans in Seam's company let out a relentless barrage of fire, shredding the canopy lying between them and Preost. The chorus of trees cracking, snapping, and falling joined the drumbeat of mortar fire as the mighty Preost forest buckled under the weight of Seam's war machines. As the attack pressed on, titans and rooks hovered over burning tree stumps and downed pines, still smoldering from their assault. The sweet smell of boiling tree sap permeated the air and mixed with the smoke that rolled through the underbrush.

Seam's titan pressed into the opened pass first, snapping down a few smaller pines that had somehow survived the shelling. The transport door was open, and the High King hung out the side, his eyes dancing in the firelight. A squadron of thirty rooks hung behind him, spread out in a fan of cover, ready to mow down any who would dare oppose them.

A hover drone flew, capturing Seam as they rode through the forest. They had cut nearly ten miles into the dense foliage, without a single sight of any of Preost's forces. Seam stared into the camera, his eyes alight with pride and fervor.

"Candor, I come before you today with a heavy heart. The alliance the Surrogator and I worked so hard to establish between Lotte and the Groganlands has crumbled. The unity of our Dominion threatens to fracture under the events that have unfolded recently. It pains me to tell you the truth. Hospsadda Gran, the mighty Surrogator of the Groganlands, is dead, falling under the traitorous hand of Willyn Kara. She has retaken the Groganlands with this final Red Death, continuing her family's reign and bloodthirsty rule. Willyn Kara has declared war on us, *on all of us.*"

Seam paused, his eyes locking with the camera before he spoke again. "But that is not the only reason I am here today, dear Candor, for there are many traitors in our midst, even those who we have long trusted. The Enclave of Alephian monks in the forest Realm of Preost has secretly been harboring Willyn Kara's allies, Grift Shepherd and the fallen Mastermonk. The neutral and peaceful Realm has become a hotbed of terrorism, networking with other cells of dissidents within the continent in a covert network that threatens to destroy our unity. I don't know how else to say this, but the monks want our land broken and divided again. They would rather have us engaged in the petty skirmishes and wars that mark our sordid history than to find and secure our own peace. Our enemies abound like wolves in sheep's clothing, waiting to devour us like lambs."

Seam roared into the camera, his eyes wide and full of fury. "No more. I will not sit idly by and see our world fall back into a second dark age. *We must rally, Candor.* Rally and protect all that we have built. Clandestine tactics and secret alliances will never avail against the mighty unification we have established! It gives me little choice but to declare a full-scale war on the brothers in Preost who have betrayed not only our continent, our alliance, but the very god they claim to serve. We will root out the poison in our body and build within this Realm a true spirituality founded on the bedrock of peace. *May Aleph help me as we march to this task.* For unity!"

The feed cut, and Seam heard a low, hideous growl within the titan. He turned, his eyes locking with kaleidoscopic eyes that flashed with rage. Abtren sneered, revealing rows of serrated teeth. Seam's heart froze at the sight as she spoke, "Why do you insist on saying *his name*? It is not wise...in this place." Bastion who stood next to her shuddered, his green eyes burning with hatred. Seam stood momentarily speechless and he furrowed his brow in mock sympathy.

"I'm so sorry, my dear friends, but how can the name of a god who does nothing terrify you? If *Aleph* does exist, then he abandoned Candor long ago." The two Serubs roared at the sound of the name, shaking as if hot coals had fallen over them.

"STOP! STOP IT!" Abtren's face morphed between wolf and woman, and Bastion fell to the ground seizing, his hands curled around his head as he shook with fury. Abtren locked her gaze on the High King, her eyes spinning with accelerated madness. "If you want our loyalty, then you should not speak the name of the false god in our presence."

Seam did not break his stare. "You've told me this before, Abtren. Let me remind you that you are *bound.* I'll do as I please."

Abtren's face broke away from the High King's gaze and she whispered, "The false god is crueler than even you, High King. More powerful than you could imagine. His invisible hand hides within *his very name* so to speak it is to invite him here. *Do not do this.*" Bastion stood up from the titan floor, a trickle of blood pouring from his nose.

Seam stood, shocked. "Bastion…I…"

Abtren lashed out as she ran to her brother's aid. "He is not nearly as strong as me, for he has not fed enough." She cut her horrific colorful eyes at him. "You see. I'm not wasting my words with you. *If you wish success, then listen to us.* You know nothing of the other side."

Seam shuddered as Abtren rushed over to Bastion, whose face was wilted and pale. She held out her wrist to her brother, and Bastion plunged his fangs into her, drinking deep. She cooed at him, rubbing her hand over his head. Seam turned away in disgust, unwilling to watch the grisly scene.

"Very well, Abtren. I will do as you say."

Commander Reed's voice flared on Seam's datalink. "Sir, we've got contact. Five monks straight ahead, and you won't believe this, but the probe is telling me they are blocking a wide open path headed in the direction of Taluum."

Seam's eyes lit up with a sick joy. "Good. I want to see what the fools will do."

Seam leaned out of the titan's hold and looked ahead. Not twenty feet in front of him stood a small gathering of Preost monks huddled in a tight circle, under the canopy of swaying firs.

The five held their circle and stood firm just feet from the massive, black titan hovering before them. The tank made them look like five ants attempting to defy an elephant from passing. The elder monk held his staff over his head and stared into the black titan's tinted cockpit.

"Is he challenging us?" quipped Seam. "This is comical. Lower the bay door. *Now!*"

The bay door on the side of the titan slid to the ground and Seam descended the staircase that dropped from the door. He strode to the collection of monks, his chest puffed out as his black cape whipped in the wind behind him.

"Hail to you, kind monks. I trust you are not impeding your High King's progress? Surely you have heard my decree? I go to war with those who seek to divide this proud world."

The monks stood like statues, their eyes locked onto Seam, each gaze filled with a mixture of anger and pity. The eldest held his staff resolute over his head as he spoke. "Your words were heard. Each lie that dripped from your lips acted to condemn you in Aleph's sight. You hope to trample on this sacred ground, but we will not allow your passage."

Seam chuckled and glanced back at his titan. "Are you blind, old man?" He pointed to the black, mountain-like tank hovering overhead. "How do *you* hope to stop my progress? With your little stick there?"

The elder monk did not sway. His voice was solemn. "We do not fight by our strength alone. May we die trying, Aleph be praised."

Seam threw his hands up in disgust and waved off the monks. "I will enjoy the show then. Pray all you want, you fools." As Seam walked toward the titan he called out, "Bastion! Abtren! Enjoy the feast."

As the words left his lips, the half-man half-beast forms leapt from the open bay door and sped across the forest floor toward the five. Abtren's form was mostly that of a woman but her face had morphed into the terrible maw of a rabid wolf. Her fangs dripped with black saliva as she screamed toward her targets. Bastion took on the form of a massive boar, running on its hind legs with little human resemblance aside from his massive arms. The two swept across the open space and leapt in the air for the monks.

The five acolytes cried out and spread out, each brandishing their staff as they formed a wider circle around the two deities.

Seam stepped into the cockpit of the titan and peered from the window. Captain Reed stammered behind him.

"Um, sir. What were those?" He was unable to pry his eyes from the terrors that had poured out of the titan.

"Unless you want to go and see for yourself, Captain Reed, I'd advise you to be silent," said Seam.

Outside, Abtren lunged atop the youngest monk and ripped at his flesh, her fingers shifting into sharp razors. The monk barred her advance with his staff, but her power was too much as she bit down on his throat, unleashing a river of red. The monk to the right slammed his staff against Abtren's jaw. The blow connected with a resounding thud, but Abtren threw a wide slash at the younger monk, unfazed. The monk continued his assault and landed a massive hit of his staff against Abtren's neck, followed by a third spear-like thrust.

Upon the third blow, Abtren roared out in pain and reached a ragged claw to grasp her attacker. She stood, hurling him against one of the massive fir trees. His back made a terrible snapping sound as he collided with the ancient tree and slid limply to the ground.

Bastion stampeded one monk and trampled him underfoot as he made way for the leader of the five hermits. The first yelped as he was crushed beneath Bastion's immense, hooved feet. The elder monk rushed toward Bastion and gouged his staff directly into his right eye socket. A black spray of liquid erupted from Bastion's face, and the massive boar stumbled forward, squealing with pain. The monk yelled out as his comrade joined in battling Bastion. "Aleph, pour out your strength as we fight!"

The elder swung again, slamming his staff against Bastion's knee, causing a loud crack to erupt. He turned, only to nail his ironwood stick against Abtren's neck as she lunged for him. Abtren stumbled back, wheezing. Soon she and Bastion stalked forward, pressing in closer on the final two monks. Abtren's face shifted back to that of her human countenance and she sneered. "We will enjoy picking the flesh from your putrid bones."

In one accord, the Serubs rushed over them, tearing into the bodies of the monks with unbridled fury. The two monks screamed out a final plea, each reaching out for the other's hand, accepting the death that came for them. *"Aleph, come please!"*

The forest fell silent aside from the ragged sound of the two Serubs as they feasted. Seam watched with disgust as the two gorged themselves on the monks' flesh. *They are like rabid animals.* He numbly sulked back to his small chamber. The conflict had been dealt with swiftly and did not bring the satisfaction Seam had hoped for. The resistance in Preost would be no match for his Serubs, much less the morels he had with him. The thoughts rolled in his mind, assuring him of his progress when a flash bolted across his vision.

An explosion of white light crashed over the two Serubs as they feasted, hiding them from view. The sound of thunder exploded within the clearing and a terrible heat pressed in on the titan. Seam had barely turned to see what was happening when hot white flames roared through the open bay door. "Close the doors!" Seam screamed as he recoiled.

The bay door slammed shut, but the claps of thunder continued outside, as the cockpit windows filled with a consuming bright light.

"What the hell is that!?" Seam screamed.

A harsh shriek rose from the white-hot tempest and Seam could make out the silhouette of Abtren, slashing with a manic fury at the vapor surrounding her. Another cry shook the titan. Bastion's beast form lunged from the cloud of white, fighting a translucent, glowing humanoid figure. Bastion's skin boiled on its surface and he screamed in agony as he dug his boar tusks into the figure that held him down.

Abtren's body erupted with a wall of black flames, and she propelled the unholy fire in a sphere around her. Her kaleidoscope eyes had been replaced by dark red pupils and she screamed, forcing her shield of dark fire to spread further and further. Bastion crumpled to the ground, thudding against a singed bed of pine needles and dirt as Abtren channeled the maelstrom around her into a single stream of onyx flame, unleashing it in the direction of the white flame's nexus.

The two fires collided with a blinding explosion, sending a shockwave through the forest that rattled the hull of the titan, threatening to lift and upend the massive machine. The rooks in the front of the formation rolled through the forest like scattered leaves, smashing against the outcropping of strong trees.

Following the collision of fire, the forest went dark. Seam wiped at his eyes, trying to regain his sight. A landscape of black was speckled with flashes of white. Vision finally returned and he peered out into the clearing. Abtren and Bastion were strewn across the ground, their breathing barely evident. Panic coursed through Seam as he screamed for the release of the bay door.

The forest floor was still searing with an immense heat, burning Seam's feet through the soles of his boots as he ran to Abtren and Bastion. The two wheezed as they fought to breathe, their chests rattling as they struggled to survive.

"What was that?" Seam exclaimed. "What happened?"

The two Serubs lay silent on the ground. Seam snapped his dagger from its holster and sliced his palms open, pressing his bleeding hands against the faces of his fallen allies. As his skin simmered with the sapping of his own blood, the two Serubs breathing steadied and they coughed and gagged for deeper breaths.

Seam pulled his hand back and leaned down next to Abtren's face. "What was that?"

Abtren's voice was hushed as she strained to speak. "Desolate."

Seam screamed into his datalink. "Medic! I need transport for these two into their quarters. Bring a dozen guards to set watch for them."

A strong wind pushed through the forest and a chill ran over Seam's entire body. He stared up into the sky, fearful of another flash of white fire tearing through the sky to consume them. He scurried back to the titan as a crew of medics assisted Abtren and Bastion to their quarters, along with the unfortunate guards chosen to assist them in recovering.

Seam commanded forward progress at top speed as the convoy tore down the open path to Taluum. He stared out the cockpit and the half-melted windshield at the dark forest on both sides of the titan and whispered to himself, "What are these Desolate? What in Candor could nearly kill two Serubs? If I can't kill them, what is it that almost did?"

He leaned into the titan's cockpit and spoke to Captain Reed, doing his best to keep his voice calm. "Have the probes analyze the anomaly that just occurred. Have them focus their scans on the forest for similar signals or triggers that brought on that firefight. We can't be ambushed like that again."

Captain Reed silently obeyed, his face drained of its color.

Seam retreated to the Serubs' private quarters and tried to quiet his mind as he marveled at what he had witnessed. Never had he witnessed such a display of raw, primal power. *Desolate.* The name of the beings of white light orbited in his mind at an unforgiving speed. *I have to know more.*

CHAPTER TWENTY-SIX

"Aleph!" The name was all Kull could manage to mumble as he knelt and crumpled at the stranger's feet, shaking with fear. "I am sorry. I did not know."

The man's strong hand took hold of Kull's shoulder and gently lifted him from the floor. Kull refused to look at him in the face until the man's voice spoke his name.

"Do not be afraid of me, Kull." Kull dared to open his eyes and gaze upon his mysterious host. Was it this new secret knowledge that made the man before him shine with a new radiance, new energy, new purpose? Or had it been there all along? Kull couldn't be sure, but regardless, the stranger he had worked with for days in Mir seemed unchanged, except his eyes. His eyes displayed a golden aura like the coming of a new day. Aleph's smile was gentle and he ushered Kull to stand.

"You have nothing to apologize for. I always intended for you to discover my identity in time." Aleph stepped to one of the mountain ledges and peered out over the landscape below. He sighed as he scanned the tops of the fir trees lining the mountains under his feet and the low-hanging clouds that floated just out of arm's reach. "Mir has served us well, Kull. But now it is time we change our scenery."

Kull sat helplessly as he tried to comprehend the fact that he was sitting with Aleph, the Gracious One, the Mighty, the Invisible Hand. The chief deity of Candor stood just feet away from him. He came in a guise Kull had not expected and his mind struggled to understand why all of this was happening to him. Kull took his time rising to his feet. He shuffled toward Aleph at the edge of the mountain, his mind brimming with questions.

"What do you mean change of scenery?" asked Kull. "Mir is always changing."

Aleph let out a loud laugh and nodded. "Well, that is true, Kull, but we cannot stay here. Not any longer. I have more in store for you."

"For me? What do you mean?" *Why was Aleph so concerned with him? Who was he to Him?*

Aleph turned to face Kull and kept his arms folded behind his back. The mountain quaked underfoot as large boulders broke free from the mountain and tumbled down its steep face. The green tops of the fir trees below swayed as if they were only blades of grass tossed by the wind. The blue sky deepened until it was a void of midnight that rocketed closer and closer to Kull and Aleph. Aleph spoke as he approached Kull's side. "You have discovered who I truly am, Kull. However, you still have not discovered who you are meant to be."

The mountain's metamorphosis continued as the granite and quartz outcrops rumbled and melted into a golden liquid. Even the rock beneath Kull's feet changed into a flowing golden substance that, despite its fluid motion, was as sturdy as the rock it replaced. The blackened sky rolled back like a curtain and Kull gasped as he peered through the void.

"Candor." The blue orb of Candor became visible to Kull, the main super-continent spread out before him in full display. Kull's mind filled with sweeping memories from his past. He trembled as a torrent of faces, sounds, and visions bombarded his consciousness. His life, his family, his friends; they all swept through him with relentless fury, yet he was able to pick out and remember each memory as it flashed by his mind's eye. The last sight of his life rose like a tidal wave in the distance. The strong, terrible Serub stepped out of the mirror at the beck and call of Seam Panderean. His blood red eyes locked on him, and he felt the pain of his essence being ripped from his body, joining with the void.

Aleph let out a deep sigh and lowered his head before turning back to Kull. "Candor is in pain, Kull. Much has happened since you came to me."

Grift peered out over the exterior wall of Taluum, perched on one of the massive stone turrets. He strained his eyes as he scanned the thick pine canopy below. A few birds rustled and called out as they lifted themselves into the sky, but the forest remained still and silent. He turned to face Adley. Her face was like chiseled stone. The nurse turned warrior did not break her gaze from the horizon, balancing the automatic rifle in her hands with certainty.

"Any word?" Grift knew the answer, but still the question came.

Adley said nothing but shook her head, her eyes locked on the limits of her perspective, sighing in the light breeze. The lush scenery around them was glorious, oblivious to the fact that Seam would soon invade and set its natural beauty ablaze. The sun shone over them, its bright light cascading from the crisp blue sky as a cool breeze rustled through the forest.

Grift shifted his position, shaking his head, his mind full of dreadful thoughts. Everything had shifted so quickly since Henshaw. Rose was dead, but Luken had returned. He knew there was no time to process the significance of all of these events, but his entire being was set on edge, ready for a fight. *Fight the person that matters.* Seam was coming and he could feel it. The black shadows of his fears would soon come into focus once more, and this time he would be ready. Ready to send his enemy to the hell he deserved if it even existed. If he failed, he would at least die trying.

As his mind played out the scene of killing the High King of the New Dominion, his eyes focused on a small black figure soaring through the sky. His hands brought up his rifle and he peered through the scope. His mouth fell open.

"Get Wael," he commanded Adley. "The monks are sending word."

Adley sprinted down the ancient staircase that descended into the living tree Sanctuary of Taluum. Her eyes hesitated to adjust to the dim candlelight of the place, but soon she saw Wael lying prostrate on the cobblestone floor. At first glance, she thought him to be dead, but she buried that fear and called for him.

"Wael!" Her heart slammed in her chest, startled as her voice ricocheted within the strange chamber. The Mastermonk rose from the mosaic of river rocks, his face tired and burdened. "What is it child?"

"Grift needs you. He says the monks are sending word. Hurry."

Wael nodded and ran behind her with uncanny speed.

As the two emerged on the tower's pinnacle, Grift pointed silently at the object flying toward them. Adley's eyes shot up as she saw the beating wings of the falcon soaring toward them. In a matter of seconds, the bird cleared meters of ground, rocketing with steadfast purpose. A high pitch screech announced its arrival and the falcon landed, extending its talons to Wael, whose eyes were wide with anticipation. There, wrapped tightly around the bird's claw, was a small parchment of paper.

Grift swallowed, his voice full of questions. "Why aren't they sending word through the datalinks?"

Wael spoke, his voice barely above a whisper. "Because that form of communication can no longer be trusted."

"How do you know?" Adley questioned, her eyes staring as Wael untied the paper from the falcon's talon. The Mastermonk unrolled the small scroll. Wael read the message and let it fall to the ground, his face becoming stony in the shining sun. He faced the falcon and spoke in the unknown language of the monks. The bird shot off like a rocket to the east.

"The scouts have sent word. All datalink communication is to cease to protect and conceal the sanctuary. Seam has crossed into the border of Preost." The Mastermonk turned to face Grift. "Willyn's report was right. He is not alone. The Serubs were spotted and confirmed, as well as a long convoy of transports that undoubtedly hold his army of morels."

"So it is as bad as we feared." Adley's face dropped as the words left her mouth. Grift scanned Wael's face for any signal of hope.

The monk nodded, but there was a gleam in his eye. "There is something more, my friends. Remember we do not fight alone."

Grift cocked his head. "What do you mean?"

"The Desolate are active. Seam and his Serubs murdered the first group of monks that were patrolling the borders. They fought bravely but fell." Wael paused and his face grew solemn. "Upon the monks' deaths, the Desolate appeared and gravely injured Seam's convoy just as we witnessed as we entered Taluum. Aleph has not abandoned us."

Grift stared at Wael, his eyes full of rage. "Let's attack them head on. Let's bring the fight to them, Wael! Let's strike them when they least expect it."

Wael stared at Grift and slowly nodded his head. "I agree with you, dear friend. If these are our last moments, they will not be of us cowering in the dark. Let us go and meet the High King."

Wael turned and called down from the tower, his voice booming from his tall station. Below, a small band of monks stood, awaiting his orders. The Mastermonk's deep voice broke over them and sent them to action.

"Ring the bells, brothers, and send word to all of our Order! Ring the bells and release the birds! Seam Panderean is here and brings to us a war, and we will fight! We fight not for ourselves but for Aleph, the Undefiled. May our deaths be a worthy sacrifice for his rule and reign, a balm for this broken and ruined land, a healing salve for the people of all of Candor against the Five who threaten to overwhelm us once again."

Grift stood silent as the forest exploded with the sound of ancient bells, a cacophony of bronze booming in the forest. Soon the empty sky was filled with hundreds of falcons who sent word over the din of bells ringing in the trees. The monks would stand together, united in their fight against Seam and his Dominion. They would all join to protect the forest Realm.

"I know that this was not easy for you, Wael." Grift put a heavy hand on his friend's broad shoulder.

Wael nodded and whispered, his words few but powerful. "None of these things have been easy, Grift. Since sending you and Willyn out, I've sought for a sign or a word from Aleph. I have pleaded with him in fasting and in prayer. Do you know what I've heard?"

"What?" Grift stood like a statue, waiting.

"Nothing. I've heard nothing, and it terrifies me. But as I live and breathe, the monks who guarded our borders were brought down fighting, slaughtered by Seam's horrible Serubs. They were sacrificed with no mercy, and their death brought on the Desolate. That is enough for me. The time for prayer is over. We bring Aleph's mighty rage and justice to the jackal king."

Adley wavered, her voice shaking. "But what about the Predecessor tech? I've just gotten it set up! We can't easily move it to the front."

"Which is why you will stay back, young Adley." Wael's voice was commanding and resolute. "For in our last moments, you will be all that we have left to keep Seam away from the last mirror. *From Isphet*. You are our last defense, and you must keep whatever comes our way *back*."

Adley nodded, her face pale. "Okay."

The Mastermonk nodded and turned to Grift. "We must move quickly. If we don't attack soon, we will surely lose our advantage."

Grift nodded and descended the stone staircase without a word.

Seam jumped at the sound of the soldiers being devoured by Bastion and Abtren. Their screams echoed through the titan as if it held a slaughterhouse. The Serubs would have to heal quickly, so there was very little use in trying to disguise their nature from his other forces. *Let them know what I wield, and let them tremble.*

Yet Seam paused in his chamber as another sound joined the chorus of ripping flesh and screams. It was an old sound, full and encompassing, a low roll of hollowness that threatened to swallow them.

"What is that? Bells?" Seam dashed to the front of the titan, his eyes wide with rage, as his voice pinned Captain Reed to the wall. "What is that racket, Reed?"

Reed had sat idling the convoy as the beasts Seam controlled were "assisted" by the other soldiers. He glanced at the High King, his face pale with all he had encountered in the last few hours. "It sounds like bells, sire."

"Bells?" Seam's face coiled and twisted with disgust. "The monks must be sounding the alarm. Very well, then our presence here is no longer a secret." Hammering down on his datalink, Seam ushered a command to his aide back in Zenith.

"Put me in contact with that useless Evan Darian in Elum."

"Aye, sir." The sound of the feed clicked over, and Seam stared at the pudgy face of Filip Darian's son, the new ruler of Elum. Shirtless, his face was covered with chocolate, and Seam heard the sound of several women laughing nervously.

"Seam! What a surprise! I dare say, you caught me at an awkward time, but I'll always accept your call, High King."

"Evan, I don't care what you're doing, but I am requesting immediate assistance. I need air support over Preost. You need to move your forces to these coordinates – fast." Seam transcribed the coordinates, and Evan's face pinched with anxiety.

"This will be very expensive, High King, but we will do as you say."

Seam growled, his eyes piercing through the screen. "Do as I say and your family's reign in Elum will not end. I find that a fair trade, don't you? I want the monks' forest to burn down to ash, do you understand me? Do it! Do it now!"

"Of course, Seam. I'll issue the commands now."

Seam snapped the screen off as he peered outside, his mind a tempest of rage. He had been worried about the white fire that the monks had called down, that had so badly damaged his Serubs. What had Abtren called it? *Desolate?* Seam smiled as he imagined the screeching sounds of jets sweep overhead.

They're not the only ones to play with fire.

Kull stood with wonder as the world of Candor rolled by the cosmic window opened by Aleph. Kull's land rolled by him like a large marble with new scenes forming and quickly morphing before him like shifting sand. Kull gasped as he observed bodies lying scattered in the mountains of the Groganlands, the fallen warriors shredded, torn, and tossed throughout the red canyon in a bloody demonstration of uncanny power.

The world shifted and rolled to the deserts of Riht where the city of Zenith stood, simmering under the desert sun. A vision of Baggers and Grogans alike being corralled appeared. They were all held at gunpoint as Arakiel stood on a platform above them, raising his arms to the sky and unleashing a shockwave of force over them. The screams of the masses rang out to the heavens and then were cut short. The crowd stood silent before their new masters. Kull recognized what had happened in an instant as a chill ran through the space he shared with Aleph. The essences of the corralled had been ripped from their host bodies so quickly, so efficiently. The window shifted again and scrolled to a landscape dominated by ancient evergreen trees. The silence of the scene was eliminated by a fiery missile exploding over the trees and igniting them in a violent blaze of flames.

The view shifted to Seam's convoy snapping proud firs like twigs and rumbling through the forest of Preost, destroying everything between them and the fortress hidden within the dense woodland. Mortars and cannons fired with no mercy, leveling anything that the mechanized giants could not roll over. Kull shuddered as Seam hung out the side of his war machine, his face drawn up in a cruel, insane smile.

As the trees smoldered and burned below, the focus shifted to a Preost fortress, the walled city of Taluum. Four figures stood, perched atop one of the wall's many spires. Wael, Luken, Adley, and Grift spoke to one another as they looked out over the horizon.

"Dad!" Kull cried out and reached for the image. He stared at them, his face darting between those he once knew; between Adley, Wael, and his father.

Aleph laid a large hand on Kull's shoulder and offered a knowing smile. "Your father has fought hard, Kull, and has lost much. Yet, he continues to fight for the good of Candor. He has shouldered great pain, but he will not stop defending this world. His spirit is still very strong."

Kull stared at his father, whose hair looked grayer than he last recalled. Large, dark bags hung under his eyes. "He doesn't look strong. He looks exhausted."

"Looks are deceiving, Kull."

"What about the others?" Kull turned to look at Aleph. "What about Adley and Wael? Do you know what is about to happen?"

Aleph rolled his hand to the left, and the images swept back to the triumphant march of Seam's mighty procession. "They are preparing to fight a battle they cannot win."

Kull ground his teeth. "There must be something we can do." He stared at the portal and pushed the window back toward his father. He stayed there, staring, before facing Aleph. "Tell me, there must be something you can do?!"

Aleph stared at Kull, his eyes knowing but distant. "There is, but it requires you to make a choice."

"A choice?" Kull stammered. His heart hung in his throat.

Aleph nodded solemnly.

"Just tell me what it is," Kull said.

Grift ripped open the door of an old truck waiting at the foot of the stone spiral staircase and whistled as he slapped the truck's hood. Luken sprinted and leapt into the truck's bed. He took his position behind a massive chain gun that was mounted in the bed of the vehicle. It was the only truck in Preost outfitted with heavy weaponry, and it was ancient, but Grift took it just the same.

"You sure you're ready, Grift?" Luken peered into the small window between the bed and the cabin.

"We don't have a choice," barked Grift. "Let's bring the fight to the High King. Who knows? Maybe you'll put a bullet through his brain."

Luken laughed as Grift turned over the ignition and pumped the gas. The old truck roared to life and a cloud of black exhaust rolled from its tailgate. As Grift pushed the truck into gear, Adley sprinted out from the tower and screamed at them, waving her arms madly.

"Grift! Stop!" Adley fought to catch her breath as she ran to the driver's side window and frantically motioned for Grift to open his door. "You can't go. Not now!"

Luken jumped from the bed of the truck and tried to assess the fear he saw in her face. "What's going on?"

Adley sucked in deep breaths as she spoke. "Jets. Coming in from Elum. They're lighting up our sensors. They're dropping lines of napalm, burning the forest down. Another squadron is headed this way."

Grift hammered his fists into the steering wheel and cursed as he punched at the old truck. "How long? How far out are they!?"

Adley glanced up at the sky and shook her head in disbelief, running her shaking hands through her hair. "Minutes...only minutes away."

Grift slipped the truck into gear and revved the engine. "Time to light up the sky!"

Luken jumped into the truck and pulled back the action on the chain gun, hitting the back of the truck. Grift hammered down the gas and the two sped off in the direction of the oncoming fighter jets.

Grift spoke over his datalink radio back to Luken. "On my mark, Luken, I want you to tear up the sky, you understand?"

"I read you loud and clear, Grift." Grift's mind roared with a quickening he had felt many times during his life. The threat of combat always brought with it a heightened sense of awareness, as if he was able to slow down the world and all that were in it. As he drove the truck through the scrambling mountain pass, Grift could *feel* the jets, as well as the distance he was from Seam's firestorm pushing deeper through the forest toward Taluum. A fork in the dirt road came up, and Grift cut the truck's wheel hard to the right. He threw his foot down on the gas and roared into his datalink.

"Aim high, Luken, and fire, NOW!" Luken whipped the gun behind him and its ear-splitting roar drowned out the world. In mere seconds, Luken saw the flash of four jets scrambling from the unexpected resistance. The spray of bullets ripped through one of the jets, causing it to careen in a chaotic barrel roll, while another broke from formation and fell back to avoid collision. The downed jet tore through the forest canopy, snapping trunks of trees as if they were toothpicks, until plunging to the earth in a blanket of fire.

The two fighters that held to their original trajectory successfully dropped their payload, unleashing another load of napalm. Grift slammed the brakes and whipped the truck around, driving the vehicle with unearthly skill.

Luken roared over the datalink, "One bird down, three more to go!"

Grift smiled and called back, "Let's hope Seam doesn't have a squadron of these things. I'd hate to think you just got lucky."

Luken leaned over and peered through the back window of the truck, flashing a mischievous smile. "Luck? Ha…"

The squall of the fighter jets ripped through the sky, and Grift screamed, "They're coming back for another pass, Luken!"

Luken swung the gun around, shooting deep, pulsating rhythms of heavy fire up in the air. The remaining jets were coming in fast, and Grift saw as the trees only yards ahead him began to splinter under their guns, ripping through the thick forest and devouring all that lay ahead.

"Hold on!" Grift steered the truck into a gully, barely avoiding the tree trunks that weaved around them. The jets unleashed another payload of liquid fire. Trees to the left and right of Grift and Luken were consumed from top to bottom and a thick haze of smoke filled the small space between the burning timbers.

Grift coughed and wheezed, trying to cover his mouth with his shirt as he fought for breath in the thickening fog of black soot. He glanced back at Luken as his partner continued to hurl hot lead into the sky, chasing the jets as they swept overhead. Grift floored the truck and turned back for Taluum. The scream of the jets overhead quieted and faded as the crackling inferno swelled, the red-hot flames leaping from tree to tree.

"Luken," Grift called out. "You okay back there?"

"I'm fine." Luken's response was quick. "We need to get back. I'm afraid that was nothing more than a distraction."

Grift steadied the truck's wheel on the uneven dirt road and held the gas down as they hurried back to assist Wael and Adley. Grift wiped at the windshield and squinted as he fought to focus on the landscape ahead through the thick, swirling smoke. Before he could see anything, he could hear the screams of the Elumite jets overhead. They had circled and were bearing down on the truck again, their machine guns thumping hundreds of rounds into the dirt in front of the truck. By the time Grift saw the strafing fire, it was too late. There was no time to turn away. The path was too narrow and the gap was closing too fast. Grift slammed the brakes, trying to delay the inevitable. He whispered a prayer as he watched the stream of raining bullets close in on the truck.

"Do something! Whatever I need to do, just let me know! Now!" Kull's plea was desperate as he begged Aleph to stop Seam's procession. "Please!"

Aleph waved his hand and the portal looking on Candor closed, disappearing into the black void surrounding him and Kull. Warm tears rolled down Kull's cheek and dripped on the bottomless floor below. Aleph turned to face Kull. His eyes were also wet with tears, but his face was set like stone.

"So much pain. So much confusion. So much hate, Kull." Aleph slowly shook his head and exhaled a slow breath. "I can feel this world's pain, Kull. This world and all the others."

"The others?"

Aleph said nothing, and Kull didn't dare ask again. Kull pointed to the spot where the portal had once stood and spoke with a bold tenor. "Why don't you just stop it all now? You can do that, can't you?"

Aleph drew in a deep breath, nodded, and paused before answering. "Yes, Kull. I could, but the life of Candor is made up of more than one moment, and this is not yet the greatest battle to fight." Aleph dipped his head and closed his eyes. A tapestry of pain, pity, and rage covered his expression. He lifted his eyes to Kull, and they shone with the splendor of a thousand exploding suns. "It is time for you to realize why I have you here. For soon you must make your choice."

New portals emerged from the darkness, exploding with celestial light. The simply framed portals looked like ordinary open doorways cut in the darkness. Kull's heart dropped as he examined each entrance. Crashing against his ribcage, his heart threatened to burst from his chest as he spun on his heels, trying to watch what was happening within the four doors at once. Each doorway held an individual close to Kull's heart: Adley, Wael, Rose, and finally Grift.

Adley, Wael, and Grift's doors showcased their every movement in Candor. Adley was scurrying about a large cobblestone staircase as she prepped a machine. She was beautiful and strong as she hustled to prepare for Seam's oncoming attack. Her long brown hair fell around her face as she toiled with the machine and tinkered with its interface.

Wael stood like a statue, watching out over the forests of Preost. Smoke rose in the distance and the chiseled frame of Wael stood tall facing it. Kull's eyes widened at what the Mastermonk wore. *Armor?* The smoke continued to bellow and grow closer to Taluum as Seam's marauding brigade tore through the forest toward his final prize.

Rose walked quietly in an open field of jasper. Long shoots of grain swayed gently, but their normal yellow hue was replaced with a brilliant red color that radiated a peaceful warmth. Kull lifted his palm to the image, and he tried to catch his mother's eye as she floated past the frame of vision.

Grift was surrounded by smoke and fire. He was driving a truck, squinting as he steered. His face dropped and he looked to the sky as a firestorm of bullets threatened to tear through him.

"There are many consequences for the choice you will make, Kull, but the choice is yours, and yours alone."

Grift closed his eyes as the white hot flashes of lead rained down inches in front of the truck. He sucked in a deep breath and held it in his chest as he waited for everything to end. The sound of the bullets thudding in front of the truck grew louder with each passing moment. Grift tightened his grip on the steering wheel waiting for the moment the bullets would end it all. They came, their sound slicing against the solid ground straight toward the truck.

Grift threw his eyes open only to observe the air around the truck shimmering as if they were in a bubble. A line of smoking holes in the ground led up to the front of the truck and continued again behind it, but none had hit them. Luken spun the gun around and opened fire, ripping through the tail of the jet and sending it smashing through the fiery canopy of trees below it.

"Luken! What happened?" Grift screamed in amazement as he scanned the truck for some sign of a damage. Luken flashed his familiar, mischievous grin and answered back.

"Just get us to Taluum. We don't have long."

"You have a choice, Kull. I will not force your hand and I will not fault you for whichever decision you make." Aleph's voice carried the softness of a gentle breeze but the power of a hurricane as he spoke. He stepped closer to Kull and placed his hand on his shoulder. His powerful, golden eyes leveled on his. "Are you ready to begin?"

Kull scanned the doorways again and the images beyond them. Adley was working feverishly to prepare the machine for the coming battle. Smoke was lifting on the horizon and Adley fought to stay focused amidst the scream of jets and the sound of war pressing closer onto them.

Wael's door was dark. The Mastermonk was prostrate on the floor, crying out to Aleph one final time. Kull could feel Wael's emotions; the fear, the dread, and surprisingly the shame. A feeling of guilt and failure draped over the Mastermonk like sackcloth. Kull glanced back at Aleph and a curious question broke from his mouth.

"Can you hear him? Can you feel him like I can?" He scanned Aleph's face for an answer.

"Yes." Aleph nodded, and his face bore the glow of love mixed with an eager pain. "Every word. Every thought. Every pain."

Kull turned back to the doors and watched his mother, Rose, as she laughed with young children and ate with friends, long since passed. She was beautiful, her skin radiant and her eyes full of life. The contrast could not have been any starker as Kull turned to the final doorway and stared upon his father.

Grift's face was haggard and tired. He was dirty, covered in sweat and mud. Grift leapt from his truck and raced into an obscure entrance along the walls of Taluum. He flashed down a narrow hallway and rumbled up a flight of gray stone steps with Luken close on his heels. *Luken. Yes, that is his name.* Somehow, in this place shared with Aleph, Kull could know things as they really were. It was as if everything he was seeing was understandable, and his knowledge of all that was transpiring was elevated. His eyes followed his father, focusing on the sleek, black automatic rifle that hung on Grift's shoulder as he ran. Grift's face was painted with determination, but his eyes were hollow and exhausted. The two men burst through a small wooden door and scurried across the top of the wall to the lookout holding Adley and her machine. Adley did not bother to greet them. She simply pointed to the forest below.

Noxious plumes of smoke rose over the thick green forests surrounding Taluum. The sky had a crimson glow as the once proud pines and hardwoods smoldered and burned away in the blaze. Grift peered over the thick stone edging of the wall and examined the destruction sweeping in from the east. He shouldered his rifle and peered down the long-range scope, sweeping his vision between the trees, trying to glimpse a sign of Seam's coming convoy.

Grift cursed beneath his breath as he realized any attempt to gaze through the curtain of thick, black smoke was a waste of time. He squinted and tried one last time to find a mark but shook his head as he lifted his eye from the scope. As he broke his line of sight, something shifted within the forest moving at an incredible speed. Grift looked back down range and felt his heart jump to his throat as he observed a mass of black-clad bodies darting through the forest.

The swarm moved in unison, unfazed by the smoke or heat of the blazing fires. Grift pulled back the trigger and snapped off five rounds. Three of the beings fell, only to be replaced by three more. Grift's mouth went dry with fear when he realized that none of the surrounding assailants reacted to the shots he fired. It was as if those struck down meant nothing to them. The army moved like a black tide, surging through the forest unimpeded and undeterred.

Luken dropped to a knee and steadied his rifle, firing alongside Grift, targeting the swarm of bodies streaming through the rows of thick tree trunks. "They're here, Grift." Grift nodded and stared down, firing shots into the wave of bodies. Suddenly, a huge chain of explosions went off, ripping through the large mass of morels with a fiery blast. A row of ancient giant trees crumpled along with the morel invaders in the sudden barrage of fire. The smoke shifted and swirled in the new open space, and the nose of a massive black titan pressed through the void with its cannon primed.

"Adley!" Grift paused long enough to scream into the datalink strapped to his forearm. "Get that thing ready now!"

Adley's voice crackled over the connection in a broken string of static. "Grift...trying to fire...time..." Grift bellowed into the device as he shot down at the flood of monsters pooling below him.

"I can't hear you, Adley! Just get the thing running and get Wael and the monks on point."

The screams of the morels grew, and Grift shuddered at the faces he saw below the stone wall. Women, men, children. *All baggers. All fresh.* "Aleph above, help us." He shot a glance down the long wall and scanned the closest spire. A group of five monks pushed against an ancient war machine. *Unbelievable.* The catapult groaned as it finally summited the peak of the tower, and the monks quickly went to work lighting its payload on fire. The men moved with one purpose, working the ancient weapon with great skill as if it were a musical instrument. A large boulder coated in flaming tar hurdled through the air and smashed into the center of the morel formation, crushing multiple attackers and setting others on fire. Another catapult followed from an adjacent spire, and the giant rock smashed into the side of the titan. The tank swayed from the contact, but continued to barrel forward, indifferent to the assault. The massive machine lifted its long cannon and swiveled its view. A loud explosion rang out as the tank sent an explosive shell into the massive wall.

Dozens of monks armed with longbows rushed to the top of the wall as it trembled below. A couple of monks carried burning torches that they used to light large cauldrons on fire. The surrounding monks dipped their arrows in the fire and unleashed a barrage of burning arrows on the oncoming swarm.

"We need more than this!" Grift screamed over the noise to Luken. "Where is Wael?"

"I don't know!" Luken never broke his concentration, continually firing his rifle downfield. "Probably guarding the mirror. Last line of defense."

"Luken!" Grift grabbed Luken's shoulder and pointed for the stairwell. "Can you bring up the chain gun?"

"From the truck?" Luken squinted down his scope and fired again.

"Yes!" Grift blindly fired a few shots in the direction of the lead titan. "We can't fight these guys with sticks and stones."

Luken nodded and shouldered his rifle. "But words will never hurt me?" Luken laughed at his own joke before jumping down from the wall. "Be back in a minute."

Grift ran and slid behind one of the wall's ramparts and grabbed for his datalink. He sighted his rifle and quickly emptied his clip on one of the rooks flanking the lead titan. The smaller black vehicle sputtered and skidded in front of the titan. The tank never broke speed and slid over the downed rook as it fired again at the wall. The explosion hit no more than thirty feet to Grift's left. The concussive blast rattled his teeth and shook his entire core. He felt the ancient stones of Taluum shift beneath him. *Please...please hold.* He struggled to steady himself as additional shots from the accompanying titans crashed along the length of Taluum's eastern rampart. *The wall can't take this for long.*

The morels had closed in on the walled city and were pouring into the deep trench that spread twenty feet from the wall. They screeched with glee, clicking their teeth together in one accord, their hollow, cloudy white eyes barely hiding their hunger. Grift glanced down as his heart filled with fear. These were not like other morels he had encountered. Those had been ancient castaways left behind from a bygone era. As he looked down on the mob of what used to be human, he saw that they had been equipped. They wore black armor and their hands were not human. They instead bore claws that flashed in the dim canopy light of the forest. It was as if their fingers had been replaced with razor blades. The throng was filling the eastern moat, clamoring up the steep stone wall like a swarm of ants. Grift saw as the beastly body of what was once a woman began to climb up the walls, her claws finding unseen finger holds. Grift's heart rocketed deep in his chest until he heard a call from behind.

"Make way! Make way!" Grift turned to see a monk leading four more with a bubbling cauldron full of pitch. In one swift motion, the monks upturned the tar, pouring the hot, viscous weapon from the wall and onto the horde of morels below. The smell of the bodies boiling in the ditch made Grift's stomach turn, but he stood amazed as more monks filed in behind him with lighted arrows. The archers fired their arrows at the tar, igniting a wall of flames that swallowed hundreds of the morels below, causing a curtain of black smoke to erupt along the ramparts of Taluum.

A chorus of beastly shrieks and screams echoed up the wall and sent chills up and down Grift's back. He turned his attention from the titans and rooks and aimed back down the wall, trying to pick off any of the morels that managed to avoid the fire trap. The beasts were still clawing up the fifty-foot wall, scaling it with ease.

Even some of the morels encased in flame still managed to scramble and climb. Grift fired at one morel after another as he yelled for Adley again.

"Adley! Come on! We don't have any more time!" Grift reloaded and scanned the burning forest below. In less than an hour, the majestic landscape had been reduced to a hellish blaze filled with nothing but death and fire.

"I've got it, man!" Luken's voice quickened Grift's resolve. He spun on his heels to help Luken prop the large gun against the wall and aim it toward the closest titan. Luken ripped open a crate of belted bullets and fed them into the gun as Grift readied his aim. As soon as the rounds were ready, Grift cocked the gun and squeezed the trigger. A stream of fifty-caliber rounds rained down on the tank, but they bounced off its thick armor. Grift cursed and swung the gun wider, strafing his fire over several rooks, ripping through the nimble black machines.

A titan explosive smashed into the top of the wall fifteen feet from Grift and Luken. The force sent Luken flying back toward the inner walls. Grift was sent tumbling across the top of the wall, hanging over the rampart. Everything around Grift slowed down, and the sounds of combat faded into an ear-piercing ring. He opened his eyes and looked down at the hundreds of hungry morels standing openmouthed below him. Even as his mind tried to catch up to what happened, stone continued to rain down from the titan's direct hit. Dust and debris covered Grift as he struggled to climb back over the rampart. Just as his strength began to fail, he felt a strong arm lock down on him. *Luken.* In an instant, he was pulled back to safety. Grift hunkered against the stone rampart, his ears still ringing when Luken set up the chain gun once more and sprayed it over their enemies.

Luken screamed over the roar of the machine gun. "Go get Adley! She needs to get that Pred tech up and running!" He turned the large gun on the mass of bodies climbing the wall nearby, ripping them away by the dozen.

Grift nodded, still shaking the stars from his eyes. He ran at a fever pitch down the length of the wall toward Adley's spire, his legs shifting beneath him like jelly. Grift stumbled onto the tower's landing and found Adley fidgeting with the machine's console.

"I think I have it!" Adley screamed. Her eyes were wide with a frustrated determination.

"Where is Wael?" Grift ran behind Adley at the weapon's console. "We need all the help we can get!"

Adley kept her eyes locked on the console. "He is underground with Rot. He is getting ready with some other monks. He knows they can't take their tanks down there."

"Fair enough," Grift grunted. A loud, rolling avalanche filled his ears as he answered and his heart sank. The wall had finally been breached. A large section of it broke loose. The city's outermost defense had been compromised. Morels swarmed for the opening, shrieking at the top of their lungs, racing to the top of the walls. They moved like a swarm of ants, leaping on the monks, mutilating their flesh or hurling them from the top of the walls into the burning tar pits below. Six rooks sped to the front of the battlefield and fluttered through the wall's opening, firing a barrage of machine gun fire and mortar rounds into the small city complex.

Women and children ran screaming from their homes as the rooks unleashed a furious assault on the inner structures. Each retreat of the innocent was quickly met by the mass of morel bodies that rushed through doors and windows, snatching the life of any man, woman, or child that dared to show themselves. Bodies piled in the streets as the swarm moved forward, threshing all those in its way, ripping through them in a tempest of bloodied claws and teeth.

A loud electromagnetic hum emanated from the Predecessor weapon and Adley let out a loud sigh of relief. "Grift, get on the platform."

Grift obliged and joined Adley on the platform behind the weapon. Again, the shield illuminated around them and the same screen Grift had seen before flashed to life. Thousands of white bodies covered the screen as Adley punched in commands. Grift roared over the sound of the shield that covered them, "Can this thing focus only on the morels?" Adley said nothing but dialed a knob up, focusing the precision of the interface. Soon the morel forms went from white to red, leaving the living bodies of the monks and the other people painted in a white glow. Adley navigated through the floating foreign text that whirled around them in a rapid pace and the machine buzzed with life. The canister discharged and the small metallic orbs broke loose from the machine's compartment. The orbs hovered for a second, only to shoot off like lightning, ripping through the swarm of morels. Dozens of them dropped with each second that passed, their color fading on the weapon's display.

The screen started to flicker and dim as its picture went in and out. Then a white flash washed out Grift's vision. The light was like a never-ending lightning bolt, eclipsing everything in a hot white fury.

Grift panicked, trying to grasp exactly what was happening below. The din of noise and chaos escalated and Grift couldn't tell if the Pred tech was even working anymore. Morels were shrieking at the top of their lungs in the chaos.

Then Grift remembered. *The Desolate.* Large figures cloaked in white fire swept through the streets of Taluum like a wave, working toward the titans and rooks. The rooks inside the city walls melted down to piles of liquid steel in seconds. The Desolate consumed Preost's enemies with an indescribable fury, forcing a retreat of all of Seam's forces. The morels spread their attack formation wider, sprinting from Taluum's wall, trying to avoid the Desolate attacks. Adley slammed her fist on the console as the weapon's screen lost life and the shield around them dropped. Grift commanded her, "Move! We've got to get underground. We've done all we can up here."

Adley nodded and followed Grift just as the Desolate ripped through two rooks that were pressing for the wall's opening. The

Desolate sped toward the lead titan like a tsunami wave of fire. The bay doors on the machine dropped, and Grift stood with his mouth agape as Abtren and Bastion leapt out from the side of the machine, each one colliding with the blazing attackers.

The four beings ripped at one another, jockeying for power. The Serubs' skin boiled beneath the fury of their enemies, but both sent powerful blows down upon the Desolate. The two gods' eyes were crazed and determined as they struggled with the elemental beings from the other side. The morels at the city wall did an about face and poured toward the Celestials, leaping into the fray, slashing and clawing to help free the Serubs from the consuming fire. Most of the morels were instantly disintegrated, but the confusion provided Abtren and Bastion an upper hand. Even as the fire burned into him, Bastion was able to gain a grip on one of the Desolate. With a gigantic snap, the Serub brought the being down, the figure's flames extinguished.

Abtren danced around the fire of the other in a blur before finally landing a deep, piercing blow to her enemy. She drove her claws deep within the fire until the guardian's form disintegrated in the forest breeze. The Desolate were both extinguished, their forms evaporating within the smoke and destruction of that cursed place.

The two Serubs collapsed on the ground, gasping for breath and clawing to pull themselves back to the titan. Grift snatched up his rifle and swung his sights on them. Adley screamed at him, "Grift, we need to get below!" Grift ignored her, his finger flirting with the trigger of his rifle when a motion in his periphery distracted him.

Oh, no.

Luken had jumped from the wall and was charging straight toward Abtren and Bastion. The remnant of morels attempted to pounce on him, but Luken was able to blow them back with an invisible force that stemmed from his open palms. Those that got close enough were torn apart as he pressed toward his fallen kin.

Luken jumped on top of Bastion and lifted the once mighty Serub's head from the ground, only to crush his fist into his skull, crumpling the giant in one swift motion. Abtren tried to yell out, but Luken shoved her back with another blast from his hands, sending her rolling across the ash covered ground. Abtren roared out as she crashed against a burning tree stump. She wilted there on the muddy soil before trying to claw her way back up toward the titan, her once beautiful form sapped into that of a withered old woman.

"Why!?" screamed Luken. "You are both fools! Why would you do this? Fight him!"

A hand grasped Luken's shoulder and he could feel an explosion of pain roar within him, draining him of his energy. Luken recoiled in pain and tried to scramble to his feet.

"Because I told them to. There is no fighting my will." Glazed, dead eyes locked on Luken as the High King of Candor stole his life away. Seam examined his palms and smirked before pointing his open hands toward Luken, knocking him back ten feet, mirroring Luken's own display of force. Seam grinned as he cocked his head to the side to meet Luken's eyes. "And now you will listen to me too, *Exile*."

Seam sprinted for Luken and lifted him by the neck, siphoning his power and life through the Keys.

Grift brought up his rifle and held his breath. "Go to hell," he whispered as the crosshairs fell on Seam. He squinted for focus and squeezed the trigger. The recoil of the shot let out a huge explosion and Seam's head snapped back. The High King's shoulder twisted as a round ripped through the side of his neck and bottom of his jaw. He tossed Luken to the side and his gaze locked quickly onto Grift's position. An orb of fire erupted around the High King and his eyes went black as midnight. The entire army of morels worked with one purpose as they swarmed after Grift.

Grift turned and sprinted, making his way for the large sanctuary doors. *Wael will be there. He will know what to do.* The thought rang hollow in his mind, but it was all he could hope for. Since the Serubs' defeat of the Desolate, Grift had lost all hope of his own survival, or in stopping Seam's progress toward the final mirror, but he had not expected Luken to fall so quickly under the High King's power. A stoic spirit filled him and he resigned himself for his end. *I go down fighting.*

His heart hammered in his chest as he pushed open the ten-foot sanctuary doors, thanking Aleph that they opened for him. Inside he was nearly mobbed by a hundred monks in formation, bravely facing the door. In the candlelight, Grift could see that those in the sanctuary were uncommonly dressed. On their faces were intricately painted ash patterns, drawn and stylized to look like flames, their bright eyes like beacons in the dim light. *So this is how the Alephian Order makes its last stand.* Grift noticed that they were armed according to their custom, with ironwood staffs, bows, and maces, weapons that Grift knew would be no use against what was coming for them.

A voice rang out in the open chamber, and Grift turned his eyes up to the altar. "Grift Shepherd, I'm glad you survived this long." There, upon the altar, stood Wael, no longer crumbled on the ground in prayer, but standing tall. The Mastermonk was decked from head to toe with a tight leather armor, and in the center of his chest plate of iron was the etched rune of Aleph. Wael's face was clear of the ash that his brothers' bore, except for the same stark rune that ran across the center of his forehead. His eyes and face were set like stone, and his countenance was like an impenetrable fortress. Next to his side was his companion, Rot, whose back was arched high, roaring with anger and agitation. Upon seeing Grift, the beast settled by his master's feet, though his one good eye kept its watch on the large wooden door.

"They are coming, Wael. The Desolate have been defeated by the Serubs, and Seam is coming."

Wael nodded and placed his hand on the monstrous dog next to him. He looked out over the hundred monks that filled the last sacred place left in Preost. His voice rang over them like a hurricane, and Grift felt his heart ignite.

"My brothers, do not bar the door for our guest. Let him come into Aleph's house so that he may meet his Lord and Master. Even in this darkness, Seam Panderean may reject his ways and turn again to the One who reigns in Aether." The brothers shuffled in the darkness, eagerly awaiting what their leader would say next. The Mastermonk closed his eyes, his voice like a prayer sung in the gloom. "But if he will not turn and submit to our Lord, then we must stand. Stand for the One who holds this world in his hands, even in such dark times of violence. Stand for the One who keeps all those dead and alive in his thoughts, in his mind, in his presence." Wael's eyes opened wide, his face seeming to glow in the darkness. Grift felt an unexpected rush of wind through the dark hall, a warm, sweet smell filling the place with an odor of wildflowers. "Do you not feel Him, my friends? He is here, even now, to greet us. To call us back to our home and to greet our dear brother, Seam. To greet the Celestials who turned their back on him so long ago, the ones once locked away. Even now, Aleph calls to these lost ones, asking them to come back to Him to turn away from the hate and rage that consumes them. We are not alone here, my friends!"

The other monks began to agree, their lips moving with their own silent prayers, other whispering, *"Selah."* Wael nodded in agreement with them and spoke once more.

"Now is the time. The time when we stand against the coming darkness that moves in our world. We may die today, and all of our Order as well. All of Candor may burn for a thousand years, and chaos may cover us all in the ruin. Yet as surely as Aleph is here with us, my friends, we are alive. We are alive in this place, in His presence, and we are alive in our death. *From death comes life!* So now...let us live."

A sudden explosion rocketed from behind the thick, timber door, and Grift shifted, turning his eyes back, pointing his rifle to what was coming. The door shuddered under the quaking force of what was behind it. Wael picked up his staff and looked upon his friends and toward the door.

"Let us greet this day, and greet those who want to enter this place. Let us greet them in the name of Aleph, the Lord on High, the One who will see us through. Steel your nerves, and know that this, this is our time. This is our time to stand, counted with the faithful. Counted with those who lived with love in their hearts. I am thankful to have been loved and to have loved each of you."

Silence fell over the sanctuary as all eyes focused in on the two thick oak doors standing between Taluum's final remnant and the jackal king. The doors swung open with a blast as a wall of black bodies pressed into the sanctuary, pausing a few feet from the first line of armed monks. Seam strolled in behind his morel army, taking his time to move toward the room's center. His eyes were as black as ravens and his face was as pale as a corpse. Perspiration beaded on his brow, glistening in the dim candlelight, giving him the appearance of a king wearing a shimmering crown.

The sides of Seam's lips curled in a smile as he gazed at Wael and then on Grift. "Ah, I will savor this moment. You continue to stand between me and my destiny? You both dare to oppose a god?"

Grift shook his head in disbelief. It was as if the shot he landed on Seam had not even touched him. His enemy's face was miraculously whole; despite the bullet he had just seen pass through it.

"You are no god." Wael lifted his staff to position and took a step forward, with Rot growling by his side. "And I will not stand by while you insult Aleph with your self-worship."

Seam burst into laughter and flexed his arms out to the sides, motioning toward his army. "I command an infinite, loyal army, monk. What has your *God* done for you? *Nothing!* He has allowed me to destroy this putrid, self-righteous city and he will stand by as I kill you, too."

The High King pulled back the long black cape hanging from his left shoulder and grasped the hilt of his obsidian sword. *"I will be sure to enjoy this."*

The morel swarm sprung to life, leaping on the nearest monks. The once silent sanctuary erupted with the sounds of ironwood staffs cracking against bone, claws digging through flesh and screams that cried out for mercy. The monks moved with a graceful unity, every man and woman playing their part, dancing with a rhythm that undulated to an invisible music. Each movement was like a note in a vicious, rehearsed melody. The morels, however, moved with nothing short of brute force. As one monster fell, another moved in to replace it.

Grift motioned for Adley and the two sprinted for the opposite sides of the sanctuary. Grift lowered his rifle and opened fire on the morels swarming through the door. Adley followed suit, ripping off one round after another from the pistols she bore in each hand. Even with the extra firepower, morels continued to flow through the open door like a black river, leaping over the dead that began to pile in the opening.

Adley muttered a soft prayer as she reloaded. "Please forgive me, Aleph." She fired a few more shots before reaching into her pack and pulling out a large explosive charge. She hurled the block of explosives toward the door, watching it skid within inches of nearest door frame. She fired twice but each shot was wide, ricocheting off the stone floor. Adley broke from the side of the room, sprinting closer for a better shot.

The morels continued to fight and claw, oblivious to their downed kin. The swarm had one purpose and one direction; *move forward*. Wael, with Rot and his monks, continued to fight the horde. Grift's attention was drawn from the sight of his rifle as he noticed Adley sprinting toward the incoming morel army. She lifted her pistol and fired at the floor. Three pops rang out, followed by an enormous explosion that rocked the entire room. A wall of flames spewed from the door, swallowing the incoming morels. Timber and stone were flung in every direction.

The room creaked and moaned, and the large doorframe snapped and crumbled in. Mammoth stones fell, blocking the door. Grift rushed into the scene trying to locate Adley, fearing the worst. *Aleph...please.* She was nowhere to be found until he spotted her, pinned beneath one of the fallen support beams against the far wall. She was scrambling to pull herself from the wreckage, wrenching at her pinned leg.

"No!" Grift's scream ripped through the room with a force only dwarfed by the earlier explosion. He lifted his rifle and aimed for the only target that mattered to him: Seam. Grift held the trigger as he ran toward the High King. Spouts of blood popped all over the King's chest as he stumbled backward. Grift collided with Seam, tackling him to the ground, pulling his battle knife from his belt. He lifted it overhead, ready to slam it through the jackal king's skull when Seam's hand grasped his throat.

The King's eyes glistened and he smiled as he smacked Grift's knife away with his free hand. His grasp was impossible, inhuman. Seam stood to his feet and lifted Grift in the air with one hand around his neck. Grift gasped for air as he pawed at Seam's grasp.

"Surprised, Shepherd?" Seam's smile grew wide as he clenched his fingers harder around Grift's throat. "Did you not listen to me? Do you not recognize who I am?"

Grift spit in the young king's face and gazed upward, muttering a quiet prayer. Seam shook him like a rag doll and screamed.

"Look at me, you insect." Grift locked his eyes on the ceiling and a small smile crept over his lips as Seam spewed with fury. Seam hurled Grift across the room, smashing him against one of the wooden pillars lining the room. A loud crack rang out as Grift connected and his limp body slid to the ground. Two morels broke away from the fight and surged over Grift's unconscious body. They snatched him from the floor and ripped him to his feet. Seam yanked his face up by his hair and placed his nose an inch from Grift's. "I know exactly how I want to watch you die." Seam motioned to the side of the room and the morels drug Grift from the fight.

Seam lost patience with his morels fighting the monk army and stepped into the fray, swinging his obsidian blade with deadly precision. He hacked away at the last few monks standing between him and Wael, bringing them down like felled saplings. Rot stood between his Master and Seam and lunged for the High King who batted his hand up, knocking the massive beast back as if Rot were nothing more than a pesky fly. Rot let out a weak whimper as he thudded against the cold, hard stone floor.

"Now." Seam's dark eyes were cold as he stared down Wael. "You will learn to bow to the one true deity in this place."

Wael lifted his staff, ready for Seam's attack, his face set in stone, determined. "I will never bow."

Seam held out his black blade, taking a swipe at Wael who easily blocked the blow, only to turn and land a side-long kick to Seam's chest. Wael made a spinning swing, slamming his staff into Seam's forearm, knocking the king's weapon to the floor. Seam opened his palm and let out a concussive blast that sent Wael tumbling head over heels.

The king snatched his sword from the ground and stalked forward, a scowl locked on his face. Wael took to the offensive, swinging his long staff from side to side, forcing Seam to block each successive advance. The two exchanged attacks until Wael landed a violent shot to Seam's cheek with his staff, followed by another hammering swing into the back of his skull. Seam fell to one knee as Wael lifted his staff for another swing.

With one lightning quick strike, Seam threw his sword forward, running it through Wael's gut. Wael let out a wheezing breath as he fell to his knees, gasping as the blade ran him through to the black blade's hilt. Seam chuckled and stood back to his feet as the monk reached up, grasping at Seam's black cloak.

"I told you that you would bow to me." Seam ripped the blade free from Wael's gut and kicked the monk onto his back. Seam stood over him and smirked as he shook his head. "I should have saved you for a slower death, but this is fitting."

Seam looked up at the exposed rafters lining the sanctuary's ceiling and then peered back down at Wael, grasping his face and shaking him as he spoke. "Look to your Aether now, you worthless monk. Say your final prayers. No one hears them because no one is there. Your faith...it is empty." Seam threw Wael's head back as the monk's eyes grew faint.

"I am God." Seam peered up again at the rafters and shouted. "Do you hear me!?" Seam stooped down and whispered into the monk's ears tenderly. "I. Am. God."

CHAPTER TWENTY-SEVEN

Beads of sweat poured down Willyn's brow and stung her eyes as she squinted through her visor display, trying to focus on the rolling dunes speeding by as she rocketed into Riht. The sands whipped around her like a dust storm, as a legion of Grogans followed her, their hearts set on waging war on the High King's city.

"ETA five minutes, men." Willyn engaged her weapon systems as she spoke, flicking red and blue switches on her controls into place. "We're going to come in hot. We leave victorious or in a casket."

A chorus of cries boomed over the datalink feed, ready for battle. "Die for the Sar, die for glory. All honor to die for our land!"

Willyn flipped up her visor and wiped at the sweat burning her eyes. She toggled her visor view over her face. Bright red displays hovered in her field of vision, highlighting the known targets that were swiftly approaching. Zenith was not without defenses. Her navigation and radar system was picking up high readings of infantry units, as well as several outfits of rooks and titans. *So many soldiers...* Her mind recoiled, her brain swarming with the memories of morels, the shambling nightmares that Seam could wield like puppets. *What you're seeing are morels...not just soldiers.* She slid the glass pane back over her eyes. "Report in, men."

Her units radioed in, their voices steady.

"Dragon Leader, here. We're ready for the fight, my Sar."

"Cobra unit. All present and accounted for."

"Rhino. Tech is steady."

"Badger unit reporting in and ready. Let's give 'em hell. Make that son of a—"

Willyn stifled a laugh as Lion unit cut through the feed.

"Lion unit to your right, Commander. Ready for the assault."

"Wolf is right behind you, Willyn. We move on your word."

Willyn's heart slammed in her chest, but despite her nerves she smiled. A strange clarity began to settle in as she glanced down at her screen, confirming her army's numbers. One hundred and fifty rooks ran point. Behind them were all that were left of the Groganlands titans: fifty gigantic war machines moving fast but still two miles behind her first wave. "Titan leaders, report!" Willyn barked out.

As her titan commanders checked in and reported their numbers, Willyn smiled. *If it comes down to it, this...is a good way to die.* Memories washed over her of blazing into Lotte after Grift Shepherd with a squadron of rooks. *I wish I had known the truth...* Her thoughts dissipated as the tip of the Spire pierced the desert horizon, rising from the sandy landscape like a black shard of obsidian glass. It looked as if the entire structure had been hammered into the earth, lodged into the very heart of the barren desert.

Willyn swallowed, her nerves causing her to tremble. *Focus, Willyn.* She called out to her men, her voice roaring over the coms. "Units spread out! Dragon and Cobra unit, swing north. We've got readings of fortifications up ahead. Artillery! *Let's take them out.*"

"Aye, commander." Sixty rooks broke from the pack and headed for the north.

Willyn stared at the navigation map, her mind moving through the strategy that was second nature to her. "Badger and Rhino unit, take the south. You will flank on my command." As the second wave broke away, she spoke and lowered her helmet's screen. "Wolf and Lion units, you are with me. Ready the new tech. Morel units are reading dead ahead. All units, you've been given your coordinates and your orders. *May our deaths be remembered!*"

All the units spoke, their voices filling the datalink coms. *"May our deaths be remembered!"*

Willyn closed her eyes and flicked a small silver button on her rook. "The first wave of Dominion forces is just over the hill.

Deploy the tech, men! We're ready for whatever they throw at us!" The armor of her machine shifted in an instant, producing a covering of fine, razor-tipped quills that hummed with electricity. It had taken three nights of constant work, but each rook had been fitted with the experimental morel armor that had long been used to help protect the Baggers on their railcars. "It's time we feast on the jackal king!"

An eager voice crackled over the datalink, the coordinates indicating it was coming from Rhuddenhall. "Is he there, Willyn?" The pain in Rander's voice was obvious. She knew it was killing him to stay in Rhuddenhall, but she needed his leadership in case she never came back.

"No intel on Seam's coordinates now, Rander. Last we heard, he was headed for Preost. All coms are going dark for now. We hit our target in less than five minutes."

Willyn muttered a prayer as the Spire grew before her, piercing the sky with each mile her forces traversed.

Arakiel and Nyx stood in an ocean of new morels under the shadow of the Spire. More than twenty thousand empty eyes and blank stares were fixed on their new masters, each and every body a puppet waiting on its master to pull the strings. Soon they would all be marched into a bloody war. Nyx fidgeted as she focused her mind on mastering the collective.

"Quite the army, Nyx." Arakiel smirked as he stared at the mass of the recently voided. "Are you up for this task?"

"Save your uncertainty, Arakiel. The morels were always my masterpiece, remember? This hive will serve us well." Nyx tore her gaze from the multitude and locked her black eyes on Arakiel. *This is our opportunity to break free, brother.* The High King made his final mistake leaving us behind. *We can make him pay."*

Arakiel roared, slamming his fist down and spitting as he screamed. "Forget that worm! He no longer matters. The game has changed. He is bringing *Isphet* with him. We must prepare for his arrival."

Nyx shot back, her eyes like black holes. "Is the mighty Arakiel nervous at the coming of Isphet? If we don't overthrow the Keeper, he will make him fall in line like us." Nyx turned her back to Arakiel and focused back on the morel hive. She whispered, her voice barely audible. "I am thinking of us, brother."

Arakiel grabbed Nyx's shoulder and spun her to face him, eye to eye. "No! You are not," he growled. "You are thinking of yourself. Isphet is coming, and my spirit is restless. I have sensed him moving within Candor for weeks now, his power growing." He locked his crimson eyes on her. "We must be ready...our brother has found an ally behind the glass and he is very strong."

"An ally?" Nyx's face twisted with hesitation. "There is nothing behind the glass, Arakiel. You know this."

Arakiel gazed out across the empty desert, his face stoic. "Perhaps you are right, Nyx, but something has...changed. I cannot think of any other answer for this." The god shook away the feeling of dread and barked his commands. "Prepare this army quickly and make sure we have enough to serve us once Isphet is unlocked. We must stay vigilant."

Nyx nodded and turned from her brother before raising her arms and losing herself to the mind of the horde.

"Help them!" Kull grasped at Aleph's tunic and tried to pull him toward the portals. "YOU MUST HELP THEM!" Kull's eyes darted from one opening to the next as he watched his father's limp body be thrown into one of Seam's titans, while Wael and Adley lay lifelessly in the sanctuary of Taluum. Seam's morel army set fire to the sanctuary, and Kull began to scream, his body shaking and his mind full of fear. "Please! You have to help them!"

Aleph stared into the mirrors, but his face was distant. He turned, his eyes locking with Kull's. "I have helped them, Kull, and I will continue to help them. That is why you are here."

Kull shook his head with disbelief. "I don't understand. How does having me here do any good? Aren't you the One? The most high of the gods? What is stopping you?!"

Aleph's eyes were sharp, his words heavy and laced with purpose. "Kull, I need you to trust me." Aleph's eyes quickened with resolve and he gazed down on Kull and then back to the portals. He held his hand out to Kull and opened it, and Kull's eyes grew wide. "The time for you to make your choice has come at last."

Kull shook with fear at what he saw. In Aleph's hand was a blue key, shimmering like a lightning bolt.

Willyn throttled down her rook and ran one last scan. She locked her computer on her prime target and pushed the throttle forward again. "All units, engage. Titans, drop mortars on my coordinates once in range."

A chorus of shouts rang over the datalink as Willyn crested the final dune separating her from Zenith. She engaged her deck gun as quickly as she leveled her line of sight on the small barricade wrapping around Zenith's borders. The explosive rounds shattered the small metal wall with little effort, but as soon as the wall was opened a flood of soldiers poured out like water from a burst dam.

Bullets ricocheted off Willyn's rook as she pressed forward, her finger held in a hard squeeze against the trigger. Bodies fell one after another as Willyn shattered them with her hammering guns, mowing down the Dominion forces that pressed in for her. "You'll have to do better than this," Willyn shouted.

Willyn scanned the horizon beyond the foot soldiers that poured out of the barricade. She spied dozens of rooks standing back, waiting, refusing to assist the men being chewed up by the Grogan machine gun fire. "Stay tight in formation and finish these hostiles quickly. They have cavalry waiting in the stables. Don't lose focus."

The ferocity of the ground soldiers' fire picked up as bullets bounced off Willyn's rook, sounding like a hailstorm beating on a tin roof. Something felt off to Willyn as she pressed forward. Three Grogan rooks sped to the front of the formation, their targets set on the Dominion war machines ahead.

Within seconds, the Grogans witnessed their first casualty. One of their rooks exploded with a magnificent eruption, followed by a violent burst of flames. As the Grogan vehicle tumbled end over end across the desert sand, the hair on the back of Willyn's neck stood up. *Something is not right.* It was as if the rook had exploded on its own. Willyn turned her eyes and caught a glimpse of something stirring beneath another rook before it exploded in similar fashion. By the time the second rook erupted in a plume of flame and smoke, she saw a magnetic mine jump from its sandy hiding place and latch onto the rook immediately to her right. Hot flames exploded from the machine, causing Willyn to whip her machine in reverse.

"Pull ba..." Before she could finish her sentence, she heard it: a loud clank. Her response was immediate. She reached down and ripped her evac cord. Her cockpit opened and shot her out just as the rook beneath her exploded, smashing across the sand in a twisted, fiery heap of metal.

Willyn's chute did little to lessen the impact as she crashed to the ground. She jumped to her feet as more Grogan rooks raced by, one after another, flying blindly into the minefield and exploding like choreographed fireworks. Willyn scanned to see if any other drivers made it out alive, but she was the only one to realize the trap. She ripped her helmet off and hurled it to the ground before barking into her datalink. "Mine field, pull back to grid TH-7. Use mortar fire to suppress."

A voice called in to address Willyn. "We're coming for your evac."

"Stand down!" Willyn screamed. "Don't come within a foot of me. Another one of those mines could be near. I will fall back on my own."

"Yes, sir."

A bullet flashed by Willyn as she tried to gather herself. She glanced down the battlefield as a half dozen Dominion soldiers ran straight for her, the lead soldier trying his best to fire his rifle while running full speed. Willyn scrambled for cover behind the burning remains of her rook. As she dove behind the smoldering wreckage, a barrage of bullets smacked the ground inches from her feet and continued to beat against her overturned vehicle. Willyn leaned out from behind her cover and sent eight shots into the crowded formation pressing in on her. Two of the soldiers crumpled into the sand, clutching their chests.

The four men remaining fanned out and slowed their pace as they shouldered their rifles and steadied their aim. Willyn popped up over the rook and fired three more shots, but none met their mark.

Willyn ducked back down and changed magazines, cursing as she slammed a new clip into her rifle. She yelled into her datalink as she peered back out, trying to pick the easiest shot. "Where is my backup? I'm pinned down."

"Lion unit has visual. Sending in heat."

As soon as the words came over the datalink, the ground beneath Willyn shook as multiple mortars exploded no more than twenty meters from her position. Willyn ducked out from the corner of hiding and scanned the field. Only two men were left and the mortars seemed to confuse them. Willyn fired at the nearest Dominion soldier and small bursts of red announced her success. She swung her sights toward the final soldier.

As the final soldier dropped, Willyn picked her path and tossed three smoke grenades across the desert sand. As each canister lit with smoke and flame, Willyn sprinted for the high ground, darting through the wall of smoke as bullets searched for her in the fog.

A voice blared over Willyn's coms. "My Sar. I have a lock on your location, coming in south of you. Copy?"

Willyn let out a sigh of relief and answered. "Copy, captain. Switch your rear gun to manual ops."

"Copy that!" The young pilot from Lion unit did little to hide his excitement.

Willyn continued to sprint through the smoke as a rook swept in on her left. She leapt on board and tethered herself into position behind the massive gatling gun. "Take us out, captain. I'm in."

"Yes, sir. Rolling out. Hot zone in thirty seconds."

The rook rocketed from the smokescreen and flashed over the desert sand, like a black sloop sailing across a hot amber ocean. Willyn squinted, trying to keep the dust and sand from blinding her as they flashed over the dunes at an incredible pace. Her datalink roared with life from the young captain steering. "Goggles below the seat, my Sar." Willyn reached for them and strapped them on, their tinted frames giving her much relief in the unrelenting Rihtian sunlight and sand swirling around the black war machine. She sat there, her eyes focusing and hand rolling over the gunning controls in the back of the rook. Willyn's bright red hair whipped behind her as she rotated the gun, readying her sights. She wired her datalink into the rook and spoke, her voice filling the ear of each man who fought for her.

"Check in, men. Status on the minefield." She heated her guns, the barrels speeding their rotation as they got closer to the battle.

"Got a lane open. Sector Z8. Ten units wide by our estimate."

There was no hesitation in Willyn's decision as she called back. "Follow me, boys. We're taking what we can. Single file, not taking any chances. Stay in the trench our titans dug out. Let's pay our tribute to the High King!"

Willyn could not help but smile as her men yelled out and shouted for her as she sped by the Grogan squadrons, taking point on the assault. The Sar was charging the gates of Zenith on the unarmored back of a rook, manning the guns, her red hair waving like a battle flag. "Follow me if you're ready to die!"

Willyn flipped her datalink over to a single feed directed to her pilot. "You ready, Captain...?"

"Mundi. Mundi, my Sar, from the Flint Mines." Willyn could feel the reverence in his voice as he addressed her.

She spoke, her voice flying as valiantly as a battle standard. "Very well, Captain Mundi from the Flint Mines. You must have no hesitation, no fear. You are my razor. Together we cut this city open and pierce its cursed heart. For the Groganlands!"

"Aye! For the Groganlands!" shouted Captain Mundi as he accelerated into the fray.

The Dominion rooks that had been holding back just outside Zenith all swarmed from the city, rushing to answer Willyn's charge. Willyn focused the barrel of her machine gun and held the fire steady on the enemy rook running point to challenge her.

"On my mark, Mundi, roll portside. Bring the aft around. No brakes." Willyn tested the tether holding her to the machine and stared back down the barrel of her gun.

"Yes, sir."

The gap between Willyn and her challenger closed rapidly. Willyn stared down the Dominion rook and waited, staring at the guns mounted on the attacker's sides. "Now!" Willyn screamed as the Gatling barrel flashed to life.

Mundi obeyed and the rook turned up on its side, swinging wildly to the left, leaving Willyn parallel with the ground below. She kept her eyes locked on the iron sights and held the trigger as her rook righted itself again. Her bullets shredded the armor of the Dominion hovercraft as it attempted to redirect its course.

Mundi did not hesitate and moved her into position again to fire on two additional charging Dominion war machines. The smaller hover vehicles swooped across the desert sand, jockeying for position, their engines roaring over the barren landscape. Willyn kept firing, the light of her shots filling her stoic face with an unnatural glow.

In less than five minutes, all of the Dominion rooks that challenged her were demolished and Willyn and the majority of Lion unit were streaming toward the heart of Zenith. The Spire rose high into the sky, welcoming their assault.

Willyn looked up, her face shielded under the massive shadow cast by the pinnacle structure.

"Let's tear that tower down, Mundi!" roared Willyn.

"Aye, aye sir!" Mundi engaged the thruster of the rook as the two ran point into the heart of Zenith.

Seam screamed over the datalink, his voice straining the limits of the small speakers on the feed. "I want a status report! Have the Grogans been handled yet, Arakiel?" Seam's eyes cut through the screen as he barked at the Serub, who stared disinterested on the other end of the feed.

Arakiel offered no emotional response in his silence. His face was set and locked like stone. After several moments of silence, he spoke, his deep voice booming as his eyes bore back at Seam. "They are exactly where I want them to be, High King. Soon your army will grow five-fold."

"Where are they? I am tired of your trivial resistance. Just tell me!" Seam saw sparks flash in his vision as he shrieked at Arakiel. Arakiel stared out in the distance, focusing on something off screen, refusing to answer.

"I said where are they, Arakiel?!"

"They are here." As the first of the Grogan rooks crested into the city, Arakiel slammed the datalink shut, cutting off all communication with the High King. The Serub roared, his voice like a booming thunderclap, and charged toward the oncoming Grogans. He held his iron scepter out toward the invaders rushing to flank their forces. His eyes fell on the Grogan war machines, and his mind paused at a strange play of the desert sun. Something about the Grogan rooks looked different. Unable to wait, he led the charge as three hundred morels swarmed toward their enemies, sprinting like cheetahs, their claws catching the light of the blazing sun. The mob poured over the first rook in an instant, but Arakiel's face froze as each morel soldier fell away upon making contact with the enemy rooks, dead before even landing a single blow. Body after body ran toward the rooks, only to fall dead to its side.

"NYX!" Arakiel boomed, calling out to his sister. He would have to move fast before more of the Grogans breached the containment wall. Even with thousands of the mindless, their numbers would be thinned out in minutes as more Grogans breached the city. He sprinted, his muscular form clearing the desert plain like a galloping horse. He slammed his iron scepter into the first Grogan rook he saw, the iron rod penetrating the machine's armor like paper. Arakiel twisted his weapon like a corkscrew until he heard screams from within, and the popping of bones.

"THE RIVERS OF YOUR REALM WILL FLOOD WITH YOUR BLOOD, GROGANS!"

Arakiel's deep voice boomed over the desert, as he tore through four more Grogan rooks, strafing and jumping over their bullet storms before they could even target him.

The Serub lord looked down on the shattered remains of one of the rooks he had just destroyed, desperate to find what was killing his army so effectively. It only took a second for his sharp crimson eyes to find the answer. *Barbed quills.* Electric quills that would fry any morel's brain at the slightest touch.

Very well, the Serub thought.

He turned, searching through the chaos for his sister. He spotted her, elevated, hovering over the ground, her mind melded with the ocean of the mindless she controlled.

"Pull them back, Nyx!" He flashed in her mind the revelation of the Grogan tech, and in an instant the tidal wave of a thousand morels began to recede from the battlefield. Nyx ran to her brother, screaming. "We have to take these rooks out now or we will be overrun, brother!"

Arakiel wasted no time. He leapt in the air, ascending thirty feet with one mighty jump. He fell to the ground like a meteor and drove his iron scepter through one of the charging Grogan rooks. The hovercraft broke apart in midair, the driver disintegrating into an explosion of gore. The Serub stared out as thirty more rooks rushed through the interior wall like a swarm of black armored yellow jackets.

He held his hand out, his fingers motioning them forward. *"Come and die, mighty Grogans. Die for that land you love so well!"* Three more rooks swarmed by him, their engines rumbling through the desert sand, daring to get too close. They crumpled under the flourishing swings of his scepter, erupting into fireballs.

The god held out his hand, his blood red eyes reading the field as more of the Grogans charged directly at him. He turned, facing his sister who had just clawed her way through a Grogan gunner.

"Get ready! I will turn these and press our advantage!"

Nyx's black eyes shined in the desert sun, the blood of the Grogan she had gored still dripping from her face. "Do it!"

Arakiel held out his hand. As the rooks screamed in for the attack formation, an iridescent sphere of energy exploded from his palm and a mighty wind tore through the place, releasing a sandstorm that clouded the battlefield in an instant. Nyx moved and her eyes clouded over, her mind searching for those whose essences had been robbed from them, taking root within their minds. The rooks caught in the wake of Arakiel's power jolted violently as something within them shifted. They spun around with an uncanny synchronicity, and to the other Grogans, it looked as if they were retreating, until a firestorm of bullets ripped through their own forces.

Grogans fought one another as those controlled by Nyx's mind ripped through the Grogan ranks, causing confusion and chaos with every passing second.

Arakiel's face and body had withered with the expulsion of his power, but he held a firm smile. The Grogans were mighty, but their strength, technology, and numbers were not enough to turn the tide. *Not against the Serubs.*

The screen went blank and Seam punched the wall, denting the iron plates lining the inside of the titan. He stomped toward his final prize and gazed into the empty, black glass.

"You took liberty to speak before when I did not request your presence. Now I seek you out. Speak to me, god in the glass."

Seam stared into the empty mirror, his reflection the only image filling the portal. Without hesitation, he unsheathed his ebony sword, slashing the razor's edge across his mutilated palm. The cut bit deep and he held his hand up to the mirror's edge, allowing the crimson of his body to flow onto the mirror.

"What?" He held it there, shocked. *Nothing was happening.* The blood rolled down the mirror without any showcase of power. The small sacrifice was impotent and void of any confirming sign of Isphet's presence.

"WHERE IS HE?!" Seam turned, his eyes wild with hate and rage. Abtren and Bastion sat crumbled in the corner of the titan, their eyes filled with fear and confusion.

Abtren stuttered, trying to find the words. "I...I have no answer for this, Keeper." She stood, pointing at the glass mirror. "Arakiel said that he was locked in the portal, just like us all. Did the monk switch it with a decoy?" She stared at the empty mirror, searching for some excuse to justify the failed sacrifice.

Seam turned, focusing on Bastion's green eyes. The Serub would not make eye contact with him, pinning his gaze to the floor. No words passed from his lips, and Seam ran, cursing to the cockpit of his titan.

"Stop the titan. Stop it now!" the High King screamed.

Commander Reed followed the order, and Seam ran to the back of the transport. The forest surrounding the convoy was still burning and even within the titan, Seam could feel the heat. Preost had become a furnace of his burning revenge against the monks. Seam ran full speed to the back of the titan, kicking in the door.

There, chained to the wall of the titan, hung the Exile. Seam wasted no time grabbing Luken by the throat.

Luken let out a muffled scream as the High King's hand clasped around his throat like a vise, his mere touch siphoning away his energy.

Seam turned to the mysterious Serub who had eluded him for so long, the Sixth who had never been imprisoned. "*You*. The last of your kin will not appear before me when I offer my blood on the mirror. *Why?!*"

Luken gave a grim smile. "I guess Isphet doesn't like your flavor, Seam. He must prefer something sweeter."

Seam sneered and Luken's body erupted with black fire. Luken screamed, pain cascading and building through his entire body.

"Wrong answer, Exile," Seam chided. "Rest assured, I will find out the truth from you. We have a long time to spend together until we reach Zenith, so save your jokes and barbs. They will not afford you any mercy from me."

Luken's eyes opened, his body still smoking from the torture brought upon him. "I'm so sorry, Seam." Luken looked up, his eyes still brightly defiant. "I'm afraid I'm going to be a big disappointment to you. You see, I'm not like the other gods you unlock from the mirrors who bow down to you because of your Keys. I'm a little more…stubborn."

Seam smiled before Luken's body ignited again with black flames. "I've got all the time in the world, Exile."

Luken's scream trailed as Seam gave up his grip on him. His voice was barely above a whisper, but the words hammered into Seam's heart. "No…no High King. You just think you do. I'm afraid your time is running out."

Grift drifted in and out of consciousness. When his mind tried to fire to life, his eyes only saw the white, glazed eyes of the morels surrounding him.

Soon the darkness relented, and Grift was able to emerge back into his horror-filled reality. The morels were packed all around him constricting his breathing, threatening to bring him into a panic attack.

Calm down. Calm down. Grift struggled to hold his thoughts together. *They aren't aware.* As Grift's heart slammed in his chest like a ricocheting bullet, he gained enough clarity to calm himself.

Each minute of motion from the transport caused the bodies to shift, and Grift braced himself for his end, fearing the mindless would awake from their slumber to devour him. The soulless faces of men, women, and children were a haunting sight, but to be this close to them, to feel them pressing in on him from all sides, was excruciating. *Baggers...all of them.*

Poor souls. How did this happen? How did Candor fall so fast? Grift's heart sank deep within his gut as a knot tightened in his throat. For so long he had fought at King Camden's side, fighting to maintain a peace and order. Peace had been earned when he was just a young man under Camden's leadership. But now, only a year after Camden's passing, Candor was burning again, full of war and bloodshed with the worst yet to come. The horrific truth of the Resistance's failure fell over him like load of bricks. *Seam has all the Keys...and now all the mirrors.*

Grift shook out his arms and exhaled as he tried his best to fight off the panic setting in. *You must fight. Don't give in to this darkness.* Grift looked at the black sheet metal ceiling and closed his eyes as he spoke. "Kull, you died saving my life. I will die trying to end Seam's..." He paused, his mind grasping for a light in the dark place. "Aleph, I don't know what else to do."

Willyn swallowed hard and took a deep breath as one of her own rooks turned on her, ripping through Lion unit. The members of Wolf unit had just breached the inner city limits before turning back.

"Just confirmed a weapon lock, sir. They are not running from battle; they are turning on us!"

Willyn thought back to the battle at the Serpent's Spine. The Serubs had taken over her forces then and decimated much of the Red exodus to Rhuddenhall. The Serubs were using the same tactics again. Willyn swung her gun's barrel in the direction of the nearest rook and steadied her aim as she called over her datalink.

"We have units compromised. If engaged, take immediate action." Willyn clicked off the line and pulled the trigger as her rook was within range of one of the rogue units. Her shot was true. The bullets hammered through the thin armor of the attacking rook and sent it smashing into a nearby building. She barked new commands to her men. "ON ME! Keep your eyes on those who have turned and take them out!" As Wolf unit scrambled on Willyn's position, three of the mind-controlled rooks broke left, while the other two swept to their right, circling around Willyn's position.

They're trying to block Wolf's maneuver! Two against one. Aleph above.

"Hard left!" Willyn screamed. Mundi obeyed and they spun around, mirroring the movements of the compromised rooks that were trying to speed around and flank them. Mundi engaged his mortar cannon and popped off three rounds as Willyn led the two rogue units with her chain gun. The final mortar blast hit directly in front of one of the war machines, catapulting it into a fiery tumbleweed, reeling into a construction site with a triumphant explosion. The second compromised rook flew straight into Willyn's line of fire and wilted beneath her guns.

"Bringing us around," Mundi called to Willyn. "Trying to locate our other friends."

The three rogues that engaged with Wolf unit had managed to keep pace with Willyn. They left themselves blind to any attack from the rear. *So self-assured. The Serubs thought those other two rooks would take us down.* Willyn opened fire and tore through the three rogue vehicles, the cheering voices of Wolf unit screaming with praise through her datalink. She settled in behind her gun and smiled, aiming her sights for her next victim when a massive blow crashed over her shoulders, knocking her flat against the thin metal decking of the rook. She felt her body collapse, as her breath was violently pushed out of her lungs.

Willyn glanced up to find a morel standing over her, its fangs exposed and its razor claws ready to pounce, but Willyn's attention went beyond the morel standing over her to the skyline behind its head. Morels were leaping from the skyscrapers onto the Grogan rooks below to avoid the quills. The mass of bodies was so immense their black silhouettes threatened to dampen the desert sun beating down on the city streets. Another morel landed on top of Willyn's rook and smashed its fist against the cockpit glass until it grasped Mundi and ripped him from his seat. Their rook lost control, teetering first, and then careening to the side, smashing through a brick wall of one of the buildings lining the main thoroughfare.

Willyn could do little to cover her head as the rook crashed into the structure. The morels that attacked the craft were tossed away, while Willyn's tether held her to the war machine as it spun like a dervish. The force of the spinning nearly dislodged her hip. She fought through the dull, aching pain and dragged herself from the wreckage into the open warehouse where her rook crashed.

The battle continued to rage outside as the sounds of explosions and gunfire bounced off the high sheet metal ceiling overhead. She could hear the sound of hundreds of morel enemies streaming into the battle, their high-pitched barks and screams filling her mind with fear. Willyn examined the wreckage and shook her head. The building had shifted with her rook's crash and sealed up the exit. She fumbled for a way out of the construction site, squinting through blurry vision as she tried to orient herself. Nausea cascaded over her and she tried her hardest not to double over and vomit from the pain radiating through her body. She fell to her knees and panted for breath.

"*Get up.*" The voice sliced through the pain and pricked her ears. "*Keep fighting.*" Willyn fought to focus her eyes as she called out.

"Mundi?"

There was no response, and no other presence. The crash must have rattled her mind. She had seen Mundi die under the morel's attack. She looked around, and there was no one there. Voice or not, she would not give in. She could not give up. *Not now.* Hagan had been inches from his death, but he never gave up his fight and neither would she. She lifted herself to a knee and got back to two feet. She leaned over to clasp her knees and took in a deep breath when a force as violent as an earthquake smashed against her and sent her sliding across the cement floor.

"*Augh!*" Willyn's mouth filled with blood as she rolled to her stomach. She fought to lift her head, gazing through her tangled red hair to find her attacker. Her heart dropped as the voice of Arakiel filled her ears.

"You got away once before, but this time I will enjoy crushing you. Your petty insistence on challenging us ends today. You and your little machines are no match for a god, much less two."

Arakiel stalked forward as Nyx floated behind him, like some demented wraith. Her eyes were pools of death, locking on the broken Sar. Arakiel bent and lifted Willyn by her tactical vest, heaving her into the air as if she were a toy, her feet dangling two feet off the ground.

The Serub sneered at her. "Did you really believe a few bullets or bombs could stop us?" Arakiel asked, laughing. He lowered Willyn so her eyes leveled with his own. "*We cannot be stopped.*"

Willyn gazed upon Arakiel's chiseled face and his brown, perfectly groomed hair. By any standard he would be beautiful, but even this gorgeous facade did nothing to hide his hideous nature. Willyn gathered spit and blood in her mouth and spat into Arakiel's face, struggling to wrench herself free from his grasp. He wiped a drop of blood from his cheek and sucked it clean before smiling and leaning in to whisper next to Willyn's ear.

"Thank you. *I wondered how your blood tasted.* I will be sure to savor it."

A voice rang out in the empty building, echoing in the emptiness. "STOP! By the authority of the High King. Stop!" The voice bounced around the room and startled Arakiel to the point he nearly dropped Willyn. He roared and turned to face a feeble man sprinting into the room flanked by Dominion troops.

"What do you want, Bronson? How dare you interrupt me?"

Bronson stuttered and pointed over his shoulder in the direction of the Spire. "Uh...the king, sir. He demands that Willyn Kara be saved for his sovereign judgment!"

Arakiel hurled Willyn to the ground and snatched Bronson by the throat. He leveled burning eyes onto the king's aid, examining his unshaven, dirty face. The Serub snarled as he inhaled deeply, drawing his magnificent face within inches of Bronson.

"Give me one reason I should listen to you, worm. Pathetic servant of an unworthy king." Arakiel's fist tightened, cutting the blood to Bronson's head. Bronson groggily bobbed in Arakiel's clutches as he fought not to pass out. "I will just kill you now and take the girl for my own. Your king would be none the wiser."

Bronson wheezed and puffed for breath as he swatted at Arakiel's forearm, trying to motion for the Serub's attention.

"Arakiel!" Seam's voice boomed from Bronson's datalink. "Her death *is my reward.* Now *stand down!*"

Arakiel ground his teeth in hot rage and tossed Bronson to the side of the room. He looked at his sister and spoke, his whisper full of spite. "Come, Nyx. There is much more Grogan blood to feast on. We will leave these broken fools for Seam."

Dominion foot soldiers poured over Bronson, their faces full of fear and concern. Bronson stood, shaken but unharmed, and pointed to Willyn. "That's her, boys. Get her up and let's move her to the holding cell. The king will be here soon."

Bronson glanced down at his datalink display and offered a smile of yellow teeth to Seam. "Soon she will be all yours, sire. She will be in holding cell five. Signing off for now."

Bronson motioned and the soldiers hoisted Willyn from the floor. They dragged her toward a small door at the back of the building. Willyn's dangling feet bounced along the gravel alleyway as two soldiers carried her, each looping an arm under her shoulder. Bronson staggered ahead of the pack as they dashed for the Spire. The sound of explosions and gunfire filled the entire city, but the war was still contained outside of Seam's impenetrable complex. Willyn groaned in pain, knowing that her forces were dying one by one as they fought against the immortals. Yet she could not believe her luck. They were dragging her right where she wanted to be, into the very heart of Zenith.

Aleph held the key out to Kull, who stared at it, eyes wide.

"What is that?" Kull's voice wavered in the dark place shared only with Aleph. The divine ran a silver chain through the blue key's intricate head and hung the key around Kull's neck. He laid his hands on Kull's shoulders and looked over him, into the portals.

"This is the final Key of Candor, Kull. Indeed, it is the only true key of power that Candor has ever known." Kull's face filled with questions, but Aleph's voice made them dissipate. "With this comes the weight and might of all my power and the ability to open many doors." Aleph turned toward the four open doorways before Kull. "Your first choice lies before you, Kull Shepherd, and it is yours alone to make. Which door will you unlock?"

Kull's eyes scanned the scenes unfolding before him. His father, crammed into a chamber full of morels, was shackled and captured once again by Seam. Willyn was being dragged to the Spire's footsteps. Wael and Adley lay close to death on the floor of the smoldering sanctuary of Taluum. Kull's heart raced with an impossible intensity as he tried to steady his breathing. His heart broke for the pain suffered by those he loved, and his blood boiled as he thought about Seam. Kull's fists tightened by his side as he exhaled.

Aleph turned Kull's shoulder to face the portal leading to Rose, her beauty and peacefulness a startling contrast to the pain and despair displayed in the windows peering down on Candor. Aleph spoke quietly, his voice full of sincerity. "Or, Kull, do you stay?"

Kull looked to Aleph, but his countenance refused to sway Kull's decision one way or the other. Kull scanned the doors leading back to Candor, as well as the one where his mother dwelt in peace in Aether. His mother, the woman that for so long he had longed to see and speak with, approached the doorway, staring right at him. She strolled toward him through the fields of Aether, stepping closer through the glowing amber stalks tipped with indigo. They swayed gently as she ran her hand over the field. A sapphire sky rolled overhead with white clouds dotting the horizon. Others joined her side as she gently strolled toward him. They were laughing and singing, all of their faces alight with such joy. Kull had never seen the others before, but he knew them immediately. His grandparents were there with his mother. *They are all there*, Kull realized. They were all waiting for him and Grift to join them. A feeling of euphoria lifted Kull's heart as he gazed on the scene that pulled at him like an invisible magnet.

Kull took another glance at the portals of Candor and then back again on his family waiting in Aether. He took in a deep breath and nodded to Aleph as he stepped forward, the Key of Candor held tightly in his hand.

CHAPTER TWENTY-EIGHT

"Drop her here." Bronson motioned toward a barren slick of the polished marble floor. The Dominion soldiers followed the order, laying Willyn within one of the Spire's lower chambers.

Bronson glanced over his shoulder and nodded at the two soldiers guarding the door. The two stepped into the hallway and shut the door behind them, leaving Willyn, Bronson, and ten Dominion guards in the dimly lit room.

Willyn stood, her body screaming with each move she made. Bronson's appearance was all that saved her from dying under Arakiel's hand, but Bronson's motives appeared to be no less sinister. He was saving her for Seam. Her mind focused on one thing: escape. *Seam will not hold me in this tower to die.* "Damn you, Bronson." Willyn spat at Bronson's feet and fought her arms free from the guards. She whipped a small blade from her hip and bolted toward her captor before one of the soldiers tackled her.

Bronson stared at her, shocked at the words. "I am already damned, for all you see is the culmination of my life's work, Willyn Kara." Willyn blinked, not understanding as she threw herself against the three Dominion soldiers holding her. Bronson continued, "This is it!" He choked back tears as he made a sweeping motion across the room with his arms. "This is all I have to give you!"

"This is what? You worthless dog!" Willyn screamed.

"The Resistance, Willyn." Bronson's words echoed in the dark as he sunk to the floor and cupped his head in his hands. "These are all I was able to muster." Bronson shook his head and his voice dropped. "You are right. *I am worthless.*"

The words stunned Willyn. "So you...did not betray me?"

Bronson offered a chuckle as he looked up with swollen, exhausted eyes. "No. Not you. I have betrayed myself, my family, my soul...yes. But I have never betrayed our cause. I've done all I could do to make sure Seam's plans would fail..."

The soldiers loosed their grip on Willyn as she stood to her feet and ran her hands through her hair, trying to gather her thoughts. Her words were gentler and she focused on her unlikely savior. "Thank you, Bronson. You've done more than you realize." Bronson looked up, his eyes a mixture of pain and hope. She continued, "Your actions saved my life, and you've unknowingly put me right where I need to be."

Bronson's face held a look of surprise. "The Spire? Your intentions were to get into the Spire?"

"Yes." The fire within Willyn's eyes ignited once more. "But we have to hurry. I need you and your men's help. She reached for her datalink but the unit on her wrist was shattered and inoperable. "Do you have a secure datalink I can use?"

"Of course." Bronson offered the datalink on his arm. "But I don't know who you will call at this point. It's terrible what has happened. It's just us. The other forces I had gathered were routed, pressed into labor into the camps and... *changed.*" Bronson's veiled words made Willyn shudder. "All communications from Lotte has been shut off since you took Rhuddenhall."

Willyn's finger froze over the datalink keys as she examined Bronson's face. Upon mentioning Lotte, he covered his face with an open palm, as if the word of his homeland was too much to bear. Seam's rebellious captain reeked of alcohol and his emotions flailed within him unpredictably. *Unstable. Broken.* He continued, his voice a ribbon of dread and remorse. "They are all captured, Willyn. The Resistance. All of them. I went dark for a while and just listened, but then you came. Maybe there is something we can do. *Maybe.*"

The glimmer of hope in Bronson's voice was brief and broke with his voice as he excused himself to a corner of the room. Willyn shook her head in disbelief. He was like a panicked animal, trying to contrive some feasible exit from his situation.

"Bronson, let's address one thing at a time. Do you have any meds here?" Willyn pointed to her shoulder. "I need them...fast."

As if summoned by her voice, a hot flash of pain ripped across her like a whip. She grimaced. "If I am going to do anything, I need help."

Bronson turned, nodding in affirmation and waved for a guard to fetch the supplies. "Take care of her, Davis. See that she gets all the meds she needs."

"Actually, Bronson." Willyn ushered Bronson to a corner of the room away from the rest of the soldiers. She lowered her voice to a whisper. "Can you allow me a few minutes alone to think?"

"Certainly." Bronson nodded and patted Willyn's hand, his mannerisms floating between genuine, awkward, and drunk. "Of course."

Bronson and the small band of Resistance fighters slipped from the room, leaving Willyn alone as she waited for medical assistance. Her thoughts sped in the dim light as she heard the sounds of war outside her prison turned safe house. She winced to think that her people were facing Seam's forces without her. *They are mighty with or without you.* The clarity spoke in the dark and Willyn conceded to accept it.

Quietly, Willyn flipped open Bronson's datalink and dialed Rander, but no answer came. Willyn grumbled as she realized the signal was not one Rander would recognize. There was no way he would answer. As she slid the datalink across the floor, its screen lit and it beeped with an incoming signal.

Willyn cautiously flipped the channel open and let out a gasp as she looked into Hagan's face.

"How did you know to reach me on this signal?" Willyn tapped at the screen and ran diagnostics to ensure the data stream was secure.

"Who else would be calling Rander from Zenith?" Hagan chuckled and shook his head. "Give me some credit, 'Lyn. All my men are monitoring the signals. We were expecting you to call, any way that you could. Are you in the Spire?"

"Yes, though I'm lucky to be alive at this point."

Hagan interrupted, "It doesn't matter. Half of the battle is already won. I'm just glad you made it inside." Her brother smiled widely and coughed horribly, his ratcheted breath causing the datalink's speakers to squeal. *He's still not well,* Willyn thought to herself. Between gasps, Hagan looked at her from the datafeed. "You need to know I am on my way. My forces will be there soon."

"What?!" The words burst from Willyn's lips with rage. *"That wasn't part of our plan, Hagan!* It's not safe! There are two Serubs outside ripping our forces to pieces as we speak."

Hagan smiled over the feed. "Willyn, do you remember our wolf hunts? I am not worried about Serubs. I am coming to help you take out the pack leader; *the alpha.* We will be there within the hour, and Seam will be none the wiser. We have found an ancient tunnel system that runs from the borders of our land into Zenith. It was used by our ancestors in the last great conflict with that cursed city. Long forgotten and abandoned, I doubt the High King expects our coming. We are closing in now."

Willyn's eyes widened. *Ancient tunnel system?* It sounded too good to be true, but Willyn accepted it. "What do I need to do?"

Hagan stared at Willyn, his eyes solemn. "Get into position as we discussed. Wait…"

"Then strike," Willyn finished.

Seam's convoy stopped at the desert ridge overlooking Zenith in the valley below. Large billows of smoke poured from the city and wafted toward the horizon. For the first time in his reign, he saw the destruction and death that the Grogans could rend on even him, and his mind was full of shock and rage. The Spire stood tall, defiant, but around it, tall buildings and defenses had crumpled under the firestorm of the Grogan raids. Seam cursed Willyn under his breath as he scanned the destruction.

The hot desert air whipped through Seam's long brown hair, and the smell of war swept over the High King. Seam held up his datalink and summoned Arakiel.

The Serub stared into the device, his face like a sulking child disappointed at the arrival of a strict parent. "Arakiel, what is the status of the battle? We are preparing our entrance into the city."

Arakiel let out a low growl before speaking. "The Grogans have been defeated, Keeper. We pushed their forces back, and they've retreated from Zenith. We have won the day."

Seam smiled, but something still didn't feel right. "What of our forces, Arakiel? What is their status?"

The Serub looked out somewhere behind the screen, as if surveying the troops. "High King, your army took many casualties from the Grogan assault, but thanks to Nyx and me, we have successfully held an adequate fighting force for you to wield."

Relief flooded Seam's mind. Grateful, he spoke, "You have my thanks, Arakiel. Truly, you do. Your leadership in my absence has been most helpful."

Arakiel's blood red eyes locked on his master's and he nodded, a small acknowledgement. "What news of Isphet? Does he accompany you, High King?"

Seam's face tightened with unspoken rage. "There is much that we need to discuss, Arakiel. Bring your sister. The Synod must reconvene in my throne room."

"As you wish, High King."

The feed was cut, and Seam motioned for the convoy to move on to Zenith. Hastily, he fumbled for Bronson's number.

Bronson's worn and aged face filled the screen with the first datalink call. "Bronson, we are making the descent into Zenith. Is Willyn Kara still secured?"

Bronson nodded. "Yes, my lord. Safely hidden in a holding cell awaiting your arrival."

"Very good, Bronson. Your actions have pleased me greatly." Seam's words were sincere, and Bronson bowed over the datalink screen.

"Thank you, my lord. I will greet you upon your arrival at the Spire."

"Until then, Bronson." Seam shut the feed, allowing his mind to tally the spoils he gained in the last two skirmishes. He had accomplished all that he had set his mind to in only a matter of months. All the mirrors were his, and Isphet would soon be unlocked, securing his full and complete reign over Candor. The enemies who nearly bested him would soon die and justice for their tyranny would soon be realized. Willyn Kara would pay for her treachery, and with her death, the Sarhood would be crushed and the Groganlands would bow to the High King of Candor.

For a reason he could not explain, his hand dialed his datalink once more, his fingers following a familiar pattern that he had not dialed in months. The feed triangulated and secured and was then accepted. The cold face of Seam's mother filled the screen, her eyes wide with genuine surprise.

"Seam...I did not expect you to reach out to me."

"Hello, mother." He fumbled for words as he tried to feign pleasantries, knowing his own mother had betrayed him, fueling the Resistance in Lotte. "It is good to see your face. I...I am so sorry it has been so long. My work in Zenith has kept me very busy."

Aleigha's voice was curt and ungenerous. "So I heard. Your adventures have been showcased as legendary all across the continent."

Seam smiled broadly, not hearing the disdain laced within his own mother's voice. "How is Lotte, mother? Our home kingdom? I was so glad that you agreed to serve as my viceroy in my absence. I trust that our kingdom is secure and you are advancing the Dominion's cause."

Aleigha stared at her son, weighing her words. "Lotte is well and secure, though I am not as I would like to be."

Seam cocked his head. "What's wrong, mother?"

Aleigha stared into the datalink, her face unwavering. "You know the anniversary...it is coming up."

Seam's face blanked with confusion, and he regretted ever calling his mother. "What are you talking about?"

Aleigha's mouth pinched up with rage. "Your father's death, Seam. The anniversary of Camden's death is only a week away. Have you thought of how you would acknowledge it, my son?"

Seam mumbled his response. "Dear woman...I will not acknowledge a Red Death...not now, not in these times. Terror has roared through our land. To acknowledge the terrorists' success would only breed more upstarts, more rogues, more villains. Camden is gone, and his vision of Candor with it. I am all that is left of him, and I am doing the best to bear his heavy mantle."

His eyes connected with hers, silently challenging her with their intensity, refusing to back down. "It gladdens my heart to tell you that Grift Shepherd has been captured and he will pay for the crimes he has committed against our family. Perhaps a public execution on father's death day would be appropriate."

Aleigha's stare was cold and her eyes burned with an unrivaled fury. "Even after all this time, you still have learned nothing. You refuse to see the error of your ways, refuse to acknowledge the guilt that has plagued you for so long. I know the truth, Seam. *You murdered your father.*"

Seam's mind exploded with hot rage. *"What you are saying, woman, is treason!"*

Aleigha cut in, her own words on the edge of screaming. "What I am saying is *the truth!* You will not stop until you see this entire horror through. I can see that now. I have prayed for you for months, begging for Aleph to show you mercy, *but you will not bend.* You will not stop from digging your own grave."

Aleigha wiped away a trail of tears that fell from her face, and her voice ran cold. "My prayers for you stop today, Seam Panderean. Hear me and all that I say to you: *You are no longer my son, and I declare Lotte's independence from your so-called Dominion.* Lotte and all her people will fight against you and the nightmares you wield until Aleph's justice is fully realized."

Seam sat as the titan continued to roll into Zenith, his face turning several shades of red to a deep purple. "So this is what we come to, mother? This is the line you draw in the sand? Very well. For months, I have known of your dealings with these terrorists." Aleigha stared unwaveringly at her son as he continued. "Then you give me no choice. For your treachery, I will see you hung on the Pass, so that crows can feast on your flesh. You will see my wonders in the end, and you will regret your treachery. You will soon acknowledge me as I truly am: a God."

Aleigha screamed into the feed, her face a violent shade of her own son's twisted rage. "So ends the house of Panderean! When I see you next, my son, it will be in a coffin!"

Grift felt the fresh rush of hot desert air roll over him as the large doors opened from the side of the cramped transport. All at once, the hundreds of morels moved out with metronomic movements, their marching measured and calculated by some unknown force. Grift was swept up in the tide of bodies like a capsized ship captain, struggling to keep his head above water.

Aleph, please help me for what is coming next. Let me die in a way that pleases you.

The morels that surrounded him split away from Grift, leaving him in the presence of the giant Serub that accompanied Abtren in Preost. The green-eyed monstrosity looked down at him with a sneer, pointing at him.

"He's the one. Lock him down and bring him to the pinnacle. The High King wishes to deal with him personally." Dominion forces were on him in an instant, holding him down and binding him with heavy chains.

Grift's heart fell to his stomach as the shadow of the High King's dark tower covered him. The last time he had been dragged to this place, he would have died if not for his son. Tears began to roll from his eyes at the thought of Kull and what he had done for him. *I've done all I could, and it still wasn't enough. Aleph, have mercy on me.*

Adley woke coughing and gagging in the smoldering sanctuary of Taluum. Her head was light and spinning and the smoke stung her eyes. As she tried to stand she remembered her ankle was pinned beneath a heavy timber. She tugged at her leg but the large beam would not move.

She scanned the floor, trying to find any way of escape. A cloud of smoke filled the dark room, obscuring Adley's vision, but as she searched for a way to pull herself free she spotted the silent, still body of Wael, lying in a large pool of blood. Adrenaline surged through Adley's veins and she pushed against the timber again, trying to reach her friend but her leg did not move. As she braced to try again her sight landed on a mace nearby, dropped by one of the fallen monks.

Adley fumbled for the iron weapon and wedged its handle next to her ankle. With all her strength she hoisted the beam and slid her leg free. She gasped for breath and tumbled backwards as the timber smashed to the floor.

The thinning oxygen made Adley's head spin and she struggled to right herself on her bad leg. Each step was excruciating but she forced herself to push further into the burning sanctuary; she had to get to Wael.

Adley ripped a sleeve of her shirt free and wrapped it around her mouth to try and slow down some of the smoke inhalation. She made her way to Wael and felt for a pulse on his cold, clammy neck.

Her heart skipped a beat once she felt a faint pulse beating. Adley rolled Wael to his back and quickly examined the seeping wound. She ripped her other sleeve free and used it to pack the wound as best she could before cutting one of her pant legs free and tying it around Wael's stomach to hold the pack in place.

"It's crude Wael. But it will have to work!" "Stay with me!"

Adley worked Wael to a sitting position and tried to hoist him to her shoulder, but her leg buckled beneath his weight. She set him down and checked his pulse again. "I will be back Wael, I promise. Just please hang in there."

As Adley jogged for the exit she heard a faint whimper. She glanced to the side and saw Rot, lying on his side trying to steady himself upright, one of his legs badly broken.

"Don't worry, boy. I'm coming for you too." Adley's heart beat quickened and she turned for the door. As she burst out into the war torn streets of Taluum, gasping for fresh air she screamed out, each word causing her smoke filled lungs to burn.

"Please! Anyone! Help me get the Mastermonk from the sanctuary!"

Grift stood chained to the floor in the middle of the Spire's throne room. All of Candor circled around the room, and Grift's hands shook as he gazed over the vast, panoramic expanse. In the west, he could see the wide, dark clouds of smoke billowing into the air; Preost was still burning. From the east, a wide and violent thunderstorm was rolling in, out of the Grogan mountains and into the Rihtian plains. Everything that Grift saw from this vantage point on the Spire bid ill tidings and dark omens.

Grift's thoughts turned toward his end. *There will be no escape this time, Grift. Today is the day you die.* He weighed the thought in his mind, holding it loosely. He saw the face of Rose, whose beauty and joy had been robbed from her life too soon. His thoughts turned to Kull, who died only months before in the very room where he was now chained.

They are waiting for you. The thought invaded his mind without asking, and it tore through him like a blazing beacon of insane hope, a small but powerful torch of light within the darkness of his soul. The torch warmed Grift's heart and calmed his nerves, anointing him for what was coming next. Grift's whole body shook with a blanketed energy, a quickening of comfort, and his eyes pooled with both grief and hope. *I'm not afraid of what is coming. Rose and Kull are waiting for me on the other side. That is enough for me. By Aleph, that is enough.*

Grift's solitude vanished in an instant as Seam Panderean broke through the large double doors that led into his opulent throne room. He stepped up on the ivory staircase that led to his throne. Each of the steps was flanked by one of the four mirrors in Seam's possession. He ascended silently without giving Grift a second glance. Two golden eagles were perched at each side of the ornate chair, serving as Seam's armrests, and as he sat, Grift marveled at the clothes the High King was wearing.

The spartan armor of the Grogans was gone, and in its stead were the royal robes of the Kingdom of Lotte. In fact, Seam sat wearing the very robes of King Camden, and on his head, he wore his father's intricate golden crown. He sat with such authority that it made Grift do a double take, as if he were looking directly at the ghost of High King Camden himself. The High King stared down on his captive, his voice booming in the high hall.

"Bring in the Synod."

The double doors opened wide, and the Celestials strode into the throne room. Luken joined his fallen kin, he too bound to the Keys of Candor. They carried in with them the last portal, like pallbearers in a funeral. Grift's body shook with fear at the sight. Seam had done all he had set out to do, and now the Five would be reunited.

There is no hope left for Candor. Aleph, have mercy on them. Grift knew in his heart that his part of Seam's grand nightmare would soon end.

Bronson Donahue shuffled in behind the Synod, bearing the ebony sword of the High King on a plump purple cushion. He trailed the Synod and placed the sword on an ivory pillar at the bottom of the royal stairs. As he placed the weapon, he turned to bow low before Seam and exited the throne room.

The Serubs erected the last mirror of their kin and stood to the side as Seam spoke, his voice ringing in the hall like a thunderclap, his eyes locked on Grift Shepherd.

"Grift Shepherd of Lotte, today is the day of my justice. As your sovereign, I find you guilty in the Red Death of my father, High King Camden and of the former Sar of the Groganlands, Hagan Kara. Your punishment will be death by my choosing."

Grift stood, the chains rattling around his hands and neck. He spoke, his voice strong and absolute. "There will be no justice done here today, Seam. Only more theatrics and hollow charades."

Seam stood and pointed at his enemy. "Then by all means, Shepherd, enjoy the show."

Seam stepped back and sat on his throne as a figure lurched through the open doors. Grift's throat went dry and his body quaked as he watched his son lumber forward.

Kull clasped the glowing blue key tight against his chest and drew in a deep breath. He glanced back at Aleph who quietly nodded. Kull paused. "What is going to happen?"

"I will be with you. Your mother will be with you. We will all be with you." The answer offered comfort, but Kull swallowed with fear as he stepped through the plane of the open portal. A blinding flash of light burst around Kull with a silent explosion that evaporated into a blanket of eternal darkness. Kull could feel himself as he was suspended in an empty void. He swiped his arms and feet but made contact with nothing. Neither rising or falling, Kull felt suspended in the darkness.

"Aleph!" Kull cried out. "What do I do?"

The void was silent and still, swallowing his cries. Nothing moved, nothing changed. Kull's heart pounded in his chest as he tried to find any sign of an exit, a platform, anything that was *real*.

In an instant, he felt his feet meet a solid floor. All other senses eluded him except the feeling of a hard floor underfoot. Kull prodded his mind. *Focus on what you were given.* Kull felt the Key radiating a brilliant energy beneath his shirt. He waited for another change.

Then, from the shadows, he caught a glimpse of five pinpricks of light gathering. He sprinted for the lights. As he grew closer, he noticed they were not lights at all, but each of the points of illumination he chased were keys. They pulsed with an incredible intensity that drew Kull in closer like a moth to the flame. The Keys clustered together as Kull reached for them.

The Keys shot forward and Kull felt a powerful blow land on his chest, sprawling him against the invisible floor. He scrambled to his feet and strained his eyes only to notice a form moving with incredible speed in the darkness. A man with the Keys lining his left arm stepped forward from the shadows, charging Kull. The being tackled him to the ground, pummeling him with a violent flurry of punches. Each time he tried to force himself up, the dark figure beat him back down to the floor.

The form continued to solidify, the solid shadow now fully the shape of a man. Kull jumped back and balled his fists with rage as he recognized his attacker. *Seam Panderean.*

"Kull!" Grift's cry echoed through the chamber. He tore at his chains, but they held tight. Seam let out a loud laugh as he gloated over Grift. The Synod set the fifth and final mirror in place behind their chained prisoner. The four Serubs circled him like sharks, two to each side of Grift, leaving him surrounded. Seam ahead, the mirror behind, and the two Serubs on each side, Grift was surrounded, but still his only focus was on Kull. His son was alive, in front of him, standing next to Seam. *How is this possible?* Grift's mind was a flurry of emotion as he stared at his son, speechless.

"Grift Shepherd, are you surprised to see your son alive? Would you beg for his release?" Seam pointed at him, standing from his throne. "Go ahead, Grift. *Beg.* You started a servant beneath my family's feet, and here you are at my feet again. Everyone will bow before me in the end, Grift. No one escapes my power. No one."

Grift opened his mouth and screamed at his son, his heart hammering in his chest. A primal energy swept through him as he furiously pushed against his bindings. "Kull. Run, son!" Grift continued to struggle against the shackles as they cut into his arms. Warm blood ran down his forearms as he fought his confinement.

Kull's eyes turned toward Grift.

"Son! What is it? What is wrong?" Grift's face emptied of its color as he realized the horrible truth. He glared at Seam, his haggard voice roaring through the hall. "What did you do to him? What did you do?"

Seam began to laugh. "Oh...my dear friend. Your son is completely fine. In fact, he is now much more useful to me than ever before." Seam stared at Grift, savoring the moment before finally speaking.

"Grift, do you know that after you strip away the faculties that inhibit a person, you are left with a machine? A very complex and frightening machine that knows only one thing: hunger. Mankind, at the end of the day, is nothing more than a self-regulated monster afraid of realizing its true potential. So, I think it is time that you meet your son for who he truly is...I can tell he is ready to meet you."

Grift's hands shook with rage in his shackles as Seam stared at his son and said, "Go see your father, Kull."

Kull turned and made his way down the ivory steps toward his father. When Grift saw his son's eyes, he fully understood the horror before him. Milky, mottled eyes stared back at him, and Kull screeched, an inhuman cry that sent Grift reeling to the floor.

What was left of Kull was only morel. His body was being controlled, and all that he had been was gone. The sudden shock of hope at Kull's appearance, and the searing loss coupled with rage sent tremors through Grift's body. His hands shook uncontrollably and his breathing seized, but then a spark lit deep inside and he bolted against his chains again.

"Release me!" Grift shook in his chains like a rabid animal. "I will kill you! I will kill you!"

Seam stood to his feet and tiptoed down the large ivory steps in front of his throne. He reached for the ebony sword Bronson left for him. He plucked the blade from its pillar and swung it in the air before handing it to Kull. He slowly turned his face to Grift as a sinister grin stretched over his lips.

"Grift Shepherd of Lotte. I hereby condemn you to death by the sword." Seam stepped to the side as Kull moved forward with the blade glimmering in his hands. Kull held the blade high above his head just as the High King issued another command. "Stop." Seam stepped in front of Kull and stared at Grift like a cat who just caught a mouse. "On second thought, let's make this fair. Unbind Shepherd and give him a blade. Let him at least try to defend himself from his son."

Luken sprinted to unchain Grift and placed a twelve-inch hunting knife in his hands. Luken's tortured eyes spoke a thousand words as he shared a glance with Grift. The other Serubs all had filthy grins painted on their faces, enjoying the scene that was unfolding. Grift clasped the knife given to him by his friend and locked burning eyes onto Seam. As the locks popped off, Grift charged forward.

Grift lost himself in the moment, lunging for Seam with all he had, as a fountain of pain erupted from his thigh. He fell to the ground, grasping for his right leg, wounded by Kull's blade. Grift rolled to the side as Kull hammered his blade down again, striking the stone floor. Grift scrambled to his feet and made a hobbled leap for Seam, ignoring Kull entirely, swiping his blade but grossly missing his mark. He fell to his stomach and felt a piercing explosion of pain in his left leg as Kull drove his blade through his calf.

"AGHH!" Grift let out a wail like a banshee and swiped back, smashing his knife against the obsidian blade that threatened to dive into him again. The force knocked Kull's grip free but Grift was crippled with pain. Heavy black shadows swirled and closed in on his vision. *Aleph...help.* Grift drew in a deep breath and pulled the sword from his leg while screaming out, shaking the room with his guttural cry.

"Stop, Kull! Please, son. Please stop."

Tears rolled down Grift's face as he cried out. He tried to push himself across the floor away from what had once been his son, but his two ravaged legs refused to obey him.

"Stop, Kull! Please, son. Please stop."

The voice was unmistakable. Kull froze at the sound of his father's voice and the shadow figure slammed its fist against his jaw, taking advantage of the opening. Kull slid across the floor before leaping back to his feet and charging his assailant. He ran full force and propelled himself into the dark creature's belly, bringing them both crashing to the floor. Kull hammered his fist down on the specter's head, but each blow simply passed through the image of Seam, crashing his knuckles against the hard floor.

"You cannot win, Shepherd. Stop fighting and accept your death."

Seam's voice sent a shiver through Kull, making him punch harder. The specter swung a heavy fist inward. Kull ducked to the side and grasped hold of the five Keys locked around his enemy's arm. He clamped upon them, refusing to release his grip as the shadowy figure of Seam struggled beneath his grasp.

"I will finish you, Seam!" cried Kull as he swung again, this time his fist colliding against a solid skull.

"I will finish you, Seam!" The words silenced the room. The Serubs gasped, each glancing at one another and then back to Seam, whose face was contorted and absent from the present fight unfolding.

Grift, laying in a pool of his own blood, reached for Kull's arm and cried out. "Kull! Are you there?"

A loud groan emitted from Seam's lips, and he blinked his eyes furiously as his focus locked onto Grift with intense purpose. Kull's hand knocked back Grift's arm, ripping up his knife. Kull held the blade and stared blankly at his father before slamming it through his chest. A warm sensation coursed through Grift, followed by a harrowing deep chill. He shuttered as the cold wrapped around him, blood gurgling from his lips. He choked for breath and reached up, touching Kull's face with a bloody hand. A tear rolled down his cheek as he fought to speak.

"I love you, Kull. I love you, boy. I..."

Grift fell limp and crumpled to the floor at his son's feet.

Seam stepped forward with arms outstretched, a warm, albeit unsettled, smile on his face. "This, my friends, is justice being served. This is the price all will pay for challenging me and my authority."

A red flash burst from behind the King's throne. Willyn surged forward bearing a long blade in her hand. With one swift motion, she swung her weapon, lopping Seam's arm clean at the elbow while a gas grenade spun across the floor. Seam roared as blood spewed from his severed stump and the Keys of Candor fell to the ground.

Kull's body collapsed to the floor, covering his fallen father as Seam's control was released.

The Synod pounced into the chaos as Seam's limp arm fell to the ground, but the room was heavy with a thick cloud of smoke. Alarms blared and red lights flashed as emergency vents clicked to life, sucking the smoke from the room. Willyn dove for the bloody bracer and lifted it in the air as she stepped back from the Synod circling her like feral wolves. She pulled a pistol from her hip, aiming it at Arakiel and then swinging it toward each of the other Serubs.

Her cold killer eyes widened with shock as they fell on Luken. Luken's own eyes were filled with a mixture of terror and relief. Willyn jumped back and edged closer to the fifth and final mirror. "I know your secret. I know whoever holds this bracer and the Keys controls you all." Willyn reached down and activated a beacon on her wrist.

"Drop them, girl!" snarled Arakiel as he pointed at Seam's withered body. "You have no clue of what you speak. *They will only kill you in the end.*"

Willyn scanned the room and locked on the door as it buckled from an explosion. Bronson and his small platoon burst in the room, gunfire erupting over the Serubs with fully automatic bursts. The bullets smacked against them, pulling their attention from Willyn as she darted for the one person she had been waiting on. Hagan pushed through the crowd and met her in the center of the room in front of the final glass mirror.

Luken turned from the fray and ran for Willyn screaming, "What are you doing, Willyn!?" Panic was laced in his voice and his eyes were wide with desperation. Willyn lifted the bracer and its five Keys into the air.

"I am giving it to the one person I can actually trust!"

"No, Willyn! No!" Luken sped forward but it was too late. Willyn handed the bracer over to Hagan, who gladly accepted it. He beamed with pride as he ripped the remains of Seam's arm from the bracer and slid it over his own. He examined the five Keys and smiled widely, sighing with relief. "Thank you, dear sister."

"No! Aleph above. No!" Luken's voice slowed and was muffled as Hagan's face transformed in the chaos. His countenance grew and swelled with power. His health and former glory returned. Willyn's heart swelled, knowing her brother had finally returned and now all would be made right again. He would be able to right Seam's wrongs, restoring the Groganlands and Candor back to glory.

Hagan looked at Willyn and he smiled his familiar broad smile until his face shifted and morphed like a pond's surface rippling with violent energy. Willyn's heart hammered in her chest as Hagan's face disappeared and transformed into someone Willyn remembered all too well.

"Hello, Willyn. Remember me?" Isphet stood beaming as he slithered out from the glass portal. "I have enjoyed our little game. My time in your head was actually quite pleasant, but I am afraid it is now complete. You have been most useful to me." Isphet flashed his serrated teeth and whispered, "Goodbye."

The fallen deity held out his hand that burned with a yellow radiant power. Willyn stood frozen in a stupor as all her hopes and dreams were ripped away from her.

Isphet raised his hands toward her, but she was tackled to the ground, just as a hot blast of fire flashed over her head. The burst of heat smashed against the marble floor, ripping through it as if it were paper. Luken huddled over Willyn and held out his hand toward his enemy, releasing an invisible attack that staggered Isphet for a moment.

Isphet blinked and stared down at Luken, smiling viciously. "Ah, my traitorous *brother*. I see you are still up to your wicked ways, loving these wretched animals."

"Isphet!" Arakiel's voice rattled the room, laced with panic and anxiety. "We have been waiting for you."

Arakiel stood at the front of the room with Nyx, Bastion, and Abtren flanking his sides, each of their eyes wide with dread.

Isphet cackled and held up the bracer in his hand. "Well, look at us all! Our precious family has gathered together once more." Each of the Serubs as well as Luken lurched upwards, dangling midair as if an invisible cord had been noosed around their necks. The five Celestials orbited around Isphet, the bracer of the Keys glowing with unholy fire.

"I do like family reunions. Such a shame that we've been so distant really." Isphet roared with mad laughter.

Pain ignited on each of the Serubs' faces as Isphet's laughter began to swell, as if his power was fueled by their pain. "Now that I have your attention, I must ask each of you, for I am very curious...what did your time on the other side teach you?" Isphet's horrible red eyes locked onto Nyx's. "Nyx, darling sister, you go first." The orbit ceased and Nyx was brought face to face with her brother.

She screamed at him like a hawk, "There was nothing on the other side! *Nothing!* Release me!"

"Wrong answer, Nyx...and no, let's not hurry this process. I'm still very interested in what others have to say. There is no hurry...I've been waiting to talk to *my family* for such a long time."

Willyn slowly shuffled back from the gods' conversation, her face a sheer white sheet of fear. As she backed away, she whispered to herself, "What have I done? What have I done?" The truth of Isphet's deception made her feel as if all her insides had been emptied out. She was hollow, empty, and dead. *Dead. Just like Hagan.*

She threw her gaze over to Seam Panderean, who lay in a massive pool of his own blood. He lay staring at the ceiling, his face blank with resignation. He muttered quietly to himself as his eyelids fluttered open and shut, fighting to retain consciousness.

Willyn shook as Isphet moved through the room, bearing the terrible Keys of Candor.

"Oh, but I can't resist. Nyx, perhaps you're right, why should we wait any longer? *Arakiel.*" Arakiel swung in toward Isphet as Nyx moved away.

Isphet paused for several seconds as he scanned Arakiel's stone-faced expression. "You still think yourself the greatest of our kind? *Our leader?* Our new majesty?" Isphet gave a quick, almost playful curtsey if not for the horrible scowl on his face. "Ha. Tell me, Arakiel, what did you learn on the other side?"

Isphet's eyes were cold and dead as he stared through Arakiel. Arakiel bore long fangs and growled at Isphet as he hung, suspended in the air. "I learned what *you are*."

Isphet offered a smirk as he drew Arakiel in closer. "*Really?* Well, that is very interesting. You're smarter than you look, brother. But let's keep that between you and I then, shall we?"

Isphet's hands flew out and clasped Arakiel's face. Arakiel let out a scream that shook the entire top floor of the Spire. The black, polished slate floor cracked under Isphet's feet as he bit into his brother's neck, releasing a torrent of black blood. Isphet hung there gorging into Arakiel, drawing in Arakiel's essence. Arakiel's form shifted in Isphet's grip as he morphed from man to lion and back again, writhing with pain under Isphet's grasp. With every passing second, violent vibrations grew, emanating from under Isphet's feet. Soon the thick glass walls of the Spire undulated and burst in unison, as the Spire quaked from Isphet's submission of Arakiel.

An empty, lifeless husk thudded against the cracked tile floor before vanishing into dust as Isphet licked his lips and drew in a long breath. His eyes lit with a new vibrancy as he stared down Abtren, Nyx, and Bastion with malice in his eyes. He turned and sneered at Luken before speaking.

"Do you feel that, brothers and sisters? Ahhh. I do. Yes, I do."

The Serubs' faces were painted with terror as they realized what had just occurred. Isphet stepped forward as they started to orbit again. Isphet stood with arms outstretched as he gloried in his newfound power, vibrating with freshly absorbed energy.

Abtren screamed out, her face shrieking with panic. "What happened to you? How can you do this?"

Isphet laughed and glared at her, licking his lips. "My time away from you has brought me much, sister Abtren. *Much even you do not know.* Arakiel's vision for us was too...limited. His scope of power far too...small." Isphet laughed, his kindred dangling around him like moons running their rotations. He eyed them, his gaze flickering over them without mercy. "What will I do with you all?" A hush fell over the room and a deep chill spread through the space as Isphet's eyes fell on the broken body of Seam Panderean. The Serubs stared as Isphet stepped forward, gazing down on the fallen High King.

There, on the floor, Seam Panderean lay, fast asleep in a deep pool of crimson. The months that he bore the Keys of Candor were over, and his body could no longer resist the exhaustion that had followed him like a tormenting shadow.

"Wake up, Seam." Isphet's command seemed to bite, as Seam's eyes flew open in a flash.

Isphet stared at Seam with as much pity as one might have for an insect. "You...you are very wise for a mortal. You came to the secret truth all on your own, with no help at all." Isphet chuckled, and Seam shook with fear under the nightmare standing over him. "Yes, I can see your thoughts, Seam Panderean, your restless, biting thoughts. Despite your torment, you came to the right conclusion about us in the end." Isphet's eyes glowed like hot coals and he stooped down, a long black tongue slithering out from his ragged maw. "*We* are not gods. Your intuition proved quite right." Isphet held up the Keys locked on his arm. "After all...what kind of gods are bound to objects such as these?" Isphet leaned in, whispering a secret as his flickering, fiery eyes bored into Seam. "But don't be too harsh with our limitations, Seam. We are only the gods that you made us to be."

Seam's face seized with dismay. "What did you say?"

"*We are only the gods you made us to be.*" Isphet cocked his head playfully. "But on the other side I found someone more powerful than you could ever imagine. I have come to bring forth his will. Now, He and I are one. The others may not be gods, but I am." Isphet stared down at Seam, a strong, clawed hand grabbing Seam's face. "I couldn't have done it without you. Thank you for your work. You've been most helpful."

Isphet stood, turning back to the broken Synod who still hung in the air. His eyes landed on Luken, who shuddered under his horrifying gaze. Isphet stepped inches from Luken's pained face.

"Ah. *The traitor*. I don't know whether to thank you or destroy you for what you did to us."

Luken drew within inches of Isphet as Willyn cried out, charging toward the Isphet in a fit of rage. Isphet held out a hand and released a force of energy that blasted Willyn back, tumbling her across the floor toward one of the shattered glass walls. "Willyn Kara, you must learn your place. The adults are talking. *Your turn is coming soon enough, child.*"

Willyn grasped at the shattered floor, stopping herself inches from the Spire's ledge, nearly sliding out to her death. She scrambled from the edge in a panic, only to notice new movement in the room. Willyn's jaw dropped as Kull stood from the floor. He examined his father's crumpled, bloody body and then looked at his own hands; his blood-soaked hands. *He's aware. He's...he's...* Kull still clutched the ebony sword that was used to kill his father.

Kull Shepherd's body shook with untold rage as he tried to understand, as he fought to piece together what happened while he was fighting to regain his mind and wield his own body again. His father was gone. He had been used as Seam's weapon. Kull turned toward the communion of the gods and faced them, his presence not yet realized. The entire building trembled as Kull's eyes lit with a blue fire and the Spire began to twist and sway with new energy.

Isphet turned and stared at the bloodied boy, *"Who is this?!"*

Kull stared at Isphet, unafraid and uninhibited. The Serub's self-assured sneer wavered, cracking under the invisible electric energy that could be felt filling the room. It built like a dam under pressure, filling until it felt like the whole room would explode. Bastion, Abtren, and Nyx screamed out curses as they gazed at Kull. It was as if all the energy in the cosmos was boiling in that one room, bubbling over with light, heat, and terrifying energy centered on Kull.

He opened his mouth and pulled out his mother's pendant. There, threaded beside the rune of Aleph, was a key, glowing and crackling with a magnificent energy, as if it had been forged from a thousand lightning bolts.

Kull's voice filled the room like a thunderclap, "Don't you know who I am, *Ma'et?* I am Kull Shepherd, servant of Aleph, the Most High. You saw me in the Sea of Souls, *you snake.* The days of the Serubs are coming to an end, for Aleph will no longer suffer your wanton destruction. The Serubs will not be used as your tools any longer!"

Kull closed his eyes, letting go of all that sought to overwhelm him; memories of his father and his mother. *I release them into your hands.* The choice he made would be painful, but Aleph had made him a promise.

"*I am for you, Kull. I am with you.*"

Kull opened his eyes and stared at the Serubs who stood silently before him.

Isphet took one step closer, his face full of rage. "Who are you to call me by *that name?!* I do not cower before Aleph! I do not cower before men, much less a boy. I am death, chaos, and rage! Who do you think you are?!"

Kull opened his mouth as the words roared out of him, "I am the Keeper of the Keys!"

Thank You For Reading!

We hope you enjoyed Keys of Candor: Sea of Souls and we look forward to connecting with you. We love hearing from our readers and taking in your thoughts and feedback. We know you have many options when it comes to reading, and it honors us that you would read our works. We invite you to write a review at www.Amazon.com to let us know what you liked.

Also, please feel free to connect with us at the resources below. We love getting to know our readers:

Online: www.keysofcandor.com

Facebook: www.facebook.com/keysofcandor

Email: eanesandervin@gmail.com

Twitter: @keysofcandor

Be sure to subscribe to our monthly newsletter at www.keysofcandor.com to get exclusive content, news about our upcoming books and more!

COMING SOON

KEYS OF CANDOR: DOMINION'S END

Kull has returned but will it be enough to sway the advances made by Isphet? Willyn attempts to recover from the Great Serub's deception and Wael's life hangs in the balance. The end is near and the future of Candor and Aether depend on the Keeper of the Keys.

Be sure to subscribe to our monthly newsletter to get exclusive news on the next installment in the Keys of Candor series.

ACKNOWLEDGEMENTS

There are many people to thank when it comes to Sea of Souls, but none more important than you; our readers. We continue to write this story for ourselves and for you. The wonderful feedback we've gotten about Keys of Candor continues to propel us to write, and we are so thankful for the amazing friends we have made along the way. So whether you saw this book and took a chance on it on Amazon, or if you met us in person at a convention we sincerely want you to know that we thank you and appreciate you. There are many things you could read, but the fact that you read our book means more than you know.

We would be foolish not to mention our deep gratitude to our stalwart editors, Laura Stallings and Susan McDonald. Thank you both for your friendships and your commitment to making our work better. We become better writers because of your both. Thank you.

Another round of thanks to those who beta-read our rough drafts of this work. A lot of you said this book was more polished than the first, which is a nice validation of our efforts to continually improve our writing. Thank you for your support as always.

Last, but not least, we want thank our families and especially our wives, Janet and Devin. Your belief in us keeps us moving forward chasing down our dreams. We love you.

Well, there is more to this tale to be told. We look forward to seeing you then.

Until next time dear reader,

   -Seth and Casey

ABOUT THE AUTHORS

Seth and Casey grew up together in North Carolina, and are lifelong friends. In "real life" they hold their posts as a librarian and a banker respectfully enough, but have always had deep interests in creating art, music, and now stories.

Keys of Candor is their first fictional series and they have grown to love the characters within Candor. They look forward to the final chapter of the saga and are excited to share the other stories and worlds that have been bouncing around in their brains. There are more stories to tell!

Feel free to reach out to us!

Online: www.keysofcandor.com

Facebook: www.facebook.com/keysofcandor

Email: eanesandervin@gmail.com

Twitter: @keysofcandor

Made in the USA
Charleston, SC
10 May 2016